THE LAST GOOD RUN

THE LAST GOOD RUN

by

Sandro Dariosto

per sempre Anita Edizione
Ferrara Seattle
2014

Printed in the United States of America

per sempre Anita Edizione
via delle Scienze 17 Ferrara

10 9 8 7 6 5 4 3 2 1

Metakuye Oyasin
All my relatives

Tasunke witko ktepi! (Crazy Horse was killed.
--notation on an Oglala winter count,
corresponding to the calendar year 1877

"When things like that happen, they don't disappear.
They linger . . . "
Mario Vargas Llosa

Evening. 12/25/89

"You can call me Crazy," Choteau said. "For short." Then he took a long swig from his cheap beer, draining it empty, and grinned at me.

At that moment, driving through a blizzard in eastern Nebraska, mopping our hot air off the inside of the Le Car's windshield with my sleeve, and steering one handed through the shifting snowdrifts, I thought he was pulling my leg.

"Wait a minute," I said. I thought about it a while, through all the beer I'd been drinking. "You mean," I laughed once and stopped there. Should I really confess to this goofy idea? But it was what I thought he meant just now, when he said that. "You're telling me that you're some sort of ghost or reincarnation or something?"

Choteau shrugged at me. "That would be one way to put it, I guess," he said.

I looked over at him, to see if I could spot anything. A cock to the eyebrows, a wink, a little smirk that gave him away. But if this was a joke, he was playing the straight man perfectly. "You're trying to tell me that you're Crazy Horse? The Crazy Horse?"

He nodded his head once, gave me this blank, matter of fact look.

"Okay, let me get this straight. I've got Crazy Horse, the great Sioux warrior from the past, the victor of the Little Bighorn, the scourge of Custer, Crazy Horse, born again, and riding sidekick in my old Renault. Right?" I was gesturing with my open hand at the windshield, for some reason.

Choteau smiled at me. "Lakota," he said, his eyes twinkled and I could see his breath in the air.

"What?"

"Not Sioux, Professor man. I'm Lakota."

1

"Oh, right," I said. "Lakota." Then I laughed and said, "Crazy Horse, huh." I threw my head back and laughed at the ceiling of the little car. "Well, ain't that a hoot," I said.

Choteau shrugged. "I knew you wouldn't believe me," he gazed away, out at the blowing snow.

But he was wrong. It was strange, and I was drunk. But right then I didn't know whether to believe him or not. Even now I don't know if I do believe him. But it's taken me a long while to know that "believing him" was beside the point.

"So I should call you Crazy," I said.

"Whatever," Choteau glanced back over at me, and he was growing quiet. He sighed, though I saw his breath again, more than heard it.

"Well, that won't be too hard," I smirked over at him in the other bucket seat. "Crazy," I added, a moment too late.

This time he frowned at me, but he was pleased. "Believe what you like, Professor," he said.

Then we both saw something moving under the snow beside the road. A figure or a form, something struggling to get free of the drifts in the ditch. It shifted around, and the smooth lines of the snow broke here, and then there. The weather was fierce outside, a blizzard blowing hard out of the far north, and in the next moment we saw it struggling up from under snowdrifts in the ditch. It was an old dog, and it was trying to scramble up to the edge of the road. It was some weak old mutt, and right then it poked its head up out of the snow.

"Pull over," Choteau yelled, but I already was. It was a dog, after all. Out there in the cold.

For the purposes of this book, you should call me Will Gentles. It's not my real name, but it's the name I deserve. You could say it's the name I earned for myself.

You see, Private William Gentles was the man the army blamed. In all their reports, in the investigation that followed the murder, it was Private William Gentles who killed him, or at least that's what they claimed. Out at Fort Robinson, on that cold winter morning in 1877, Private Gentles was the one who did it. He shoved his bayonet into Crazy Horse's back twice, during a scuffle in the doorway to the jail. Then Crazy Horse collapsed in the snow, and later, after dark had fallen, with his parents and his old friend He Dog at his side, he died on the floor of the adjutant's cabin.

But you know, if you had to blame someone for Crazy Horse's death, Private Gentles was pretty darn convenient. He was there, for one thing. He had a bayonet. He certainly could have done it. But most of all, by the time the investigation was over and done with, and the army's full report was released, Private William Gentles was dead. The Private died in May of 1878. You see, asthma got him, months before the investigation was done. So he was as dead and almost as gone as Crazy Horse himself, when the army laid the blame on his head.

So like I say, I'll go by Will Gentles here. Associate Professor Will Gentles to you, thank you. I think it's the name I've come to deserve.

Either that or what Choteau sometimes called me back then. Little Big Man.

Every little square inch of my existence is different now. Bernard Choteau turned my life over like so much dirt ready for planting, and there was nothing I could do about it. And for all of that, I still can't put a finger on him, can't hold him still long enough to see him clear. He picked me over like gravel in his garden plot, and I still can't even tell you who he was. Not for sure, anyway.

But I do know who I am. I'm the man who murdered him.

I know, the news reports all say he was killed while resisting arrest. An escaped convict killed by the citizen he'd kidnapped. or even better, by the police during his arrest. Gol-

3

man made sure the story came out that way. And after all, there were a few dozen police officers involved in the killing, too.

But "killed" is for folks who drive too fast in blizzards. "Killed" is for people who step off the curb on busy streets, for dogs who chase cars. "Killed" is for earthquakes and tornadoes, for Pompey and San Francisco and the Land of Oz. It's not for what happened to me on December 28th.

I murdered Bernard Choteau. I murdered him with a paring knife. I murdered him in the back. I murdered him. On Thursday, December 28, 1989.

His blood was all over my hands, and I can look down right now and see the scar snaking around at the base of my thumb and onto my palm. Those dozens of cops, all they did was finish the job I started, no matter what Golman says.

Choteau would say I murdered Crazy Horse.

And the more I think about it, the more I remember what happened, the more I go back over the details of what went down that morning, over and over again in my memory, the less I know what to believe. Maybe I did kill Crazy Horse.

But I'm jumping ahead of myself again. Maybe if I just put it down in order, just the way it happened, chronologically, the way I learned in school, maybe it will make some sense. Maybe. So this is our history. Let me back up, all the way to the night we met. Crazy Horse and I.

12/23/89. Late.

I slipped my hand up under Terri's pajamas until I gently held her breast, and things were looking up. "Will," she scolded, and squirmed a little. But she giggled, and that meant we were going places. So I bent over then and bit her white neck, right at the base, by her freckled collarbone.

It was cold outside, and late enough all the town Christmas lights were out for the night. Tomorrow we'd be up at her parents' house for the holiday, and we'd have to listen to all her brother Mike's stories about "the Bureau," and we'd have to put up with his two spoiled boys messing into everything. We'd drink too much eggnog and eat too much deer sausage, and then at midnight when we were all tired and full and two thirds looped, we'd have to go to church and try for two hours not to fall asleep or pass out. On top of all that, this year my sister-in-law wouldn't be there. Jacki and Mike Golman had separated two months ago, and now Golman was frantic to make his two sons merry on Christmas Eve, even without their mother. That was the happy holiday we had waiting for us.

Still we had tonight. I ducked down under the comforter and slipped my head up beneath Terri's flannel pajamas, and I licked the spangle of freckles around her navel. That really made her squirm. "Will," she said, without the scolding this time. So I licked farther up, one long stroke across the white skin of her stomach. Then she was still, and she whispered something I couldn't make out through all the covers and pajamas rustling, not to mention the pulse that was rushing in my ears. It was probably some little complaint about how I was giving her a chill, or something. And I knew how to warm her up, I did. But I noticed she didn't shiver or tremble, she was just perfectly still. And that was odd.

5

I stopped for a moment and listened, but all I could hear was my heartbeat. Terri didn't say a word. She just lay very still, like she was waiting for something. So I leaned up a little to kiss her nipple and make it blossom.

"Will," she said. But this time it was different. Not exactly angry, but it wasn't playful anymore. Then she said something again that I couldn't make out.

It took me a lot longer than it should have, at least if I was graceful about it, to climb out from under her flannel nightie. Then I got tangled up and lost in the sheets and the quilt. I kept pushing a forearm out, trying to come up for air, but mostly I just pulled the covers loose at the bottom of the bed. Terri said my name again. But it took me a couple more seconds to poke my head out.

"What!" I said.

"Didn't you hear it?"

"Babe, I didn't hear nothing but the sap rising."

Terri laughed at that, but then she said, "Someone's knocking at the door, Will."

"Well, who the . . . ?" I said, and stopped short.

"Listen," she said. She started to laugh and then held her breath. Her eyes were so green I'd swear even now they were lit. It was probably just the hormones in my blood that lit them up, but at that moment I didn't care if it was fireflies. Those green eyes loved me.

Then I heard the three heavy raps on our front door.

"Shit," I said and flopped over on my side in the bed. Terri started to laugh again.

"Coming," I bellered at the door. "Just hold your horses." I sat up with a jerk, muttering, "I'll get it," and Terri held her laugh down to a giggle. "What's so funny?" I said.

"You," she said. "Didn't you hear that knocking before?" Then she chuckled at me again. "Getting a little heated up, were we, Will?"

"What time is it anyway?" I said, as I got my feet on the floor and reached for a robe. Terri was still chuckling about how lost I was playing submarine, but she stretched out and picked up the alarm clock. Then she read it at me, "11:15."

"Who the hell comes knocking at this hour?" I said.

"Santa?" Terri was still giddy, I guess.

"He's a day early," I said, "the old codger."

But I had this foreboding, you know. Good news doesn't show up at this hour. It waits for morning and daylight. It's emergency and tragedy that comes knocking in the middle of a winter night. All the news you could sure wait to hear, even when you know you can't.

"If that's your brother out there . . . " I muttered and stood up. It was strange, I thought, there was no more knocking. This was a patient emergency, all of a sudden.

"What would my brother want?" Terri said.

"I don't know. You know how Golman is. It's always an emergency with him. Maybe Jacki's filed for divorce, huh? Or maybe its some FBI shit he thinks is all important. Who knows?"

"It's not Mike," Terri said, with a little edge in her voice. "Just go get the door," she said.

"Right," I said, and walked out through the hall into the dark living room, thinking about what might have been, back under those rumpled sheets.

See, Golman and I have had our differences. It goes all the way back to Vietnam, and it covers nearly everything since then. He was a good marine, back in those days, and I dodged my draft notice with a student deferment. And then there was what happened with my book. But that's a long story, and a different one than this.

I walked past the empty fireplace, and something brushed my shoulder. I nearly jumped loose of my pajama bottoms before I realized it was only the mistletoe. We'd hung it just that morning off the nose of the Indian mask above the mantel. Two days before Christmas and we'd finally put up our decorations. But better late than never, you know. When you teach, and you're trying to get those final grades in, sometimes Christmas trees and mistletoe are a last minute thing.

I patted the big bear gently on the nose. It was a big wooden mask, a dance mask from the Northwest, carved into the face of a grinning bear. He had eyes made of abalone shells and they filled his face with tides and mystery, even when he had a ball of mistletoe dangling from his nose.

I stared out the arched windows in our front door, through the old leaded glass filled with ripples and distortions. The porch light was on, shining yellow against the black night, but I couldn't see anyone outside. Normally, you can look out right at the top of someone's head there, unless it's a kid. Pulling my old robe around me tighter, I walked over to the entryway, switched on the light, and answered the door.

But no one was there. I glanced around, back and forth, shrugged and said, "Hello?" to the dark streets out past the lawn. Maybe this was all just a college prank from some old student of mine. Knock on the door and run, you know? I was beginning to think about Terri and her freckled stomach again.

Then I heard a rustle in the bushes behind the front stoop. I pushed the screen door open and stepped out with one foot onto the porch, to see what was going on. I was about to say, "Hey, who is it?" but I didn't get the chance.

Whoever was out there was short and huddled low down, and he moved quickly. He shoved right past me and shot inside the house, and he found the light switch in the entryway like he'd lived here all his life. The light went out, and I was still standing with one bare foot on the cold concrete in front of my own house. "Hey," I yelled, and stepped back inside beside him. The storm door slammed behind me, and he pushed the big front door closed once I was inside again.

All of this happened so quickly I didn't have time yet to be frightened. At least not until I realized who it was. When I recognized him, I caught my breath. I suppose my mouth was hanging open. "Choteau?" I said, finding it hard to believe. A chill went through me then, but I wasn't cold.

Bernard Choteau stood between me and the door now. He didn't smile or stick out a hand, he just nodded recognition at his name. A moment passed while both of us tried to measure the situation, I think. He may have been afraid of me, too.

He had long black hair going gray in broad streaks, and he wore it loose. It hung past his square shoulders. He was wearing sneakers and a pale green jumpsuit that didn't fit him very well, and he wore no coat or jacket or anything warm at all. It was winter in Missouri out there, and the cold air radiated off of him. Above his breast pocket, right below a tong of gray and black hair, there was a number stenciled in black.

"You escaped," I said.

He didn't respond, he just stood there in the shadow of the front door, with the porch light shining in a halo behind him, and his eyes frantically scanned the room around him. They rested, only once and just for a moment, on that mask of the grinning bear above the mantel. He almost smiled at that, or maybe at the mistletoe. I wanted to ask him then what he wanted from us, but I didn't say a word, I think because I was afraid of what his answer might be. Then I heard in the distance the first sirens winding through the streets.

"Who is it, Will?" Terri said, from the other room.

It was nearly fifteen years ago when these troubles really started. For all of us, for Terri and for me, as well as for Bernard Choteau. It all leads back to a morning in the summer of 1975. Of course, I was somewhere else then, lost in graduate studies in California. In fact, I hardly knew any of this was happening.

It began about midmorning on June 26, 1975, when two FBI agents drove down onto an acre or so of ground that belonged to June Little, near Oglala, South Dakota. They were in separate cars. They came from different directions, but they joined forces as they approached the Little property, near the center of the Pine Ridge Reservation. They were cautious about entering the vicinity alone. They had read their reports.

I was probably sitting in a seminar room talking about historical methods. Or maybe I was in the library reading about John Brown's trial in the Congressional Record. Or I might have been out soaking up the California sun. I'd watched the news reports a few years back about the siege at Wounded Knee. I was interested in the history. But I didn't know a thing about what was happening out there on the reservation that day, or any other day for that matter.

Those two FBI agents knew a thing or two about Pine Ridge, though. Ever since 1973 and the conflict at Wounded Knee, the FBI had focused their attention in South Dakota on the American Indian Movement. And they thought they'd learned a few things, too. Somehow they'd come to believe that AIM was planning a campaign of terror, planning to disrupt our bicentennial celebrations. In fact, the FBI believed AIM was planning an assault on Mount Rushmore sometime soon. Anytime in the following year.

Special agent Jack Coler was only twenty-eight years old, just a few years younger than me. But he had training in special weapons, and the Bureau office in Denver thought a SWAT man could be of help in Dakota that summer.

So that morning, Jack Coler linked up with special agent Ron Williams, just to be safe. They were looking for a young Indian named James Theodore "Jimmy" Eagle, age nineteen. Or at least that's what the Bureau report later claimed. Jimmy Eagle was wanted for stealing a boot in a Nebraska bar, down off the reservation. Not a major offense, even if it was a white man's boot. But it gave agents Coler and Williams a chance to take a look around the Little compound. And this was some property they were dying to see close up.

After all, Jack Coler and Ron Williams didn't team up just to handle a punk like Jimmy Eagle, and find an old boot for some Nebraska drunk. They both knew, from all their briefings, there was an Indian camp just below the Little's house. Down in a hollow among some trees along White Clay Creek lay an encampment run by the American Indian Movement.

And those two men, approaching that compound, probably believed what rumors and reports had told them: that the AIM camp on White Clay Creek was surrounded by bunkers. Later on of course, after the damage was done, no one ever found any trace of anything like a bunker, because they weren't there. But it didn't matter in the end because Coler and Williams drove down there assuming the AIM camp was filled with Indian subversives, heavily armed and committed to disrupting the reservation, waiting for them behind those vanishing bunkers.

At around 11 o'clock on a summer morning like that, I'd have been thinking mainly about a coffee break, I suppose. The Katz Deli was across the Ave from the main library, and for a buck you could get a coffee and a different kind of bagel every day. I was probably trying to decide whether to have the poppy seed like usual or go with something different, like rye or onion.

But in South Dakota, at around 11 o'clock, an exchange of gunfire began. How it started, and who exactly was involved, remains unknown. I'm sure agents Coler and Williams were jumpy. Probably they had their sidearm drawn going in. But those who were there, and the few others who know what occurred there, all refuse to say a word. Still we do know this. Sometime just before noon, someone approached those two stranded FBI cars and killed both agents with at least one high-powered rifle, at very close range.

In the hour and a half that followed, whoever was at the Little property and most of the Indians in the immediate vicinity fled in every direction. At the same time, FBI forces, Bureau of Indian Affairs police, South Dakota Patrolmen, and quite a few local white volunteers gathered and surrounded the place, setting up road blocks on every road out of there. Around 1:30 p.m., in one of the many skirmishes that occurred near the compound, a bullet struck Joseph "Little Joe" Stuntz in the forehead. He was killed instantly.

It was late afternoon by the time the FBI were able to enter the Little compound. Both the hollow by the Creek and the encampment were empty. They found the bodies of Coler and Williams at about 6:00 p.m.

By that time I was, most likely, tossing down a few beers at the Glocamora, shooting some pool, and talking shop with Mick Hagerty, or Jud Elrod, or any of a few other grad students. Jud teaches European at Cal Tech now, and Mick owns a beer distributorship in Indianapolis. They're doing well these days. And back then, they were always good for a brew and a little eight ball.

It took only a few hours before the FBI labeled the two killings at Oglala the Reservation Murders, and the "ResMurs" investigation was underway. The murder of Joe Stuntz didn't count for much though. They didn't really include Little Joe in the investigation, because he was killed while resisting arrest. But even with simplifying the numbers, it took the Bureau better than five months to press charges. In the end, five men were indicted. After years of extradition hearings and trials, and after the tireless pursuit and prosecution by the Bureau, only two of those men were ever convicted.

One of those two convicts disappeared quietly into the federal prison in Marion, Illinois, and later was transferred to Leavenworth. He never pressed for an appeal, didn't even offer much in his defense. He sought only anonymity. An orphan, he chose to silently serve his time, waiting without hope. Until one night, fifteen years later, just before Christmas, when he stood huddled in my doorway, with his eyes scanning the holiday decorations in my living room, as my wife called out from the bedroom, asking me who he was.

He was Bernard Choteau.

Terri came to the edge of the hallway and stopped there. "Will?" she said.

I didn't turn to look at her until I saw Choteau's reaction. He seemed to coil up and go tense. He was in his late fifties, at least, maybe early sixties. But he looked tough, like he'd seen a lot more of this world than I ever would. His arms cocked back a little, and I thought he might spring. What I would do, if he did, I had no idea. But I knew I didn't want Terri involved.

"Get back," I turned and said to her. I don't know where I wanted her to get back to. I just wanted her gone. And fast.

When I saw her there, across the room in the shadows, I almost ached with fear for her. I thought I might lose what little control I had right then. I might come apart. Moments before I was kissing the cleavage between her freckled breasts, and now I could lose her. All in a moment. She stood there in her big, plush robe, white and heavy with thick velour, and I called it the "marshmallow" for a joke, because of the shape it gave her. But she was more beautiful than ever, hidden in that shapeless robe. She held one hand up covering her mouth, and her black curls were splayed out and disappearing into the dark hallway. But I think I saw her like there were spotlights on her, so I could see even the sweet motion of her breathing.

"Will?" she said again.

"Terri, go," I pleaded, but I didn't know where to send her. I was afraid then to look back at Choteau. Let him jump me from behind, with my eyes closed. Just let her go.

But Terri moved a step toward us, out of the hall. Her hand dropped from her mouth, and she said, softly, "Bernard Choteau?" She knew him, because her brother was with the FBI, and because I had spent some years studying his case. Bernard Choteau had been my ticket to a tenured position at the university, you see.

We'd met before, Choteau and I, but only in a room at Leavenworth, a room with lots of bars and guards. And only long enough for him to make it perfectly clear to me that we had nothing to discuss. He wanted not one word written to re-mind the world of his existence. He wanted me to give my re-search up. He wanted to be left alone.

I ignored all his wishes, I'm afraid. And for a lot of rea-sons I called "professional," reasons that suddenly sounded a whole lot like excuses.

And now he stood here at my door, and I had the gall to wonder why.

"You know me," Choteau said to Terri.

I looked back at him and he seemed to have relaxed. His hands closed into loose fists and he let his arms drop. When he wasn't coiled up for a fight, he seemed older, and

13

softer somehow. The porch light cast a yellow glaze on his cheeks, and he seemed tired then. I felt for him, suddenly, cowering in my doorway alone. But I was still afraid of what he might do next.

"What do you want?" I said.

"Will," Terri said, cautioning me.

"Stay back, Terri."

His eyes glanced around him quickly. They rested for a moment on the bear mask, as if he recognized it. But then they shifted back to the windows in the living room.

"Draw the curtains tight," he said. Oddly enough, it sounded more like a need than a demand. Terri moved to follow his order, though, and I stopped her.

"Terri, get back in the bedroom," I said. "This is between Mr. Choteau and me." But what it was between us, I didn't know.

"Stay here," he said. Then he crossed the room and drew the curtains tight himself. He leaned awkwardly around the Christmas tree, knocking off an ornament or two, and pulled those curtains tight, too.

"What do you want, Choteau?" I said.

"Your neighbors?" he asked, with his back to me. He turned and seemed like a tensed muscle again. I just stared back at him, but I think we both knew my tough front was a sham. I noticed he didn't seem to be armed, though. That was some small relief.

"They're all gone," Terri said.

"Terri," I said. "Don't tell him anything."

She looked at me, and I saw the fear in her eyes. She was going to do whatever he wanted, until he left us alone. She'd already decided the course to take with him.

"Over there, they were just students," she said as she turned her eyes back to Choteau. "They've been gone for a week or so. And the Carters, next door, they left yesterday. For the long weekend."

He nodded and moved away from the windows and the tree. I saw how his long hair was streaked with gray, and his face was lined and worn. He seemed old, but not frail. He stopped near the cold fireplace, and stood facing that bear mask over the mantel. He was standing between us then, between Terri and me, and I felt trapped.

"What do you want from us?" I said.

"He needs our help," Terri answered, instead of Choteau. The old man looked down at the floor before the fireplace. "Can't you see that, Will?" I looked past him at Terri, in her plush white robe, and I realized she was as afraid as I was but she knew what to do. Resisting him in any way would mean more trouble. Trouble of some kind we didn't want. We had to help him, so he would leave us alone.

That's when Terri walked quickly over to the fireplace, right to Choteau's side. She put a hand on his shoulder. I wanted to reach out for her, to pull her away, and I said her name in a feeble effort to hold her back.

"My God," she said to him, "you're freezing. You're wet. And look what you've got on, in this weather. This . . ." She gestured down at the pale green jumpsuit he wore, not really knowing what to call his prison clothes. "This suit," she said finally. "And it's getting ready to storm out there."

At the touch of her hand, he lifted his head and seemed completely helpless and lost. For the first time, through my fear, I wanted to help him. The thought came to me like a dawning craziness.

But then, like some warning that I'd gone too far, that I'd lost hold of the rudder of reality, outside a siren wailed. A wake up call from Dr. Sanity, its red and blue lights flashed softly against the walls. We all were still.

There was a long time then to think about being caught between Choteau and the police, about being held hostage in the middle, about what he might do if he was really cornered. About how dangerous he was. Only that bear mask on the wall kept grinning, with his mistletoe hanging from his nose, and Mr. Bear seemed fiendish, in a way, now. The idea of decorating it for Christmas didn't seem so funny now.

Slowly, the lights and the siren's whine passed by on the street, and they didn't stop. I began to breathe again, though I didn't know until then I'd even stopped.

15

"Let's get back out of here," he looked at the doorway. "Have you got a back room, or something?"

I don't know whether you could say he ushered us or we led him, but we moved back to the bedroom, away from the street and the front of the house. I saw the rumpled sheets on the bed, and they seemed to belong to a different, quieter century.

"You need to get out of those wet clothes," Terri said, and moved for the closet in the corner, behind a dresser.

He watched her very closely as she opened the door and reached in. I saw his eyes glance over and notice the telephone by the bed. Terri pulled out an old robe of mine and walked toward him. He stood by the door, and she held the robe out to him. "Put this on," she said. "You'll make yourself ill in those wet clothes."

Choteau took the robe from her, but did nothing with it. I felt caged in my own bedroom, and I expected him at any moment to jerk the phone cord loose. I wanted to ask him how he'd escaped, but I think I was afraid of the answer.

I knew he'd been hospitalized here. Out on the west edge of town, the federal prison system had a hospital, wrapped in razor wire and guard towers. Inside it, federal prisoners were treated for serious illnesses. I'd seen the story on him in the paper, a week or two back, and a couple of my colleagues had mentioned it to me. Choteau had been shipped down here from Leavenworth. There was something wrong with his eyes, and he was undergoing tests there at the prison hospital.

But he sure seemed to be able to see now. And he sure didn't look ill. So I thought about those guards and all the coils of razor wire, and I wondered how he got out. But I didn't really want to know.

"Why us?" I said. "Why did you come here?"
"Will," Terri said.

"No," I scowled at her and looked back at him. "I want to know."

Choteau glared right back at me. I saw his jaw muscles work and he took a deep breath. He set the robe down on the bed, to free his hands, I guess.

"Is there somebody we should call or something?" Terri said. "Do you need to contact someone?"

There was an angry silence then, while he ignored our questions. A gust of wind outside shook the bedroom windows, and seemed loud in the silence. It was followed by the sound of rain or sleet rattling on the glass.

"It was because of your book," he said, and then he seemed weaker for a moment, because he seemed so alone. He pulled in a deep breath, glared over at me, and that weakness if it was ever there, was gone." It was because you sent me that book, Professor."

My big study was really only a monograph, but I suppose to him it seemed like a book. And it would have been a book, instead of just an empty gesture to earn tenure, if he'd cooperated with me. If he hadn't shut me out completely. I sent him a copy anyway, out of spite.

"I didn't think," he said. "After what you said in there . . ." He trailed off and didn't finish the thought. But I realized we were it for him. He didn't know anyone else around here who might help him. He didn't even know if we would. But we were all he had.

It didn't sound like this jail break had been long and carefully planned. Haste seemed to be the key.

"Why did you break out?" I said.

I didn't expect him to answer.

"I didn't think you would turn me in, Dr. Gentles," he said. He was asking us for help. For just a moment I wasn't afraid of him. The hard winter rain ticked against the window panes, and I made the mistake of relaxing a bit.

And then we heard someone else knocking on our door.

*　　　　　*　　　　　*

17

Choteau grabbed Terri by the arm and pulled her toward him. She let out a tiny, stifled cry, and held her breath. Her eyes, as she looked at me, welled up.

He pointed a finger at me and said, through his teeth, "Get rid of them." With a jerk of his head, he tossed the long hair back out of his eyes. "Whoever they are, Dr. Gentles, get rid of them."

The knock grew into a pounding at the door for just a moment, then it stopped.

I nodded to Choteau and stepped past them into the hallway. "No funny business, either, Professor. We don't want anybody to get hurt," he said. "Do we."

Terri moved stiffly alongside him as they stepped back further into the bedroom. "I'll do my best," I said to her instead of to him. Terri was silent, but she blinked back the tears.

"Do better than that," Choteau said. "Get rid of them."

The third knock came echoing down the hall then.

"Coming," I yelled, and backed away from the bedroom door. I didn't know what to do.

This time I could see who was out there through the arched windows in the front door. The storm door was closed, and the two policemen outside were wearing their hats in the cold rain and sleet.

"Professor Gentles?" one the officers said when I opened the door. It was a familiar face, though I couldn't place it right away. Over his partner's shoulder, I saw the dark patrol car sitting in our drive.

I tried to remember how a person looked when he was calm, but I felt like I was trying to smile into the face of a gun.

"Evening, Professor," the younger cop said. "Sorry to disturb you."

"Come in," I held the storm door open for them. "Come in. It's raining."

As they stepped inside, I pointed a finger at the officer who'd spoken first. I recognized him. He'd been a student of mine a few years back. "You're . . . ?"

"Bob," he said, taking off his hat. His partner followed the younger cop's lead.

"That's right. That's right. Litzberg, isn't it?"

He nodded his head, and grinned like a cub scout. "Litzberger, Professor." The other cop closed the front door snugly. It could have been to keep the cold and rain out. But it also meant they were staying, and I had better start thinking fast.

"Let's see, Bob, that was," I tapped the finger I'd pointed at him on my chin. That gesture seemed, even to me, contrived and obvious. "History of the Mississippi and West, right?"

"Yeah," he laughed. "I didn't really think you'd remember, Professor Gentles. That was five years ago."

But I remembered him clearly enough. Bob Litzberger was a good student, if not an especially bright one. In fact, he may have been a little too good. Always there, always on time, always with an answer to my every question. And always the exact answer you'd expect. No Surprises Bob, that's what I called him in my head. I had him figured for the Business School.

But now old Bob had come back to surprise me.

"So you're a police officer now," I said, and chuckled a little at that. I hoped it didn't sound forced. He took it to mean I was proud of him.

"It's my third year," he said, his head bouncing in a nod.

His partner, the older officer, started shuffling his feet then. "Well, good for you, Bob," I said, wondering how to get rid of them. "But is something wrong? You're not just dropping by to say hello at this hour, I hope."

"No, Dr. Gentles," the older policeman saw his chance to jump in and he took it. "There's been some trouble over at the Federal Hospital.   There was an escape there tonight, Dr.

Gentles. We're just checking on you. You haven't seen anything unusual here, have you? You haven't seen anyone sneaking around, or anything?"

"No," I shook my head. "Should I have?" I gave them my best worried frown.

"Well, Professor," Litzberger said, "the man who broke out was Bernard Choteau."

"Ahhh!" I said and arched my brows. It felt like they were believing me. I'd never lied to the police before that night. Now I discovered it had a strange thrill to it. "I did read that he'd been sent down here," I said.

The rain washed across the windows again, and I wondered why it was so easy to lie to them. Was it just for fear that he might hurt Terri? Or had I begun somehow to trust him?

"We knew you'd been a friend of his," Litzberger said.

"Only if you call meeting him once for twenty minutes a friendship," I laughed. "I met him just long enough to find out he wouldn't cooperate with me on what I was trying to do. That's it, Bob, I'm afraid."

"But you did write that book about him," he said.

"It wasn't just about Bernard Choteau," I stopped, and reminded myself that I was supposed to be concerned, not defensive. "I did send him a copy of it, though. But I suppose you know that. Its probably in your records, or something."

Neither of them took the bait and told me what exactly they knew that brought them here. It was the older cop who spoke. "We do think he knows you live here in town, Dr. Gentles. And he may even think you'd help him," he said, and paused heavily there. "You're sure you haven't seen or heard anything unusual?"

"Nothing. Nothing but this Christmas rain."

I noticed the older officer was using the time to look the room over carefully.

"Would you like to come in and look around?" I held my hand out to invite them in further, bluffing for all I was worth. What would I do if they took up my offer?

"No, no, Professor, that's all right," little Officer Bob said. "We just wanted to check on you, make sure everything was okay." His face was flat and his eyes were bright with concern, but the older cop's glance was still nervously flitting around the room. "It would be smart to keep everything locked up tight tonight, though, Professor. And for the next couple days, too. Well keep an eye on the place, but you just call us if you see or hear anything. Anything at all."

They put their hats back on as I thanked them and held the door for them again.

"You won't mind if we check around the house and the backyard a bit," the older cop said once he'd stepped outside.

"Please do, Officer. In fact, my wife and I would appreciate it if you did."

He nodded once like he was taking an order, and as Litzberger stepped through the doorway, I followed him out onto the front step. "Was anybody hurt out there, Bob, when he escaped?"

"There's two guards in the hospital, Professor, " he said. "I guess one of them got hit over the head with a length of pipe. He hasn't come around yet."

"I see," I nodded and pursed my lips.

"Be careful, Dr. Gentles," the kid said, looking too young to be a cop. "He probably knows you live here."

"Yes," I said, stepping back inside the house. "Yes, I suppose he probably does."

I locked the door behind them.

In the bedroom I found Terri tucked under the covers. When I walked in, she rolled over in bed and, acting like she'd just been roused from a deep sleep, said, "What's wrong, Will?"

It was a beautiful ploy.

"It's okay. I got rid of them. They're looking around outside, but they'll be gone soon. I think." I looked around the room for Choteau. "Are you all right?" I said to Terri. She nodded her head mutely. I wanted to hold her, but I didn't see anyway I could comfort her.

I followed Terri's gaze over to the shadows in the corner then, and I found him. He was crouched down near the floor, behind the dresser, just out of easy sight, ready to spring on whoever might walk through that door. He looked hungry.

"Stay down until they're gone," I said. And it felt good to regain some control. "I'll let you know when it's clear. But I'm going to fix us something to eat. That will look natural."

He didn't really move out of his crouch, and he didn't protest my orders. After all, he still had Terri there as a hostage. "No funny stuff," he snarled at me as a warning. But what else could he do?

I went out and lit a fire in the fireplace. As it began to catch, I watched the pale lights flicker off the bear mask grinning down at me and listened to the fire's crackle mix with the rain and sleet riding the wind outside. I began to think about the one thing I had learned from all the research I'd done on Mr. Choteau. He was a victim. His trial had been a farce, and if he'd bothered to appeal, he'd probably go free. Except of course that the Bureau of Investigation, my brotherin law included, had it out for him.

In the kitchen I sliced up pastrami and some cheddar with dark bread, and watched out the window for the patrol car to leave. It occurred to me that Choteau had not come here to hurt us. He had come for help. And the more I thought about it, the more sense it made to help him. When the headlights switched on and the patrol car backed down our short drive, I parted the curtains and waved to them from one of the living room windows. I was still holding a paring knife in my hands. Their lights glared off the wet pavement, as the patrol car pulled out on the street.

"They're gone," I heard Choteau say behind me. "For now." I hadn't heard him come in. He reached out and took the knife from my hand. "Let's eat," he said, and then he tossed back his head and laughed out loud.

We sat on the floor in front of the fire then, and the food tasted good. I'd brought us out a round of dark beers, and they went down easy, too. I think I needed a drink after all of this. Choteau was too busy wolfing down the pastrami and cheese to speak, and I was lost in my changing thoughts about him. I wanted to help him, now. But I wasn't sure how.

"You need to know about my brother," Terri said to him, and ended the hungry silence. "We don't want any surprises."

Choteau seemed unconcerned. He picked up another slice of pastrami for the plate, and added it to his sandwich. Then he took a long swallow of the beer I'd served him, and emptied it. He was still in his wet prison clothes, but at least he had the robe over the top of them now. He looked like some hospital patient sitting there.

"My brother works for the FBI, Mr. Choteau," she said. "You should be aware of that. His name's Mike Golman," she said, implying that he might recognize it.

Choteau shifted his gaze from the fire over to her, but he didn't say a word.

"It's even better than that, Choteau," I told him. "Golman went through school or training, or whatever, with Ron Williams."

He didn't blink at the name of one of the men he was serving time for killing.

"And he knew Coler too, I think. And he was in on the ResMurs Investigation afterwards. So Golman," I stopped to consider the right wayto go on. "He knows who you are. And I guess you could say he's interested in your case."

"I see," Choteau looked back into the fire. He picked up his empty beer bottle and held it in both hands.

"And we're supposed to spend Christmas Eve with him tomorrow," Terri said. "At my folk's place, up north at the lakes."

Choteau set the empty bottle down, and heaved a sigh. He was nodding his head as if to say, "It figures." But he was quiet.

"I don't know how long it will be safe for you here," Terri said.

She was rubbing her arm unconsciously, right where Choteau had grabbed her. I couldn't figure out what she was up to, then, why she was sharing all this information with the convict in our house.

But I felt my allegiances shifting. Though he still scared me, it was only physical fear working. Fear is no small thing, but on another level, I had changed sides. I needed to help him in his escape, because he had been wronged. And I knew he'd been wronged. The right thing to do was to help him get to his freedom. But that decision itself scared me. I knew what should be done, but I didn't know if I had the courage to do it. And I didn't know where these flights of morality and principle were going to take me.

And I wasn't sure of Terri either. She seemed now to want to help him too. Part of me wanted to believe she had changed her mind like I had. The force of moral action had swept away her doubts, or at least left them in a dust heap behind us. Still I couldn't help but wonder. Could she just as easily be acting out of simple, practical fear? Go along with him now, give him whatever he wants, and then he'll leave us alone. And the more we help him along his way, the sooner he'll be gone out of our lives.

I looked at the tired red in her eyes, and I watched her rub that arm, and I couldn't say where she was.

*　　　　　　*　　　　　　*

24

"How well can you see?" Terri said to him. "It's glaucoma, isn't it? That's why they sent you here?" She'd read the article in the paper too.

He stopped chewing on his sandwich, and ran a hand through his hair and held it up in a ponytail. "Well enough," he said.

Then he looked down at the empty beer bottle in front of him. "Do you realize how long it's been since I had a beer?" he said. "Thirteen years. Thirteen long years without a beer. Christ."

Terri laughed at that, but I thought it sounded forced. I was sure now she was playing him for information. "What does that mean? You can see well enough?" she said. From where I was beside him, I noticed he wore some sort of dark jewelry behind his ear. But then he let the hair fall and I couldn't make out what it was.

He picked up the paring knife and cut a square of cheese. "Well," he said as he chewed on it, "that depends." He set the knife back down on the plate where the food was heaped.

"Depends on what?" I said.

Choteau snorted once and then, without a grin or even a hint of humor in his voice, he said, "Depends on whether I need to see or not." Then he looked straight into my eyes. "Depends on whether I want you to know if I can see," a little smile curled his lips, "or not."

After he spoke he kept staring me down until I glanced away. If he couldn't see out of those eyes, I sure couldn't tell. It was malicious enough, that the old physical fear welled up in me again. I wanted to get up and walk away. Terri seemed to draw down into herself.

*　　　　　*　　　　　*

25

"Isn't there somewhere we can take you, quickly?" she said, her head down. She was pleading. "Is there somebody we can call?"

When I remember it now, I think Choteau really was lost at that moment. I don't think he knew where he was going then. Not for sure. Or maybe he was just embarrassed to say. But what he did next, to distract us, I still don't understand.

He stood up and ran his finger along the face of that mask over the mantel. His fingers followed the bear's grin down until he came to where that mistletoe dangled from its nose. It took him just a moment to pull the tape loose carefully, but he took the decoration off and let it drop to the floor. The mask grinned down at us happily.

"It's a nice piece," I said. "Isn't it?"

He nodded, but didn't speak.

"It's Kwakiutl," I said.

Then, without looking down at either of us, Choteau slipped his hand back behind the wooden mask, as deftly as if he'd practiced the move for years. Suddenly the bear's big grin split wide. Its head opened up like it was growling, but then as it reared back, it turned into red and black wings, and a raven's long black beak jabbed out between them, where the bear's tongue should have been. In the bird's eyes were white crescent moons.

Choteau looked over his shoulder at both of us.

"You knew about its trick," I said, and laughed like a kid. "It has two faces."

Choteau's smile showed his teeth, white in his dark face. "Oh, it does?" he said. His hand was still hidden behind the mask. Suddenly, as if he'd beckoned to it, the raven's beak began to part. It split in two, opening like some kind of screeching bird. But it wasn't screeching, because inside there was another face, a third face, and one I'd never seen. This mask was a human face, with black, oriental eyes and bright red lips, scowling out at us. And it seemed angry to be found.

26

"How'd you know about that?" I said. Choteau cocked his head back, so he could laugh deep from his gut and loud. "I didn't even know about that," I said, and I started to laugh a little with him.

But then, just as quickly, he pulled his hand away. The mask slapped shut. First the raven's beak clapped closed, and then with a wooden clack the bear grinned down at us again.

"It has three faces," I said, still surprised.

"No, Professor," Choteau said. "It has four." Then he patted his stomach. "Now. If I could have another one of those fine beers, and a safe place to sleep, I will think about this brother of yours," he said, wearing a big phony frown for Terri. He had no plans to leave us just yet, it was clear.

"Four?" I said. I had my hands behind the mask then, feeling for the leather pull string.

"Think about it, Professor," Choteau said. He paused and then he laughed at me. "That's your job," he grinned just like the bear, "isn't it?"

Terri showed him the old couch back in my study. She did it with no hesitation, and when I tried to glance at her, to figure out what she might be up to, she just stared blankly at me.

"Why don't you turn in," I said to her. "I'll take care of this. Get some sleep."

She nodded blankly and left, and I wondered if she was in shock or something. Then she turned and said, "Will?" She looked down at Choteau sitting on the couch, cradling his second beer in his hand. Then she said to me, "Don't try anything, Will. Don't be a hero." She turned and left the room.

The study there is walled all around with books, right over the two small windows. I seem to get more done when I can't stare out of windows, and there were always too many books. So the windows were gone, behind bookshelves, and now it became the perfect hideout. A little cell to hide our secret sharer. But for how long I didn't know.

"This is where you wrote your book," Choteau said.

I nodded yes.

He took a long swig from his beer, and then seemed to make me a promise. "Maybe you'll learn something from me, Professor. Maybe this time, if you're really up to it, you'll learn something here."

"I don't need to be bribed to help you, Choteau."

He shook his head no, then toasted me with his beer bottle. "Good night, Professor."

I went out and picked up the scraps of food and the three empty bottles by the fireplace. A wave of exhaustion rolled over me. It was midnight or later, and the evening had been long, much longer than I ever expected. The adrenalin rush had died and I just felt worn.

But the bear was grinning down at me like some jester, and I couldn't resist. I opened his smile to see the bird. I knew that trick. But no matter what I pulled, in the dark there I couldn't find a way to open up the raven and see the scowling human face inside.

As I felt around the raven's beak, it dawned on me suddenly, where the fourth face was. I thought I understood what Choteau meant. It was the dancer, of course. The fourth face belonged to the one who wore the mask. But if that was true, I played around with his ideas in my head, then what was behind the fourth mask? Or was it a mask at all?

I was feeling proud of myself, because I was as clever as old Mr. Choteau. I carried the plates and bottles to the sink in the kitchen. Setting them there, I chuckled at that crazy mask and Choteau's little stunt with it, until I noticed that the little paring knife--the one I used to slice the meat and the cheese--was gone. The knife he'd taken from my hand at the window. The knife that was sitting there on this plate just moments before as we ate. I went out and looked around on the floor by the fireplace, but it was nowhere to be found. It had disappeared.

"Does he scare you?" I whispered to Terri. I was holding her as we lay in bed, listening to the sleet and wind outside. The house was dark and quiet, but not empty. Neither of us could sleep.

"Yes, " she said, her head was resting on my shoulder. Then she sighed. "We need to help him, though."

"He won't hurt us, Terri. I'm sure of that."

"I know," she shifted her head and gazed across the bed at the closed door. "He came here for help. But I'm not so sure that won't hurt us. In the end."

I thought about the missing knife and where it must have gone. "Did he hurt you?" I said, and touched her arm where Choteau had grabbed her.

"It's nothing that won't heal," she said. Then she looked over at me. "Does he scare you, Will?"

A moment passed while I weighed whether to lie to her or not. Would this be any easier if I played some macho part? Probably not.

"Yes," I said. "He scares the light of dawn out of me. I don't know what he's going to do next. I can't predict him. Not at all." I reached over and picked up the phone receiver. "I mean, look at this. He trusts us. He left us alone in here with the phone. He knows we won't turn him in."

She rested her head on my shoulder. "Or he knows we're too afraid of him to try."

"We're going to help him, Terri," I said.

"I know," she kissed my shoulder. "But I'm not sure I really know why," she said.

A lot of reasons why came to mind. There was the way the FBI and the government had hunted him down and tried him in the past. There were the real doubts I had about whether he was guilty, whether he'd really pulled the trigger and killed those men out at Pine Ridge. And I suppose there was good old White Man's Guilt as well. Not to mention his strange promise to me just now, a promise to finally tell me his story. Any of those might have been reason enough to help him. But they weren't it.

It was just that this harried man came to our door in the middle of the night, needing our help. And he seemed to be headed toward something important. And I believed Terri sensed that in him too.

So we stared at the darkened walls and listened to the strange winter rain, and it took a long while to fall asleep. Once, after a long silence that didn't lead to sleep, Terri said, "You don't think he shot those two agents, do you, Will? Like Mike says he did."

"No," I said, "he's innocent." And though I believed it when I said it, those words sounded empty in the air. They sounded like a lie.

It was over a month later we learned Choteau made a phone call that night. We didn't find it out until the bill came. He must have waited until we were soundly asleep. Then he placed a call in the middle of the night to Grand Forks, North Dakota. To Room 315 at the University Hilton. And he talked to her there for half an hour.

The sound of cracking and popping, like the sound of some distant war, woke me in the dark. I lay still for a long time in the confusion of near sleep, trying to remember where I was, and what I had to do this day. Outside the sleet crackled like a fire, broken only by strange pops and sizzles.

30

I sat up in bed then, remembering slowly the weather, and then Choteau in the other room, and then all the police who'd been hunting for him, and then that it was Christmas Eve and we had to travel. Each of these details came like bursts of ice water in a hot shower. So I was alert and standing beside the bed by the time the last shock had passed. Gradually, warning sirens were winding up and crying all across the city.

"What is it?" Terri said sleepily.

"I don't know," I groped my way toward the door and said, "Watch your eyes," as I switched on the light. Nothing happened. Slowly I understood that the power was gone. As I felt for my robe in the dark, Terri reached over to the night table by the bed.

"We've still got telephone," she said. She was so much more collected than I was; she was clear and thinking already.

The house felt cold and the night was punctuated with the sound of cracking wood as limbs broke outside. The warning sirens sang in crescendo and then fell down into moans, over and over, in a kind of ragged unison.

I walked out through the dark living room, and back to the rear of the house. Bay windows there looked out over the backyard. Choteau stood beside them, wrapped tight in his robe, looking out in silence.

I moved up behind him. A thin coat of ice plated the glass, so the dark world outside was warped and blurry. "Ice storm," Choteau said, without looking back at me. Something in the way he said it had the quality of a command.

Probably I was just half asleep and confused, but it's seemed ever since in my memory that he called for that storm. He caused the ice to fall in sheets and weigh down trees, toppling them into the wires to knock out power. It was part of his escape. Nature was contributing, an accessory after the fact.

Evidently he'd been standing there watching for a while, because I could make out nothing through that coating of ice.

Terri came up behind us then, carrying a lit candle. Its soft light caught every angle and wave in the frozen coating, and blinded us entirely to the outside.

"The trees are cracking under the weight of the ice," Choteau said, in that same commanding tone. I felt like I was going crazy, like the storm belonged to my senses and not to the outside world.

"How can you see?" I said. Then I remembered his blindness, and decided he was using his ears.

"Blow out the candle, Terri," I said, "so we can see the yard."

But Choteau flashed a hand out quickly, and took the candlestick from Terri. In the light of it I saw he wore little, if anything, under the robe. His prison clothes were gone. I thought he'd blow the candle out, but instead he held it up close to the window pane. Slowly, in strict silence, we watched as the heat of the flame began to warm the glass and melt a hole in the layer of ice outside. We stood, hushed like we were waiting at a peephole to gaze into some magic show.

Choteau's face was close to the candle, and I noticed again he wore something tied behind his ear. It was a small, brown pebble, not an ornament, because it was too hidden for that. It was an amulet of some kind. And then, at that moment, I remembered what it was, and why it seemed so familiar.

"Look," he said in his commanding voice, and blew out the flame. Terri and I put our heads together like children, and stared out the peephole in the ice. Out there, wires lay in the frozen grass. Our two apple trees had fallen over on their sides.. They lay on the ground, uprooted by the weight of ice, mounds of the broken earth behind them where the roots had pulled up the soil.

In just moments the sleet outside and the fog of our breath closed the hole and we were blind again. But we'd had our glimpse of the storm.

Choteau laughed loudly with great, fat pleasure. He knew the storm had locked up his pursuers, it had helped him in his escape. At one and the same time, he was as free as he'd been in a dozen years, while he was trapped, caught in this house by the elements.

But without any electricity, there would be no heat. The house was already growing cold. And there was nothing any of us could do about it until morning. Choteau crept back to his couch in the study, and we crept back to our rumpled bed to stay warm. In the light of morning, we would worry about power companies and repairs, and about hiding this stranger through the rest of the storm.

Before long I could hear the sound of Terri sleeping again, breathing regularly, curled beside me. But I lay awake for a time, listening to the breaking limbs, cracking like the world was cracking, and I thought about that little stone Choteau wore.

You see, I knew it from my dissertation. But I didn't know why Choteau wore that little pebble behind his ear. He hadn't said a word to me yet about who he was, or who he said he was. But I remembered from a lot of old research that someone else had worn a stone just like that one, a century ago. A little amulet like that had been part of the strange vision that shaped a man's whole life. A man who was not unknown.

But that night, struggling to keep warm in the heart of an ice storm, I thought Choteau was just imitating a hero, emulating a great figure from his Lakota past. In the spirit of the long ago ones, you know. In the spirit of Crazy Horse.

12/24/89

A phone call from Golman woke us. "Got any electricity?" he said, not hello, or good morning, or Merry Christmas. He was all business.

"Well, at least your phones are up," he said. "You guys are in a disaster area," he chuckled.

I explained to him that we were still under the covers keeping warm. Our heat was out, the lights were gone, and I hadn't got out yet to survey the damage. But Golman was glad to survey it for me. The ice storm had knocked out power in parts of Missouri, Oklahoma and Arkansas. All three Governor's were asking for federal aid, and the shelters were opening all around for people without heat.

"Well, don't you worry," Golman said. "You got a fireplace, right? Just sit tight and stay warm and we'll come down and get you, this afternoon. All right? Once they clean this up a little. I'm at Mom and Dad's, and the kids are already here. So all we need is you two. Hey, pal, let me talk to Terri, would ya?

It took me a moment to say, "Yeah, she's right here." I was letting the facts hit me. An FBI agent was coming to my house, and I had an escaped federal convict in the back room sleeping on my couch. Not to mention, this convict was of particular interest to my agent brother-in-law.

"By the way," Golman said with a laugh, "haven't seen your buddy Bernard Choteau, have you?"

"What?" I said. I know my surprise at that question sounded genuine, because it was genuine.

"Choteau escaped last night, chum."

"But how would he get here from Leavenworth?" Now my playing dumb seemed so obvious, I wished I'd just shut up.

"He was in Springfield, buddy boy," Golman said, then paused while he thought about my question. Or at least that's the way it felt to me as I kept my mouth shut. "He was in your backyard when he hopped the fence. Left two guards unconscious in his hospital room. One of them's still in a coma. So be careful, brother, he knows who you are," Golman paused, then said, "I believe."

"Well, I'll check the couch to see if he used the key I sent him, Mike," I said. I was getting better at this lying game.

"Hey, no joke, buddy. The man's dangerous, and you've tried to contact him. He may be coming your way. So watch yourself. Let me talk to my sis, huh?"

I handed the receiver over to Terri, who was lying with her eyes closed. But she was listening. "Golman," I said.

"That's my name," she muttered, knowing who I meant by it. I didn't answer her. I knew it drove her crazy that I called her brother by their last name, but like I say, Golman and I, we just didn't agree about much in this world, or any other.

Choteau appeared in the doorway in his robe then. His frown told me he'd heard me mention Golman's name. I nodded yes to him anyway. He just glared at the whole room in response. His hands, at his sides, began to work like he was holding loose beads.

"Let me talk to him," Terri whispered, as she held the receiver up and covered the mouthpiece with her hand. "I can handle him," she mouthed, more than spoke.

"Don't tell him anything," I whispered back at her.

She nodded at me. Then she said, "Mike?" into the receiver.

With a jerk of his head, Choteau led me out into the living room. I followed him out there happily, putting on my robe. I didn't really want to sit and listen to Golman run Terri through the wringer anyway. She was going to hear all about how much he needed us up there, for the sake of his two boys, and so on. I was glad to miss it.

Choteau had already started a fire in the fireplace, but it was small and the house was still frigid. He began to pace. He might have been pacing to stay warm, because he was still wrapped only in that robe, but I guess he had other reasons as well.

He stopped pacing long enough to look me over. He was measuring me. Then suddenly he seemed to decide that even if I didn't measure up, he had to take a chance on me anyway.

"Can we trust her?" he said.

It was a funny question, because he'd just left her in there talking on the phone with an FBI agent. I think he was testing me then.

"Yeah," I said. "You can trust her." I remembered the two of us lying in bed the night before. I remembered the way she asked me if Choteau was guilty of those two murders, and the way my answer sounded uncertain in the night. "She knows your story," I said, and sounded like I was defending her.

Choteau nodded, but he was still eyeing me. "Sure," he said. "But whose version? Yours or her brother's?"

That made me a little angry. It was all right for me to nurture my secret doubts about Terri, but not for him. "We can trust her, Choteau," I said, more sharply than I meant to.

He stared at me silently for a while, and I wondered if I'd passed his test. Then he nodded yes, and turned away. He walked straight to the front door and threw it open. "Look," he said. With a push, he opened the ice coated screen door too.

"Careful," I said, and stepped toward him. "Somebody out there could see you."

He gave me that big laugh again and said, "Don't worry, Professor. Just look!"

When I finally did look outside, I understood. The city was perfectly still, and everything was coated with at least an inch of ice. It almost seemed artificial, like one of those glazed ceramic villages you put under a Christmas tree. Everything out there glistened in the morning sun. The storm had passed, but what a world it had left. The bare trees, the light poles and all the wires, some of them down and on the ground, every car

36

parked along every curb and in every drive, all the street signs, the fire hydrants, right down to the brown blades of grass, and even the beer cans littering the gutters in front of the students' house next door, everything was transformed by the glaze. It was a glass world out there, sparkling, still, and fragile.

But it was as foreboding as it was beautiful. Limbs and whole trees and even some poles were down, strewn in the streets. The only sounds were the far off scraping of road crews working to clear the main streets, the sizzle of hot electric wires on the ground, and the high groan of trees rubbing against one another as they tried to hold up under the weight of the ice. In our front yard, our pretty magnolia lay over on its side across the sidewalk, its trunk broken into splinters. The weight of the ice on its leaves had cracked it like a twig.

And out past that ruined tree, not a soul was moving yet on our street.

This glassy devastation left both Choteau and me quiet. Inside all our private worlds of worry and effort, nature was a ticking time bomb, waiting to show us our real priorities: warmth, food, shelter. The bomb had gone off last night. So we gazed out at that crystalline ice and silently rearranged our worries.

Then Terri strode into the living room, wrapped in her marshmallow robe, and dropped the next bomb on our laps. "My brother's on his way," she said. "He's leaving right now."

For a moment we all stood there, looking dumbly at one another. Slowly, I shoved the front door closed.

"How long will it take him?" Choteau barked. His fists closed, and he was nervous as a cornered animal again. I think he was wondering what Terri had told her brother, because I found I was too. When I talked to Golman, he was going to wait until afternoon to come. Now he was on his way here. What had hurried him up?

It was an hour and a half drive, in good weather. And as we told him that, we began to discuss what to do next. I took him off to my closet, and with the help of some rolled sleeves, a couple of safety pins, and one torn waist, we got him dressed. A flannel shirt, some gray wool slacks, and a pair of old work boots dotted with paint did the trick. With a couple of stretched out sweaters and one old hooded sweatshirt for the cold, he was ready to run. It wasn't high fashion, but at least he wasn't wearing any numbers.

Choteau was strangely quiet the whole time. He seemed lost in thoughts, and the longer he brooded over it all, the more he seemed to relax. I think he was making some decisions then, keeping it all to himself.

My idea at the start was to hide him right there, in the house, until we got back from the holiday. Then we could drive him somewhere, wherever he needed to go.

"That won't work, Will," Terri said. Choteau stood by the fire and watched her carefully, while she explained why. She seemed almost angry about it, but she was right. There wasn't any heat in the house. And if he tried to use the fireplace, someone was bound to notice. Repairmen were going to be all over, working their way through the city. And then there were the police. We knew they'd be watching the house. This was not the place to hide.

I wondered, as I listened to her, why she'd thought this through so well. She was helping Choteau, yes. But she was also getting him out of our house as soon as possible.

But Choteau waited for her to finish, watching her, and then agreed. "This is my shot at it," he said. "I need to use this weather to get ahead of them."

I knew they were right.

We began to gather up supplies for him, and put them by the door: blankets, a sleeping bag, a bottle of water, some food. I offered him the use of my car, though I wasn't even sure where he was headed. I guessed it was north to Canada. I knew he'd escaped there, to Vancouver Island, years ago. But it was probably best, with a federal agent for a brother-in-law, that we didn't know where he was going. Not even the direction. And I told him that.

Choteau was watching me then. He didn't say a word about the car, or all these preparations. Terri moved like a skater, though. I heard her laugh for the first time since Choteau had stepped in our door. She was seeing the end to our abduction, if you could call it that. She could see safety and Christmas out there just past afternoon. It buoyed her up.

But Choteau was quiet through it all, and I was trying to hide the disappointment I felt. I couldn't say why, but this quick way out the door with him made me uneasy.

My next idea came from that uneasiness, though it didn't last long. I decided Terri and I together should drive Choteau to his safety, wherever that was. No one would stop a middle-aged married couple driving cross-country on the day before Christmas. Choteau could just hide in the back seat. We were the perfect cover for him.

Terri's glare was a mixture of anger and disbelief. She wasn't laughing when she said, "What about Mike? If we don't show up at Mom and Dad's tonight, he'll have every cop in the Midwest out looking for us. With photos, descriptions, license plates."

"And he'll know I'm with you," Choteau said.

"He needs to go alone, Will," Terri was flushed rosy red. She glanced at her watch, "And soon, too."

I nodded. "It was dumb. I just . . . "

But Choteau didn't seem in any hurry yet. He bent down and prodded the fire a little, hefting the poker in his hand. It was cold in that house and the cold seemed to make it all clear. Choteau needed to take my car and drive alone to Canada, as soon as possible. Terri and I were done with him.

The escape was almost over for us. Except for a car he could abandon in Canada, and we would claim was stolen, we had done our part for Bernard Choteau.

"It makes sense," I said, trying not to sound too disappointed. I thought about how much I might learn from him, if we had just a few hours alone together. I thought about my phony monograph with just half the story, and how it might have been a book. And I thought about the adventure of it too, I suppose. About driving to Canada with a political prisoner, fleeing from the FBI. About taking a gamble, running for the border, daring to set him free. "Okay, Choteau," I said. "Let me get the keys and hop into some clothes, and I'll show you the car. Its got a full tank, you know. I topped it off yesterday, when I heard the storm warnings." I couldn't help my sigh then. "You need to get on the road."

But Choteau still didn't move from the fire.

"I want you to come with me," he said. Then he stood up, put a hand on my shoulder in camaraderie, and stared straight into my eyes.

"Come with you," I repeated.

Terri moved over to the couch, and sat down. She put her head down in her hands and was quiet. A long while passed, and then she looked up, her hands still covering her mouth. Tears ran down her cheeks.

"Yes," Choteau said. He let go of my shoulder.

I wanted to go. But I looked over at Terri and saw the way her hopes were fading. Moments ago she was sure this was almost all over with, but now it might go on further than she could see. I was going to be in danger, and there was even the chance I might not come back from this. It could stretch out and touch every moment of the rest of her life.

"I don't know, Choteau," I walked over and touched her hair. She didn't make a sound.

"I'm not asking, Professor. An Indian, driving alone in this countryside. I stick out," he said. "We don't have time to argue about this. There are some places I won't get through alone. Some places I need to be driven through, Professor. I need you to come along." He was still holding that poker in his right hand. He made no gesture with it, but it was there. and in my mind, so was that missing knife.

"We're on your side, Choteau. Don't threaten us."

Terri stood up and moved away from my touch. "No. He's right, Will. You need to go with him." With her fingertips she wiped the tears off her cheeks and sniffed once or twice.

"I don't know, Terri . . . "

"Just do what he says, Will." She walked over to him and took the poker out of his hands. As she set it down in the rack by the fire, she said, "It's your eyes, isn't it?" She wasn't quite able to hide the tremor in her voice. "You can't see well enough to drive yourself all the way to Canada. You need someone to take you. Because you can't see."

He shook his head no. "I can drive," he said. "I can see well enough. But how far will I get, alone? I stick out, Mrs. Gentles."

"You still don't trust us, do you?" she said. She sniffed back her tears again, and the tremor was gone when she said, "You don't deserve to be in prison, Mr. Choteau. I'm scared of you, but that doesn't me you deserve to be in prison." Then she looked at me and said, "You need to go with him, Will. He can't see."

"Look," she walked over to the hall closet. I watched Choteau as he watched her open the closet and pull a cap out. It was a bright red ball cap. Then she walked back and handed it to Choteau. The cap said "K.C. Chiefs" on the front. "Put it on, and stuff some of that long hair up in it," she ordered him. She was putting on a brave face, I thought.

Choteau tucked his hair up under the hat as he slipped it on. And he did it easily. This was not the first time he'd hidden all that hair under a cap.

"There," Terri said. "Now you two will just be a couple of old boys from Missouri on your way north. The two of you together, driving, you can make it to the border in a day, if you drive straight through. Nobody'll even notice you." Then she turned to me, "Just drop him off and get back here." She stopped there, and then said, "There isn't another way, Will."

"How are you going to fool your brother?" Choteau said. His head cast down, he stared at Terri from under a heavy frown.

"All you need is a day," she said. "I can keep Mike busy with Christmas for a day."

But Choteau just kept glaring into her eyes, holding them the way he'd grabbed her arm the night before. Was she really a part of this escape? Or was she just cooperating out of fear? Maybe she didn't know for sure herself. But Choteau kept staring at her, trying to read her.

"This Mike Golman," Choteau said. He let go of her eyes finally. He adjusted the hat on his head and walked away from the fire. From the rear, he looked like some hillbilly who'd wandered into town. I knew the look, because I'd seen it a hundred times. I'd seen it on more than a few of my students. He looked lost, but defiant. "If he's a fed, then he's sharp. He won't be easy to fool."

"I can handle him," Terri said.

Then, without turning around or pausing, Choteau told us how it would work. It was all so clear and complete, it was obvious that he'd been thinking about this for a while. Maybe all night. Just like he knew I was going to drive, he knew the lie we were going to tell. And it was simple enough to work.

When Golman showed up, Terri would just tell him that I was down at my office on campus. The ice storm had knocked down a tree and broken a lot of windows in my building. So I was down on campus moving my things, files and records and books and so on, into storage. It might take all afternoon, so they shouldn't wait for me. And there were plenty of faculty and custodial staff, so Golman didn't need to help. What he needed to do was get his sister home for the holiday.

Later on, when everything was in order, I was supposed to follow them up to the lakes. But of course, when that time came, I would be iced in for the night. Stuck until morning at least.

"We will stop somewhere along the way this afternoon," he said. "The Professor will call and tell you then that he's stuck." I would simply tell Terri on the phone, with Golman listening if he wanted, that I figured it would be safer to drive up in the morning, when the roads are clear and sanded. "Who's going to argue with that?" Choteau said. "A cop?"

"By the time he catches on," I said, "we'll be across the border." I laughed at how simple it was, and suddenly I felt good that I was going along. It would be quick, it would be safe, it would be over before anyone knew what was happening. "We'll be long gone down some Canadian Highway, before old Golman even figures it out.

"And when I come back, I can just claim I was kidnapped." I reached out and put an arm around Terri's shoulders. "Its easy," I said. .

Terri put both her arms around my waist, and said, slowly, "It will work. Won't it?"

Choteau nodded yes, but didn't say a word more.

"How much time do we have left?" I said. And I went to get dressed. Now there was work to do.

When Choteau saw the car he groaned. "It's not exactly a Cadillac," he said.

I laughed and patted it on the hood. It was an old Renault, bumble bee yellow, with a hundred and fifty thousand miles on it. "She'll get us where we need to go," I said. But he still didn't seem happy.

We warmed the car up, loaded it with our things and Choteau slowly scraped the ice from the windshield. I went back inside and gathered up all the cash we had in the house. It wasn't much, but it would have to do.

As Terri opened up her purse and pulled out the few bills she carried in there, I had a moment to think clearly again. She looked worried and suddenly this adventure didn't seem so great. We were just going to be apart on Christmas. I was just going to drive away to somewhere with a stranger and leave her alone in the middle of a disaster area, without power or heat, waiting for her FBI brother to save her. "Merry Christmas," I muttered.

"Are you okay behind this?" I said. It was the first chance we'd had since Golman's call to talk alone.

She didn't look up at me as she handed me the bills she'd found in her purse. "Just be careful, Will. Do whatever he says, and he won't hurt you."

"He deserves to be free," I said.

"I know he does. But that doesn't mean he will be. Or that they'll let him be. Does it?"

"No, it doesn't," I said. I looked over at the dark Christmas tree in the corner, and it only seemed dried up and dangerous. "But we're gonna try, Terri."

She nodded her head, and then the tears really did come. I hugged her and she muttered, "Be careful," into my shoulder.

"We'll do Christmas when I get back, okay?" I said. "We'll do the presents and stuff then."

She wiped the tears off her cheeks, sniffed once, and then said, "I have to wait to open my presents?"

We both laughed then, and it eased some of the fears. I kissed her, and then she hung onto me for a moment. I tried to memorize how green her eyes were. I was about to tell her that I loved her, but she said, "You trust him, don't you, Will?"

Choteau stepped inside the front door before I could answer.

If we had any doubts about whether he'd been listening to us, they died in a moment. He stood there, in that wrestling stance he fell into so naturally, and said, "It doesn't matter, Mrs. Gentles. Whether he trusts me or not, he's driving."

He drew a deep breath that seemed to swell his chest, and made that practiced toss of his head, the one that tucked his hair back in place. "And it doesn't matter if you trust me or not, either. Or if I believed your speech a little while ago. Because, Mrs. Gentles, I won't hurt him. But if you don't fool your brother, if your brother finds out, then all his many, many policemen friends will be after us. And your husband," he looked over at me. "When they find us, he will be in the middle of it all."

"Is that a threat?" Terri said, her voice rising.

"Terri."

"It doesn't matter if you believe me or not, Mrs. Gentles. I won't hurt him. Not even a whisker on his chin. But," he held his hands out in front of him, palms up, "when the feds come crashing in, they're not always careful. I know. I've seen them come crashing in a time or two. It's dangerous, when everyone is scared."

I felt her arms tighten around my waist.

His tone grew dark and angry then. He was all business. It was a lot of prison years talking. "Just remember. The best thing for all of us is that your brother never knows. The longer you can keep him fooled, the better off we all are. Everybody. Mr. Golman included. Remember that."

He leaned back then and opened the front door. "We better roll, Professor." He stepped outside, and waited holding the door open for me. "We don't have all day."

She didn't let go of me for a moment. I said, "I love you" one last time, and kissed her. "It'll be all right," I whispered to her, and I believed it too. For some reason. Then I pulled out of her arms and followed Choteau to the door.

"Be careful," she said. "Both of you." Then she struggled to smile. "Mike'll be here in an hour or two. I'd better go get ready for Christmas Eve," she said.

But she followed us to the door and watched as we drove away.

The wheels of my old Renault came loose with a crack. Even though the engine had idled for quarter of an hour, we had to break the ice to move. After that, it was a free for all.

There was no such thing as brakes on those streets. Basically, I just pointed the car where I wanted to go, got up what momentum I could, and rode along. It was like canoeing through fast rapids on a narrow stream, but with less control. The only way to stop was to coast slowly until we were still, or to find something soft to hit. Even then, we had to be careful we didn't bounce.

The old Le Car handled the ice as well as anything could, but I'm afraid its heater was more like a hand warmer. My defroster was really a rag I kept tied to a knob on the dash. With both Choteau and me in the car, and both of us breathing, I think we were wiping the windshield clear constantly.

The roads were littered with limbs and downed wires. We drove right over the branches that looked small. But in some places, where a whole tree was down or where wires looked hot and dangerous, we had to resort to driving through yards or on the sidewalks.

The Renault was small, and that was good. Three times Choteau and I had to climb out and rock the car enough to jump a wheel over the curb, just so we could go on. The third time, as we rocked the car over a broken gutter, I slipped on the wet ice and slammed my knee hard on the street. I felt my ankle and knee twist a way they weren't supposed to. It wasn't really all that painful at first. But the minute my kneecap struck the ice and concrete, I knew I'd done some real damage.

I felt weak for a moment, but it was too slick out to try to walk it off. So I held myself up in the car doorway and eased my weight down on that leg a few times. With Golman on his way, there was no time for anything more than that. So I hopped back inside the Renault and set myself to drive. Somehow, with that knee beginning to swell and stiffen, we drove on and got through town.

Only once, for a moment, did we talk about what was ahead of us. "Head north, I guess?" I said to Choteau, not long after we'd slid out of my driveway.

"Right," he said.

"Through Kansas City okay?" I said. I was wiggling the steering wheel, trying to keep a straight course as we slid between an uprooted redbud tree and a downed light pole.

"North," was all he'd say.

For a moment then, I wondered about this. What was I doing? Had I lost my mind? Leaving Terri in the middle of an ice storm on Christmas Eve and going on the lam with some convicted cop-killer?

But fortunately, the narrow space between that uprooted tree and the icy curb was all I could handle for the moment. It kept my conscience and my common sense iced over with a slippery layer of numbing cold.

It wasn't until we reached the edge of town and drove on out into the icy countryside that I really had much time to think. Out there, headed north under a gray white sky in an ice-plated world, I had the time to remember what I was leaving behind. Choteau wasn't talking, and the cold road was lonely, and that's when the memories started coming at me.

*   *   *

47

I met Terri Lisa Golman on a Friday night in a grocery store, when we both reached for the same bottle of wine. It was nothing special, just a cheap bottle of Rhine wine. But I was alone, new in town, just hired to teach at the U. She was alone, not wearing a ring, and pretty enough to turn heads. So I suggested we share the bottle.

Really it was just a joke. And a lame one at that. But she looked back at me with bedroom eyes and said, "Sure." We went to her apartment and then we talked and talked all night long. When the sun started to rise and that bottle of wine was long gone, along with half of another one, I suddenly found myself wrapped in her legs, making love, seeking visions. I woke up at noon on her floor, with carpet burns on my behind and some real terror in my mind. You see, one reason I'd taken this teaching job was to escape an entanglement that had started a lot like this. I wasn't very good at these things, once they became entanglements.

When I asked her that afternoon why, she shrugged her naked shoulders and said, "A gentleman wouldn't ask." Then just as smoothly, she told me I looked a lot like this married doctor she'd had the hots for at work for years. Except I wasn't as stuck up as that doc.

"Oh," I said, and I suppose I looked disappointed I wanted to be told about my animal attractions or my intelligent eyes or my urbane wit. My smooth come on. Not that I looked like somebody else.

"You asked," Terri said, with a scolding look in her eyes.

Six weeks later we moved in together and two years ago we were married, and we bought this house. The empty bottle of Rhine wine still sits on our mantel, right below that grinning Kwakiutl bear, like a memorial to our first night.

*   *   *

A few years ago, before we were married, I was driving this same stretch of highway in the middle of the night, except I was headed south instead of north, headed for home, and I was alone in the car. It was June and muggy even after dark. I was driving back from a month or so of research out in South Dakota. I'd spent some time in Denver and in Minneapolis interviewing FBI sources on the ResMur case, the people Mike Golman had lined up for me when I couldn't get Choteau to talk. And I'd spent two frustrating weeks around Pine Ridge, trying to gather information there from people who didn't want to talk to me. They'd all gone silent on me since my brief, useless interview with Choteau.

It was about one a.m. I was late. I'd called Terri that morning from a motel in York, Nebraska, and told her I'd be in that evening. Early, I'd said. But along the way, I detoured over to Leavenworth, and wasted three hours trying one last time to interview Bernard Choteau. The key to the whole research project.

But all I heard, from one guard or another, was that Choteau didn't want to speak to me. Eventually, Choteau claimed he was too ill--headaches from his glaucoma--and he didn't want to be disturbed. It didn't matter, since no one could make him see me. I was wasting my time.

So I was late getting home, and I was tired, and frustrated at my core. The only sources I really had were the ones Golman had got for me. Which meant the FBI sources. I whirled across the deserted streets of town, running a few of the flashing red lights. I left my luggage in the car and slipped quietly into the house, feeling a bit guilty about the worry I'd probably caused Terri. It had been a long, hot ride, growing more and more humid as I drove further east, so I peeked in at her sleeping under the sheets, and then I took a quick shower.

The cool water didn't really revive me, it just reminded me how hard the last hundred miles had been. I was beat.

I walked into the bedroom with only a towel wrapped around me, but feeling fresh after the sticky Missouri air. Terri was gone. The bed was mussed and open where she'd been asleep, and now in the dark, across the room on the dresser, three fat candles were burning. Their flames shone inside stained glass vessels, and the white walls flickered with red and blue and gold light.

I looked down at the colors moving on the empty, white sheets. Then, someone jerked the towel away from me.

"Hello, stranger," Terri said, sounding throaty.

She stood in the flickering shadows behind me. All she wore was turquoise jewelry and enough black lingerie to make, maybe, a tea bag. Her black curls were thick with shadows, and seemed neatly arranged around her face. Then, before I could answer, she literally tackled me.

I crashed into the hardwood floor with Terri riding on my back. I felt her bite the very point of my shoulder hard, and the pain of it, lying face down on the floor, was so sweet it was hard to bear. It was filled with all of our pent up absences. I curled and squirmed to get free, but she clung to me tight.

With a good shove, I flopped us both over onto our backs, then turned and pinned her with my body. The shove had broken her bite on my shoulder, and Terri's head fell back laughing. Her hair still seemed arranged around her face.

"You greet every stranger like this?" I said.

"Only if he showers first," she grinned. She licked what must have been the blood from my shoulder off her lips.

"Mailmen don't shower," she said, and touched her tongue to her upper lip. "They're far too salty a treat."

"Bad for the heart?" I said.

"Then try this," she said, and wrapped her legs up around my waist, locking her ankles behind me so I couldn't get free. She made love to me then, first from under me, then rolling me over so she rode me on top. It seemed to go on and on, and I came up for air not knowing where I was.

At dawn we were lying tangled on the living room floor, two rooms away from the bed I never reached. In the morning light I couldn't tell where my body ended and hers began. The candles still flickered in the empty bedroom and I hadn't slept all night. We'd left a trail of black lingerie and silver trinkets across the floor.

My shoulder, where she bit me, was black and blue, and I felt bruised from the hard floor too. I realized slowly that I was marked all over, from my knees on up to my ears, I'd been bitten and beaten into submission. I ached like I'd been through a war.

Terri lay peacefully beside me, wearing nothing at all. Her lips were as red as if she were wearing bright lipstick. But she was wearing nothing at all.

And her green eyes were closed, and she slept the sleep of a child.

"I'll tell you, Professor," Choteau was shaking his head and had to stop talking in order to laugh. "The names you got for towns in this state," he said. He rested his forehead on the car window and chuckled away happily.

I wasn't in the mood to see much that was funny in the world just then. Not only was I missing Terri, I was driving too fast across ice and salt, playing with the wheel to keep the old Le Car steady. The windows were still fogging up. And then there was my knee. It was my right leg I'd banged on the concrete, and now every time I pushed the accelerator, I could feel that knee resist the move. It was stiff, probably from swelling.

"What's so funny?" I said.

"Humansville," Choteau said, then cracked up again.

We were driving past the outskirts of Humansville, Mo. Just a water tower, a lot of smokeless chimneys and ice-laden trees, in the distance. And a green highway sign: "Now Entering Humansville."

"That cow barn over there," said Choteau, " that must be Bovinesville, right, Professor?" He paused to enjoy his own joke for a while. I still wasn't laughing.

Then he said, "I know. They should build the Missouri State Pen here, Professor. Call it In-Humansville."

"Well, you're the specialist when it comes to prisons."

I regretted it the minute those words slipped out.

But it didn't even give Choteau a pause. With a chuckle, he said, "Just call me Professor Penitentiary, the Doctor of Detention. At your service, Mr. Gentles."

How did he get to be so cheerful, I thought. But then I remembered I was the one leaving my home. He was headed for something somewhere that had to seem a lot more like home than Leavenworth, Kansas. He should be chipper, I thought.

"You know," I said, at least half-conscious that I was trying to dampen his spirits. "That's Cherokee, Choteau. Humansville. A lot of Cherokee names include that word human. It's a common last name in Cherokee, or part of a last name. Like 'Mankiller,' you know. Some Cherokee, probably some escapees from the Trail of Tears, founded that town. The Trail of Tears went through just south of here, in 1836."

Then I stopped. This was a learned pause, you know, a teacher's pause. I was waiting for Choteau to catch up in his notes. I had paused, instinctively, to leave time for questions.

But Choteau wasn't taking notes. His thick hand grabbed my shoulder, and I thought he was going to shake me. But it was just his excitement. "When I was in the prison hospital, he said, as if he hadn't even heard me, "I studied the Missouri highway map."

Now there came a truly pregnant pause, as we both thought over why he was reading maps.

"Anyway," he said, after a moment, " I got a big kick out of the town names down here. You know. Halfway. Peculiar. Licking. Humansville."

At "Humansville" he squeezed my shoulder. From then on, his words were punctuated with chortles and half laughs.

"So I started this game, to kill time, you know, Professor? I started making up headlines. Right? This is my favorite one.

"Let's say this guy from Peculiar, you know, starts dating a girl from Halfway, Missouri. Some Saturday night, hey, there's a dance or a party or something down in Licking, see. So this guy gets his date and they head down there and, what the hell, they have a couple beers on the way. or a little snort of wine and some smoke, or maybe you know, the guy's thinking how pretty and brown her knees look, or something, you know how it goes, right, Professor?

"Anyway, they get in a car wreck, man, and they both get killed. Right?

"So, what would the headline in the paper read?"

Choteau stopped right there and waited for me to guess the answer. "I don't know," I said, gruffly.

This time he did shake my shoulder, and his head bounced with joy, and he was still wearing Terri's Chiefs hat. "Okay, this is what it'd say, right? It'd say: 'Peculiar-Halfway Couple Killed in Licking Accident.'"

Choteau absolutely fell back into his seat and rolled around with delight. I swear, he hugged his knees and just about squealed. I laughed along politely, but mainly I worried about keeping the Le Car on the road.

"And then there's Tightwad. Tightwad, Missouri. This state's got the goofiest names," he was off on another story, to be followed by another.

But suddenly, as we approached a stop sign I was planning to run straight through, he yelled, without any change in his jolly mood, "Turn here, Professor. Let's not be too predictable, right?"

I cranked the wheel and we slid off 13 onto highway 54, bouncing gently off the far curb, and drove on due west toward Kansas. The side road was a rougher, more winding

53

route, and the pavement was icier for lack of traffic. I slowed down to a crawl and we spun along deliberately, picking at the miles.

Still chuckling a touch at his headlines, Choteau settled himself back into the seat. When he seemed comfortable and still, he adjusted the visor on his cap. "So, will she lie for us, Professor? You think she'll stall that FBI brother of hers at all?"

He said it as if we'd been discussing Terri all morning. In a way, I guess we had. I know she'd been on my mind since we skated out of the driveway back there.

"Sure she will," I said. "She'll do the best she can."

He nodded his head, but didn't say anything to agree. His silence just seemed to ask more questions. The engine of the Renault sounded loud and noisy for a while. "That's good," he said then. "Because having this Golman guy on your ass, man, that's a bitch for us now."

"How do you know he's on my ass?"

He snorted a laugh out, then he said, "I can tell from the way you two talk about him. What you say to one another. All of it. Your wife calls him Mike, for example." Choteau raised his eyebrows at me. "And you don't."

I didn't tell Choteau that he was behind it all himself in a way, this bad blood between Golman and me. You see, when I was working on my book, and everyone else seemed to be interested in Leonard Peltier, somehow I decided that Choteau was really the key. He was some kind of holy man or something, a shaman or a seer, and that was behind it all. Somehow. It was religious, in some way I couldn't quite explain yet. Then all those folks out on the reservation, and people like Dino Butler and Bob Robideau who were there the day those agents were killed, suddenly all of them, everybody closed ranks and shut up when I started asking questions about Bernard Choteau. Then I knew I was onto something.

Maybe it was just the murders, you know, but it seemed bigger than that. It seemed like it had to do with the siege at Wounded Knee in '73, and it was deeper still. It had to do with the spirit of these people, I decided. And I was getting close to the truth of that.

But in the end it didn't matter what I thought. Because my sources dried up. Suddenly I was stuck, after two years of work. Nothing. Dead end city, you know. Nobody would talk to me.

And that's when Mike Golman stepped in. He listened to me complain about the wasted hours, and the frustration of it all, of being so close to figuring the whole deal out, when all my avenues in closed down. And I'm sure Golman knew, from Terri and from listening to me, that my hopes for tenure--for a safe, secure position that meant not traveling around the country with his sister from one temporary job to the next--they were all hinged on this research.

Like I say, Golman's a good marine, you know. He came through for his family. Even if he and I had done our share of wrangling about Peltier and Choteau and the conditions out on the reservations, he came through for me. He set me up with all the Bureau information I could handle, interviews with every agent and every secretary and file clerk and janitor who had anything to do with Pine Ridge in the early '70's

And that's why Mike Golman still feels betrayed. Because when I sat down to write, I found out I didn't have a book about Bernard Choteau, about this strange man who was maybe the spirit of the Independent Oglala Nation. But I did have a pamphlet—**Twisted Visions and Forked Tongues: How the F.B.I. Mishandled the ResMurs Investigation**—about the lies and intimidation the Bureau used to convict two Native Americans of murder. When the monograph was published by the University of New Mexico Press, it earned me my tenure. And it made a friendly enemy out of my brother-in-law. It is a sore that Golman and I have been picking at ever since.

"Well, we've got a couple hours on old Mike Golman, no matter what he finds out," I said to Choteau. It sounded feeble the minute I said it.

55

Choteau nodded his head again, but he didn't seem any more convinced.

"Besides," I said, "Terri doesn't even know which way we went."

Those words sounded particularly empty then. They seemed to fog the windshield and blur my view of the slippery highway. I grabbed for the defroster rag and wiped away at the glass. Still it was hard to see the road clear, and maybe it wasn't all on the glass, you know.

He lifted up the K.C. Chiefs hat and let his long hair fall out over his shoulders. The streaks of gray in it matched the gray sweatshirt he was wearing. My gray sweatshirt. We were both quiet for a long while. The icy roads seemed enough to keep us busy.

We crossed the state line into Kansas and I felt homesick, suddenly. In the end, I broke the long silence.

"Choteau?" I said. "Why am I along with you on this?" I kept my eyes firmly on the road as I spoke, though my peripheral vision was locked on him. "Why did you trust me?"

He glanced at me and just a faint hint of a smirk touched his eyes and his lips.

"I don't mean why you need me along, or anything like that," I said. "Not for your cover, or to get you out of the country or any of that. It's just, well . . . "

"Why are you here?" he said for me. His head absolutely swaggered as he said it. The cocky bastard.

"Yeah," I said. "That's what I mean."

"That's easy, my friend."

"What?"

"It's easy," he pulled his hair back over his shoulder, and I noticed that tiny stone tied behind his ear again. Crazy Horse, I thought. "Guilt," he said.

"What?" Now I turned and looked at him.

"It's guilt, Professor, plain and simple." He nodded his head, mostly to himself. His face took on that relaxed look of comfortable understanding.

"You're an educated guy, Professor," he said. "You know the history, and anybody like you who knows the story, I mean honestly knows the whole story of this country, feels guilty."

I grunted. I didn't care much for this easy analysis. Especially when it was laying out the blame. And I didn't care to be so transparent, either. Because, you see, he was right. At least partly. Still, we'd all, every one of us, heard this old guilty white man stuff over and over. Even when it's true, it gets old.

"But see, Professor, you're different than most people in a couple ways," he said.

"How do you know?" I used the road to avoid his eyes again. "You've known me all of about 24 hours. You'd hardly even talked to me until yesterday. Where'd you get all this expertise."

He shrugged and grinned. "You asked," he said. Then he eyed me a while. "I read your book, my friend," he said, finally.

"Monograph," was all I said. Then, "You can't read me just from reading fifty some pages of something I wrote."

Choteau looked over, tilted his head. He wore one of those chummy grins, with a lilt in his eyes. He adjusted that bright red cap and his grin said, 'Who are you trying to kid?' He laughed.

So he got me to grin along. It was infectious, and I didn't want it to mean I agreed with him. But he took it that way.

"You know, Professor," he said, "a 'skin don't get to be pushing sixty in this world, without getting to know something about white folks. If you don't learn a few things about white people, you end up dead, or dead drunk, in your thirties."

He slunk down in the seat, and said, "I ain't thirty no more, brother."

I liked that. The sound of 'brother' on his lips. It made me proud. Much more proud than 'Professor' or 'Doctor' ever had. I was a brother.

"And like I said, you're different than most white folks, in a couple ways. Number one, you know what's been going down in the LAST hundred years. Not just the four hundred before that.

"See, most white folks like their Indians to be a hundred years old, sitting on one of those ponies with their heads drooped down, maybe with a big, hound dog tear in their eye. The Vanishing American. 'Ain't it too bad what our gran'parents did to those poor people,' they like to say. But progress marches on, right. White folks like to feel bad about that, about Sand Creek and the Bear Paw. About Wounded Knee in 1890, and the Trail of Tears. Ain't it all just too bad.

"They don't like feeling bad about Pine Ridge or Big Mountain, or the Trail of Broken Treaties, man.

"You see, Professor, they figure since they like Indians so much, their government must treat them poor Injuns' good nowadays, what with welfare and monthly payments and give-aways. Because they sure feel sorry about what their ancestors done. Them sad, awful ancestors. But when you tell people that ain't true, that their government hasn't treated Indian peoples any better, white people usually get upset and refuse to believe you.

"That's one way you're different, professor. You know it ain't true."

He was nodding his head slowly as he spoke and his eyes stared out at the icy highway. But he was still grinning.

"You're different, Professor, because you know about the Allotment Act, about the BIA and Indian Agents, and about assimilation and them boarding schools, and about termination of the reservations, and relocation programs, about strip mines and fishing rights wars and uranium mine tailings. You know what's been going down for the last hundred years on the res'. So you're different than most white folk. You ain't no normal wasicu, baby."

I'd seen the disbelief and denial he was talking about in most of my students' eyes, because I'd been inserting those same sad stories into my history classes for the last five years or more. I'd watched one student after another, over the years, start by doubting me and the details of the past, and then proceed to ignore it all, saying it's all in the past, and there's nothing to be done. I sat there now in the car silently listening to Choteau lecture, because he was right about them. And maybe he was right about me.

"You're different in one other way, too, Professor." Choteau looked thick as he sat low and comfortable in the Renault's seat. Suddenly it was hard for me to imagine the car without him there in it. He watched the icy pavement roll by, seemed to talk to the bent and broken trees, instead of to me.

"Most people, when they feel guilty, they send a check to the heart fund, they attend church regular for a couple months, or they go shopping. They shake their little heads and feel bad, and say, 'Wish it wasn't so. But what can we do?'

"But you, Professor, you had to do something, so you wrote a book." There he was with that easy praise again, and I ate it up. "And I suppose you taught your classes all about it, too. And still nothing got changed, so you kept feeling guilty. For a guy like you, it gets frustrating. You were just bursting to do something."

"So you knocked on my door," I said, "and gave me something to do."

"Yup," Choteau said, with one resolute nod. He looked over at me and his eyes glowed with pride at his own cleverness.

But me, I felt so predictable and obvious. I always thought I was opaque, a true mystery. At least I seemed that way to myself. I turned out to be clear as mountain water, simple as a chunk of solid rock. And it made me angry.

It's an odd feeling to have a stranger explain you. Like being caught in a mirror, through the looking glass, here in Kansas now, but on the way to Oz. But I still felt like Toto, just tagging along for the ride.

"Doesn't that mean . . . " I paused to negotiate a slippery bend in the very real road, feeling the car fishtail out of my hands like I was trying to hold onto a dream. I held my breath. Suddenly we wove all over, covering both lanes and some snowy gravel shoulders too. Choteau yelled out a broad, "Wahooo!" and it fogged up the windshield.

He was still laughing and hooting when we came around straight. I wasn't breathing yet. I was shaking a little, afraid I'd lose control of the car again. I grabbed the rag, once the Le Car seemed steady, and I wiped the inside of the windshield off.

"Nice drivin', Professor," Choteau muttered and I didn't know how he meant it.

"Doesn't that mean," I said finally, after I'd caught up with my held breath, and we were down the road a few miles straight and easy. "Doesn't that mean you're using what you call my 'guilt' to get me to do what you want?"

"Yup," he said, with that nod again. "You could put it that way. But it'd be about as true as your driving."

"Well, how would you put it?" I felt the ice under my wheels still, but I took the next corner without slowing down.

"Oh, I'd say I asked for help from someone I thought I could trust, somebody who might help me."

"Somebody you knew was a sucker."'

Choteau paused. "Same difference, Professor," he said, "Ain't it?"

"If you say so, Mr. Choteau." I didn't like his laugh, or his attitude, suddenly. I didn't like being so obvious, or being used.

"Shit, Professor, it's however you want to put it," Choteau threw his head back against the seat and shook it slowly no with exasperation. "I needed a hand. You were nearby, and I figured you were willing."

"So I got used," I said.

Choteau closed his eyes and sighed. He sighed at me. "This is going to be a long trip, baby, if you cop an attitude like that," he muttered. Then, without budging, he opened up and really let me have it.

"Professor, your guilt is only the part I knew about. I figured you'd be eager to help, because of what you wrote, and because you kept trying to reach me in jail. But there's a bigger reason you're here, and I don't have anything to do with it. You're running away from something, for some reason.

"I don't understand it. I don't even pretend to, man. Looks to me like you got everything, baby. You got a good life, man, a job that means something, people counting on you. You look like you got it all figured out, Professor. You even got the makings of a little family. Your wife seemed like a good, strong woman to me, someone you'd be proud to be with. But I don't pretend to understand it. All I did was offer you a fast way out, man. And you took it, Professor. Without asking hardly a single question. Man, you jumped at the chance like you were getting out of the joint after hard time.

"So don't blame me if you're feeling lonesome or scared now. 'Cause I ain't it. It is back there with your pretty wife, and your good life.

"If you want to blame me, then I'm done talking about it. We're here, that's that. But," he sat up in the seat again, and carefully kept his eyes away from me. "If you want to talk about what's eating at you," he paused and then turned toward me in the seat, "Professor, its a long drive we got ahead . . . "

I squirmed a bit, and the car seemed deadly quiet. Every spit of gravel, every dip and weave seemed loud and enormous. It went on like that for miles and miles. It got to where I was looking to hit some ice and go for a nice, distracting spin again.

Maybe this was all his game. I think back on that now, and I see how it all fits in to what was going to happen. Maybe Choteau just turned the tables on me, spun me around to keep me driving toward our secret destination. Maybe he was being clever, using me like a toy.

But even now, after everything that's happened, I think he meant it. Here he was, on the lam, a federal prisoner with most of the FBI still gunning for him, still looking for an excuse to cover their quick, hungry revenge. And he wanted to talk about what was bothering me.

61

But I didn't have the guts to face it then.

That may be part of why I'm writing this down now. At a moment that might have made a difference in my life, I changed the subject. See, it seemed like it fit in the conversation, at the time. I papered it over to sound good.

But it was a dodge. Let me tell you, it was. And we both knew it.

"Why do you need me along, Choteau?" I said.

I was a worm.

Of course, I didn't know then about Mary Red Skies and how he loved her. I didn't know about what he'd given up in the past, or the chance he was taking right now, for her. Maybe if I'd known about Mary Red Skies then, I'd have opened up to old Choteau. Maybe I wouldn't have been a worm. But the fact is, I didn't. Mostly it was because I didn't know what was wrong myself. Choteau was right. I should have been happy. I had everything I'd worked for years to achieve. And now I was risking it all to take a joy ride with a convicted murderer who'd busted out of jail.

"That's one thing," Choteau sat back and turned away from me, "I can't tell you."

We were quiet the long rest of the day.

Just after dusk somewhere out in Kansas from a phone booth outside a gas station, I made the phone call we'd planned. The sky over the flat stretch of snow had turned a dirty orange and brown. Terri picked up the phone. She was waiting.

"How are the roads, Will?" she said.

I knew by the way she said it that she wasn't alone. Somebody else was listening.

"They seem pretty bad," I said.

"Well, Dr. Gentles, old buddy, got your office all cleaned up?" Golman butted in.

"Yeah, but it took all afternoon. A tree crashed through a bunch of windows."

"Anything get ruined?" Terri said quickly.

"That's funny," Golman laughed. "Sis' told me it was a fire from some downed wires too."

"No, it was just the snow and ice blowing, but they were afraid of a fire, I guess." It didn't sound like things were going very smoothly back there with my brotherinlaw. "We had to move a bunch of stuff back into the hallway is all. But it was a pain in the ass," I lied.

"Don't they have any maintenance people to do that, down at the University?" Golman said.

It was hard not to let any anger rise in my voice. I had to stay calm. "Not for my files, they don't?" I said, and forced a chuckle. A semi pulled out of the gas station and made a roar as it arched up onto the slick highway.

"What was that?" Golman said.

"I think I'm just going to light a fire here, and sleep by the fireplace. I'll drive up in the morning."

"The roads will be better by then," Terri said, but it came a little too quickly, I thought.

"Right," Golman said with a laugh.

I looked over and saw Choteau filling up the Renault. He was walking around the car, checking the tires. It was damn cold, and snow was falling again, as the light of day died out in the west. I was standing on my good leg, but that right knee was still aching, going stiff again in the cold.

"Listen, I got to go get the fire started again. I'll call in the morning," I said, "if I still can't get up there."

"If the phones are still up," Terri said.

"Right," Golman goes again. Then he laughed. "I think you're holed up down there with your Indian buddy."

"Sure, Golman," I laughed back at him. "That's why I gotta go. He's roasting weenies on the fire right now. They're just about done."

"No kidding though, buddy," Golman's voice went flat and serious then. "They still haven't found him down there. He's still loose, you know. And that one guard he nailed with the pipe hasn't come to yet either. This Choteau character, he knows where you live, Will. So be careful down there tonight. All right? Have you got everything locked up?"

"I'll watch myself, Golman," I said, as I watched Choteau clean the snow and salt off the car's windshield.

"He's dangerous, pal," Golman stuck to the flat tone, sounding more parental than ever.

The phones were silent a moment then. Finally Terri said, "Could we talk alone for a minute, Mike?"

"Oh," he said, "sure." The line clicked.

"Merry Christmas, Terri," I said.

"Will, you heard what Mike said. Are you okay?"

"I'm fine. A little cold."

"Well don't be too . . . " Terri stopped there. "Be careful, will you?" she said.

"Terri, don't worry. I'll be fine. See you tomorrow. Right?"

"Right," she said. "I love you." Then she hung up.

"I love you too," I said, but she didn't hear it because she was already gone. I was about to hang up, and go to pay for the gas, when I realized the dial tone hadn't come back.

"Give Choteau a kiss good night for me, pal," Golman said with a chuckle.

"Merry Christmas, Golman," I said, "you son of a bitch."

"Be careful, buddy," I heard his voice say as I hung up. I knew the rest without even hearing it. "He's dangerous," Golman said, in my ear.

Christmas Day, 1989

Crazy Horse. You might have forgotten about Crazy Horse, the strange man of the Oglala. I mentioned him right at the start. The natural leader of his people. The visionary. The warrior, the conqueror of Custer. A man of high principle, and man of his people. The victim, the martyr. Betrayed, held by the arms and stabbed in the back. September 5th, 1877. Crazy Horse.

Not to mention, the man I think I was driving across Kansas.

When he was just a child, not quite an adult, Crazy Horse who was still called Curly then, saw an old chief die. It started when a group of Mormons traveling the Oregon Trail lost a cow. That old cow was so ill, it fell behind the immigrant train as they pushed west to Utah. It was just a straggler.

Back then, in 1854, the Lakota called the Oregon Trail the "Holy Road," not because it was sacred to them, or anything even close to that, but because the white men insisted everything that traveled on the "Holy Road" should travel safe and untouched. It seemed odd to them, but the Oglala had to treat every dog and every wagon wheel as sacred. Even the whiskey wagons on the "Holy Road" were sacred, it seemed.

But then a sick, old Mormon cow straggled behind, got left and forgotten on the Holy Road, and wound up a sorry meal for some Lakota braves. It wasn't buffalo, they said, but it was easy.

At least until the immigrants complained and soldiers came to arrest the "thieves," and Conquering Bear called it all to a halt.

He was their chief, and an honest friend to the wasicu, the whites. But he decided no one from his band was going back with the soldiers just for eating some sick old cow that was tough and wasn't any good to the taste anyhow. In the argument that ensued, the soldiers' guns blazed, and in the end Conquering Bear was shot. Shot in an argument over an old cow that couldn't keep up.

Young Curly, who would become Crazy Horse, crept up to where he shouldn't have been, and peeked beneath the robes covering the travois. Under there he saw Conquering Bear, a "peace chief" who signed treaties with the whites. The old man was ashen gray and feeble, bleeding to death slowly as the Lakota fled away from the Holy Road. He was the Conquering Bear, the man of peace and deals, dying over an old cow.

This sight of the old chief dying scared the boy. It rattled him enough that he wandered off alone, into dangerous country filled with white soldiers, wanting to seek a vision, something that would make sense of what he'd seen, something that would give him power. But unfortunately his search was all wrong. He wasn't properly prepared to go crying for a vision. He hadn't been purified. And what's more he went searching alone.

But young Crazy Horse had seen sudden, violent death, had seen one of the Big Bellies fall without reason. One day Conquering Bear was a thick, echoing chief of the people, and the next a man dead in life. For the first time Crazy Horse saw the white world touch his own, and he understood in the wisdom of childhood what would happen when they met.

He would see it again, of course. In fact, it would become the pattern of his whole life: the resounding and deep red touched by the white, and turned ashen gray.

But this was the first time.

So young Curly went seeking a vision to try to understand. And a vision came to him, though he did it all wrong.

His vision rose and gave him his power. And behind his ear, everyday he lived after that, Crazy Horse wore a tiny stone, because it was part of his dream.

Among many other things.

But this was no vision I was driving toward the Twin Teepees Motel in Hounddog, Kansas, last Christmas Eve. No, it was Bernard Choteau sitting beside me there. He was flesh and blood there, and his blood was as real and as easy to spill as yours and mine.

And the Twin Teepees was his idea.

He thought it was pretty funny. He laughed out loud when he saw the sign. And suddenly he decided we should stop and spend the night. "Pull over here," he yelled.

I did what he wanted, but I said, "Shouldn't we drive straight through? I thought the idea was to put as many miles down on the way to Canada as fast as we could."

"I been in the joint for almost fifteen years," he said. "I'm gonna do just what I want, Professor, without the Man on my back."

"What ever you say," I shrugged. "It's not the plan, but you're the boss."

"Screw the plan," he said.

He tucked his hair back up inside the K.C. Chiefs hat and strutted inside to sign in. The Motel had two concrete wigwams for an office. They were both peeling red paint and chimney smoke poured out of one of them. A neon Indian stood next to a plastic Santa, and pointed at the "Vacancy" sign.

"Wickiup for two," Choteau said to the little old man who answered the counter bell. "Just for one sleep," he said, and then gave out a Tonto grunt. His arms were crossed on his chest.

The old man missed it all. "Merry Christmas," he said as he hauled in my cash.

Snow was falling steady now in big, pretty flakes. Nothing but a Seven-Eleven was open in Hounddog, so we bought gas and beer and sandwich stuff, and headed back to our Teepee.

While we ate our bologna and cheese and drank Bud, I asked Choteau about that little stone he wore.

"This?" he said, touching it behind his ear.

Remember, he hadn't said a word to me yet about who he was. It was enough that he was Bernard Choteau, the holy man of the American Indian Movement. It was enough for me that he wore it in the spirit of Crazy Horse. I didn't expect him to say he was the spirit of Crazy Horse.

And he didn't, just yet.

"You know," I said in my history teacher voice, "Crazy Horse wore a stone like that. He saw a figure in his vision who wore blue leggings and just one feather in his loose hair. He had a lightning streak across his cheek and hailstones on his chest. A storm followed him in the sky, and a small hawk with red on its back flew over him. And the man in the vision wore a pebble behind his ear." I shook my professorly head.

Choteau ate his bologna and cheese quietly, without looking up. He seemed not to hear. I took it to mean he was, properly, humbled before the memory of Crazy Horse. But then he slurped out of his Bud can, and said, "ahhh!" He held the can up lovingly and admired it. He seemed to read the label. Then he burped with his mouth closed.

"Crazy Horse dressed that way when he prepared for battle," I said, and ignored the burp. "The leggings and the lightning bolt on his cheek, and so on. But he wore that little stone behind his ear all the time. It was like a talisman, or an amulet. A center to his power."

Choteau tipped it up and drained the Bud can then. I watched his Adam's apple jump as he swallowed the beer. His Chiefs cap was off now, and his hair fell free around his head and shoulders.

"But I guess you know all about that," I said, trying to break through his indifference. or what I thought was indifference. So much for reverence.

68

"Because that little stone you wear behind your ear," I said, "that's just like the one Crazy Horse wore."

He pulled off his sneakers and let loose with a broad belch. He sniffed as if to enjoy the smell of it. Then he looked at me through half lidded eyes, through strings of long hair, and said, "Like?"

Choteau plopped down on the bed then, pulled the covers up over his clothes, and promptly went to sleep.

Bernard Choteau snores. I mean, not the polite little snorts and wheezes of an older man. He snores. The blinds rattle, paper moves around the room. You wonder if the walls quake. How I'd missed it the night before, I don't know. It tells me how hard and heavily I had slept, or how little he did. But when I heard him that night, on Christmas eve, I wondered if he'd even slept a wink the night before.

After two beers, I was still wide awake. I needed the rest like Choteau did, but I wasn't even weary. I sat thinking about the drive, about Terri, about what Choteau had said. I rolled over and lay at the foot of my twin bed, and switched on the little black-and-white TV in the corner of the room. I suppose a part of me was missing my flannel pajamas and my heavy robe. But they were all part of another, different world now.

The picture was tilted sideways. 'John Wayne was shooting over our heads at someone. I popped open another Budweiser. With the sound off, I listened to Choteau snore as the gray Duke in a white hat chased one enemy or another crookedly across that little screen. Most of his enemies seemed either oriental or Indian. Probably they were Indian, because he kept riding uphill across some John Ford view of the Monument Valley. But I didn't watch close enough to care who the enemy was. I just sat and remembered it was the early hours of Christmas day and wished John Wayne could be Jimmy Stewart. I just wished it could be a wonderful world.

I watched the tube the way you watch a fire. Meanings didn't register. I just basked in the flickering gray and white light, and sipped my beer.

Then suddenly the Duke was chasing us. or it seemed that way. Choteau's face popped up on the screen. Front and profile. Holding that little, impersonal number at his shoulders.

We'd gone from John Wayne to some rerun evening news without a break, at least in my mind. What little Christmas spirit I felt disappeared then. I didn't have time to be lonely or sad, or to wish I had a guardian angel like Mr. Stewart did. We were on TV.

"Choteau," I yelled.

He snored on, without even rolling over. "Hey, Choteau," I yelled again. I leaned forward and turned up the sound. Then I stopped hearing anything.

It was right about that moment, when I touched the volume knob, I came on the screen. There I was, standing beside the spoonbill we'd caught last April. I was in thermal coveralls. I wore a big, half drunk grin, like a happy thief. I was holding a bottle of Busch by the neck. The eighty pound fish hung on a limb beside me.

My father-in-law took the picture. He caught the fish, too. That's why I was grinning, see. He'd already caught his limit, so he gave me this fish. Then it won the spoonbill tournament that day. I won two hundred bucks and a trophy, and they ran my picture on the front page of the local weekly.

That's why I was grinning like a thief.

My father-in-law kept the trophy, though it had my name on it. We split the two hundred, but spent most of it on beer and bait that summer. It was all still the family secret, while I became the champion spoonbill snagger of central Missouri.

We never told Golman though. Golman is too straight an arrow.

It was bad enough we made the county paper with this little lie. But now, there I was on national TV.

They zoomed in close on my face, and that big spoonbill disappeared. That's when I realized they weren't worried about how I cheated in a fishing tournament. I was the fishing professor, the good old boy with an education, who'd been kidnapped by a wild Indian.

"Choteau," I yelled.

This time he grunted and the snoring paused. But he wasn't awake enough to answer.

By this time the announcer was simply saying the Highway Patrol had reported we were probably armed and certainly dangerous. Then we were gone and it was flooding in the Carolina's and the weatherman was tracking Santa on the radar.

Armed and dangerous, I thought. There was that word again: dangerous. I sure was running into it a lot these days. What a laugh. It was all built up on Choteau's reputation. Get anywhere near the death of an FBI agent, and the rest of your life you'll be considered "armed and dangerous." All we had were a couple of screwdrivers and a set of wrenches in my trunk, and a little mystic stone that Chief Crazy Horse wore. Or one like it, anyway.

Not much the FBI couldn't handle.

"Choteau?" I walked over to his bed and shook his shoulder. He was awake though. His eyes popped open, and he looked at me clear and straight.

"We've been on TV," I said. "They're looking for us. They've got my picture, too, so they know we're together."

Then I went silent. It hit me suddenly. There was a reason the authorities knew about me so quickly. We hadn't been gone but eighteen hours or so, and they had me pinned. It didn't happen that fast by accident. Somehow Golman had got some kind of information out of Terri.

"Don't worry, Professor," Choteau said. "I'll take care of it later. Just turn off the tube and get some rest. We're gonna need it the next week or so."

"Yeah," I said. "Right."

I did as I was told, in something like a trance, not really hearing him mention those words "week or so." I'd been mostly thinking in days since the start of our run. A week sounded a lot more serious, somehow. But it didn't matter. One of his instructions, no matter how hard I tried, I couldn't follow. I couldn't sleep.

I lay there a long while staring at the ceiling of the Twin Teepee. I wasn't thinking. I was just numb.

"Choteau?" I said.

"Yeah, Doc."

"The TV said we were armed and dangerous," I said, then tried to laugh.

"I heard," Choteau said. "Get some rest, okay, Professor?"

I fell asleep, eventually, to the rhythm of his snores.

It was the silence itself that woke me, I think. I lay there a while, piecing together where I was, in the dark. It was Christmas morning. I was sleeping in a twin bed in a motel in Hounddog, Kansas. It was snowing lightly. An escaped convict slept in the next bed. But then I suddenly connected. There was no one snoring. I looked over, and he was nowhere to be seen.

"Choteau?" I said.

There was no answer.

My eyes were already used to the dark, so I spoke his name again, and scanned around the room. His bed lay open, and at the foot I could see his clothes lying neatly folded. But Choteau was gone.

"Choteau?" I said again and got up. The minute I moved, I remembered something else. My knee. It screamed at me when I put my weight on it, but it did feel better with each step. Maybe with time I'd walk the sprain off.

I'll admit that for one brief moment the thought that Choteau had left crossed my mind. Maybe he'd stolen the car and left me stranded here. A wave of relief I couldn't help rolled over me. I would call Terri; I would go home; I was safe. It was Christmas morning, after all.

But as I wandered around the motel room in the dark, stepping gingerly on that weak knee, I knew I was wrong.

Wherever Bernard Choteau had gone now, he wasn't gone from my life. He wasn't done with me yet.

Out the front window of the room I saw the Renault parked. It had a nice dusting of snow on it, maybe half an inch. It seemed ready and waiting. Only one other car sat outside the Twin Teepees. An old blue-gray Buick parked near the office. I'd have taken it for the owner's car, except it wore Missouri plates.

I noticed, too, the trail of footprints in the new snow. They stood out, because they were clearly so fresh. They circled the Buick, and they trailed around the front of my Le Car too. It was as if someone had been checking on the autos.

I felt myself begin to tense up at that thought. Rather than worry about who was messing with the cars, I lumbered back toward the twin beds.

Choteau's clothes, actually the clothes I'd given him, were neatly folded there at the foot of his bed. I felt guilty, but I couldn't resist. I began to check through them, listening all the time for any sound of his return.

I don't know what I hoped to find there. After all, these were clothes he'd worn for less than a day. But I wanted to know what else he carried. Maybe what he was toting would give away our destination, prepare me for what we had in store. In his pocket I found another small pebble, and some change. There was also a tube of white, frost lipstick, the kind Terri liked to wear.

The only other thing he carried was an old wallet photo. There was no name or date on it, not a mark. It was just a color snapshot of a woman in her late thirties. She was Indian, at least partly. But she wore her hair curled and frizzy. She had dark brown eyes, and a come hither look in them made you wonder who was taking the picture. Especially since there was a little white kid, a boy of about six or eight, sitting beside her in the photo. He wore a white shirt and a little black bow tie, and you could almost see him squirm in the still photo. Except for that look in her eyes, the whole thing looked like one of those dime store family shots, and both mother and son were strained.

I put the photo and the other things back in his pants pocket, and I felt pretty cheap. Here I was peeping into some guy's life, going through his pockets. But I picked up the flannel shirt anyway, and something fell out if it.

It clattered on the linoleum floor. In the empty room, the noise rang like an alarm. I stood still and listened. But everything was quiet as snowfall. Wherever Choteau was, he was out of earshot, I guess.

I reached down to the floor and retrieved what had fallen out of the folded shirt and made such a racket. What I found made the snowfall seem loud. The knife.

I remembered then how Terri and I bought it a few years back at a country store down in Arkansas. It was a beautiful, little, handmade tool, with about a six inch blade in a carved wooden handle, whittled to fit the hand comfortably. It was made for everyday use. A strap or two across a whetstone, and that knife was sharp.

Though it felt right and comfortable in my hand, familiar as an old friend's handshake, there at the foot of Choteau's bed I didn't know what to do with it. It sat there in my hand and asked me, in that solid way the world has of making the abstract real, how far do you trust Bernard Choteau?

The FBI was right, you see, we were armed after all. But were we dangerous?

Then a faint noise drifted in from outside. I'd never heard anything like it. It sounded like a human voice, moaning or wailing. It wasn't loud, and I couldn't identify whether it was male or female. But it had a musical quality, a kind of melody line, simple and repetitious, and filled with sadness. And the hushed tones of real terror. Whatever it was, this song or cry in the night, it moved something down in me that had never been touched before.

For a while I stood there not really knowing where I was. Then a horrible sense of foolhardy, fearless loss rolled over me carried by that song, and I was fixed, and afraid, at once.

Maybe it says something about my state of mind then, I don't know, but eventually the song lured me toward it. The fear in it became a love song, and I was drawn across the darkened room toward it.

I think now it was really very quiet. The song he sang wasn't loud. It was probably just a whisper. But it had reached into me so far it seemed to roar.

I looked out into the snowy night, out the bathroom window. The glass was frosted, but I stood on the toilet seat and looked out the top, clear pane.

Outside, facing away from me, Choteau stood with his arms raised. The sharpest sliver of a moon floated right over him, blurred with white light, slicing through the moving clouds. He sang, or chanted, or spoke in some genderless voice. They weren't words I understood, if they were words at all. He was still, and the snow fell gently around him. I think he was stark naked in the cold.

Then he stopped. Clouds covered up that sliver of moon and Choteau's arms curled around his chest as he hugged himself.

He turned toward me, toward the room, and muttered, "Shit!"

When he turned so abruptly, it startled me. He seemed to be coming straight toward me, in a balled up, curled tight run. He seemed to be speaking to me. I guess I jumped, because my foot slipped on the stool lid, and I fell off the toilet to the side. I caught myself on the shower rod with one hand, and righted myself. But I had twisted around enough that my swollen knee screamed at me. The knife I was holding in my hand clattered into the shower stall.

As I pulled myself back up, I heard the motel room door open and close. I grabbed the knife out of the shower and

75

realized then I was wearing only my boxer shorts, and suddenly the knife seemed enormous.

"Holy shit," I heard Choteau say. Then he let loose with a loud "Brrrr."

I flushed the toilet, lifted the tank lid, and set the paring knife inside. By the time I limped out into the room, my knee was worse than ever. Choteau was buttoning his pants up.

"Geez, it's cold," he said.

"Well, if you wore some clothes out there, it might not seem so fierce," I said and leaned against the wall to take the weight off my aching knee.

"Yup, you're right," he reached for the flannel shirt. If he noticed the missing knife yet, he didn't let on.

Choteau had white dots painted on his chest. Hailstones, I remembered. So I looked and, sure enough, on one cheek he had painted a jagged lightning bolt. All of this was done with Terri's frost lipstick. They were the "power" markings that Crazy Horse wore whenever he went into battle.

"Crazy Horse," I said to him.

He looked up, blandly, buttoning his shirt, as if to answer to that name.

"Those are the markings that Crazy Horse wore," I said.

Choteau grinned.

I heard the toilet tank still running in the bathroom. Choteau walked past me and switched on the light in there. Both of us squinted. He let the hot water run. I hobbled around so I was facing him again. The stool was still running and I realized that the knife must have lodged itself in the way of the plug. It was going to make the toilet run all night. And give itself away.

"You know, Choteau," I said, as he began to scrub the lipstick lightning off his cheek, "those markings are very personal, aren't they? I mean, they come from a vision, right. They belong to a person, I believe."

Choteau ignored me and scrubbed away. He groaned a little with pleasure, so the hot water must have felt good on his hands and face. I limped a step or two over to ease my leg into a comfortable position. There didn't seem to be one.

"So," I said, eventually. "Should you be wearing Crazy Horse's war paint?"

"Should you be hanging that bear mask over your fireplace, Professor?" The lightning strike was nearly gone from his cheek.

"What do you mean?" I said.

He stood up straight and away from the sink and turned the water off. He smiled at me. In a way he seemed proud of me. "You're doing very good, Professor. You read all those books well. And you may just get the answers to all your questions sooner than you think."

He finished in the bathroom and seemed not to notice the running toilet. Then he switched out the light in the john and nearly dove past me into his bed. He curled up in his clothes under the blankets and moaned at the pleasant warmth.

I worked my way over to the bed and crawled in, arranging myself so my leg was something near comfortable. or as close as I was going to get. We lay there in the dark room and I knew in moments the sound of Choteau's snoring would drown out the sound of the toilet running.

"What were you doing out there?" I said.

My voice sounded loud. He smacked his lips a while before he was ready to speak. I think I saw him shiver again.

"I said I'd take care of you, Professor," he said.

"What'd you do?"

"I took care of the car, since they know you're with me."

"What?"

He laughed deep and rolled over on his back. "Were from glorious Kansas, now."

"What do you mean Kansas?"

"I took care of your plates," he chuckled to himself a little. "I switched your Missouri plates for the plates on the old guy's car."

"But," I said, "what for?"

"Maybe I guessed wrong, Professor, but I figured that old guy won't notice he's got out-of-state plates on his car for a couple of days. It'll give us a couple days run before they figure out they should be looking for a Kansas auto. It'll give us a little more room."

"Isn't that illegal?" I felt dumb the minute I said it.

"Only problem is, why couldn't you be driving some kind of Ford pickup, or a little tan Chevy. No, you gotta be driving an old French car the color of a warning light. You don't make it easy, Professor, taking care of you."

"Sorry," I said. Then we both laughed. "It's a good car."

"Get some rest, Doc, " he said. "I think were gonna need it the next couple days."

"Choteau?" I said. "What were you doing out there just now? I mean, I get it with the license plates and all. I think. But what was that chant, or whatever? What was that?"

He was very quiet then. Noticeably quiet.

"If you don't mind me asking," I said.

"Soon enough, Professor," he rolled over on his side again. "You'll know. Soon enough, you'll know."

I woke early, and it was light and clear. The snow had stopped, leaving a fresh, white coat across Christmas morning. Choteau was sawing away. Between his snorts I could hear the toilet rattling on.

I limped over to the bathroom, as quietly and quickly as I could on a knee like a rusty hinge. With the door closed, I flushed the toilet and took the knife from the tank. I dried it off, then waited for the water to stop running in the tank. When it was done, Choteau was still snoring away. He didn't seem to have budged.

So I hobbled back to bed. Along the way, I left the knife on the floor a few inches under the foot of Choteau's bed. Right where it might have fallen when he got undressed for his little horse raid, I thought. Right where he'll think he dropped it.

I thought.

On Christmas morning I called her again. Choteau was outside, scraping ice and snow off the Renault. A warm shower had loosened up my knee some. But I was sitting on the bed, resting it while he warmed the car.

I knew it was stupid. I knew that Golman was probably there, and that any word from me might give Choteau away. Hell, it'd give me away, too, I suppose. The phones were probably tapped at the house. It was just foolish to try.

But it was also Christmas morning.

I gave the operator my first name only and called collect. My father-in-law George answered, gruff and half awake.

"Hello. Uh, I mean, Merry Christmas," he barked. He didn't sound particularly festive. I must have given them all a long Christmas Eve.

The operator did her spiel about accepting a collect call. When he heard my name, George went through a quick litany of "What? Where? Who?" and so on. Then there was a pause, and he said, "Sure. Yeah. Put him on. Put him on."

Suddenly, he sounded much more awake.

"Merry Christmas, George," I said.

"Where are you?" he said. "Are you all right?"

"I'm fine, I'm fine," I said. "Could I talk to Terri?"

"She's not up yet. Where are you? Is that convict still with you?"

"George, this has got to be quick and I just want to talk to Terri. Could you get her?"

"She's had a long night, you know. But," he stopped and I heard his heavy breath hit the receiver. "I'll see if she's awake."

The way those words came across the phone lines, they seemed like an electric shock. "George?" I said, hoping to catch him before he left. "I'm sorry," I said.

There was a long enough pause now that I thought maybe he'd already gone, maybe he hadn't heard my lame apology. And that was just as well, I guess. But then, out of nowhere, he said, "Be careful out there, would ya', Will? I'll go get her."

"How's it going, Pal?" Golman said.

There was no click of connection. Nobody picked up the line. He'd been listening all along.

"Where's Terri?" I said.

"She's coming. Boy, you sure did a number on her, pal. She's a mess. The kids are all upset. We spent the whole of Christmas Eve arguing about it."

"I bet you did," I said.

"Listen, buddy, why don't you just tell me where you are? I'll call the authorities, and we can get this over. Have a little Christmas left besides. What do you say, pal?"

"If she's a mess, Golman, it's because of you."

"Sure, tell yourself that, Will," he said.

"I just want to talk to Terri."

"You know, Will, he's dangerous. Don't trust that Choteau character. Don't turn your back on him. I been looking at his file from Leavenworth. He's been caught making knives out of pieces of his bed frame, and a couple times out of stones in his cell. Don't trust him, Will. I'm telling you, brother-in-law, he can't be trusted."

"I'd say you got that message across, Golman."

"You're not in any trouble yet, Will," Golman said. "I can still fix it for you, pal, if you just tell me where you are."

"Mike. Get off the phone." Terri's voice cut in and sounded like sweet salvation on the line.

"I'm just trying to help, Sis'."

"Get off the line, Mike."

"Sure. Sure thing," and I heard the line click.

"Will, don't trust him. Even if Mike's not listening, somebody is. They've got this line tapped, I think, so don't say anything you don't want them to hear."

"I love you," I said. "Is that safe?"

Terri laughed, and it made me feel strong and right, across all those miles. "Yeah, I don't think they can arrest you for that," she said. "Did you get there? Don't say where, but did you make it?"

"No," I said, "We stopped last night. He's still with me."

"Stopped," she said. Then there was nothing for a moment. "I thought you were driving straight through the . . . "

"He wanted to stop. He doesn't seem to be in such a big hurry now."

"Careful, Will. They're listening to us."

"I know, I know," I said, and the trap we were in made me angry. "Terri, how did they find out so fast? What did Golman pull? Did you tell him . . . " That last question trailed off into a lot of silent blaming I didn't really mean.

Terri was quiet then. That's when Choteau came in the door. "Be careful, Will. I'm really worried now," she said. "I thought you'd be there, or almost there by now. They know, Will. They know a lot. So you better get going." She stopped, and I said her name, and then her voice cracked when she said, "Get going fast, Will."

I looked at Choteau and he cut a flat hand through the air. But how in the world could I hang up then. "I love you, babe," I said, and listened to her crying. "Terri?"

81

"Be careful, Will. He 's . . . Mike told me about the trial and . . . "

"Don't believe any of it," I said.

Then Choteau took my choice for me. The moment he heard me say Terri's name, he walked across the room. He waited a moment longer for me to hang up, then he set a thumb on the cradle and cut us off.

"Have you lost it, or something?" he said. "That call is being traced right now."

I nodded my head. "Right." I put the receiver down. "I just thought . . . "

"And that's just what they expect you to think," he said, pointing at the phone. For a moment he seemed too angry to speak. Then he barked out an order. "Let's get rolling. Now." He turned and seemed to march out the door. He left it open behind him, too.

I stood up and walked on my leg, testing the knee. It hurt, but I could use it. It was more useable than my limping emotions just then.

I felt betrayed, as I picked up my coat. But I don't know what I expected. Choteau was furious with me, Terri was up-set, and Golman's police were on our ass. Somehow they'd found us fast, and Terri was mixed up in how that happened. But what else could I expect?

What could she do with an FBI agent for a brother, a cop right there in the room, listening in? Of course he'd try to use her. Of course, they'd fill her up with horror stories. Her own brother wouldn't think twice about terrorizing her to get what he needed. But it wasn't Golman who was to blame; that was too easy. I was the one who put her in that position.

With my emotions twisting in the winds like that, I nearly limped out and forgot to check. A cold gust blew in the door as I hobbled back and looked under the foot of Choteau's bed. The knife I'd laid there was gone. In its place sat Terri's bright red Chiefs hat.

The tires squeaked on the snow as we pulled out of the Twin Teepees Motel. There was an angry quiet between us. I didn't know what I could do to end it, or if I wanted it to end. Once we were on the road, though, Choteau surprised me.

"Sorry," he mumbled.

He was looking away from me, out the window across sleepy Hounddog, just waking to the snow their Santa had brought.

"It was just damn stupid. Just what they were waiting for you to do. Calling home," he shook his head. "But I shouldn't have yelled at you."

We were quiet again. I drove out of town into corn stubbled fields. Yellow and gray stalks jutted through the snow, so the fields looked the way I felt, like I could use a good shave and a fresh start.

"I'd have done the same thing," he said to me then, but with an awkward failure to look me in the eye. Kansas corn was not enough to hold his gaze, but he stared out at it anyway.

"How is she?" he said.

Looking at his feet on the floor of the car, I found myself wondering if he kept the knife hidden in his socks.

"How are you?" Choteau said, when I failed to answer his last question.

"I don't know," I said.

Sporting our new license plates, we drove across eastern Kansas for the better part of that day. We were quiet and somber through the morning. I drove, though I shouldn't have, with my knee. It began to stiffen with the cold, and the back roads we traveled were covered with snow and ice most of the time. If we'd gone into a skid, that knee could have killed us. But I kept thinking about that little paring knife, and Golman's little warnings kept echoing around in my head. So I drove.

It was flat, rolling countryside. One stubbled cornfield after another, all newly decorated with holiday snow. But as the miles drifted by, and I drove further and further from where I was supposed to be, my taste for this adventure went flat.

Like most adventures, it looked better from the start than from the middle.

Early in the afternoon, it began to snow and before long the wind began to blow in gusts. Christmas day was so clouded and gray, it felt later than it was. On the back road we took, there were soon drifts to negotiate. My knee began to throb at the workout I was giving it.

Almost as if he couldn't stand all this glumness, Choteau began to talk. He laughed first, then he said, "Woman troubles, Professor." He shook his head. "She's driving you nuts, isn't she?"

I didn't answer. Chatting with an escaped convict about my marriage didn't really fit my travel plans just then. Besides, I didn't think Terri and I had any problems. But I was in the mood to blame him for all my troubles at that point. Though it would be a lie, it would be a handy lie.

"You know, Professor, there's a lady who's been driving me crazy for better than thirty years." He laughed at himself. "Some things you just never grow out of, you know?"

The wind blew, and buffeted snow against the car. The wipers, when I used them, were so snow crusted they just smeared the glass. But at least they shoved the snow aside. It was not an evening to be driving, even with good knees and "Grandma's house" for a destination. It was an evening to sit by a fire and frown out the frosted windows.

"Is that the woman in the picture?" I said. I expected to jar him. It was what I wanted to do. I wanted to admit I'd been through his pockets and shake our little situation up. He should have been surprised, but it didn't even give him pause.

He carefully took that photo out of his pocket, then slunk down in the seat. Holding it cupped in one hand, he said, "Mary is her name, Professor. Mary Red Skies."

Choteau looked like a teenager swooning over a pinup girl. Suddenly it was hard not to like him, slouched there so vulnerable, a man in his late fifties with his heart aching like a kid's. I tried though.

"Who is she?" I said, sounding as gruff as I could.

He laughed once, through his teeth.

"She was a year ahead of me all through school," he said. "I was so crazy about her, I thought she was about as beautiful as springtime. But she was a junior, you know. She was dating all these older guys. Guys out of high school, you know. She didn't even know I was alive. What was I to her, you know; I was just a kid." He cocked his head back and looked at me out of the corner of his eye. "I was bashful, too."

Then he roared with laughter and only got quiet when he looked at her photo again. "I bet you didn't think I could ever be bashful, huh?"

"It's a little hard to picture," I said. I wanted to stay sullen and quiet, I wanted to mope, but he was making it difficult.

"Shit, that first time, professor. Mary Red Skies and me," he sighed, shook his head.

Wind slapped the car, and we hit a drift that slowed us down with a jerk. Then, just as quickly, the wind shifted and we were past the drift.

85

"I was walking back to the dorm at the mission school one night in a snowstorm," Choteau said. "Not quite as bad as this. But bad enough. It was after basketball practice and I hung around to shoot some. So my hair was wet from the showers, and I didn't have a hat on or anything. All I had was this lined jean jacket, you know the kind. So I was pretty cold, and I had a ways to walk.

"Here comes Mary Red Skies in her mother's old Chevy. She sees me walking in the snow. She's like a junior and has got a home and a family in town, and I'm just a sophomore. I don't have nothing. But she pulls over and asks me if I want a ride. 'You must be cold,' she says. I guess she felt sorry for me. But I remember her saying that, leaning across the car seat toward me, out in the snow.

"So I get in and the car's even got a heater that works. I'll never forget this. Some of my hair was frozen, from the walk, you know. We were stopped by the side of the road, and she reached out and touched my hair. She said, 'You poor thing, it's frozen.'"

Choteau took a deep breath then. He laughed at himself, shaking his head again. "I still can't believe all this happened," he said.

"Where was this?" I said. He'd drawn me into it.

"North Dakota," he said, and looking over at me, his eyes seemed dark and hidden in the dusky light. "Fort Totten Res '. You know, Professor, I was poor as gravel then, but I do think that's the happiest I ever was. That year."

"What happened?"

The falling snow had pushed on over into a blizzard by now. It was dangerous out there, but we were both in a different snowstorm, in our heads.

"See, she touched my hair and I came apart, Professor. I felt her warm fingertips and I just fell forward into her lap. Right there in the front seat of that '48 Chevy. I was so full of all my kid fears, and I was so bound up I couldn't talk or even swallow or anything. But I was aching for her the way only a kid can ache." He stopped there, as if he was thinking about whether that was true, whether only kids can ache like that. "It was all I could do. I just fell over toward her and my head landed in her lap.

"The amazing thing is, she didn't laugh at me, or anything like that. She wasn't even surprised. She stroked my hair. that's what she did. I lay there in her lap and looked up at her, and I couldn't speak. I was so embarrassed. But she ran those long, pretty fingers of hers through my hair.

"She understood, Professor. Somehow. 'Cause then she drove that Chevy up off onto a back road, someplace she'd been taken to before, I'm sure. I remember, when she took off her coat, she was wearing this baggy, old gray sweatshirt, and there was nothing under it, Doc. I could see it the minute I looked at her.

"You know what else I remember. She smelled like an apple. You know, when you bite into a red, shiny apple, that sweet smell there is. I kid you not, Professor, that's what she smelled like."

He sat up then, seemed to come out of his memory. "An apple, yeah," he said, and he laughed at the word. "Seems appropriate now," he muttered, his mood changing like the blizzard.

It dawned on me then that this is where we were headed. To North Dakota, to a reservation there. This was the great secret destination, this was what he needed a driver for. I was chauffeuring him to Mary Red Skies. He was risking his life, and mine, to get back to her.

He had turned his head and sat staring away from me, out the window into the snow. I saw the stone behind his ear, I saw the long graying hair trailing down his shoulders. I saw the color of his skin.

87

When I turned my eyes back to the highway, that color stayed with me. The shade of cinnamon sugar, roughed and lined and cracked with wear. That skin so different than mine. My winter white pale.

Would I be here, I thought, if his skin were like mine? Then all those old questions came at me, the ones I hate to admit, even now. No, I'm wrong. They didn't come at me. They came out of me. If his skin were my color, would I be out here in a blizzard on the Kansas prairie on Christmas Day? Wouldn't I be home, drinking eggnog and rubbing a belly full of turkey, yelling at football players on the TV? Belching on the couch between my father-in-law and my brother-in-law?

If he were like me, wouldn't I have kept that knife? Wouldn't I have tried to escape? Wouldn't I have told my brother-in-law where we were?

If his skin was the same shade as mine, would I have even opened the door to him that first night?

The answers I kept coming up with for all my questions made me uncomfortable. But I couldn't back away from it. If his skin, just his skin, and just the tincture of it was the same as mine, I would never have even known him.

So what did that make me? What kind of hypocrite? What kind of liar? or just plain fool?

So what was I doing here?

"Let's get something to drink," Choteau said. He didn't look over at me.

For a moment I thought he was reading my mind. He'd seen into my little race game. He'd felt my confusion, at all this buried hate. I glanced over at him, and again all I saw was that tawny shade to the skin showing behind his neck. How ice white my skin would be right there, where it never sees the sun.

Choteau laughed. "Damn," he said. Then he grinned at me. "Woman troubles, Professor. Don't they get to us all."

I kept my eyes on the drifted highway.

"I could use something to drink," he said. "Gotta be some kind of store out here." He laughed again. "Somewhere," he said.

I'd escaped again. The whole time Choteau was thinking about this woman. This Mary Red Skies of Indian Reservation, North Dakota. I'd snuck my little stare at his color, my little bout with hate, right past him. He wasn't all seeing.

Problem was, I hadn't snuck it past myself.

We crossed the state line into Nebraska in midafternoon, and found a country store near the border with its lights on. It glowed like Grandmother's house through the heavy snow. But it sat at a four corners called Kaw City that won't appear on any current Rand-McNally.

"There," Choteau said.

"That's not a bar," I said, pulling into the snowed over lot anyway.

"They'll sell beer," he said.

"What, we gonna sit and drink in the car?" I said. "In this weather? We'll get drifted over."

"Right," he pulled his loose hair back behind his head and tied it tight with a rubber band. "'Cept we ain't gonna sit." He cracked the door open into the snowstorm. "Got any money?" he said.

I gave him a ten out of my wallet full of spare bills. He rubbed his face once, then looked out at the blowing snow.

"Shouldn't I go in?" I said. "Somebody might recognize you."

He shook his head. "Out here," he said, "a strange Indian buying beer on Christmas won't look near as odd as a strange white man. Besides," he reached over and poked my shoulder, "we all look alike, right?"

While he went inside, I sat and wondered if maybe he had read my mind. And I rubbed at my sore knee. One thing was clear, he had learned to use our ingrown hate to his advantage.

I expected him to come back out with a pint or a six pack and a handful of change. When I heard the door to the Kaw City General Store bang shut and saw him trudging across the drifted lot, he had one twelve pack of cheap beer in each hand. If he had any change, he kept it.

He tossed the beer into the back seat of the Renault, laughing happily. "They'll stay cold enough back there, won't they?" Then he shivered and slammed the car door closed behind him.

Leaning in to the back seat, Choteau pulled two cans from the cardboard and handed me one. "Here's to Miss Terri," he said, "and Miss Mary." He popped his can open and flopped back into his seat.

I took a long swallow, and the beer seemed just cold and bittersweet. But Choteau let loose with a belch right off, drained his can and tossed the empty over his shoulder into the back.

"Let's get rolling," he said as he reached back to pull another can out.

I looked at the beer in my hand and the snow heaping up on the road ahead of us. In the new dusk I switched on my headlights and it only seemed to make the snow fall harder.

"I don't think it's too smart to drink and drive in this weather," I said. "Or any time," I muttered. Then I took a drink of the cold beer.

He downed a good slurp, then said, "It's not too smart to go running around the countryside with a murdering Indian, either." He laughed at that.

I just sat and looked out the windshield at the moving Nebraska snow.

"Want me to drive?" he said.

I didn't answer, and I didn't start the car either.

Choteau wiped the steam off the windshield with a forearm, slurping at his beer the whole time. "See, you get some experience with drinking and driving, living on the reservation."

I wanted to say it was stupid, it was dangerous and un-necessary. I wanted to say all those things. Instead I started the car, resolved not to have anymore of this bad beer, and drive like he said.

I think I was afraid of him then. Maybe, seeing now how it all turned out, maybe I should have been more scared of him than I was.

At that moment the door to the Kaw City store opened and a short, white haired man with a stoop and a shotgun stepped out. He raised the gun awkwardly, like it was a racing flag, and he pointed it at us. "What's with the old . . . " I said.

Choteau let out a big whoop and then said, calmly, "Professor, I think it's time now to drive."

The shotgun back there on the stoop went off, sounded like somebody big stamping his feet on a wooden porch. Then a bunch of buckshot rattled across the bottom of the old Re-nault like someone throwing gravel.

"He's shooting at us," I said softly.

Choteau was laughing now, but I wasn't sure if it was at me or the old man and his shotgun.

I jerked the car through the snow and back out onto the drifted over black top. With the little wheels spinning on the Le Car, we spurted and then shot down the road. "What's he shooting at us for?" In my mirror, I watched the old guy try to manage the shotgun with his stooped back. Choteau let out some kind of rebel yell, and then kept laughing.

"We're having fun now," he yelled.

The wind gusted up and beat at the car, but as I drove down the road, The Kaw City Store and the old shotgun guy disappeared into a white wave of snow. I heard the whomp of the gun again, in with the wind, but the snow never even cleared off enough for the store's honey-yellow lights to show in my mirrors. "I thought you were some kind of holy man," I said, maneuvering the car down the road. "Aren't you some kind of example for your people, Mister Suffering Martyr Bernard 'Persecuted' Choteau," I said. "Would you look at yourself a minute? What are you doing?"

With a toss of the wrist and a laugh, his second empty can flew into the backseat of the Renault. "Aw, hell, even 'holy man examples' gotta have a little fun sometimes, Professor." Then he sat and chuckled merrily to himself.

"What was the guy shooting at us for? Did he recognize you?"

Choteau shook his head no. "Lighten up a little, would you, Professor?" he said. Then he leaned over again onto my shoulder and pulled a fresh beer out of the back, along with a cellophane pack of Slim Jim sausages. He tore the paper packages off the meat with his teeth. "Drink up. That knee must be killing you," he said.

He took a bite off the string of sausage, then handed it to me.

"Don't you know how this stuff is killing your people?" I said, biting off a chunk of meat. I found out I was hungry.

"What? Slim Jims?" he said, with a chuckle.

"You know what I mean."

"Hey, right now I don't much want to discuss alcohol and the res. All right?" he said. He pulled another pack of summer sausage out of his shirt pocket, tore it open and began to eat. Then, with his mouth full, he said, "People who live without hope sometimes live with a lot of alcohol. Okay?"

"Right," I said. "But I don't buy it."

"We didn't either," he laughed at his own joke.

I took another bite, and finished off the meat in my hand. Then I chased it with beer, and I hated to admit it tasted good. "Cheap excuses," I said. But I took another swallow.

Choteau pulled a third package of sausage from another pocket, tore it open and handed it to me with a, "Here." Then, "Need another beer yet?"

I hadn't noticed, but he was right. When he got me a second can out of the back, he said, "For a guy who doesn't drink and drive, you sure handled that first one pretty fine."

"We shouldn't be doing this," I said, but took a longer swallow. I drove through the snowflakes rushing toward the car and, though I know it was the beer working, it began to feel a little more like Christmas. "So, that old guy at the store must have recognized you, huh?"

"Hey, I was feeling bad about an old girl friend," Choteau ignored my question. "And you're missing your wife. It's pretty lonely out here for both of us. I don't think a beer or two will hurt us any. Not if we don't talk ourselves into feeling bad about it."

It was a lie, of course, but I took another drink and decided to believe it.

That was when Choteau reached into the backseat and pulled out a brick of Cracker Barrel cheese. He tore the foil wrapper open with his teeth, took a bite and handed it to me.

I bit a big chunk off the cheddar, and chewing on it said, "That must've been some store. Ten bucks went a long ways."

Choteau laughed for an answer, took a long pull on his beer can, then grinned at me. "I'll say." He reached in his sweatshirt pocket and pulled out a folded bill. Rubbing it between his fingers, he let the ten dollar bill fall open.

"Holy shit," I mumbled. "You stole all this stuff." Then I gulped some beer.

"No, no, no," he said, grinning the whole while. "I just explained to the man that I was a hungry In'din and it was Christmas. Then he donated this care package to our cause."

"He didn't recognize you," I said. "He was shooting at you cause you were robbing him." At the same time that I felt relieved we were still invisible, I was wondering how much else Choteau had stolen.

"Not robbing," Choteau shook his head. "We're In'dins. We were foraging."

I found myself laughing along with Choteau then. It seemed pretty funny suddenly, and right then he handed me my third beer, and I said, "Yeah. Foraging."

"Living off the fat of the land," he said.

"The fat," I said. I raised my beer can and he raised his, we toasted to our success. Even the ache in my knee began to feel better.

Somewhere along in there, Choteau slipped my ten spot back into his pocket. I guess he was foraging again.

Just a few more miles down the road and he told me. Maybe I should say a few more beers down the road. I do know it was the beer talking when I asked him, "So, Choteau, my man, what's with all this Crazy Horse stuff anyway, huh?"

He smiled at me, that distant, mysterious grin of his. The Buddha smile. The one that makes you think he's pulling your leg.

"These little stone amulets you wear. The war paint and all. Running around naked on winter nights. What's the scoop on you and Crazy Horse?"

He didn't answer, but the smile slipped over into a chuckle now.

"Is he a hero of yours, or what?"

Choteau shook his head no, grinning still. Then he said, "Maybe you're ready."

"Ready for what?"

Now he laughed loud, a grand though brief guffaw. It could be it was the beer talking in him too. Because then he gazed out the windshield into the snowstorm. He took a long, leisurely drink from his can. "I guess I owe you that much of an explanation. Don't I, Professor?" He paused. "I don't know if you're ready, though."

This time, wisely, I kept my mouth shut. We were getting close to revelations time. True stories revealed. Honest Injun stuff. All of that. If I kept my big trap closed a minute or two, I knew I might learn something here. Really learn something.

"But first," Choteau said, "let me get you a fresh one." He leaned back again into the back seat and came up with a beer. "You're gonna need this, Professor."

I drained the can in my hand. He took it from me, tossed it over his shoulder into the backseat without a glance, and handed me the new one.

This time I didn't argue about drinking and driving. I didn't even think about it. I was on the verge of learning something, and I'd do what he asked to keep him in the true confessions mood.

Choteau pulled the rubber band out of his hair, shook his head and let the long hair fall loose again. It was draped over his shoulders, and I wondered for a moment why he didn't wear it braided, since it was plenty long enough. Then I remembered; Crazy Horse kept his hair free.

He looked over at me, still wearing that bodhisattva grin of his. "I am Crazy Horse," he said. Then nodded his head once. I almost believed him.

Right then we drove into a drift of snow. We crested a hill, and the snow lay waiting. It sent the Renault into a skid and I turned into it, one handed. We straightened, and with just a twist of my wrist, we were headed direct down the snowy road again.

I didn't even slosh the full beer in my other hand. I took a big swallow of it, then I said, "Come again?" I laughed. "You know, I thought you said you were Crazy Horse?"

He smiled and nodded his head once more. Then he repeated it.

"I am Crazy Horse."

There was just road noise for a moment, while I absorbed that.

"That's what I thought you said."

Then he hit me with that favorite line of his. "But you can call me Crazy, for short."

I laughed at that.

"Take another drink," he said. "It'll start to make sense. Maybe."

"Crazy Horse is dead."

"I know." The Buddha grin was back. He took a swallow of beer, and then looked me straight in the eye and said, "I'm sort of his reincarnation. That's the way you'd put it, anyway."

Choteau grinned and I drained my beer. He took the empty can from me and I wiped at the frost from our hot air on the window. Anything to give me time to think about this.

And that gets us back to where I started this whole story. Back where I asked him to say it all again, only slowly this time, hoping the whole while that Choteau was just fooling with me. You see, everything made some sense to me up to that point. A foolhardy, exciting kind of sense. But now were right back to the place where I got truly confused. And I have been ever since.

"So," Choteau said again, grinning, "you can call me Crazy, for short."

"Well, that won't be hard," I said, and added "Crazy" just a moment too late.

Ahead of us, at the edge of the road, something moved under the snow. The drifts were blowing around in the headlights, but this was different; it was something hurt and alive there. Something under the snow.

I think Choteau and I recognized what it was at the same moment. A dog, crawling into the ditch to stay out of the storm.

"Pull over," Choteau said, but I was already off on the shoulder and braking. We snaked a little, but as we came to a stop, the snow changed. It was no longer rushing at us; now it floated down in slow, heavy streaks.

This dog had crawled down into a snow filled Nebraska ditch.

Choteau climbed out of the car, or maybe I should call him Crazy Horse now. Anyway, he pulled his hair back and tied it again. Then, looking over the top of the Renault at me, he said, "I don't expect you to believe me."

"Right," I said and laughed. Mainly because I didn't know what else to say.

"Not yet, anyway," he said, as we headed toward the ditch.

You could see where the poor mutt had crawled under the drifted snow. Already the blizzard was filling in its tracks though. The snow smoldered around us like smoke rising off burnt ground.

"Protector," Choteau called out, as if he knew the dog's name.

We were pretty drunk, I guess. I was out there in a flannel shirt and I barely felt the storm. We followed the dog's trail down into knee deep, then thigh deep snow. I limped on my bum leg, but it didn't hurt in the cold and the alcohol.

"Protector?" Choteau called, crouching a little, extending an open hand.

A flat nose poked out of the drift, sniffing like a vacuum, moving the snow around like the storm. I half expected a growl or a snarl, but it was only that black nose sniffing us over.

"Here, boy," Choteau said, stepping down toward it. I was at his shoulder. Then a gust lifted the snow and covered over that snout. It disappeared in wafts of snowy dust, like fog moving in across cold water.

"Easy, Protector, easy, boy," Choteau said.

Maybe the dog was just responding to the snow drifting over it, but the way it moved then it looked like it was answering to Choteau's voice. Slowly its head rose out of the drift. A flat, square head the color of red mud, with a huge black muzzle. It was a big bulldog mug.

"Protector," Choteau said, in a whisper that blended with the wind.

The dog leaned forward toward Choteau's outstretched hand. Its sniff worked Choteau over. As it leaned close to him, my instinct told me to grab the dog. This storm was too fierce for us to spend a lot of time out here coaxing a frightened bulldog out of the elements. But Choteau stood still and let his open hand bear some bulldog examination. The whole time his voice rattled low and soft. "That's a good boy. Easy, easy," and so on.

I shivered, but Choteau stood still in the cold, wearing less than I was.

The dog stepped closer and Choteau began to stroke its head. In a few moments, he was holding the mutt. It seemed natural. Choteau had grabbed the dog, or the dog had come to Choteau. Whatever happened, he turned slowly and strolled back to the Renault like it was a summer's day and he was carrying a lap dog or a pussycat.

But Protector was no pussycat.

By the time we climbed out of the ditch, snow had drifted up to the wheel wells on the car. The sky was growing from gray dusk to black night, and as I started the Renault, I knew it would be slow going, if it was going at all.

But we pulled out and began, now, to creep along the highway. Choteau held the Bulldog on his lap and it panted, steaming up the windows. "Good fella, Protector," he said, stroking the bulldog's head.

"Where'd you get the name?" I said, as I wiped the dog's pant off the windshield.

"It fits," Choteau said, "Doesn't it?"

"Maybe it's a little backwards."

98

The old bulldog mutt was almost heaving now, he was so pleased and at home on Choteau's lap.

"Protector," Choteau said. "It fits fine."

"Kind of like your name," I said. "Crazy."

A few miles down the road, Crazy Choteau began to feed the old dog some of his "foraged" goods. It was amazing how much cheese and sausage he had stuffed into that old sweatshirt of mine.

I was beginning to sober off a little then, since the driving was hard work. I began to think about robbery as a concept.

"You didn't take any money, did you?" I said.

Choteau didn't answer. He just laughed, I think because the old bulldog, once he'd gotten a bit to eat, began to drool. Or maybe I should say slobber. It fell like an overflowing eave trough, dripping down between the seats, and when Protector decided to pant along with the drool, my end of the car was awash in spray.

I drove along, mopping his steam off the windshield. Wind smacked the car around and, when it gusted outside, we got near white out.

The weather and the dog and the beer wearing off began to make my head ache. And my knee--the same knee I had barely noticed as I plowed around in the drifts moments ago-- now began to throb.

Meanwhile, Choteau and his dog were splitting a package of Canadian bacon.

Out of the blizzard and the dog's slobber rose a sign at the side of the road.

John Brown's Cabin
Sportsmen's Park

Down in a patch of brush a little cabin was nestled, drifted under the snow. "We're stopping," I said.

"Sure," Choteau laughed through his bacon. "We've got provisions."

I didn't find it funny.

I trounced on the gas, harder than I planned, but that bum knee of mine needed a stretch. We shot down into the snow along where I thought there was a lane. The car slid past a barbecue grill and by a nearly buried picnic table, until we came to rest between the cabin and a rusted, swingless swing set.

The dog woofed, once we were stopped. I'd killed the engine with my little race maneuver. Choteau, bellowing with laughter, handed me a chunk of bacon and said, "Look."

He was pointing at a little sign on the cabin door. "Members only," followed with a list of rules about fishing and picnicking. Sure enough, about ten feet ahead of us stretched a patch of ice dusted clean by the blizzard.

We'd stumbled on one of those little seeded fishing ponds that small towns out here build and maintain. Since the local fishing is so poor, folks pull together and stock a manmade pond with bass and walleye and such. You pay your yearly dues, and you drive out here to fish. You pay your dues to pretend you're in Minnesota or Canada, and not in Nebraska.

The door to the cabin was padlocked, but Choteau had it kicked open before I was out of the car. The twelve pack we had left was under his arm, and the bulldog was trailing at his heels. It was obvious he'd made a friend.

Protector followed him straight inside the cabin, walking stiffly like an old lady. I grabbed a flashlight and the sleeping bags from the trunk, and then. limped inside too.

By the time I threw our bags in the corner, Choteau was pulling the "Members Only" plank off the door. The old dog had curled up next to a stone fireplace at the end of the one long room. Behind Protector, like a Godsend, sat a stack of cut, dry wood.

In a few minutes we had the door shoved closed and the beginnings of a fire started. We were going to be cozy, warm, safe, and hidden away by the storm. We'd found a home, for now. I think we all felt it, but none of us more than Protector the bull pooch, the king of the slobberers. He basked beside the growing fire and in the safety of the cabin in the way only a dog can.

The bulldog curled up next to Choteau, and put his big square head on the convict's lap. There weren't any tags or collars on him, nothing to identify an owner. He was all stray, and so he was all ours. But our new dog was no purebred, either. He was pure mutt. Mostly bulldog in the face and the squat build, but with pointed terrier ears and patchy black spots on his tawny side. Handsome he wasn't.

On top of its head, the fur had gone gray, and a salt and pepper streak ran right down his black and brown back. He was bone thin, and those bones seemed frail, too. I remembered the gimpy walk it had as it followed Choteau into the cabin. Arthritis, probably. At least in the hind legs. Maybe worse. I think we had adopted somebody's abandoned old mutt. Someone had dumped old Protector by the side of the road in the middle of a prairie blizzard. He'd been left to die, to freeze to death before he starved. Put "to sleep" by the cold, with simple country cruelty.

I reached over and stroked the old dog's head. He looked up at me through foggy eyes, and slobbered on Choteau's lap. I don't know whether the poor mutt could see me, but out of somewhere came its trust. It lapped my hand with its big speckled tongue. And my hand was wet.

That was all it took. He was part of the band. Another blind misfit on the run, trying to escape his checkered past, but too old to stay ahead of it for long. A member of our tribe.

As I got warm and full and a little drunk again, I forgot about the ache in my head and in my knee. I started to feel at home, oddly enough, though I couldn't kick the loneliness.

"So," I said, scratching Protector's ear, "you think you're Crazy Horse."

We spread sleeping bags out on the stone floor in front of the fireplace. With the dog in between us, we lay there and drinking the rest of the beer and eating our stolen sausage and cheese.

Choteau threw his arms out and stretched beside me, a long leisurely working of his muscles, and then he settled onto the sleeping bag. "No." He drew the word out slowly. He sipped his beer.

"But you just claimed . . . " I sat up, laughing at all this.. Protector lifted his head off my good knee, then settled it quickly on the floor. The dog sighed and fell straight back asleep.

"I didn't say I thought I was Crazy Horse," Choteau said. He was grinning at his beer can, holding it in folded hands on his chest. "I am Crazy Horse."

"Oh, excuse me." I got up and stood by the mantelpiece above the fireplace.

"I did say, however," he looked up at me from raised eyebrows, "I didn't expect you to believe me, Professor."

"Yet," I added. I surprised myself when I said that.

Protector rolled over a bit on his back, front paws drooping in the air.

Choteau laughed and took a drink. "That's right," he said.

"You're nuts," I said to him. I was trying to hang onto my sense of perspective. So I laughed at him. Then I felt bad about it.

I stood on my good leg and soaked up the warmth of the fire on my front. Flannel pajamas and my old terry cloth robe seemed a lifetime away just then. Part of another history, something I'd have to study in documents and imagine now. But I didn't feel bad about that, just intrigued. There was an oak picture frame on the mantle next to where I rested my arm, and I picked it up.

"Maybe I am," Choteau slurped.

Protector began softly to snore. 'Great,' I thought, 'now I've got a dog and a prisoner to saw away in tandem all night long.'

"Maybe I'm not," he said.

I wasn't sure what he meant. Did he mean maybe he was crazy, or maybe he was Crazy Horse?

The frame on the mantle was glassed over. Inside it held a small gray photo of John Brown pasted at the top of a piece of parchment. It was just a little photo, clipped out of some history book or slick magazine. But, of course, I recognized him immediately. Old John Brown. My friend. My nemesis.

"Maybe you're just trying to lead me on," I said to Choteau.

He laughed and said something. But I missed it, because I was reading the hand printed notice under that little photo of John Brown. Somebody had hand lettered the parchment, with calligraphy from some evening craft class, I suppose. It was neat and perfect as the parchment. As I remember it now, it read something like this:

Here on this spot, in a cabin much like this one,
John Brown and six of his followers hid out on the
nights of the 15th and 16th of May, 1856. Brown and
his band had murdered five proslavery settlers near
Lawrence in the "Bleeding Kansas" War.

Beneath this were listed the names of the six "followers." At the bottom of the page, in florid gothic print, the calligrapher had drawn out: "His truth goes marching on."

"He lies a moldering in the grave," I said out loud. Just a mutter, but it came out involuntarily.

Choteau burped then. Even though I'd been eating it too, I could smell the Slim Jims wafting in the air.

"What?" he said.

I picked up the framed parchment and handed it down to Choteau. "Look at this," I said. He took it. I drained my can of beer. "What is it?" he said. He tilted the frame toward the fire and played with it. I thought he was adjusting it to the glare of the glass. But then he rubbed at his eyes and I remembered his vision. "What is it?" he said again.

"John Brown slept here," I said. "Just like us."

John Brown, the fanatic. John Brown, the abolitionist. John Brown, the first warrior of the Civil War. The murderer, the saint. The madman.

"Well, Glory Hallelujah," Choteau handed the frame back to me, unread.

Did he know who John Brown was? Beyond the phrases of an old song? I had my doubts then.

"Can you grab me another beer?" I said as I took the frame. And then I told him my story.

I'd written my masters thesis on old J. B., you see. I spent a year reading out of the Congressional Record, poring over old letters and newspaper articles on microfilm, studying maps of Lawrence, Kansas and Harper's Ferry, Virginia. In the end I narrowed it all down; I wrote about the stretch of weeks John Brown spent in jail between his conviction and his hanging. It was a time when, with great dignity, Brown held court with the nation from inside his jail cell. His visitors, the great and the unknown, Henry David Thoreau among them, lined up daily outside his jail waiting for their audience with the wise old patriarch wearing that Mosaic beard and sporting those fierce, relentless eyes. His messages became the headlines of the whole world's papers. His hanging echoed through the conscience of the whole country, and the "Battle Hymn of the Republic" got a new set of words.

I leaned on the mantel and grinned at the little photo of Old John Brown. His stern, Old Testament face eyed me back. Eyeball to eyeball with 1856, and riding around the prairies with 1877 in 1989, time began to seem a matter of personal preference suddenly. This is worrisome to a man who made his living studying the how's and why's of yesterday. It made me uncomfortable. And here I was talking about 1975.

"When I finished that thesis," I said, "after a whole year's work, it was almost turned down. It almost failed. The committee approved it finally. Grudgingly. But only after a lot of argument."

I could feel Choteau's eyes on me. Could he care about any of this? He was born and reared on a Reservation, an orphan educated in mission schools. He'd spent a dozen years or more in a federal prison. Could he possibly understand my little problems with a graduate school world, with petty academic fights on an intellectual battlefield? Could he know that, in their way, they tore you up too? It all seemed small then.

So I didn't turn around. I just kept my eyes on old J. B.'s patriarchal gaze and tried to explain it.

"They said I missed the major question of the whole study. I nearly blew a whole year's work.

"You know what was wrong? You know what question I forgot to ask? The question that never crossed my mind? Not once in a year of reading his letters, not once in all the reports of all those folks who saw him. Not once."

The cabin was surprisingly quiet. Only the snoring of Protector the bulldog and the crackle of the fire disturbed the blizzard's hard silence. I heard Choteau take a sip, but not a grunt or a hum came from him.

"'You let yourself get too close to the subject,' they told me. The committee said I had 'fallen under the spell' of old

105

John Brown, just like the nation had back then. I'd lost my historical perspective, so I never asked the most basic question of all. The question everything else hinged on.

"I never asked: 'Was John Brown mad?'"

I tilted my beer up and toasted the little photo of J.B. "That's the question that nearly cost me my degree."

"Hm," Choteau said.

I think I was getting more than a little drunk then. All the pain was gone, in my knee and in my memories. I laughed at it all merrily.

"You see, Crazy Horse," I said and grinned down at Choteau on the floor. "Old J.B., he was so right, I never once, not in a year of living with him, I never once wondered if he was nuts."

"Maybe he wasn't," Choteau said. The first words he'd spoken in a while.

"But you see, I never even asked," I said, then drained the rest of the beer from my can. "It's a mistake I could make again," I said. "Right, Crazy Horse?"

"You're asking me?" he said.

I took a nice, long drink from my beer. "No," I said then. "No, I suppose not."

Outside the snow buried us in John Brown's cabin. Choteau, or Crazy Horse, or whoever he was, lay in his sleeping bag with the bulldog snoring beside him, and drank beer. "Can you understand what that meant to me?" I asked him. "I mean, it may not seem like much to you, with what you've been through, but it was a year of my life almost wasted. It was," I paused and looked for the right word. "Humiliating," I said finally.

Boy, did that sound stupid the minute it left my lips.

"Every single body hurts in its own way," Choteau said. He was trying to be understanding, but there was distance in his gaze.

"Prison, Choteau," I said like a fool. "You've been in prison. That was like a prison to me, you know?" I'll give myself a break here, and claim the alcohol in me was really talking now.

"No," he said, flat and stoic. "It wasn't."

The tone he used settled me down some. I got back down and laid myself in the bag and shut up. After a while, I muttered a "Sorry."

"Don't be sorry, Professor," he rubbed the dog's chest and old Protector snorted in his sleep and squirmed with pleasure. "Hurting comes in a lot of flavors."

Then Choteau set his beer can on the floor. He folded his hands behind his head and stared at the ceiling. I wondered if he could see that far, or if he was just gazing into some fuzzy blindness. We were both quiet for a time. In between the dog's snores, I listened to the fire crackle and the wind whistle around the cabin. And I drank.

After a while, out of his quiet thoughts, Choteau said, "There was a kid I grew up with on the res. Professor. Lennie was his name." I wasn't sure what any of this had to do with my little attack of self-pity. Choteau just seemed to be talking. "He was four years older than me, in school anyway. While he was in the mission school, that is, before they tossed him out. He was a tough kid, too. I was scared of him, man. I was.

"See, he used to carry this bottle opener around in his pocket, you know the kind. I flat little piece of steel with a pointed beer can opener on one end and a bottle opener on the other. This was back in the days before we had these nice pop tops on the cans, and you needed something sharp to open your beer, remember, Professor? Lennie took that opener and he hammered the pointed, can opener end down flat and then he sharpened it into a knife. Seemed like whenever I saw him, he was always leaning against something, a tree or a building, and fooling with that opener of his. Cleaning his nails. Picking his teeth.

"'This end opens up beer bottles,' he told me, 'and this end opens up beer bellies.' And I believed him, too.

"One day, when I was about ten, I was walking back to the dorm and Lennie comes driving up in this pickup. He doesn't have a license, I know, much less a pickup. But he leans over and pops the door open on my side. 'C'm here, Bernard,' he says. When I come over, he says, 'Hop in, Bernard. I need your help, little brother.'

"I was too scared not to get in, even though I was plenty scared of getting in with him. 'Where'd you get the pickup, Lennie?' I said after I closed the door behind me.

"'Oh, I just borrowed it to run some errands, little Bro',' he says to me. And off we go down the road to Sheyenne, which is about a mile off the res'. See, Lennie was going to get something to drink. In those days, there was no liquor on the reservation. So we were headed off the res' for alcohol. Even I knew that right away."

I was looking away from Choteau into the fire, remembering the way I popped off about drinking and driving in the car. As if I could tell him anything about it. As if he didn't know a world about alcohol I couldn't even imagine.

"He drove us up to Mulgrew's, was a little general store outside Sheyenne. Lennie parked in back and left the truck idling. He didn't have any keys, you see, Professor. And with what he had in mind for us, he had no time for hot wiring the truck again. So he let it idle.

"'Bernard,' he says to me. 'You go in there and keep Mr. Mulgrew busy for a while. You're a smart kid. Think of something, okay? Just keep him away from the door for a while. Will ya?'

"Lennie had that opener-knife thing in his pocket, I knew. I didn't think he'd use it on me, but I wasn't sure. I was more afraid he might use it on Mr. Mulgrew, who had a nice beer belly on him. So I sure wasn't gonna say 'No, Lennie,' at that point.

"'You got an idea?' Lennie asked me, like I was thinking it over.

"I figured out then why Lennie picked me for his helper. I was a 'Good Indian' back then. I didn't start out as any rebel and convict, Professor. I'd just finished second in the school spelling bee, and I was going to a sixth grade speech contest in Bismarck. I was 'a nice kid for an In'din,' you know. I got written up in the mission bulletin and the local papers around there. A nice, clean boy for an Indian. Almost white.

"I was the last kid anybody would figure on for a liquor store robbery."

Choteau laughed and I heard him pick up his beer can again. I wasn't looking his way just then.

"'So, you got an idea, Bernard?' says Lennie. I nodded my head yes. 'All I need is about two, three minutes,' he says. 'I'm fast.'

"Into the store I go, slowly, because I don't have the slightest idea what I'm gonna do. In a couple of minutes Lennie is going to come flying in and ransack the place, and I'm going to be stuck between his can opener and old man Mulgrew's belly.

"First thing that happens is I hit a stroke of luck. It isn't Mr. Mulgrew inside, it's his wife. She's about four foot tall and four foot wide and still likes to wear stripes that make her look six foot wide. She's also a softy, since her and Mr. Mulgrew don't have any kids.

"'Well,' she says as I walk in, looking more than a little lost. 'What can I do for you, little Poncho?'

"White people, for some reason, like to call Indians Poncho. They always seem to think it's cute, or clever, or something.

" 'My name's Bernard, Ma'am,' I say. Not because I was standing up for myself or anything. I just didn't know yet what else to say. But right away I knew I shouldn't be handing out my name.

"'Say, you're that little Indian boy, the smart one,' says Mrs. Mulgrew. Then she grabbed my cheek and pinched. 'I saw your picture in the paper. Such a cute little one.'

109

" 'No, Ma'am," I said. That wasn't me.'

"All I know right then is Lennie is about a minute from coming in the door and popping Mrs. Mulgrew open like a beer can. The only thing between Lennie and her was my ingenuity, which was straining pretty hard at that point. I didn't want to see the insides of old lady Mulgrew. And I didn't want to see Lennie after he popped her open, either.

"Out of the corner of my eye, I see a shadow moving outside the front door. 'Ma'am,' I say. 'I need to use the restroom.'

"Now, this was the honest-to-God truth, but it was also a stroke of genius. See, at that time, folks didn't like Indians using the public restrooms too much. Oh, there weren't any signs or anything. But the white folks out there, they figured we were all nature boys or something anyway. And you learned if you were off the res' it was better to find a tree or a ditch outside of town, than to be using the local gas station. If you know what I mean.

"Plus, I knew there wasn't a public restroom in the store, just the Mulgrew's own, in their house attached to the store. Mrs. Mulgrew, she glances out the window, like she was looking for some tree for me somewhere. But that just wasn't acceptable either. Not in front of her store. Her hand went up to her lips.

"Please, Ma'am,' I say, adding a little urgency to my voice. Some real urgency, to be honest.

"'Well, since you're such a sweet one,' she says, glancing around to be sure Mr. Mulgrew is gone. 'Come on back,' she says like we're breaking some big, secret rule. 'But don't you tell anybody about this.'

"So she leads me back to the bathroom in the house part of the store. I try walking as chicken legged as I could, so I looked like it might take me a while when I get in there. It wasn't hard.

" 'Now don't you lock the door,' she says, 'and I'll wait right here.' She posted herself in front of the bathroom. 'Be quick, little Poncho,' she says, 'Mr. Mulgrew will be back anytime now.'

110

"That was advice I didn't need. Suddenly, I didn't need to go so bad. I turned the water on in the sink and flushed the toilet. I kept seeing Mr. Mulgrew with that can opener stuck in his belly. So I slipped the hook latch down on the door and crawled out the window. I hit the dirt running, but by the time I was around the house, Lennie was already in the truck. Fact was, I thought he hadn't even left it for a moment, and I was angry, 'til I saw the quart bottles of beer on the seat.

"Lennie already had one open, and he was grinning happy. 'Let's roll, little brother,' he said and pickup threw gravel and dust behind us as we hightailed it back to the res'."

Choteau stopped to take a swallow of beer. A memorial swallow, I suppose. Or maybe just to wet his lips.

"Schoolboy drinking stories," I said, in the gap. Then I laughed. "I remember my first time when . . . "

Choteau butted right in. He wasn't anywhere near done with me yet. "I didn't want any beer or anything. I just wanted to get away from Mulgrew's store and never go back there. And for once I was glad that all us 'In 'dins' looked alike to them.

"But Lennie hands me his halfgone quart. It was warm and it tasted bitter and thick as spit to me, but I drank it. I drank it because I was still afraid of Lennie. Not just of what he'd think either. I was afraid of what he might do to me, if I wasn't in on it. All of it.

"So we drove around 'til the pickup ran out of gas, drinking warm beer and listening to the radio. Lennie had the happiest grin the whole time, but his eyes were red and full of blood. He drank most of the beer, 'cause I didn't need much to get blasted. But even after I was feeling happy, I kept seeing how red his eyes were.

"I slept in the yard behind the dorm that night, threw my guts up the next morning. I never went back to Mulgrew's, and we never got caught. When I think about it now, I don't think those Mulgrew folks ever figured out they were robbed.

"But Lennie did go to reform school in about another year. And you know," Choteau laughed, "I can't remember what it was they sent him up for."

111

He took a swallow of beer and smacked his lips.

"Which one it was for, anyway," he said.

He paused for a while, rubbed the bulldog's chest. Old Protector's eyes opened a crack and his big flat snout went snuff a couple of times. I'm sure all he smelled was the beer.

"The reform school didn't dry Lennie out, though. Not for good anyway. He was gone from Dakota for a couple years. After he got out, he bummed around the country for a while, ended up in Portland. He got busted there for stealing wine and somehow they sent him back here. I mean, to the res'. He took to sleeping in the ditches around Devils Lake. He got work doing construction now and then, when the money for the Air Force bases was flowing. But he always seemed to end up back in some ditch just off the res'.

"See, when you go to the city you never feel at home anywhere, and someone always wants to buy you a drink. So you run away from that and come back to the res'. But then there's no work and nothing to do. And somebody's always saying 'Com'on, pal, what else you got to do?' So even if you dry out for a while, you never get away. There's always the boredom, and always the invitation.

"'You can handle a little drink, can't you?'" Choteau said in a funny deep voice. Then he grunted a "Big Chief" grunt and swallowed some beer. "You don't know how tough it is, Professor."

"Time of the '50 census, I was a senior in high school. Lennie'd been in and out of reformatories in more states than most of us could find on the map. But he'd come home, then. You know what Lennie listed as his address for that census? The Ramsey County Jail." Choteau took another little swallow,

112

then said, "You can look it up, I suppose. Somewhere. But it was honest. Shit, that's where he lived, mostly, I guess. If he lived anywhere. Anywhere with an address."

"Tough," I mumbled, shook my head: Choteau gazed over at me, wearing a placid face. He seemed pleased that I was learning. But he wasn't done with me yet.

"One time, it was the last year I was in high school, I was walking along out in the country, trying to get away from the school and the dorms and all. And then I heard Lennie's voice. 'Hey Bernard, little brother,' he says. Sure enough, there he is leaning up against a dead car in the ditch.

"'How you doin', little brother?' he says, and tries to stand up a little, but he's pretty shaky. I noticed right away that he looked all yellow. His eyes were bloodshot, too. As red as that day in the pick up seven or eight years before.

"So we talked for a while, and then he gets around to his point. 'Bernard,' he says, 'can you get me something to drink?'

"I knew the stuff was killing him. His hands were shaking like he had some old man's disease, or something. He was all of twenty-three or four, and he looked like he was in his fifties. But I also knew he'd been through half a dozen dry-outs in as many years, and none of them stuck. I knew he was dying for lack of it just as much as he was dying because of it. Or that's what I told myself anyway. So I said, 'Sure, Lennie. You just wait here 'til I get back.'

"I wasn't legal myself, but I pocketed a pint bottle from a gas station out on Highway 281. The mechanic there kept a bottle stashed in a drawer in the shop; I knew where 'cause I'd worked there some on weekends, when they got behind. I was a good In'din, remember. I brought that pint back to Lennie. He was waiting inside that dead car, and when I got close I realized he hadn't heard me coming, because he was crying.

"But then I found out maybe he wasn't crying. See, he had blood all down his face and I knew then his eyes were bleeding. When he saw me with the bottle, he brightened right up. He took a big swallow or two and then mopped at his eyes and his cheeks with his sleeve. The sleeve on that flannel was stained brown where he'd mopped up blood before. 'By golly, Bernard, by golly, little brother,' he kept saying, as he tossed the whiskey down.

After a couple more drinks he starts laughing and asking me, 'Geez, little bro', you remember that time we ripped off the old Mulgrew store? You came out the bathroom window with your wheels spinning like a hot rod. Shit, you was scared, huh? Bernard? But they never did figure it was you. Did they?'

"I shook my head no.

"You know why, don't you?' Lennie laughed and took another quick pull. 'Cause when old lady Mulgrew said she thought it was you, everybody said, naw, not that Bernard. He's a good Indian, man.'

"Lennie took another couple of pulls, and held himself against some pain in his stomach, I guess. Then he did start to cry and the tears were deep pink, you know. And he starts saying, 'Jesus, Bernard, I'm thankful you come around here. But you stay away from me, hear? I'll get you into trouble. You stay a good In 'din, man. Stay away from me. Hear?' He kept repeating that, one way or another, and crying those red tears.

"I couldn't stay away from him though.

Choteau stopped there and, after a moment, he let out a big breath. He sat up and crawled over to the woodpile, then gently set another log in the fire. Red sparks flew up the chimney, glowing in the dark room. The bulldog woofed just once, then rolled lamely over to me, because I was still and warm. I wanted to ask Choteau why he couldn't stay away from this Lennie guy, but there didn't seem a way to say it. Still, I didn't understand why, not then anyway, and Choteau didn't offer any explanations, as he stretched back out in his bag.

"I couldn't stand to see him crying and whimpering like that. It was hard to imagine being afraid of him once, like I was. He just seemed hurt and dying.

"So I asked him, 'Remember that can opener you used to carry, Lennie?'

"That memory worked. He sat up straighter, and he brightened up. He wiped the bloody tears out of the corner of his eyes and started to laugh. 'That was some trinket, huh? I forgot about that. Shit, yeah,' he says.

"'You still got that thing?' I asked him. And he laughed and laughed, and threw the empty whiskey bottle out the glassless window. It crashed and tinkled against the rocks out in the
ditch somewhere.

"'Oh, Bernard, they took that little toy away from me a long time ago.' He reached in his pocket. 'But I got a grown up one now.'

"Out he came with this sweet switch blade, flicking it open in his hand. There were no more tears, just a lot of laughter as he fingered it. He played with it just the way he did when I was a kid. Then he laughs at me, I think. He says, 'Get outa here, Bernard. Get lost. And stay away from me, will ya?'

"He was the old mean Lennie again. But I wasn't scared. Not now. And besides, we both knew I couldn't stay away."

Choteau laughed and swallowed some beer. "That fall, I had this big idea. I was going to save Lennie. He was gonna come to the mission school and talk to some of the high school classes about drinking. About what it does to you. I got him cleaned up, and he sorta half dried out, too. I made all these arrangements with the school, and everything. They seemed to think it was a good idea. Lennie thought it was a great idea. 'Who can tell 'em better 'n me about boozin'?' he says. 'I know how to scare it out of 'em.'

'I'll show 'em these,' he said to me. Then he pulled off his right boot. He wasn't wearing any socks, so I saw the point right away. He didn't have but one toe, his middle one, left on that foot.

"'Frostbite,' he says. 'I passed out one January night up here. Couple years back.' He laughed at himself. 'They cut 'em off at the state hospital. But not before I got these.'

Lennie rolled his jeans up then and showed me the brown pink scars running up his shins. 'What **are** those?' I said.

"'Gangrene,' he says. Then laughing some more, 'That oughta scare them kids off de boozin', huh?'

"While he laughed I tried telling him that maybe those scars of his might be too much, you know? They're just kids.

"'No, no, no, Bernard. That's what they need to see, little brother.'

"But then it all fell through. He never talked to them classes, and instead he went on a real bender."

"How come?" I said. I finished the last can of beer just then and, though I had quite a buzz going, it didn't feel good anymore. It had all gone pretty sour, and we'd gone pretty drunk too.

"Lennie didn't make it through that winter. He was maybe in his mid-twenties. One of those big Dakota storms blew through and cooped everybody up for about four days. When we dug out from under the snow, a road crew found Lennie under a drift on the edge of the highway. They were trucking along when thunk goes the plow and there's Lennie Red Skies. Frozen solid as a two by four." Choteau shook his head and laughed low down. "They had to thaw him out to take the bottle out of his hand."

"Red Skies," I said.

Choteau nodded. "Here's to you, Lennie," he said and downed the can of beer in his hand. The last can of beer. Now we were dry, even if our thoughts were pretty cold and damp.

"Lennie Red Skies?" I asked.

"So don't you be giving me any lectures about alcohol and my people and that shit. Don't be thinking, Professor man, that I don't know all about it."

I turned over on my side, gently, trying not to disturb the dog. "That's why you couldn't stay away from him," I said. "Isn't it?"

"Problem with Lennie was he didn't know who he was. It was his own damn fault," Choteau started to rub his cheek with a hand, but I noticed he was checking that stone behind his ear. His Crazy Horse stone. I guess Choteau knew who he was. He was Crazy Horse.

Right?

"He killed himself, man, that's what he did. He wasn't a white man, even though he lived in a white world. Anybody who grows up Indian in North Dakota knows that. Even in a mission school, you know that. You may not understand it, but you know it. You ain't white.

"But Lennie's problem was his other edge, man. That's what it was. He didn't know he was a Lakota, see. He wasn't white, but he forgot he was Indian, so he didn't know who in hell he was. And that killed him.

"I've seen it happen, Professor. Folks like Lennie," he turned his head and his eyes moved up and down, scanning my face. I wondered how much he could see, with those eyes. Could he see enough to read me? "Don't think you'll ever know what I'm talking about, professor," he said. It wasn't bitter, though it sounded that way to me. He was just stating a fact, the way he understood it. "I've seen it happen, over and over."

He shook his head at himself, I think. "Aw, hell, that's a bunch of crap. I don't know why Lennie drank himself to death. I don't know shit about it. I'm just trying to explain it to myself." He closed his eyes and frowned hard. The firelight flickered off the furrows in his brow. "Now I'm laying it onto you."

After he was quiet a moment, he said, "Sorry, Professor."

"He was related to this Mary Red Skies, wasn't he?" I said.

117

Choteau nodded his head curtly. Was he giving me these clues to himself on purpose? Or was I just learning to read him? Or were we both just too drunk?

"Her brother?" I said.

"Older brother, by a few years."

"And that's why you couldn't stay away from him, isn't it?"

"Yeah," Choteau sat up. He pulled the bag open and the bulldog rolled away from me and over onto its side. Protector lifted his head and yawned.

"I gotta take a leak," Choteau curled up his legs and stood up.

But I wasn't letting him off that easily. We were close to something, and old Crazy Horse Choteau here was trying to piss his way out of it. So I got up too. The room was cool and Choteau was headed for the door in his stocking feet. The bulldog got up on his front feet and shook his head to wake up. His stiff hind legs stayed lying on the bag though. I reached down and lifted the bulldog's hind end up. He whimpered at the pain, but he stood up, and seemed to understand the help.

By the time Protector and I made it over to him, Choteau had the door open and he was peeing out into the drifting snow. I must admit, the cool air of the cabin did start all the beer in me to moving.

I stood beside Choteau, spraying out with the wind. "That's where we're going, aren't we? Were not headed to Canada. Were heading for this Red Skies lady, aren't we?"

But Protector moved in to save Choteau, almost as if there was an instinctive link between them. The bulldog limped out into a furl in the snow and then hunkered his hind legs down like an old farmer checking the dirt. Those hind legs trembled from the pain and the cold. And so, the poor dog proceeded to shake so much he peed all over himself, trembling out there like a bare twig in the wind.

"Would you look at that poor dog," Choteau said. And when he was done, Choteau walked out into the drift and went to work wiping off the dog's front legs with snow. "Poor old

Protector," he cooed, stroking the dog's head at the same time he scoured him with snow. Then he carried the bulldog inside.

The old mutt was shaking from his snowy bath. Choteau laid it down gently in his bag and then lay down beside it. He covered them both up and held the dog until it stopped trembling. Then the dog heaved a big sigh, and they both fell asleep.

I was the one left to shove the door to old John Brown's cabin closed against the storm. Then I scurried across the cold stone floor to my own sleeping bag by the fireplace. I was racing against the onslaught of both Choteau and that bulldog snoring, and hoping maybe a bloodstream full of alcohol would rush me off to sleep ahead of their racket.

But Choteau had a bellyful of beer too, so I lost that race. He and the dog seemed to start snoring as soon as they were warm. I lay there awake for a little while, hearing the wind outside blowing in tandem with the dog and the convict. Another big attack of self pity was coming over me. I could feel it. But this time I was learning, I was. From Mr. Choteau, the spirit of Crazy Horse, and his lesson in yarns. I was learning, because I relaxed and let the lull of alcohol drift me away.

"Merry Christmas, Crazy Horse," my alcohol said, and I started to laugh. The snores and the wind were my only answer. "And you too, old John Brown. Wherever you are. You, too."

Sleeping on a stone floor next to an old, arthritic dog and an escaped Indian convict, I felt pretty good.

12/26/89

With some considerable measure of cottonmouth and headache, we got up the next morning and dug our way out. I know I felt as lame as that old dog, what with my sprung knee and my barking head, lying on stone, next to a cold fireplace. But we did it. We even did it happily.

The wind had died, but a hard, clean cold rode in on its heels. The kind of cold that makes the sky blue as turquoise, while the temperature hovers around zero under the midday sun. Choteau and I scooped the powdery snow away from the car. With the dog sitting up in the back seat, and both doors open, we rolled the Le Car forward through two big drifts and out onto the roadway. It took us all of forty-five minutes, I suppose, to get the car free. But the work and the warm blood running in me against the cold did wonders for my head, if not my knee.

The Renault turned over on the first try, only to tell us we were low on gas. And this was no day for running on empty.

But the idea of a big breakfast settling down with all that beer and sausage in my stomach sounded fine, too. So we stopped at the next little town on our way, a little place called Tecumseh.

The gas station at the edge of town had an empty cafe, at least by midmorning when we got there on the day after the blizzard. We filled the car and parked it around behind the place, just to be safe. It was the kind of joint that didn't mind the dog, especially on a zero day. So Protector sat on the floor next to our booth and drooled on napkins I put on the linoleum under him. A fair haired, fortyish woman brought coffee and

120

the newspaper over with a Xeroxed menu on a plain white sheet of paper.

"Cold enough for you boys out there?" she said, and didn't seem to recognize us. I took it as a good sign.

Choteau bummed the change from me for a phone call. He didn't say to whom, but I could guess. I curled up around the paper and the coffee. A kerosene space heater sat by one of the plate glass windows, kicking out dry heat to contest with the weather.

It was the Omaha paper, and it looked like the storm had run us off the front page. The country was in a mess from Great Falls to Atlanta. All across the continent, you could take your pick: mercury freezing temperatures, heavy snow, hard winds, ice storms, tornadoes, floods, mud slides and fog. It was all there on the front page, next to a big picture of some folks shoveling snow in Omaha, dressed like they were on an Arctic expedition.

But the big news as far as I was concerned was this: we weren't there. Nowhere on the front page.

In fact, it took me a couple pages into the front section to find us. But when I did, I had a surprise waiting.

There was no picture. Just a story, and that's when I discovered I had become a victim. "Choteau and Hostage Still Missing," it read. I had become a kidnap victim. The poor little professor caught in the middle. Golman's fingerprints were all over this. We may not get along, Golman and I, but I was still family and he was taking care of me. He'd saved me a way out of my little predicament, even though he knew me better than that.

Choteau strolled back then and grumbled something about no answer. "Hey, Choteau," I said brightly. "Guess what? I'm your hostage now."

I handed him the paper and he scanned it, holding it close to his face. Right about then our food came, and he carefully folded the paper and tucked it down beside him in the booth. At first I thought he was hiding it from the waitress. It seemed smart of him. But after she was gone, we ate in silence, and the quiet seemed strange after all the talk of the night before. I'd ordered the bulldog a bowl of Cream o' Wheat, and the cereal disappeared in one or two big gulps. Then Protector begged the lion's share of pork sausage from both of us. But the food was good and plentiful. It restored us. We washed it down with juice and bottomless, bottomless cups of black coffee.

When I was full, I leaned across the table for the paper. Choteau's hand came down gently and held it in place. "What's with this?" I said. "I just want to read what it says about me."

His hand rested there on the paper a moment, but then he gave in. I think he realized I was determined to see it. or that whatever was in it that he didn't want me to see, I'd earned the right to know. He cracked a big grin, as if it was all a joke. The dog woofed and Choteau used his newspaper hand to give Protector a slab of greasy hash browns. "Think I'll try that phone again," he laughed and got up. Protector's big jaws smacked up and down on the potatoes. Choteau gently scruffed the dog's neck, shoved the paper toward me across the table, then he strode away.

I turned open to our page hungrily. On the radio in the cafe, Paul Harvey began to drone on about weather and congress and wedding anniversaries. I couldn't find what Choteau was hiding from me for a long while. But somewhere toward the middle of the article it jumped out at me. When I saw it, I knew immediately what Choteau was covering.

He was up for parole. Or he would have been.

The paper posed it as a question. Why would a model prisoner due to be reviewed for parole in six months suddenly break free and kidnap a hostage? His motives were a mystery to the paper and the police, and for a moment or two, to me.

But then I thought of him over at the pay phone, standing in a hallway between the cafe and the garage, trying desperately to get through to someone. It wasn't clear to me, but I knew the answer had to do with Mary Red Skies and her brother Lennie. I didn't know how yet, but I knew it was them. And I knew I was going to figure it out.

Choteau walked back to our booth in just moments. "Nobody home?" I said and he nodded. The bulldog gazed up at him lovingly, but through its cloudy eyes.

"We should keep rolling," he said what he always said. But he didn't notice the routine. He just stood gazing out through the frosted windows. I couldn't see anything through that glaze of ice. But he seemed to see. I think his own eyes were so bad that the fuzziness of frost didn't really change the world that much.

"Let me try to make a call," I said. "Okay?"

He jerked a glance toward me. Then he tilted his head down and looked at the paper lying on the table. He nodded, but he said, "Be quick about it, Professor. They'll be tracing it, you know."

"If Terri doesn't answer, I'll hang up," I said.

"Be quick," he said without glancing up from the open paper. "Go talk to your woman," he said.

He understood, in his own way. I knew then for certain it was Mary Red Skies he was calling. She was where we were headed.

Terri picked up the phone. "Hello?" she said, and I said her name.

It was a coincidence, I thought. A stroke of dumb luck. But no, she answered it because she was waiting for me to call, she knew I would call. She knew me and she was waiting. I felt my spirits lift at the sound of her voice.

"Are you okay?" she said.

"Yeah, oh yeah," I said. "I'm fine."

"Did you stay out of the storm?"

"We holed up in a fishing cabin," I realized I was smiling as I spoke. "Just as cozy as could be. Terri, get this. He tells me yesterday he's Crazy Horse. Would you believe it?"

I chuckled as she said, "He what?"

"He claims he's the reincarnation of Crazy Horse. See, I was right about this stuff in my monograph. At least my original idea about the Ghost Dance was right. But nobody'd talk to me, is all."

"You be careful out there. He sounds like he's a mental case, or something."

"Oh, he's not goofy at all," I said. Then, just to egg her on a bit, I said, "Who's to say, Terri? Maybe he is, you know. I suppose he could be Crazy Horse, in a way?" The minute I said that, though I meant it as a joke, it made a scary kind of sense to me. I kept looking for the logic behind it, you see. Maybe he'd gone so far into his history and culture, that in a way he was the Spirit of Crazy Horse. I was trying to argue it around with myself. If Choteau really believed it, then from a certain angle of vision, I suppose he was.

Terri was quiet on the other end when I said that. Then, once I'd laughed, she said, "You're as crazy as he is, Will. You watch yourself."

"Well, why couldn't he be Crazy Horse?" I said. I was less and less sure of who was kidding who now.

"Listen to you," Terri laughed at me, just once. "I'm not even going to answer that."

I was in love with her, as wildly and foolishly as I ever was. That little laugh of hers rang in my ears like some kind of home team anthem. Rah, Rah, for our side, it sang in my heart.

"Terri, this phone is probably tapped. I want to talk to you somewhere where they won't be listening. Can you get to a phone booth or something? Fast?"

"Yeah, sure," she said. "Sure, I can," as some idea came to her.

"Good. Get to a phone and call me right back. Fast as you can, okay?" Then I read her the number of the pay phone. They would take that number and it would tell them where we were. But if Terri was quick, if she got to another pay phone in a few minutes, this would buy me the chance to talk to her without Golman and the boys listening in, at least for a moment or two.

I went back into the cafe and lied to Choteau. I told him Terri didn't answer, but I had to use the john. I gave him the money to pay our bill and told him I'd be back in a flash. He filled up his coffee cup from the pot, winked at me and said, "Don't hurry, Professor."

By the time I got back to the phone, it was ringing.

"Terri?" I said. She answered and I knew we still needed to be quick. "Where are you?" I said.

"At Moore's grocery." The tone of her voice had changed. She seemed angry suddenly.

"Listen," I said. "First off, how long are you staying at your folks?"

"I'm going back home tonight. I've got to get back to work. I'm going nuts with Mike and all his Bureau friends hanging around here."

"All right. If I need you, you'll be at home."

"Somebody will be listening on our phone at home, you know. Mike's got them watching me close."

"But they won't know this. Choteau and I are in Tecumseh, Nebraska. They'll know that soon. But they won't know we're driving north, Terri; I thought we were headed for Canada, but I think now we're going to find this woman friend of Choteau's first. Mary Red Skies is her name. That's all I know right now. But if you can find her, Terri, I'm pretty sure you can find us."

There was a long silence on the other end of the line. Then Terri said, "Why are you telling me this?" That question was strange. Her anger was still there, and for a moment I wondered what she meant by it. After all, she was part of this whole deal.

"I want you to know where I am. That's all." Still, the way I said it those words sounded ominous. They carried echoes. In case I can't reach you, in case something happens to me, in case you don't hear from me again, they seemed to say. Though that wasn't what I meant.

"I can't lie to Mike. I'm no good at it," she said. Then she was quiet, and I figured she was trying to digest all this.

125

"Terri?" I said to the silence at the other end. "I miss you."

"Oh shit," she said. "What?"

"Oh no, not you," Terri said. "It's Mike; he's walking down the hill from my folks' house. Shit."

"Did he see you?"

"I gotta hang up. He's gonna have a million questions now."

I could see Golman coming down the hill. Big grin on his face. That 'caught ya' twinkle in his eye. His erect, Semper Fi strut.

"Goodbye, Terri," I said.

"Be careful, Will. Choteau sounds like he's sick, or something. He may not know what he's doing. He might be dangerous."

"He's not a fruitcake, Terri," I laughed. "He's Crazy Horse."

But she just said, "I love you," quickly, and the line went dead.

"I love you, too," I said, to the dial tone.

"Bathroom, eh?" Choteau said, and startled me. He stood in the door to the hall, counting my change with the bulldog drooling at his heels.

"Well," I mumbled, "I . . . "

"They're tracing that call right now," he said, and pocketed the change. But at least this time he'd paid for the breakfast. Maybe he was beginning to worry about leaving a trail. "We better hit the road, compadre."

"No, were all right. I called her at a phone booth," I said. "They were both clean phones, I think."

"You think," he said. "C'mon, boy," he said to the dog, but it sounded in my ears too. Choteau opened the door and we walked around back to the car. He picked up Protector and set

126

him gently in the back seat, then climbed in himself. "Woman troubles," he said. "We're gonna get ourselves killed over them, Professor."

He laughed, but I just started the car. "Choteau," I said. "I told Terri where we are."

He found something richly funny in that, because he laughed harder than ever, shaking his head from side to side. But he wasn't laughing at me, it was at our whole predicament. And at himself, too, I thought. I noticed, though, he didn't ask me why.

"Can we trust her?" he said, still shaking his head.

I pulled the car out onto the highway. "Yeah," I said. "Yeah, I think we can." The acceleration down the road felt good, and so did feeling close to Terri again.

Choteau's laugh settled down. He laid his head back on the neck rest and reached over to stroke the dog. "Protector, old boy, what did you do with your lady friends? What did you do, old fellow? Does it get better when you get old?"

The bulldog just drooled a little and panted away, happy at the attention.

"We're not going to Canada, are we?" I drove north on the old pavement out of town. Nebraska stretched out in front of us, amazing to be so completely flat.

"Eventually," Choteau said, "I hope." Then after a moment he added, "Maybe."

"So, what's with Mary Red Skies?" I said. "Where is she?"

He grinned at me. I guess he grinned at the way I was reading him. "Grand Forks," he said.

"Well," I revved the engine a touch and we spurted ahead, throwing us all, the dog included, back against our seats. "To Grand Forks, it is. I guess it's on our way, isn't it? On the road to Winnipeg, huh?"

I chuckled and maneuvered smoothly around snow banks collapsed onto the pavement. "That's what they'll call this when were a tv movie, Mr. Crazy Horse. 'The Road to Winnipeg.' Starring Bernard Choteau as the Indian Chief. Right?"

Smiling, Choteau patted the bulldog gently on its gray head, and a big dollop of drool fell from its mouth. It rang tinny on the beer cans heaped in the backseat. "Ugh!" said Choteau.

"She's the reason you couldn't stay away from Lennie Red Skies, isn't she?" I said, not really asking.

Choteau grew very quiet and he stayed with stroking the dog's ears. He was still smiling, but his eyes were still and firm. He shook his head slowly, slightly now at something.

"You know, after she took me for that ride on a winter night, we were inseparable. My last two years at the school, Professor, you just couldn't keep us apart. I saw her everyday. Even after she graduated and went to work in Devils Lake, at the clinic there, I saw her every night." He paused a moment, then said, "She was beautiful, Professor, you know? That straight black hair, man, dark eyes.

"Every guy in Ramsey county wanted her. Not just on the res', either. She had her pick of us, man. White guys, too. Not just skins. Mary had her pick."

"But she picked you," I said, and looked over at him. Though he tried not to respond, he grinned.

"Yeah, I was just a kid. A year or so younger than her. And she'd been around, you know. Older guys had taken her everywhere. All the way to Minneapolis, once. That used to seem like it was the end of the world, man." He stopped, blinked his eyes a few times, and seemed lost again. "She told me, later on, that before she met me she was just using her looks to get what she wanted. She knew what she was doing. And then, with all of that, she picks me." He laughed sweetly, with a chiming in it I hadn't heard in him before. "You know why? Why she picked me? Because my dumbest move was my best move," he laughed.

128

"See, she'd heard every line there is, man. Heard 'em all. Then I come along, just struck dumb as granite, and fall over in her lap. She told me it was the first genuine thing anybody ever said to her." Choteau sunk a little in his seat and smiled out at Nebraska. "Imagine that, Professor," he said. "After all the smooth talk, after all the promises and clever little jokes, she fell for the klutz who didn't know what to say."

He winked at me then. "Remember that, Professor. Works every time. Just shut your mouth and fall over in her lap."

"Right," I said. "Let's see. Shut mouth. Fall in lap. Works every time. I think I got it, Chief."

"Put that in your book, Doc," Choteau grinned.

"Except, Mr. Crazy Horse, sir," I smirked back at him. "When I met Terri, we talked all night. She said what she liked about me was that I didn't try to hit on her all night. I just wanted to talk. I walked her home from the wine counter in a grocery store and we yacked and yacked all night, until the sun came up. I didn't try to make some fancy move."

"Well," Choteau shrugged, "whatever works for you." Then he cocked a head toward me, "But how long'd it take before you did make a move."

"When the sun came up."

"Good," he nodded. "I was worried about you for a moment there, Professor."

We took side roads around the edge of Lincoln then, and drove on to the north, talking about his high school days at the mission in North Dakota and about Mary Red Skies mostly. Funny thing was, the more we talked, the more I missed Terri. I'd throw in what I remembered about us, but we never got far from the North Dakota in Choteau's mind.

"Mary graduated when I was a junior, you know. But she took a job in Devil's Lake. She was pretty enough they didn't mind she was an Indian working at the clinic. She looked really good in that white uniform. And the doctors, they were always hitting on her, man. But she stuck with me, Professor. Mary Red Skies and me, we were going places.

"You know, I was a world beater back then, Professor. I wasn't any fucking lifer in the joint. I was going places, man." He stopped there for a moment. It was just enough of a pause for me to doubt him. How did I know it wasn't all a lie? How did I know he wasn't just some fast talking con telling me his sob story? How he lost it all? But it wasn't his fault, you know? It never is. Funny, but it was easier to believe he was Crazy Horse, in a way, than it was to trust him on his life story.

At least the Crazy Horse story was fresh.

"I wasn't no convict, man. I wasn't any 'political prisoner' or nothing. I was just one Indian kid smart enough to get an education. I had big plans, you know. I'd seen enough of the res.' Enough hungry winters and rusty pickups, man, I was getting out.

"The people in Fort Totten knew it, too. I was gonna get out of there and do something with myself, but they didn't know what. I was just the golden boy, you know. The star, babe, I was their kid."

He stopped again and touched his chin with three fingers of his left hand. The sun was shining hard on the snow and making the world very clear, and very cold. "Maybe she knew that, you know? Maybe I was just her ticket off the res'," he said.

"She must have had better chances than you, if that's all she wanted," I said.

But it didn't brighten him up any. He just said, "I suppose. Yeah, I know she did. But there are all kind of tickets-- some you like and some you don't--that'll get you where you want to go."

"You said there were doctors after her, just now," I offered him. "But she chose you, Choteau."

He laughed bitterly, and all traces of that chiming in it were gone. "Yeah, there sure were doctors after her, Professor. There sure were." Then he went dead silent. He wasn't in the car for a while. He was off searching something out his memory.

"How come you're blowing your chance at parole?" I said.

It pulled him back from wherever he'd gone in his head. He grinned his Buddha grin at me, and seemed to be in control again. He just eyed me for a time. It was as if he was measuring how to answer, how much to tell me, how much he could get away with.

"They wouldn't have paroled me, Professor. I'm like number two on the FBI's hate list. Right up there next to Leonard. Don't fool yourself. They'll never let me out of the can."

"Well, busting out is one hell of a way to convince them to give you a chance, wouldn't you say?" I kept my eyes on the road, but I still felt his little grin.

"It's got something to do with Ms. Red Skies, doesn't it?" I said. "That's why you blew parole."

Choteau looked over at the bulldog. "He's good, ain't he?" he said to Protector. The old dog looked at me, and licked the slobber off his chops.

But I wouldn't let Choteau slip away this time. "That's why were headed for Grand Forks. Were headed for Ms. Red Skies, aren't we?"

"Nordstrom," Choteau said, still holding his grin. This was his next curve ball.

"What?" I said.

"It's not 'Mizz Red Skies,' Professor," he said. "It's Mrs. Nordstrom."

Immediately I thought of Terri, of the dead end I'd handed her on the phone. She wouldn't be able to do a thing with the name "Mary Red Skies." It was useless to her. She couldn't use it to find me, and she suddenly seemed miles and miles away again.

But Golman and his FBI chums, to them this name was a tip they could work with; they would have files and access to the records that kept track of name changes. "Mary Red Skies" was a key to our direction, and a key they knew how to use. If they found it.

"She's got a son now. Nordstrom is a doctor in Grand Forks," Choteau kept his grin, though it must have been a labor now. "He worked at the clinic." It was becoming scary, that solid as ice grin. "Mary Nordstrom is her name now."

"Oh," I mumbled, and felt numb. So now Terri was far, far away again and the snowy pavement seemed lonely. It was hard, coming right on the heels of that connection I left for her. That dead end connection. "She's married," I said.

Finally, his grin cracked. Choteau gazed down at his feet on the floor, shielding his eyes a moment. Then he looked up and they were steeled again, and he said, "Separated. She left him a week ago Saturday. I got her letter two weeks back. Then I called her."

The little car made the only noise for a while. We drove along to the sounds of the heater fan blowing and the suspension squeaking and the dog panting. After a time, I said, "You're right. She is beautiful, Choteau." Somehow calling him Crazy now seemed wrong, though certainly it still fit.

"Yeah," he said, almost whispering. "She was, man." He was frowning at the floor on the car now. "But how do you know?" he said, as an after thought.

I'll admit it, I enjoyed having the edge on him. For once, no, for the only time, I had him confused.

"I found the picture of her. The one with the little boy and her. I guess it's her, anyway."

He nodded. He seemed older then, the gray streaks in his hair seemed more prominent, the weathering in his face more harsh.

"When was it taken?" I said.

He stopped and seemed to add it up. "Better than thirty years ago," he said. "She sent it to me, when I was in the service. With a note that said, 'I'm happy. Hope you are too.'" He laughed a bitter laugh at that, then said, "She looked white, you know, in that picture. You wouldn't know she was Indian, with the curl in her hair and that little boy dressed up for the photographer and all."

I didn't mean to drive him into himself like that, so I thought I'd try to lighten up the mood a bit. "But now she's left the guy, huh?"

He raised his head and looked at me.

I said, "Better late than never, right? Crazy?"

The grin returned. I think he regained his Buddha cool, but you never know what's behind a grin like that. Sometimes not even when you're wearing it.

"So, Mr. Professor," he cocked his head and glared at me out of the corner of his eye. "You've been going through my pockets, eh?"

"Me?" I said.

And then, there it was. The knife again. That stolen, hidden, re-stolen paring knife; the one we thought about a lot and never mentioned.

"Not me, Crazy," I said, frowning and shaking my head. And not saying a word about the knife.

He laughed, then said, "I got you, Professor."

"Red handed?" I said, emphasizing the 'red.'

"Ind'in giver," he said.

"That little boy of hers must be all grown up by now, I suppose," I tried his trick, changing the subject.

Choteau let the knife issue disappear again, with ease. If I wasn't going to press it on him, he wasn't going to own up to it. But whatever little doubt there might have been left about who knew what, it was gone now. He was carrying a hidden weapon, I knew it, and he knew I knew it. And we never mentioned it.

"I guess so," Choteau said.

"So tell me, Choteau, what happened to you two? How'd she end up married to a doctor, playing white lady of the suburbs?"

"Maybe she didn't. Maybe the picture just looks that way, Professor."

"But you said it yourself. It's the curled hair, you know, the permanent," I said. "But what gives, Choteau? How'd she end up married to a white doctor?"

"Listen, Champ," Choteau gazed blankly up at the roof of the car and grinned, "you don't need to know everything about me."

"Not right now, I don't," I said.

He laughed. "Not ever."

"Not yet," I said.

Back in the days of my research, I was working on the Ghost Dance. I was convinced that some remnants of the old Ghost Dance religion were behind all the troubles out at Pine Ridge and Rosebud in the 70 's. That was my theory. At first, in the early interviews and research, I seemed to have touched on some truth. People opened up to me. Letters and old files and Congressional testimony made a sudden, new sense. It was all easy, because it all fit so well together.

The Ghost Dance wasn't really forgotten, see. That old, apocalyptic religion that swept across the mountains and plains of the West in the 1870 's and 80 's, it was at the root of all the blossoming pride and independence in South Dakota. This faith in an end time, when the grasses of the prairie would roll out new and cover over all the pillage and construction of White America, when the buffalo would run once more across that new, reborn prairie, and when the people who kept the faith in the bad times and lived right as part of that old natural order, they would come to life and this old island continent would follow the good red road again. This idea, this dream was behind Wounded Knee, behind the massacre in 1890 and the revival in 1973. That was what I saw.

And somehow, Bernard Choteau was the key. The trails seemed to lead past the activists, past the Peltiers and the Robideaus, and even past the holy men like the Crow Dogs, always trailing back to Bernard Choteau. But whenever I tried to touch on him, the trail disappeared. Documents and testimony came to a dead end. The people shut up. Choteau wouldn't talk, and nobody would talk about him.

So when he told me he was Crazy Horse, the old, trained history professor in me sat up. It fits. I wasn't clear yet how it fit, but it did. You see, I wanted him to be Crazy Horse. Logically, it would work somehow. I could find some primitive myth, or some old formula, some native belief, and I'd make it fit. Bernard Choteau was Crazy Horse. I just had to figure out how.

And then I'd write that book. The one I couldn't write before. The one I had to drop to write the little book that made Golman mad, and my career safe. But now I was back to the real task. The book. The true book. The one I meant to write from the start.

The one, I suppose, I'm trying to write now.

We crossed into South Dakota about one o'clock, and Choteau had me pull over at a truck stop near the border with a public phone. He stood outside in the frigid cold and dialed his North Dakota number.

I took the bulldog for a walk. Or maybe I should say a limp, since we both were pretty hobbled by our ornery joints.

Still it was good to get out of the car. Protector hunkered down beside the Renault to pee again, trying to mark his turf, I guess. But the old dog was too crippled to lift his leg, though his sense of territory was still alive and burning. What it amounted to, though, was the poor mutt dirtied himself again. So I gave him another quick snow bath, and then set him back inside the Renault where it was at least tolerably warm.

Protector was licking at my hands and I was drying him off with the edge of a sleeping bag, when Choteau came strolling back with a couple of micro waved sandwiches and black coffee.

"Do we need to run?" I asked him.

"Nope. All bought and paid for," he said, as he fed the dog corned beef from his sandwich. "Bad place to forage," he said. "Owner's got a .45 by the register."

"Hmmm," I said through my ham and Swiss on rye. "Nice place."

After we'd chowed for a while, Choteau said, "Nobody home." As if it wasn't obvious from the short time he was gone and the way most of it was spent on lunch.

I started up the Renault and we drove northward again. Choteau seemed quiet, disappointed. But not me. We may have been on the lam, pursued by federal forces, crossing the hard plains in dead of winter, but the road made me lighthearted again. On these back highways, eastern Dakota was an expanse of rolling snowfields. The little yellow car trudged across it with a warm heart. My knee ached on the throttle and I missed Terri, and I don't think Choteau could see much past the short hood of the car with his bad eyes, and he must have been wondering why Mary Red Skies Nordstrom didn't answer, and the arthritic dog drooled uncontrollably onto the empty beer cans in the back seat, but our bellies were full and we seemed somehow to have a bright purpose ahead of us. It was called Grand Forks, land of the Red Skies, filled with promise. We'd be there that very night, so it all seemed Grand, indeed.

And the FBI was nowhere in sight.

Still, Choteau was distracted, lost in his thoughts about that unanswered phone and this Red Skies woman he was risking everything for. "You know," I said, trying to pry him open, "You've had this trouble before, Crazy Horse."

It didn't even give him pause when I used that name for him.

"What trouble is that?" he said. He had a point. There were a few ways you could interpret that word 'trouble' in Bernard Choteau's life.

"Last time around," I said, "it was about your biggest mistake, I'd say."

"Which?"

"Oh, you know," I took a slow sip from my paper cup of coffee, just to stretch the moment out. "Falling for the wrong woman, Crazy Horse."

He laughed and seemed to follow what I was talking about. But he might have been faking it. "My biggest mistake, huh?" he said.

I was kidding him, and trying to pry a little more of his story out of him, too. But at least a part of it was a test. If this guy was who he claimed to be, the spirit of Crazy Horse, then he would know what I was getting at.

"Last time out," I said, "in your last life, you got yourself in big trouble over a woman."

"That was last time," he chuckled.

I wouldn't let him off that easily. He couldn't dodge my test by playing coy. I guess it was my academic training switching on again. I knew I had Choteau cornered, and I was going to press him until I found out if he had anything of Crazy Horse in him at all. It was dissertation defense time out on the old range.

"You might say it was your fatal weakness, Crazy," I was careful not to give away any details, but I made it clear what I meant. That is, if he was Crazy Horse.

He was smiling at me, puckish, his eyes crinkled up with delight. "So you don't believe me, huh? I knew you wouldn't."

I laughed, I think because he'd read the situation so clearly. But I didn't say a word to give my little test away. I just laughed and waited.

"Don't you know, Professor, you can't prove something like this. You either believe me, or you don't. I am Crazy Horse returned, or I'm not. But you can't prove it, one way or the other."

"Right," I said.

"It's all a matter of belief, Professor."

I nodded.

He laughed, then said, "You're asking the wrong questions, Doctor Gentles."

I looked over at him, tried to make my face go serious, then said, "So why don't you answer anyway?" Then I turned back to driving and couldn't hold back. It was all just too wacky, driving along with a convict testing him to see if he was reincarnated. I started to laugh, and I laughed so hard tears came to my eyes. Choteau, or Crazy Horse, or whoever the hell he was, joined me and even the dog woofed along with our noise.

"Mary Red Skies is different," he said, carefully using her maiden name again, I noticed.

"Oh yeah?" I said. "How is that?"

Choteau, or Crazy Horse, I guess, he glanced down for a moment and he pulled his loose hair back behind his shoulders. He touched the stone behind his ear, as if to gather memories. And then, he let me have it.

When he looked back up at me, he'd gone dead serious. "You're hinting around about Black Buffalo Woman. When I was young I spent a lot of time courting her. I'd go to her parents and her mother would drape the blanket over us. That's the way it was done then, you know? Not like nowadays."

He was talking about old Lakota courtship practices. Young couples were never left alone together, so when a boy wanted to speak to a girl, when courting was going on, someone would hold a blanket over them. That was as close as they got to privacy.

"She promised herself to me," Choteau said, "but Black Buffalo Woman was beautiful, Professor, and I wasn't the only one talking under the blanket with her. There were a lot of others. She wanted me to prove I was a great man first. A real warrior, worthy to share a life with her. So I went off on a war party against the Crows to prove myself. But while I was gone," he paused there, and seemed not even to breath. "She left with one of those others, with No Water. She went away and became No Water's wife. I'd lost her."

He shook his head slowly. "I still don't know why," he said.

"So how is she different?" I said. I was impressed with what he knew, and with the serious way he spoke about it. He almost had me believing him.

"This all happened after I became a shirt-wearer, Professor. There were five of us who were chosen, and as shirt-wearers we became the leaders of the camp during times of war, and whenever the camp moved to another place. It was our duty then to keep order and make sure everyone was respected. We made sure no violence ever happened in the camp. Most of all, it was our duty to look out for the helpless, for the poor ones and the sick. The Big Bellies charged us to always put the good of our people first. Never to think of our own wants and needs. It was a great honor, to be a shirt-wearer then. Before it all changed."

There was a proud lift to his chin as he spoke. Choteau seemed a different person to me then, not the smart ass convict he'd been moments before. But, I guess I wanted him to be different.

"There was a saying, and we heard it when we took the shirts. The old men, the Big Bellies told us, 'Now, you must never again think of yourself. If anyone does you harm, no matter how severe, you must pay no more attention to it than you do when a dog lifts its leg near your tipi.' "

"Unless its old Protector," I said. "Then you got to take off your shirt-wearer's shirt and give him a bath." I slapped the steering wheel once with my hand, and chuckled out, "Right, Chief?"

But he didn't join me. He just paused there and his head sunk a little. He stared sadly away. "I kept my vows, Professor, for many years. I kept them through all the little battles and the lean winters, and with less and less game to hunt. And then, when I'd seen enough, after I'd watched my people suffer and my friends die, and all for nothing, I decided. Life was short. I was tired of being alone. I had no wife and no children, nothing but those vows of the shirtwearer and even though I kept them carefully, our old way of life seemed to be dying. I was tired of gazing at Black Buffalo Woman across the fires, and watching her gaze back at me. It was too long.

"This all happened in the spring of the same year when Custer came and found gold in the Paha Sapa. Right at the time when my people needed my vows the most, I slipped away with her. Black Buffalo Woman ran away with me. By our laws, she had the right to be with whoever she chose, and she wanted to be with me.

"We stayed together two nights," he said, and then he stopped again. He sat there, as if he was lost in some memory, as if he was talking about Mary Red Skies and high school nights in North Dakota, and not about a hundred years before.

"On the second night, No Water came. Little Big Man was with us, with Black Buffalo Woman and me. The three of us were sitting together, laughing and talking in the evening. No Water burst into the tipi and he was carrying a revolver. I stood up and drew my knife to defend us, but Little Big Man yelled, 'No,' at both of us and he held my arm back. Then No Water said that I was a dog and he fired his gun. The bullet hit me here in the jaw." Choteau's hand rose up, and it seemed involuntary. He held his cheek. Then he trembled, hard, next to me in the car, as if he felt the bullet travel through him again. "I fell forward into the fire, and Little Big Man pulled me out. No Water turned and left me for dead. He ran away. And Black Buffalo Woman crawled out the back and fled. But I saw her

140

when she ran. I remember it. The blood from my face had spattered onto hers. As No Water ran away in one direction, I heard her screaming and I saw her holding her face, clutching at hers where mine had been torn open." Slowly he let his hand drop to his lap again.

"But it wasn't my time to die, Professor. Not then. I lay there and Little Big Man and He Dog and some others took care of me and I healed. It was in my vision, you know," he began to slowly nod his head. "I should never fear the white man's guns, because only the hands of my own people would hold me back and lead me to my death.

"No Water was one of the Bad Faces, and I was Hunkpatilla, Professor. For a while, it seemed there would be a feud between our two bands over us. But I got well again, and Black Buffalo Woman went back to No Water. And he gave a gift of three horses to my father. I wanted only one thing. Black Buffalo Woman should not be harmed. And that was how we kept the peace between us, between the Bad Faces and the Hunkpatilla.

"But even with that, I had destroyed my vows. Custer was out finding gold in our sacred hills, while I was driving my people away from one another. I had put myself before the people. And though I never did that again, it still was all over. I was not a shirt-wearer. Not in my heart.

"And there never was another ceremony after that. There were only four shirt-wearers left, and I had broken their authority. Some men claimed, in those days after that, to be shirt-wearers, but there never was really anymore of them again.

"So you see, Dr. Gentles, I was the first break in the sacred circle. After that, it seemed the time had come for everything that was Lakota to end. And I wore a scar on my face to show it."

Choteau, or whoever he was then, sucked in a deep breath. His eyes were squeezed tight. His fists clenched and he shook like he was fighting a seizure. It scared me enough I started to pull the car over. The bulldog let loose one insistent bark at him and then Choteau sank down in his seat again, still.

"You all right?" I said, not knowing what else to say. And then I really said it. I mean I said it for the first time and believed it. "Crazy Horse?" I said.

Okay, now you're sure I have gone off the deep end. Yes, I knew most of what he said he could have found in half a dozen different history books. Rationally, it could have been just a great performance, and yes he was a con artist, what with his acting like he could see and his "foraging" and with this whole pilgrimage to Mary Red Skies and all. And don't get me wrong, I don't buy voices and channelers and deja vu, or even reincarnation, for that matter. I don't believe any of that. All I can tell you is I sat next to him in a compact car on some South Dakota back road, and for a while I started to call him Crazy Horse. It wasn't anything I thought through. It wasn't a decision, or a change of mind. Its just that for a while there, the name seemed to fit him. Crazy Horse.

I believed, sooner or later, I would figure it out.

Not long after his little attack of the shaking Willies, Choteau started to laugh. "Whoa!" he said, as he straightened his hair again. "How was that? You believe me, now?"

"Well, let's not do this too often," I said. I sounded a lot paler than I wanted to then.

"You do believe me," he said, and nodded his head with satisfaction. "Maybe there's hope for you after all, Professor," he said.

We rode along for a while then, and Choteau or Crazy Horse, I guess, was quiet like I was. There didn't seem to be much to say that could make any kind of sense. So we listened to the dog pant. Then suddenly, out of nowhere, he said, "Mary Red Skies is different."

That part, that was the old Choteau speaking, the one I'd grown half used to.

"Sure she is," I said, and tried to sound convincing.

Arriving at the idea that you're driving across South Dakota with Crazy Horse in a Le Car is not easy. It calls for a certain stretching of one's sense of the limits of reality. A sense of reality I'd spent thirty-eight years constructing. A sense I'd come to depend on. I'd always called it my common sense.

I'd just taken a sharp left turn out of the land of common sense and driven off into the great, uncharted territories. The Yukon of the fishy and the questionable. It was a wide open expanse out there, and I for one didn't know where I was headed. I was lost, because all my old maps were gone. And I hadn't given up on them yet. Most of me still believed the old maps would work. I suppose that's why I was lost.

What I didn't need right then was a cop.

But you don't always get what you need.

"Uh oh," I heard Crazy Horse say.

Then I saw the red and blue lights flashing in the rear view mirror.

"Shit," I muttered. "What should I do?" I looked over at Crazy Horse and saw Choteau the escaped convict sitting there. He seemed as lost as me.

"Pull over," he said. "Fast. He's gonna be calling in our borrowed plates."

"That's right," I said, distracted.

"Pull over now," Choteau yelled.

I hadn't been driving my best, and I realized that now. It wasn't the car or our stolen plates that had attracted the South Dakota Highway Patrol, at least not yet. Crazy Horse had been resting up from his little fit of memory making, in a daze I guess. Meanwhile I'd been doing the old weave and swerve down the state highway. These tiny glimpses of Nirvana and apparent truth are hard on your driving record, you know.

I pulled the Renault over onto a dirty snow bank. The patrolman was right behind me. Before the car even came to a rest, Choteau had hopped out. "I got to distract him, before he gets a read on our plates," he called back to me as he sprinted toward the patrol car. I had this sinking feeling it was already too late.

I watched it all in the rearview mirror. I was remembering how good Crazy Horse was at laying out a decoy in the old days. It was his favorite trick, leading the cavalry over the hill and into a trap. Custer was his biggest sap, you know. And now there he was in my mirror, trying to head off the South Dakota Highway Patrol.

"Stop where you are," boomed a godlike voice over the patrol car's p.a. "Do not approach the car."

Crazy Horse charged on like there'd been no announcement. He was at the officer's window before the last words were out of the loud speaker.

It was pretty gutsy of him, seeing as how he met a pistol barrel when he got there. The cop swung the door open enough to make him back off. Then he climbed out of the car and held the renegade Indian at bay.

Choteau raised his arms over his head, I assume because he was ordered to. But it had worked. He'd lured the cop away from the radio.

Protector growled in the backseat and worked his sore bones around to watch. I just sat, eyes on the mirror, waiting for doomsday as this High-Po waved Choteau forward with his pistol. They came marching toward the Le Car then, Choteau first with the cop a few steps behind him holding the gun.

Choteau let his marching steps wander a little along the way though, and once he tripped over the edge of the pavement. Was it an act, or his eyes? I wasn't sure. But with every

144

misstep, I heard the cop bark something out at him. And each time, Protector growled low down in his throat, back at the cop. The old dog followed it all, moving around in the back seat slowly without a whimper, despite the arthritis in his bones.

Officer Dakota looked impressive; he was dressed to give orders, he was. Tawny pants with a cowboy hat to match, and shining brown boots. He wore a dark brown leather flight jacket with a tawny fur collar like the hat and trousers. And of course, reflector shades. Black gun in hand, his gun belt with the radios and beepers and handcuffs and such stuff tinkled at each step, and he sported a nice big star badge on his chest. He looked like authority itself, the way he was supposed to: Mr. Dakota Ranger, sir, with a bookshelf of John Wayne videos at home next to his Louis L'Amour's.

He flagged Choteau over next to the front fender of the Renault, then ordered me to step out. I swear I heard him mutter something about a "white lad" as I turned to open the door. Choteau was sneering and he rested his behind against the car. The Renault leaned under his weight.

What with that attitude and the gun waving and all, I figured the jig was up. Old Crazy Horse had been too late. By the time he made it to the patrol car with his delaying action, Officer Dakota had a bead on us, and he'd called it all in. The FBI were out there now, bearing down on us across the plains. It was surrender time, or maybe massacre time, but the party was over.

"C'mon, step out here," Officer Dakota said. "Keep your hands where I can see them. And let me see your ID's, lads."

Protector growled deep, then let loose with a flurry of barks against the rear window glass. His ugly mug charged at the glass and he was beginning to froth at the mouth. It was not pretty.

"Keep the dog in the car," Officer Dakota added, quickly. I think that is when he noticed the beer cans. There were better than a dozen of them back on the floor, and they were flying around some now as old Protector kicked up a fit in the backseat.

"Step out here," Dakota nearly shouted. "Now."

Choteau started to chuckle. The cop glared at him, said, "You, stand up. Step away from the car."

Choteau had his arms crossed on his chest. Somewhere on his person he was carrying that paring knife, and as I turned to step out of the car, I remembered that. Maybe it was the thought of that knife, and the way Choteau ignored the cop and just leaned there against the Renault. Maybe it was the news of the last half hour, the idea of riding with Crazy Horse. Maybe it was just too many hours of mindless driving on my bum knee. But I proceeded then to pull one of my most graceful moves.

I turned, leaned forward to step out of the car. But my good leg was numb from sitting, and the foot on my other, bum leg got hooked on the brake pedal, or something. A sharp pain shot up through my side when I tugged it free. But I already had the forward motion started. The leg that was asleep folded up when I put my weight on it and, well, I fell out of the car and onto my face beside the pavement.

In fact, I practically smacked my forehead on the High-Po's boots. He jumped back a step. I guess for a moment he thought I was lunging at him. Choteau, still leaning comfortably against the car, started to laugh now.

I did too, as I struggled to get up. What else could I do? I had one leg tangled up with the stick shift in the car, and screaming at me in pain. The other leg was fishing around under the car, while I did pushups off the pavement, trying to get loose.

"Geez, little buddy, can't hold it, eh?" Choteau croaked. He guffawed, and staggered a little himself, as he wobbled around the door and bent down to help me up. As he reached to pull me up, he glared in my eyes. Then he said in

146

this goofy new croak of his, "Straighten up, buddy. The officer wants to see your license."

I got it. We were playing drunk. I wasn't sure why yet, but I knew enough to play along.

It wasn't hard, because I had trouble standing, even once Choteau got me up and untangled. My bum knee throbbed anew, and the good leg was tingling with pinpricks, and wasn't any too steady.

"Having a little too much fun on the highway here, aren't you, Chief?" the cop said to me. I thought for a moment he was talking to Choteau, because of that 'Chief' he tacked on the end. But after a beat, I realized he was talking to me.

"Sir?" I said.

"Let me see your license, Chief," he nodded at me with that cowboy hat.

Now, I've got dark hair, but I'm as pale and blue eyed as any white kid in Indiana. I look about as much like an Indian as I do a Martian. So it hit me as a shock: through the blinders Officer Dakota here was wearing that afternoon, I'd just become another drunken Indian. Guilt by association, I guess. Or maybe by miscegenation. Imaginary miscegenation.

When the cop holstered his revolver, saying, "Come on, let's see your driver's license, Chief," I began to understand Choteau's game. Play to the audience's expectations.

I handed him my Missouri ID, thinking all the while about those Kansas plates he must have called in. But Officer Dakota wasn't too sharp that afternoon. He didn't catch the discrepancy between my plates and my license. What's more, my name didn't mean anything to him.

I was actually a little disappointed at that. I guess I'd been growing famous in my own mind as I drove along with Crazy Horse himself. Here I was, about to be caught, and the cop missed it.

Officer Dakota seemed a bit distracted though. First off, he had to deal with my partner. "Identification?" the officer said to Choteau.

He just shrugged and held his empty hands out in front of him. "Don't got none," Choteau said, smirking. "But I know who I am?" he said.

"No identification?" the officer's voice rose a note in pitch and volume.

Choteau shook his head no, looking at his empty hands. "You got to read a piece of paper to know who you are?" he said, raising his eyebrows and cocking his head.

"Stand up," the cop said, to both of us. I was steadying myself on the open door of the car. Choteau was beside me, leaning on the Le Car again. "What's your name, Chief?" the cop said.

Choteau grinned at him. "Crazy Horse," he said flatly.

I nodded my head. "He is," I said. But Officer Dakota didn't believe us.

Behind me, I heard Protector shove his way between the bucket seats. The dog was panting with the effort, and grumbling as he went.

"You fellas think this is funny, huh?" Officer Dakota said. "Well let me tell you, boys, I was off duty just now. I live right up the road here, at the edge of Bancroft. I was headed home for the evening, fellas."

Protector had made it down out of the front seats to the floor of the car, panting hard through his wet drool.

"I got two young sons up there and on a day like this, they might just be building a snow man in the front yard. They're just youngsters, fellas, and they might even be building their snowman too close to the road. Sometimes they get so involved in playing, they forget what I told them about staying away from the highway, you know, fellas? Maybe?"

Protector was right behind me now, and not listening to Officer Dakota's speech about family life on the plains. The bulldog was slowly setting himself to step down out of the car. I could hear his feet shuffling and digging in the car's thin carpet, and his worried snorting.

"So I don't like anybody drinking and driving, fellas. I especially don't like Indians drinking and driving. I've seen too much of it, you know. So, here I come, driving home to my wife and kids, and I find you boys driving toward my town, right toward my house, toward my two little boys on the day after Christmas. And you," he looks directly at me, puts his arms akimbo. "You can't stand up, much less keep your automobile on the road.

"I have a tendency to get upset about things like this, fellas." He shook his head and looked thoughtful for a moment.

"I kind of lose my sense of humor, Mr. Crazy Horse," he glared over at my partner. "If you know what I mean." Protector got his front legs stepped down out of the car, and stopped there. But the bulldog never let out a whimper. The way the dog stopped and panted in that awkward position, the pain in its hind legs must have been fierce.

But his loyalty was fierce too.

"So, maybe before I give you guys the blood alcohol test, maybe you'd like to humor me a little and tell me who you are."

"I'm Crazy Horse," said Choteau.

"He is," I said.

The cop's jaw clamped tight and the muscles in his cheeks worked hard. Protector stepped out of the Renault onto the gravel behind him. Then the dog stood stiff a while and rested.

The officer glanced at my license and barked out my last name. "Count to ten on your fingertips like this," he said. Then he quickly counted by touching his thumb to the tips of his fingers back and forth across one hand until he reached ten. "Do it," he ordered.

I smiled, held out my hand and counted it out. It was easy. At least when you're sober. Choteau started to chuckle again.

That only made the cop more angry. I was defying him by following his orders.

But his next test wasn't going to be so easy. Not with the condition of my legs. "Get out here," Officer Dakota said.

He pointed down at the white line on the edge of the pavement. "I want you to take ten steps, toe to heal, down that line. Count them off loud as you go."

Then he stood at attention out on the pavement and waited. I limped my way over to him, keeping a hand on the car door as far as I could. One leg was still pin-prickly, the other was swollen stiff and tender at the knee. Suddenly the South Dakota wind seemed hard, and it was tough just to stand toe to heel on that line, much less take a step.

"Let me tell you what's going to happen here, Chief, so you can think about this as you walk," the Officer said to me, not to Choteau. He still thought I was an Indian. "If you don't make it, Chief, I'm going to haul your ass down to Bancroft and set you in jail. There's a fifteen hundred dollar fine for first offense on driving under the influence. Assuming this is your first offense, Chief."

Protector had crawled out of the car and down behind Choteau. The bulldog stood there collecting himself after his big effort. Officer Dakota, evidently, was so intent on nailing my behind to the pavement that he'd forgotten about the old bulldog.

"You'd need $150 dollars bail money, if you got it. And even if you do, Chief, sometimes it takes the bondsman a couple days to get through, when the weather's like this."

I had enough of his "thinking words" about then, so I started my parade across South Dakota. For the first step I used my good leg and counted one loudly. The Great Plains wind was cutting across the highway and through me. I had my hands out like I was walking a tightrope.

The next step was the tough one. When my weight rested on that swollen knee, jerked around by my little tumble out of the Le Car, I felt myself leaning forward. Somehow I quickly took the third step and managed to stay standing, and squeaked out, "two-three."

"That's enough," the cop said, stepping toward me. "You ride with me to town, along with Mr. Crazy Horse here, the big chief who won't cooperate." He grabbed me by the elbow and said, "Come on, fellas, let's get in the patrol car. We don't want any trouble."

I jerked my arm loose and said, "Wait a minute; I can do it."

I saw Protector then, limping over toward the cop. He seemed to be on the same tightrope I was, walking that painful straight line even when his body wouldn't cooperate. But his high wire was built of arthritis.

"Don't make any more trouble for yourself, Chief," the cop said. Then he reached for the cuffs that dangled from his belt and started reciting the Miranda list at me, from memory. It took him a while and he hesitated once or twice. I think he was new at being a HighPo. Choteau stood up and pulled his hair back off his shoulders. But it was old Protector who was really on the move.

The bulldog hobbled slowly up behind the cop and, just as the young office told me anything I said could be used against me, that dear, old arthritic pooch raised its hind leg. He lifted that stiff old limb right up in the air. Even if he did hoist it slowly.

Protector let loose with a good hosing onto Officer Dakota's right boot. I'd seen this dog piss a couple of times before, when we'd had to bath the old boy with snow as a result. But I'll tell you, this was pissing in a new dimension. This was not precious relief, not need, this was malicious attack. The cop didn't even know he was under a bulldog cloud burst until Protector had soaked his pant leg.

Right in the midst of his "in a court of law" spiel, the officer felt that warm pee on his leg. "Hey," he yelled, and turned. With a backhand he swatted down at the bulldog and sent poor Protector yelping away.

Before I knew what I was doing, I grabbed the patrolman's other hand, and growled at him, "Don't. No more."

Officer Dakota glared back at me, and then at my hand on his wrist: "I wouldn't if . . . " he started to say.

But he didn't get to finish that sentence.

In the next moment, Protector turned and fought back; the old dog clamped his jaws on the High-Po's clean pant leg and started to pull and growl. The cop was about to kick Protector loose, when Choteau landed on the officer's back. I shoved my shoulder into Officer Dakota's chest, and we all tumbled over: High-Po, bulldog, reincarnated Indian chief, and me.

"This is assault," Officer Dakota squeaked as he went over. His cowboy hat went bouncing away under the Renault, as we wrestled him to the ground. In a few confused moments, I was kneeling on his back and had hold of his wrists. Choteau had his legs pinned to the pavement and Protector was chewing happily on the clean boot.

I didn't really think much about what this meant just then. See, I'd just closed my escape hatch. Without a thought, I'd gone from a kidnap victim to assaulting an officer. And it was all just an instinct. He swatted at old Protector, and about the next thing I knew I was kneeling on a highway patrolman, pushing his face into the gravel and twisting his arms behind his back. But it was right about that moment, when it was too late to look back, I realized what I'd done.

"Now what?" I said to Choteau. I found myself looking up and down the highway, wondering about witnesses.

"We got to cuff him," Choteau said. And then my next big revelation hit me. When they come, those revelations, you

152

don't have a lot of time to duck, you know. And it seems like with me, they always come in clusters.

I found out, then, just how bad Choteau's eyes were. "Grab the handcuffs," I said. They hung there from Officer Dakota's belt. They were not small. They were not hard to notice. They were also not something Bernard Choteau could find.

"Where?" he said.

I heard the old bulldog happily slobbering away on boot leather. I hoped it wasn't foot, but I couldn't be sure.

"There, on the belt," I said through my teeth. "I can't get them," I was tied up with holding Officer Dakota's arms.

"This is a mistake," the cop groaned. But pressed there in the salted gravel, he'd lost all his authority. It had bounced away under the car with his hat.

Choteau began to feel around for the belt, believe it or not. He couldn't even find the belt on the guy he was pinning to the ground.

"And you offered to drive?" I said.

He just grinned and shrugged at me. "Highway's bigger than a belt," he said.

"You'll regret this," the cop said.

"Shut up," I said. I surprised myself. I sounded like I knew what I was doing. "Over to your left, and up a little," I said to Choteau.

He groped around on the Highway patrolman's behind, and I was imagining how this was going to sound in court. Officer groped during assault while two suspects resisted arrest. But then Choteau found them, and I was amazed at how deft his fingers were once he'd located the cuffs. It was as if he could see, as if he'd become Crazy Horse again, but I realized it came from years of compensating for his deteriorating eyes. He'd learned to fake his way through a world of prisons and holding cells, while his eyesight narrowed and narrowed into a tunnel of dim light. He was looking at the world through a periscope that was shrinking. And what little he saw wasn't kind. So he'd learned to adapt.

The minute he had those cuffs in hand, he took over again. He handcuffed the cop and then, pulling Protector's rope collar off the dog's bull thick neck, Choteau bound Officer Dakota's legs tightly. "We got to get him upright," he said. "Let's carry him back to the car." I took the cop's shoulders, expecting Choteau to grab his legs. But it didn't happen that way. "Keep those shoulders up," Choteau came around beside me.

"Why you so worried about getting him up?" I said. I thought Choteau was just being kind to the cop, trying to keep him comfortable.

"Because these guys wear an alarm deal, Doc," Choteau bent down and took one of the officer's arms. With a grunt, he hoisted the cop up into a sitting position. "It goes off if he's prone for more than a couple of minutes. Come on, Professor, heave ho!" We lifted him up by the shoulders and dragged him toward his car, with his heels leaving a trail in the frozen gravel.

Officer Dakota's eyes were wide with terror the whole time, but he was scared enough now to be quiet. And once we gagged him anyway with a piece of his shirt tail and his handkerchief, he never made another peep. I guess he was remembering all those mysterious reservation murders he'd heard about, and all the Indians he'd hauled in over the years. He'd heard one too many stories about disappearing persons and slit throats and drunken Indians. He didn't even struggle.

Choteau kicked a file box off the seat, and crawled into the back of the patrol car, dragging the officer behind him. I crawled in too, kneeling on the seat. We sat him up straight between us in the patrol car. It was a tight fit back there, with the plexi-glass windows that rose from the front seat of the car and caged us in. They don't give you much room in the back seat of a cop car. This was my first look inside, and it gave me claustrophobia.

Choteau couldn't resist one last dig then, one last shot at the John Wayne visions in that cop's head. "Nice hair," he said, and stroked the patrolman's flat top. Out of somewhere, he pulled my paring knife then and he tugged at the cops bristly hairdo a little. Officer Dakota's eyes nearly bugged out. The High-Po shook his head frantically, and moaned out a 'mooo' sound through his gag.

"Not enough to take," I said, playing along. "Looks like somebody beat us to it."

"Guess you're right," Choteau shook his head slowly. "It's a shame though. We'll just take his boot instead," he said, " for Protector."

"Good old Protector," I said.

The bulldog, standing right outside where he'd followed us, woofed once for joy when I pulled off the cop's clean boot, the one with the dog slobber and not the piss on it, and handed it out the door. Protector snatched it and pranced back toward the Renault like a puppy. "Well, looky here," said Choteau, and pointed at a hole in the patrolman's white sock. A fat, pink big toe stuck out into the cold air. Choteau tugged on the end of the sock and pulled enough loose to knot the end, and cover up that bare, rosy toe. "Wouldn't want you to get frostbit out here," he said. I think he meant it, too.

Protector was already back up the highway and climbing into the Renault with his new chew toy.

"Hope his feet don't stink," I said absently.

Choteau pushed open the sliding center pane of the plexi-glass window. Then he leaned forward into the front seat and switched off the flashing red lights with the tip of the knife. He knew right where the switch was, too. And he flicked it off like an old pro, even with his bad eyes. Just like he knew how to push those guard windows open. I guess he's spent some time in patrol cars before.

"Put the knife away," I said. It was the first time I'd mentioned the unmentionable. Choteau looked over his shoulder at me. He smiled, his long, graying hair draping over his chin.

"It bothers you, huh?" he said.

"Just put it away," I said.

He shook his head and closed his eyes a moment. Then with a flip he tossed the knife around in his hand so he held the blade. Then he reached out to me, holding it out handle first.

"Take it, then," he said flatly.

"Well, I didn't mean . . . " my voice trailed off and I felt like I'd violated some bond or trust, something we maybe didn't have.

"You keep it," I said, after an awkward moment of silence.

He was still grinning, and with another flip he had it in hand again and he slipped it up his sweatshirt sleeve. It disappeared so adroitly, I started to worry about it again.

Then the radio crackled, and a row of letters and numbers came across it. After it, a voice said, "All clear, Frank."

Choteau started to chuckle, and officer Dakota groaned. Choteau stopped a moment, picked up the microphone and answered. What he said was another row of letters and numbers and followed it with a "thanks." What Choteau seemed to know about the inside of police cars and how they worked was apparently endless. The knowledge of long experience.

The voice over the radio answered with numbers too, and then a "see ya." Choteau chuckled easily and said, "We better get rolling, Professor. It won't take them forever to find Officer Frank here." He patted the cop's flat-top gently. The officer lay very still.

"What was that?" I said.

"That was our license plates." With a nod of his head he drew my eyes to the Kansas numbers on my Missouri car.

"You mean," I said, "all clear?"

Choteau laughed broadly, but held his fingers up to his lips too. Then he pointed at our bound and gagged patrolman.

"Right," I said.

So we crawled out of the patrol car's back seat by opposite doors. "Goodbye, sir," I said to the cop, following some dictum from my childhood that said be polite to policemen. He just glared at me in what was, I think, fear, as I closed the car door.

156

"Will he be all right?" I said to Choteau, looking across the patrol car cherries at him.

"Better off than we'll be, if we don't get moving." He turned back toward the Renault. "They'll find him before he gets too cold. All he's got to do is lay down, you know."

I limped along behind Choteau, who was laughing again as his feet squeaked in the dry snow. The cold, evening air felt good then, and the wind felt free. My good leg was awake and my bum knee was stiff enough to feel numb.

"So our plates got an all clear," I said.

"Yup," laughed Choteau. "That old Teepee motel guy hasn't noticed he's from Missouri yet."

"Then we'd have been okay," I said. I was suffering those second thoughts about assaulting an officer, now that it was too late and all over. And Choteau was reading my mind.

"'Okay, until he called in your ID." He opened up the rider's side door of the Le Car. Then he flipped my license to me over the roof of the auto. "Until he figured out why I don't have any ID." Then he hopped in and shut the door behind him.

I crawled in and settled myself in the seat. Slipping the license back in my wallet, I was quiet as I thought about how close our pursuers were, and how close they had just come. I shut my door, and used my hands then to adjust my bum leg near the accelerator.

"Can you drive?" Choteau asked.

I grinned, but I wasn't sure if he could see it. I chose not to answer his question and, in a moment, he got my point with a laugh.

"I guess it does help to see clearly when you're driving," he said. "Let's get outa here, Professor."

I turned the car key and the Renault went right into a smooth purr. Then Protector's big mug shot up between Choteau and me. In his mouth was the boot, wet and shiny with bulldog slobber. Choteau patted him on the head, and kept chuckling. They were enjoying our little victory.

I lifted my leg slowly, through the pain, and put my foot on the accelerator. As we spun out, throwing a little snow,

I saw Officer Dakota's cowboy hat in the rearview mirror. It floated up into the air with the snow and then, like a frisbee, it drifted down and disappeared into the ditch near the quiet patrol car.

The December sun turned cool orange as it started to set over all the drifted South Dakota snow, and we rode north through the strange, white dusk that followed it. We pushed on, ever northward, I thought. The dog was curled up in the back seat, enjoying his boot.

"Did you notice how that cop called me 'Chief'?" I said. Choteau nodded.

"It's like he thought I was an Indian, or something," I chuckled. "Just because I was with you, now I'm an Indian, huh?"

I looked over at Choteau, but he sat in his own quiet. He was resting his head on a hand and leaning on the door. He gazed off down the highway, following our headlights through the strange dusk.

I laughed a little awkwardly, a laugh that admitted I liked being mistaken for an Indian. "That's what the cop thought, anyway," I said, and turned back to driving.

After a little while, Choteau said, very softly, "Maybe you are."

My head jerked as I glanced over at him. Then I laughed. "Oh yeah, right," I said. "Maybe in an earlier life, like yours, huh?"

A small grin crossed his face. Enough to make me think I'd caught him at his own game. But he didn't say another word for a long time.

A few miles went by to the sound of Protector's happy gnawing in the back. Then Choteau said, "May be." He made it two clear, distinct words.

He seemed so quiet and serious, I was suddenly un-comfortable. We drove along in an awkward silence. Or at least it was awkward for me.

Once, later on in the dusk, he said, "White people." That was all. Then he shook his head.

But I don't think he was talking to me.

It was at a gas station in some little town on Highway 25 that Choteau finally got through to her. The sun was disap-pearing beyond the far western snow, and its odd pink going brown light, like the light of a dirty fire, was fading with it. I was filling the Renault with gas, standing under the faint pur-ple of the station's big driveway lamps. Protector was in the back seat, sleeping next to his boot. Choteau was over around the corner, out of sight, at a pay phone again.

I went in and paid the attendant. Then I walked back through the garage toward the john. "How you doin', Will?" a familiar voice said when I stepped inside and the door had closed.

He was wearing a down parka, but under it he had on a suit and tie. His little mustache was so straight it made me think of my scruffy two-day growth. "Don't panic, Will," he said. "We've been following you for a while now." He didn't say exactly how long. Then he reached over and snapped the lock down on the bathroom door. "We don't need any surprise visitors for a minute or two, do we, pal?" he said. "Not while we talk."

"What are you doing here?" I said to Golman.

Then I glanced over at the one stall to see if we were alone. Did Golman have agents with him? Was it all going to be over this easily? Just a stop at a gas station, and we give up?

"We need a little help from you, buddy," Golman said. He ran his thumb down along the line of his mustache.

"How'd you find us?" I was frightened about what was coming next, but I was strangely relaxed, too. It was all over.

Just that quick. Snap of the lock on a bathroom door, and it's done. "That cop we jumped. That's how you did it. You found him, didn't you? I knew that was a mistake."

Golman laughed. "What cop?" he said.

"The highway patrolman. We left him tied up back down the road, this afternoon."

He snapped a radio up out of a coat pocket. "Which highway?" he said.

"You didn't find him," I said, slowly.

Golman rattled off the information about officer Frank into his radio and someone let out a mechanical "Check!" on the other end.

"How'd you find us then?"

"We gotta be quick here, pal," Golman slipped that little radio back into his suit pocket. "I don't want Choteau suspecting anything. We need your help, Will."

"How'd you get here?"

He paused a moment there, looked down at the dirty brown tile on the floor. Then he said, "Terri." He looked up and straight at me. "She told us about your call this morning, and about the Red Skies woman in Grand Forks."

I walked over to the greasy sink then and washed my hands with some powdered soap. I did it so I wouldn't have to speak.

"She's been a big help to us today, Will. Now we need your help too."

"I don't believe you, Golman." I just pulled a paper towel down and stared at my hands as I wiped them.

"If you help us now, I can make sure everything will go all right for you, pal. In the end."

I turned around and looked back at him. He still had one hand in the pocket with the radio. "I don't know how you got here, Golman. But you're lying. Terri wouldn't do that. I know she wouldn't."

Golman shrugged. "Believe what you like, buddy. But this is what we need you to do." He took his hand away from the radio and reached into the inside pocket of his suit. "You've got his confidence, Will." He pulled out a small pad of paper

160

and wrote something down on it. "We want to see where he's headed, and what he's up to out here. We want to know who's involved with him on this. And what their plans are. And you're gonna be our inside man." He looked up. "I hope." He handed the slip of paper to me, and there was a phone number on it. I read it once. "Memorize that, Will. Then throw it away. And remember, we'll be tailing you all along the way. If you get scared, if you feel like you're in danger at any time, you just call that number, Will. Our people will be right there. Right there," he snapped his fingers.

"You just want him to lead you to the old timers, Golman."

"No," he said, frowning sincerely at me, shaking his sad head.

"You're trying to get as many of those vets from the Pine Ridge days arrested as you can. You guys are just hoping to get even."

"No," his frown disappeared. "We're just doing our job, Will."

I balled up that scrap of paper and threw it at him. But Golman caught it in front of his face, then he reached over, dropped it into the stool and flushed it away.

"We'll take care of things, Will," he said.

I turned away and flicked the door unlocked. He stepped back into the stall as the door opened, to stay unseen. "Don't worry about Terri, pal," he whispered, as I walked out.

But crossing the empty garage toward the door outside, I found I had that phone number in my head, like it or not, as clear as new ice.

When I limped back out into the cold, Choteau was sitting there inside the car, waiting. As I climbed in and adjusted myself in the seat, moving my bum leg around until it was settled, he stared straight ahead. He didn't say a word. "Nobody home again?" I asked. He didn't answer.

In fact, he seemed shaken. I'd never seen him like this, so silent in front of something like fear or confusion. I don't know why I didn't tell him about Golman then. It may have been his desperate mood. It may have been my own fears of what he might do. It may have been the way Terri was involved, and I didn't want to lose trust in her. But whatever it was, I kept it all to myself.

Choteau's poor eyes, gazing blankly out at the highway ahead of us, seemed to me to bring on the dark. Night fell on us quickly then; his dark mood was the cause.

"Did you get through?" I said, this time trying to sound concerned. It was heart to heart time, and I suddenly knew more about what loving a woman wrong meant. But no matter how I sounded, it didn't help.

"Let's go," he said.

I knew he was right. We were pursued and they, whoever they always are, were closing in on us. They were right behind us, lurking in bathrooms, waiting to pounce. There was no time for broken spirits. I started the car, looked around for other cars, found none, and drove.

A few miles north on the highway he said, out of his silence, "Turn here." Just as he spoke, our headlights struck a gravel road off to the left. Did he know it was there? Was he planning this all along? How exactly he saw it, I'm still not sure. But I followed his orders. I slowed and turned off to the west. There were no lights anywhere behind us. The highway was black. We were completely alone, or at least we seemed to be.

The gravel road was rough and drifted over in places, and at its best it was icy smooth. But the car trudged along it, riding precariously up on the frozen ruts left by pickups and wagons and tractors. Protector, after a while began to snore, and the noise he made was welcome. It papered over Choteau's heavy silence, and covered the noise of the laboring car besides.

Choteau was changed. It was not just a mood he was in, and I seemed to sense it right away. This was more fundamental than a mood. Up to the moment we turned west, our whole ride together had seemed a crazy adventure, a quest without anything but a general direction for its end. We were headed north, toward some vague freedom across a distant border, some illusion we both chose to look far past and believe in deeply at the same time. Salvation lay out there, across the line, to the north. But we planned only as far as the next gas station.

All that changed when we turned off the northbound highway and trudged westward. Our good red road was over. North was nowhere we could ever reach, now. We were on the black road to the West, the way of war and death and troubles deeper than that. The sunset land of endings, happy or not. I knew it the moment he said, "Turn here," in the dark. It was night.

"You talked to her, huh?" I tried desperately to reach him. But Choteau was lost in a distant silence.

He was different now. See, he was always a puzzle; I never understood him. But now he was a different puzzle. And he wasn't just broken hearted, it wasn't just disappointment. At least, that wasn't the main part of the way he changed. It just seemed now, once we turned toward the brown dirty sunset and drove into gathering night, we had reached a new resolve. We had a purpose, not just a direction and an illusion. We were rushing down a short black road. I was the only one who didn't see where it was we were headed, but I was only driving. I was only the means. I was transportation, not destination.

I guess I'd say he didn't seem like Bernard Choteau anymore. He'd shed some last few vestiges of that. Now, he'd already shaken me enough to make me believe he might be Crazy Horse born again into this world. Enough so I'm not sure even now what to think of him, not sure who he was. But from that moment we turned off the good red road, it grew harder and harder to think of him only as Bernard Choteau.

He didn't answer my question about Mary Red Skies and the phone call. Never even tried. He just sat in the growing dark, silent and blind but full of some purpose, and it all seemed irrelevant suddenly. As irrelevant as asking Crazy Horse about some white doctor's wife from Grand Forks,

North Dakota. As irrelevant as telling him about Mike Golman hiding in that gas station restroom. As if any of that mattered.

There was one other thing he did, though. As I drove along, balancing the car on the rough ruts made of frozen Dakota mud, he gave me a name. He called me Little Big Man.

"Turn here, Little Big Man," is what he really said.

And we all know what that means, what Little Big Man did. He was the one who held Crazy Horse by the arms, while someone stabbed him in the back. On the night Crazy Horse died.

The first time.

I think.

*

We seemed to creep along that awful road forever. Every time I made the slightest wrong twist with the steering wheel, down the Renault would plunge into a rut. Over and over, the bottom of the car scraped the frozen ground. My shoulders winced, and somehow, working the wheel and the clutch and the gas, I'd wrestle it back up on top of those deep ruts and we'd inch along further.

I had visions of broken axles, ruptured cables, ripped tires. Every time I slipped and we went scraping down, I saw us bottomed out, tires spinning on air and dusty, dry snow. I saw us spending the night in the Dakota cold, losing fingers and toes to frostbite, dying in a lonely frozen ditch like Lennie Red Skies.

So my eyes strained along the headlights and I drove a foot at a time, negotiating the holes and pits and never daring to glance up the roadway, for fear I'd lose it again. My hands grew tired of griping the wheel, my back ached from stooping forward to see, my knee throbbed at holding the accelerator steady and slow. Though my eyes were burning, I dreamed of other, safer highways, crowded with oncoming headlights.

Through it all, Protector snored and Choteau was as still as the cold.

I'm sure we drove until the early hours of the morning, while that road only grew worse and worse. "We've got to stop, Choteau," I said, finally. "I need to rest a little." I was about to just roll to a halt, and then slouch for a moment. Maybe get out in the cold and stretch.

But the minute I spoke, the very instant I gave it up, the sign popped up beside us. Now, I'll admit, I was staring at the tractor ruts in front of me, and I may have been lost in my driv-

165

ing, hypnotized by the rugged road. But still that sign seemed like an answer to me.

"Medicine Wheel, S. D." is all it said.

You can try to look it up. You won't find it. I've pored over every atlas in the University Library. I spent days in the Map Collection room, perusing every inch of anything related. I wrote to the state Highway Department and read the voter registration logs, and I even went back through old census figures and settler's claims from the territory days. Medicine Wheel, South Dakota, isn't there. Not anywhere. Last summer, in desperation, I drove back out there. I found our turn off Highway 25, or one that looked like it anyway. In a rented four wheel drive I roamed around every lane and followed every pair of ruts I could locate. I spent three days and thirteen tanks of gas, and I never found anything but a few ranchers who shook their heads no and squinted at me like I was either nuts or the advance scout for some army of East Coast snobs with big real estate money to spend.

"Ain't no such place," one of them--burnt red right down under the bill of his feed cap--said to me. "And never has been." Then he cocked his head and squinted some more at me.

We passed the sign and the rutted mud quickly turned to rock and gravel, and the road widened out into a flat, gravel lot.

"Pull in there," Choteau said. Then he called me Little Big Man again. In the headlights I could see several houses scattered without much order around the gravel lot. They were all square and identical, the way government projects are. Only one of them held any light. It was the one Choteau pointed at.

I pulled up in front of it and above the door a stenciled sign shone in our lights. Inipi Motel is what it said.

I grunted at the bad pun. "A motel called the sweat lodge? Sounds inviting."

Choteau opened his door. "Let's go in," he said, like he knew where he was headed. He was out of the car in a moment and then lifted Protector out gently onto the gravel and snow. I noticed the Renault was the only vehicle in sight. There must have been a dozen dark houses around, scattered about like some insane barracks. It was late and I guess everyone in Medicine Wheel was asleep. That figured. I'd lost all my sense of time, but it felt like it was late. And it was certainly dead of winter, so they should be in bed, tucked soundly away until daylight.

But one thing did bother me. Where were all those tractors and trucks that had rutted up the road? I couldn't see a single vehicle anywhere. There was only my little, tired Renault. Way out here on the prairie, how did these people get around? It was so still and empty, it felt vaguely like some old ghost town. Except for the light in the building that claimed to be a motel.

I followed the dog and Choteau into the Inipi. Inside an old Indian man with a face eroded like the Dakota Badlands sat in an overstuffed chair.

"We need a room," I said to him, and I pulled out my wallet. The house felt hot and stuffy after the bitter cold outside. The old man looked at me, and then over at my companions. Then they all laughed. Everyone except me. I took a few bills out of my wallet, thinking this couldn't cost too much.

The old man put his hands on the arms of the chair and shoved himself up onto his feet, moaning as he climbed. But at least half of that moan was meant to cover the sound of his fart. It leaked out of him with a tweet. He laughed at the sound, and his face was so deeply wrinkled and toothless it looked caved in. He squinted at me, then said, "Come on, Butch." He snatched the wallet out of my hands. Then he scurried down the hallway, ahead of his own smell. He was spry, and quicker than I expected.

I hobbled along behind him, with Choteau and Protector following me, and with a fistful of bills in my hand. The building was bigger than it seemed from the outside. We scurried down the narrow hall a good hundred feet or better.

When we came to a plain door, the Old Badlands Face stopped. "Here you go, Butch. Number Seven." Then he reached in my wallet and extracted the rest of the cash, as well as a couple of gas cards. He handed all of this to me. Then, with another bright laugh, he danced on down the hall, and disappeared back into the lobby.

"Hey, wait a minute," I yelled at him. The old fart was strutting away with my empty wallet. Empty except for my driver's license, and all those worthless personal things you can't replace. Pictures of Terri at her college graduation, old college ID's, my father's obituary, those worthless invaluables.

"Don't worry," Choteau put a hand on my shoulder and guided me into the unmarked room, the one the old man had called "number seven."

It was black as a cave inside. If there were any windows to this room, they were shuttered tight. I was lost entirely, once Choteau closed the door behind us. He moved around the room with ease, though. The blind have definite advantages when it comes to a moment like this.

I felt around the wall by the door for the lights. "What kind of room is this?" I said. There was no switch to be found.

I could hear the old bulldog panting and Choteau's steps. Beyond that, the room sounded empty. "I don't like this," I said. I was so sightless and disoriented I could barely tell what was up or down. "Where the hell are we?" I said.

Choteau's steps halted. "Where is 'hell'?" he said.

I remembered an old anecdote about Crazy Horse. A trader had once told him the white people back East thought he was a "murdering hound of Hell." Crazy Horse didn't understand. What was this word: Hell? What did it mean? But when the trader tried to explain, it only confused Crazy Horse more. It didn't make any sense, you see. How could the great good powers make a place like Hell? The more it was explained to him, the more Crazy Horse was confused.

"Never mind," I muttered, echoing the words of that old trader, I suspect.

"Come here," Choteau said in the dark. I heard the dog lick his slobbering chops. "Sit down," Choteau said.

"Where the hell are we?" I was feeling my way across the room toward his voice. But there was nothing to feel. It was an empty room, as far as I could tell.

"Come here," he said. "Sit down."

My hands found his then and I could sense Protector was nearby, too. As my eyes began to adjust to the dark, Choteau guided me down to sit on the floor. It felt soft as worked over earth, and warm as July grass, even in the middle of the Dakota winter. Slowly my eyes began to adjust to the dark, and I could see Choteau like a shadow, and he was changed.

A quiet fear, deeper than any I'd ever felt, even deeper than what was to come, clattered around in my soul. I started to sweat because I was afraid, and questions began to pour out of me.

"What is this place, Choteau? Where are we? And what happened to North Dakota and Mary Red Skies? Where are we going?"

I almost said, "Where are you taking me?" But I stopped short of that.

His hand squeezed my shoulder gently to still me. It was that simple reach across a lonely gulf, that physical contact that comforted me. I began to see the shape of him more clearly, though the room was gone. If it was a room. I felt like I was outdoors, without any walls, warm and comfortable as a sweet fall night. Indian summer. And Choteau, or Crazy Horse, was changed.

He was dressed in buckskins and moccasins, blue leggings and a plain white shirt. One eagle feather was tied in his hair, cast downward, to the side. He wore a breastplate of bones and quillwork from his neck to his waist. In one hand he held a fan made of the tail feathers of a hawk.

There are no pictures of Crazy Horse, you know. He was never photographed, and always refused to have any likeness made, not even a sketch. There are descriptions of him in the historical record, of course, from friends and enemies alike. But there is not one drawing or sketch or photo, not one likeness of him that anyone can trust.

Still, I knew him straight off. I was looking Crazy Horse in the eye.

"Where are we?" I whispered.

He smiled softly. Protector rested his head on Crazy Horse's leg and sighed. As my eyes grew accustomed to the low light, I sensed we were not alone. There were other figures slowly making us part of a circle. They seemed to be dressed, like Crazy Horse, in traditional clothes, but I couldn't make them out. They were just shadowy figures in the dark.

So I whispered again, "Where are we, Crazy Horse?"

He smiled and his eyes almost wrinkled closed. Then he said something I couldn't understand, something in Lakota I guess.

"Where?" I said.

He just laughed, and said the Lakota words again. "It's not a place, Professor. It's a way to begin."

"What is?"

He said the same phrase again, and the words seemed familiar now, even if I still didn't understand. Crazy Horse paused a moment and thought before he spoke. He touched his fingers to his chin, and then said, "It's an old prayer, you would

170

call it, I think. A simple one." Then he said it once more, slowly, and they made sense. I don't know how I understood them, but I knew what he meant. "All my relatives," is what he said, but he still spoke in Lakota.

I wanted to ask him "What does it mean? Not the words, but the prayer?" But I think I was still in shock that I had somehow understood Lakota, suddenly, without any prompting.

"You know, Professor," he said next, "the old man will come close to you." He was nodding his head a little as he spoke.

"I'm lost," I said.

"We know that," Crazy Horse smiled. "But we're trying to help. Remember this, Professor. When the old man is so close you can't bear his stink, try to remember the questions he asks. Got it?"

"Uh huh," I said, looking around for the door. "When the old fart lets loose . ." But I was still lost. It seemed like I'd gotten to the point where every question I asked just got me deeper into the woods without a map. I wasn't even sure what language we were speaking anymore. But he seemed to be waiting for me to speak then, leaning forward a little, his head cocked to listen to me closely. I saw the brown stone tied behind his waiting ear, and I said what he had said, "All my relatives." I think I spoke those words in Lakota.

He leaned back and grinned proudly, and this time his eyes did wrinkle closed. "When I was very young," he said to me, "I went off by myself, out crying for a vision, you know?" His eyes were still closed. "But after two days of fasting and staying awake and praying, I hadn't seen anything. Nothing. Not even a shooting star. I was just thirsty and hungry enough to eat dirt, and I was tired. So I gave up.

"I walked back to where I'd left my pony, tethered in a meadow beside a pretty blue pond. As I walked, my steps got heavier and shorter, and I began to feel like I couldn't make it all the way back. But someone or something seemed to lead me to a bank beside that pond. I staggered over near the water's edge and flopped down there, under a black ledge. There was a hollow in the shadow of that ledge, like some bear's den, and I crawled down in it to rest, and to get out of the sun. That hollow was filled with loose, flat shale. The gravel clacked and rattled like old bones as I collapsed in there and curled up on my side. But it felt comfortable, pressed into my bare shoulder.

"I didn't know then whether I was going to throw up or shit all over myself. But I knew it was going to happen. I was going to empty myself, maybe out of both ends at once. I was dizzy with weakness and I couldn't even sit up. But there was nothing in me to vomit out, you know? Not after two days of fasting, and staying awake, I was empty. Like a hollow, dead tree, tipped over on its side and just waiting to rot away.

"My pony was right there in front of me, over on the other side of the pond. But I didn't have the strength or the will to go get him.

"I lay there in that bed of loose rocks and waited to die, I guess. I was so weak and foolish, I wanted to die, I think. There was nowhere I could go. Not like that. It was an end."

He opened his eyes then, but kept them cast down. His loose hair was tossed over one shoulder. I waited and listened for him to continue, and I sensed the others in the room, who-ever they were, were waiting and listening, too. Protector sighed softly in his sleep, and then lapped at his chops.

"I curled up around the pain in my knotted stomach, and it started croaking like a bullfrog," he said. He shook his head and smiled at the memory. "The dry heaves, Professor. These belches were roaring out of me and that hollow I was in made them ring like an echo in a canyon. My pony looked over at me, I was burping like a big drum, and his eyes frowned like he couldn't figure me out. Then he snorted, answering my sour croaks. He was laughing at me, I think, Professor. The whole pond was laughing. But all I could do was taste the juices from my stomach in my spit, and wipe the hot tears out of my eyes, and wait for the next wave.

"My pony threw its head back, and her gray mane streamed around her like a blanket. It was a hood draped around her face. I waited for the sound of her laugh again, but there was only silence. There was only that movement, a gesture like a laugh, but without a sound. Then she turned toward me and someone was riding her. She shook that gray mane, and then a strange man was on her back. He rode her right across the water and I watched them, galloping without touching the pond or the ground. And as they came, she kept changing colors, Professor. The pony was a bay at first, but then she changed to pinto, then blue-black, and then more colors than I can tell you now.

"And all around my pony, " his hands made the shape of a ball in the air, "there were enemies, and they kept attacking the man riding her. But he rode straight through them all. The arrows and the bullets flew at him, but they never touched him. Not even one of them. He wasn't even scratched."

Crazy Horse stopped there. He drew a few deep breaths, as if he was preparing for something important, for an ordeal or a test. Three times I heard the breath sigh from him, his mouth closed and his eyes hard set. I was afraid to make a sound, for fear I'd disturb his preparations, whatever they were for. Everyone in this goofy circle of ours was waiting silently too.

"The man riding my pony never said a word, but he spoke to me, Professor. He told me things I needed to know then. He wore his hair loose, with one eagle feather, like this," Crazy Horse brushed the feather in his hair. "And he wore a brown stone behind his ear. He told me what I should do to prepare for the wars to come: before every fight, he said, I should throw a handful of dust over my war pony and then rub some of the dust into my hair and on my body. If I do this, my enemies will never harm me. They will fall away like the arrows flying around him.

"I knew he was the one I had to become. That man was me. If I ever stopped puking, he was what I had to become, Professor. Fearless, untouchable, a leader. He told me to always live for the people, and never take anything for myself."

Crazy Horse smiled at the memory of him. Then he winked at me. It caught me off guard. Who was that winking at me across the room? Was it Choteau beneath his Crazy Horse mask, tipping me off to the joke? Letting me see past the

173

tricks? Or was it someone else? In the next moment, looking straight at Crazy Horse as he spoke, I wasn't sure he'd ever winked at all. I'd been imagining it, my mind playing tricks on me. I think.

"A storm rose up out of the hills behind him then." Crazy Horse's free hand rose from his lap and made the shapes of the clouds in the air. "The sky was filled with blue and white streaks of lightning and suddenly, as if it had always been there, the ground around me pattered under the hail. I felt the ice striking my face, and melting. On the man's cheek one of the lightning bolts shone, flashing blue and snow white, " he touched his cheek and then he laid his flat hand on his chest. "On his body he wore some of the hail. But it was there, cold and hard, it wasn't melting like it was on me. Then I heard this loud screech over his head, and I saw a little red-tailed hawk, riding with him just like the storm." He lifted the fan of hawk feathers then and held it between us in the dark, creating the motions of the bird. I could make out other faces in the circle, familiar faces some of them. Several of those shadows were nodding along to the rhythm of the story. They could see the whole hawk in the motion he made with that fan of feathers, I think, because I could too, then.

"More enemies came, rising up from the ground. But these were people, like us. Human beings, not Crows or Cheyenne or Shoshone. But people, you know? They tried to grab hold of him, to pull him back and hold him down. One of them reached up and grabbed hold of the man's arms and held them back. When I saw that these shadows were human beings—not the enemies from before, but his own people—then he was gone."

Crazy Horse let his hands drop to his lap again. Protector lifted his head and left a wet spot of slobber on the Indian's blue leggings. The bulldog licked his chops, and Crazy Horse stroked the old dog's head until Protector rested it again on the blue legging. The dog sighed heavily and closed its eyes.

"When I woke up, I was lying there in that hollow of shale all alone," Crazy Horse said. "The world was like it was before. My pony was grazing out beside the pond and the skies were clear and blue. Only one thing was different. Perched in the brush near the banks of the pond there was a red-tailed hawk, Professor. It sang its simple cree out once, then flew away in that empty, cloudless sky."

In the black around me I began to see more clearly. I was nodding to the end of Crazy Horse's story, like many of the faces in the circle with us. Men and women both were there, and some of them I began to recognize.

Crazy Horse broke the silence with a goofy laugh. "What is it about?" I said. He tossed his head back and his long hair streamed back toward the ground behind him, and he laughed like he'd lost his mind. "Who was he?" I said.

"It's not much really," he said, as he settled down. He beat his flat, open hand on the ground in front of him. "To the stars and the sun and the endless wind. All my relatives. And it's all a story, Professor. We are related to everything that is.

"That's not so high and mighty, is it?"

"All my relatives," I said. I still can't tell you what language we spoke in right then.

He smiled gently across at me and said, "How do you know for sure who the dancer is?"

I shrugged at him, but only because I didn't know what he was talking about.

"When the old fart comes to your room, alone, ask him this, Professor. How can you tell the dancer from the mask?" Then Crazy Horse winked at me again. "Remember that." There was nothing of Bernard Choteau in that wink.

I remember then I just wished I could be the old dog sleeping beside him. If I could forget all this goofy advice, this mumbo jumbo in the dark, if I could just curl up and go to sleep. If it could just be that simple.

Then the old man with the badlands face stood up out of the circle. He carried a pipe and, holding it up to the four directions, began to mutter some prayers. He lit it and smoked. Soon he was passing it from person to person in our circle and the dark began to fill with the smell of sweet smoke.

Some of the people began to ask Old Badlands Face for advice, or for help. As the pipe went around, the people asked about illnesses, about the hunger and craziness that alcohol brought on, about the wives and husbands their children were choosing, about journeys or hunting parties that were planned. Sometimes the old man would answer. Other times he would lift his hands up and mutter prayers to the four directions.

As all this healing and hoping went on, I started to see everyone clearly and know who they were. The first one to take the pipe after Old Badlands Face was someone I'd seen staring out of old photographs in a dozen history books. But now he was alive and breathing, drawing in the smoke from the pipe. I was looking at He Dog, Crazy Horse's old friend. It was He Dog. Then there were others I knew the same way and I began to recognize them, too, one at a time. There was Spotted Tail, Crazy Horse's uncle. And there was Touch the Clouds, all seven foot of him, and Pawnee Killer, and then I saw American Horse, and Red Cloud, and Young Man Afraid of His Horses. All of them in the circle now, smoking in turn as Old Badlands Face handed them the pipe.

Before long I was recognizing people in that circle I couldn't possible have known. Indians from the nineteenth century who were never photographed, some of them never described, or even named. But I knew them, somehow. I knew who they were.

I'd been taken into some room that had opened wide and filled up with Crazy Horse's life. Everyone was there. His father Curly, once called Crazy Horse, too. His mother. And Black Shawl, his wife. His little daughter, who died as a child, sat beside her. Hump, the old man who taught him to hunt and ride, was there. Little Wolf, his younger brother. They were all there. Even Black Buffalo Woman, with No Water sitting beside her.

Every part of his past had gathered there, drawn into a circle with him. They were smoking the sacred pipe and praying, for health and understanding, and for a wholeness to life, to be real human beings. And I was there now, a part of that circle too.

I felt as complete as I ever have, at that moment. I was part of a community, connected with a past that reached back further than memory, part of a whole that was larger, sounder, more sacred than me. I was not alone. I was whole.

Then, in the very warmth of that moment, as Crazy Horse beside me took the pipe from Old Badlands Face, I realized who was missing. It fell on me, like the weight of loneliness. Everyone in the circle of Crazy Horse's life was there, everyone except for one person. Everyone except Little Big Man.

Beside me, Crazy Horse smoked from the pipe. He did not ask a question of Old Badlands Face. And instead of handing the pipe back to the center, to the old man, Crazy Horse turned and handed it directly to me. "All my relatives," he said.

As I took the pipe, my hand touched his. Just brushed against his rough fingers. That's all. But I saw, at that second, the shadows from his vision. They reached up and grabbed hold of him and held his arms back. They were dark red, then white, then pale yellow. Then the shadows I saw turned black and were gone.

I held the pipe and turned toward the center, and Old Badlands. As I drew in the smoke, I looked around the circle at all these faces I knew. It was my turn to pray, to ask for help and understanding.

As I breathed out the smoke, my words rode with it. I had no choice. I looked up into that weathered and lined face, and the question welled up from inside me.

"Where is Little Big Man?"

Old Badlands Face wrinkled up with a smile. Then he gave me his first answer. He belched in my face.

I have to stop here and try to explain. It seems silly, I know. It was a goofy, paranoid question. But there are a lot of ways to ask for help.

You see, I was afraid at that moment that I was Little Big Man. But when I breathed out that question, I was asking more than just for a missing figure in the circle. My question carried a lot more freight than that.

For a moment I'd been part of that circle. I'd felt grounded and connected and whole. But if I was a Little Big Man, then maybe I was alone again. For one moment I'd been whole, but now I was back to old times. It was back to me, the guy who was breaking Terri's heart, who was running from work that should have seemed important and fruitful, from a life that was useful. It was back to me, with no direction, nothing to believe in, maybe no one to love. It was back to alone.

That's what I had loaded onto my question, and all those spirits in the room knew it, too. They knew what I was asking. If I held you down, if my hands were the ones that dragged you back, and maybe destroyed you, then am I really alone?

And where does the circle end?

Old Badlands Face cracked wide open and laughed. I could taste the sour breath of his belch in my mouth. I drew on the pipe again, to kill that taste.

"Where is Little Big Man?" I said as I exhaled the smoke. I thought to look over at Crazy Horse then, but I couldn't. I didn't have the courage to face him. Not if I was who I thought I was.

"He was going to go to college, you know. He was going to be a lawyer, and help the people," Old Badlands Face said. His pink and gray tongue lapped over the wrinkled lips then. He seemed to be holding in his laughter now.

He took the pipe from my hands and handed me a bowl. Around the room I heard the talking and laughing start. He Dog was chatting with Hump, both of them eating warm stew out of wooden bowls with their fingers. The same with Spotted Tail, Black Shawl, American Horse and all the others. The prayers and petitions were over, ended by my loaded question it seems. We were at a feast now.

Crazy Horse patted me on the shoulder. "Eat," he said and laughed. "It's good."

I looked back to Old Badlands Face. He still seemed to be holding back his laughter, trying to hide it from me. And not doing very well at it. "Little Big Man went to law school?" I squinted at him in disbelief.

The old man and Crazy Horse, and a few others who heard, laughed at me then. Old Badlands Face chuckled as he said, "No, no, no. Not Little Big Man. Bernard Choteau," he said, with heavy emphasis.

I turned to Crazy Horse and saw no sign of Choteau in him at all. There was no wink, no grin. My partner, my problem, my whatever he was, my friend Choteau, he was gone. It was just Crazy horse sitting there. And that's all, just Crazy Horse.

It dawned on me then these people were good at answering my questions out of order. If you just waited long enough and listened close, you found out what you needed to know. They might be confusing, you know, but they were honest.

"Eat," said Old Badlands Face. So I dipped my fingers in the stew and tasted it. It was lamb, I thought, maybe with some pork too. A simple stew made with mild onions and carrots. I was hungry, and it tasted good. Once I started to eat, the old man was so filled with glee he could hardly restrain himself. But then he sucked in his stomach, and I thought he was going to burp at me again, until he settled down and his face sobered.

"The last year he was in high school," Old Badlands Face looked over at me as I ate. "That was what did it for Bernard Choteau. He had it all arranged that winter, you know, for Lennie to come to the boarding school and give a talk. It was all set up, just like Bernard's scholarship for college. He was going to go to a little Jesuit school in Nebraska. It was done and planned out. It was a sure thing.

"Or it was until she found out." He stopped there, and then rustled around settling his behind on the ground. His bent finger began to point at the dirt as he went on.

"When she heard what Bernard was planning to do with her brother, bringing him to the school to talk, Mary Red Skies was so mad she was wild. 'You're not going to make my brother into some sideshow freak,' she said. They argued about it for days, but she could never see it. She said, in the end, that he was making Lennie into a circus animal. That's what she said.

"But Bernard was a stubborn kid, Professor. He just knew he was doing the right thing and once Mary saw what happened because of it all, she would be happy too. He didn't think he could lose her, you know. He really didn't.

"But they didn't talk to one another or see one another, or anything, for three weeks, and maybe longer that that. And they were always together, every day, you know, before this all happened."

Old Badlands Face shook his head and stopped talking to eat from his bowl. I did too, and held a piece of meat up with my fingers and grunted to him and to Crazy Horse. The three of us all nodded that it was good while we ate. But the old man had to look down at the ground to keep from laughing suddenly, at something.

*   *   *

180

"When the big day comes, Bernard is pretty excited, Professor," Old Badlands said, smacking his lips. "Lennie's stayed sober now for a whole two weeks, and the kids at the school are all ready to hear him. The brothers there have got them boys all primed and ready. They're going to listen and it'll make a difference. Bernard really believes that, you know? They're going to see that boozing it up is this big trap. And they only fall into it because they're so mad, and so bored on the res'. They'll understand that when they hear Lennie. And then Mary will understand it too. She'll see it wasn't no sideshow. So they will be back together, and that's a big part of why Bernard is all excited."

The old man winked and leaned forward to whisper to me, but loud enough so everyone could hear, "Bernard was horny as an old bachelor, you know. He'd been getting it pretty regular up till then, Professor." I could smell the stew and the old gas on his breath and I leaned back away from him a little. Several laughs broke out around the circle at that.

"So him and Mary will get back together, and then he'll go off to school, and everything will be better," Old Badlands said, as he sat back. "It was them Jesuit fathers that taught him that, taught him to think ahead and make plans for his life. And little Bernard, he learned that lesson well from them, after all those years at the boarding school. He's got it all planned out in his head how he and Mary Red Skies will get married, and then when he finishes school, they'll come back to the res'. That's when he'll practice law to help the tribe, and he'll be a big man. He can see it clear, he's got it so well planned.

"But then Lennie doesn't show up." Old Badlands paused, either to think about what that meant, or to hang his mouth open and let a little belch out. It was hard to tell if the gas was the only thing slowing him up. "The whole school is all assembled in the little basketball gym and waiting for Lennie, all seventy or eighty of them kids. From little ones all the

181

way up to high school, waiting. But there's no Lennie. He's nowhere to be found.

"The brothers try to cover it up, you know. But it's pretty obvious what happened to Lennie, so before long some of the older guys start laughing and giving Bernard a hard time. The Jesuits try to keep them quiet, but it's pretty hard right then. 'Cause Bernard is their star pupil, you know, the teacher's pet, and they've got him now. The whole deal turns out to be one great, big lesson in reverse, you know?"

The old guy let loose with one of his crazy laughs, like the cackle he'd had out in the hall. But this time nobody seemed to be joining in. I noticed then, the more he told of this story, the harder it was for me to see the other faces in the circle. Hump and He Dog and the others, they were fading away into the dark.

"Bernard doesn't know what to do then. So he walks out of the gym and goes wandering around looking for Lennie. He's hoping to find him in a car accident or something, you know. With broken legs on the highway, or in a hospital with a heart attack. or maybe he got arrested for something he did a long time ago. Something, you know. But down deep, he knows better.

"It takes until evening to find him, which gives Bernard a lot of time to think. About himself and about Mary, and about how far apart they really are. About how she seemed to want to leave the res' and live a better life. About how little she thought of her brother.

"Lennie is hiding in a dead car in a ditch. That's where Bernard finds him. Turns out he'd been sneaking a little to drink for most of them two, three weeks he was supposed to be dry. But then, as the time got close for his 'class,' he realized he was screwing up again. He was coming in between Bernard and his sister, and he was lying to them all. So he decided to really try it cold turkey.

"It's a freezing December night and Bernard finds Lennie shaking and hallucinating out in that dead car house of his. 'Bernard,' he says and tries to laugh. 'Little bro, remember when we ripped off old lady Mulgrew.' And Choteau gets the point. Turns out, Lennie hasn't eaten anything since he tried to quit cold. Couldn't keep anything down, when he did eat.

"Bernard sees him there shaking with cold and sickness, and talking to the dead car. He figures, what the hell, anyway. Everything else is going wrong."

I could hear the muttering conversations and the chuckles from the feast, but I couldn't see a one of them anymore. Hump and Curly and Red Cloud, they were all distant except for Crazy Horse beside me and the old man telling Choteau's story.

I set my bowl down and grunted out a, "Good." I was licking my fingers when Crazy Horse spoke.

"We eat this to remember," Crazy horse said.

"Remember what?" I said.

Old Badlands laughed so hard he nearly fell over. He had to steady himself with one hand, while he rubbed the tears from his eyes with his other. Then all the laughing gave him another gas attack, and he belched out the smell of stew.

Crazy Horse didn't even smile. "To remember the hard times, in the old days," he said. "Times when we were at war, times when it was winter and we were on the run and trying to escape, when the buffalo and the game were all gone." He nodded his head as he spoke, and then he licked his lips and wiped his mouth with the back of his hand. "We need not to forget those times. We should remember," Crazy Horse said, "when we had to eat dog to stay alive."

I stopped licking my fingers. I looked over at the old man, and he was holding his breath. He looked almost ready to burst. My tongue moved around in my mouth, tasting that stew again. "You mean that was?" I said, and stopped short.

I looked from my soiled fingers to the bowl, and then to Crazy Horse and Old Badlands Face as they nodded yes.

"It was?" I said. Crazy Horse smiled.

But the old man almost lost control. He slapped both hands on his thighs and roared with enough laughter he was almost choking. His toothless mouth was open so wide the deep crevices in his face smoothed out. He moaned hard, then finally, he blew a fart so loud I thought he'd shit himself.

That's when I remembered the old bulldog. I jerked my head around looking for him. "Where's Protector?" I said.

The old man was waving one of his hands now to clear the air. It needed clearing, too. His laugh had settled down into short, hard bursts of giggles. "Don't worry," he said, and then giggled. "It was nobody you know," he said.

He was right. I saw Protector there beside Crazy Horse, happily slobbering and snoring away. The Indian was stroking him behind the ears. They were a picture of contentment.

Old Badlands Face quieted down slowly, and he heaved a big sigh after a while. Then he looked over at me. The smile caved into that wrinkled face again, and he said, "We better get to the end of this." He cast his dark eyes down, and seemed to be looking inside himself. "This isn't so much fun as feeding you dog." He chuckled once at that, and then went quietly, soberly on with Choteau's story.

"That night Bernard thumbed his way off the res' to Devils Lake, the same town where he used to go to see Mary, where she worked at the clinic. He was on his way to get Lennie something to drink. And the way he was feeling then, I think Lennie and him were going to split whatever he found.

"But of course, Bernard didn't have any money, and nobody up there was supposed to sell liquor to him anyway. But that wasn't about to stop him. I guess he wasn't thinking too much about college and law school right then." Old Badlands Face swallowed his lips then and seemed to chew on his toothless mouth. His face about caved in, and roiled around like a mud pot. Then, suddenly, he laughed bitterly. I guess he was ready to go on then.

"Little Bernard walks into this grocery up there. They got the liquor stocked up behind the counter where the cash register's at, but that's all right. Cause there's only the one clerk running the store in the evening, and the place is empty except for her. She's a white girl, going to high school, you know, and her dad owns the grocery.

"She's out dusting and straightening selves, not at the register. So its easy, you know. Bernard just slips behind the counter and pockets two pints of Ol' Grandad. Simple as picking fruit, you know. One in each pocket. Except for his mistake.

"See, Professor, Bernard is behind the counter when he spots the bread rack across the room. He remembers how Lennie hasn't eaten in a couple days. So he steps out from behind the counter and, instead of getting long gone, he walks over and picks up a loaf of bread. It was Wonder bread, that's all. But he tucks that loaf under his coat and that's when she sees him."

"'Hey,' she calls out, because her father taught her about shoplifting and Ind'ins. So Bernard turns and runs out the door. But that little lady is quick, and she heads for the phone. She's learned what to do well. The town cop has caught Bernard before he's run two blocks.

"'You got a receipt for those items?' says the cop. Of course, even if he did have a receipt, the cop still had him for the liquor. But Bernard knows, the way we all learn to know, he's in bigger trouble here than just a loaf bread and a couple pints. He's in the river deep now. But what's he going to do?

"'Dropped it somewhere,' he lies. But nobody's getting fooled.

"Bernard gets to ride back to the grocery, where the clerk girl is all wide eyes and scared, and says, 'Hi' to Bernard when the cop brings him in. She was only doing what her daddy told her to do. That's what her sad, buffaloed eyes say."

"Along the way from the cop's 'Is this the guy?' to identifying just what he stole, it turns out there's supposed to be a few hundred dollars missing from the cash drawer. Just enough to qualify Bernard for a felony. Of course, that money never left the register. But Bernard knows that's gonna be his word against a cop and a pretty white girl. So he can see where it's all headed.

"'You're that Choteau boy, aren't ya?' the town cop says, not really asking a question. 'From over at the mission. The one going to collleech?' he says. He likes the way 'Leech' can be attached to that word. He's used it that way before. Bernard can tell."

"But this time Bernard's hard work and smarts go against him." The old man's tongue reached out and lapped over those sagging lips. But he barely stopped talking. "All the way down to the town jail, the cop rambles on and on about his days in the army. He's a World War II vet. Fought in the Pacific against 'them nips.' Made a 'man' out of him, and all that sort of stuff. Bernard doesn't have any idea what all this is moving toward now. Not yet anyway.

"The cop lets him sit in jail over night. Then he shows up about 3 a.m., carrying the arrest record with him. He's got a way that he and Bernard can fix this 'little mistake' up, he says. 'I know how we can tear this up and start all over, boy,' he says, waving that arrest report in his hand. The way he explains it, Bernard's got two choices. He can wait it out and get charged with robbery, and not with shoplifting either. Or he can join up and go to war. Serve his country and grow up.

"I guess that cop thought the army would make a man out of Bernard. You know? Or maybe it was 'them Chinee' and the Korean 'commies' over there looked enough like 'them nips' to keep the officer happy.

"Anyway, you know what happens. Bernard makes his decision and the cop rips up the kid's new record. Then the two of them take a dawn ride down to Grand Forks, and Bernard gets himself enlisted in the army."

"Next couple weeks roll by pretty fast. Lennie is still missing and Mary is still angry. The Jebbies at the mission are disappointed, surprised their star pupil has enlisted, but they don't know what happened. The fathers just write it off to some Indian war ethic, or something. And it wasn't the time for them to object to any boy enlisting. Especially an Indian kid.

"When Bernard gets to Louisiana to boot camp, he gets a letter. One of the priests at the school sent it to tell him about Lennie's death. About the snowplow and the body, and about how glad they are now he didn't talk to those classes. He writes to Mary, then, a couple times. But she never answered any of those letters

"Then, about the time he's done with training, Bernard gets the other news. It turns out, to everyone's surprise, Miss Red Skies has slipped off and become Mrs. Nordstrom. Her and one of the doctors from the clinic ran off to the Twin Cities and got married, and then just as quick they moved away.

"That last punch just about put Bernard Choteau out of the match. His whole life, all those plans he had, they just crumbled in his hands. All in one night, it seemed like. So what does he do?" Old Badlands Face held his hands out, palms up. When he paused, I glanced around me at the dark. I looked at Crazy Horse sitting quietly, one hand resting on his blue legging, the other stroking the sleeping dog.

187

I felt dead tired myself and yawned a sleepy sigh. It never crossed my mind that there was any hint of Bernard Choteau in that man beside me. It didn't seem funny at all to be sitting there talking about Choteau in the third person. In fact, it seemed right.

The bulldog rolled on its side and stretched its front legs while it snorted. I noticed the silence then. We were alone in the dark on that warmed ground. No one else was there. Just Crazy Horse, Old Badlands and me. I leaned over and rested on my side, I was warm and full and sleepy. "So what did he do then?" I said. I was too tired to be really curious. I just wanted the story done, so I could sleep.

"He volunteers for the war," Old Badlands Face said, then clapped his hands. "What else!" he squeaked, and I waited this time for him to fart, but it never came. He just laughed that bitter, crazy laugh of his. I lay down on my side entirely, and rested my head in my hand. That clap should have startled me, but my legs ached with the long day of driving and my eyes seemed filled with grit.

"The next thing he knows," Old Badlands Face said, wearing the loony grin I was growing used to, "Little Bernard is a foot soldier at Inchon, huddling his way through a winter that reminds him of Lennie and the way Lennie died in North Dakota. Bernard feels pretty alone and useless out there. But out of nowhere he gets a letter. Not a word in it, Professor. Just the postmarked envelope and a picture from Grand Forks, North Dakota. A little wallet picture wrapped up in a couple blank pieces of stationary. That's all."

The drowsiness was heavy and I laid my head down on my arm. I was having a hard time following the drift of all this information. I was just too weary to put the puzzle pieces together, to fit this in with all the rest of Choteau's life, with everything I'd been learning for days now.

188

I knew that if I could just stay alert, it would all come clear. The old man was explaining it all to me. I was going to understand something. And it was something important.

But it was a mighty effort just to stay awake.

"The picture was of a little baby boy, wrapped up in a baby blue blanket, wearing a little blue bonnet. That baby was reaching out at the camera and squinting his eyes closed at the light." Old Badlands Face shook his head. I felt alone with him in the room then. Even Crazy Horse was gone. It was just me and this loony old man. "It looked like that little boy was reaching out to Bernard the G.I. for help, you know," he said.

I closed my eyes to rest them. They felt hot when they were closed and it took great effort of will to open them again. When I did struggle and open them, I realized I'd missed something. some of the story had gone by me, and Old Badlands had become a droning voice in the dark. He wasn't even visible anymore.

"It said, James Richard Nordstrom' on the back," he chuckled. "But Bernard knew that it was a lie. He knew it."

I fought it hard but it was pointless. The voice went on, but I let my eyes stay closed and I drifted in and out of sleep. There were many more things I heard but most of them were meaningless, after that, and so they're gone from my memory. Only one of them remains, and only because it shocked me enough to make some sense. It must have pulled me out of my sleep when I understood. Because I can see Old Badlands Face say it, and I remember seeing nothing else.

"Little Jimmie Choteau," he said, his eyes wrinkling up into a frown, and him wearing that crazy grin of his, and his head nodding, bouncing on each word. "Little Jimmie Red Skies Choteau," he said, like it was the line to a song.

Crazy Horse has a son, I thought.

Then his crinkled face turned up to the black sky and Old Badlands sang. "All my relatives," is what he sang. "All my relatives."

*

That night, wherever I was, I dreamed of Terri. She came to me just the way I left her, before all this happened. But she was barefoot and wearing a baggy gray sweater that hung down to her thighs. Her knees were dimples and she had silver jewelry around both her ankles.

When she came close, I could smell strawberries in her hair. It seemed to have a life of its own, her black hair, because it moved toward me. The way it brushed lightly against my shoulders and chest, I needed to hold her. But I couldn't. I couldn't move or speak. I was frozen still, a paralyzed heap. There were three freckles on her cheek, in an odd little triangle, and I needed to kiss them. When she smiled and laughed, they moved like shooting stars and disappeared.

But she was always across the room. She took off that gray sweater then, just pulled it away with one gesture like it was paper, and underneath she was round and plump, big with child. She stood there naked, unashamed. She walked back and forth in front of me, proud of her roundness, proud of the rich color of her skin. The silver on her ankles sparkled as she stepped. She lifted her arms up with a dancer's smooth grace, and her breasts were fat, pale moons above the broad, brown sky of her stomach. Below it was the dark triangle of her sex, waiting like the ground, warmed by the sun, soft and comfortable.

She came toward me, stood right over me, exposing herself. Then she lay down on me like a heavy sleep and took me deep inside her, laughing all the while. It was laughter about the deep joy in all things, about that center we miss while we fret over the details, about the earth that moves far

191

down inside us all, that we can only taste at moments like this, in the last moments of sex, the lost moments of devotion, when you disappear into the grains of dust on the floor. You become the grit in the back of your mouth.

When nothing else matters.

When it is all related.

Sometime Wednesday Morning

When I woke up she wasn't there and the room was cold. I was sleeping in my clothes on a cot with sheets as gray as dry Dakota soil in August. There were black soot stains on the ceiling. My head ached with some drugged hangover, and I discovered that dull ache when I lifted my head to look around.

The wind rattled the board walls then, and a December draft moved the dust and scrap paper around the dirt floor. Next to the cot where I'd laid my head, a small wood stove stood, cold as the draft in the room.

I heard a snort, and turned to find the toothless old man asleep beside me in the cot. Old Badlands Face himself was curled up next to me, stealing the warmth of my body. His hand, the color of the dust on the floor, was resting on my pale chest. He smelled of sweat and dirty linen, so I rolled out and sat at the edge of the cot, holding my aching head.

What had happened to the hallway and the motel of the night before I don't know, I was looking around at a one room, windowless shack. There was a heap of scrap lumber, some of it from stolen highway signs, by the doorway. The door latch was rope. The walls were arrayed with junk, scrap metal, old tools and farm implements, chunks of harness leather and lengths of rope, rusted cast iron pots, and leather bundles holding God only knows what. Snow drifted in under the doorway as I watched. There was a table and a many times painted chair in the center of the room, chips and nicks showing two or three previous colors. The table was heaped with more junk, and dirty dishes sat beside it in a galvanized tub.

At my feet, wrapped in a couple blankets, lay Bernard Choteau. He slept, and I'd barely stirred the old man snoring behind me. But Protector looked up at me. The dog was curled up in the blanket with Choteau, and it gazed up at me with those big loyal eyes that said, "What next, Kemo Sabe?"

I couldn't answer.

I rubbed at my face a couple times, trying to drive out the sleep and the haze of whatever they'd slipped me. Then I massaged my temples, trying to drive the ache away. Every time I opened my eyes, I saw Choteau lying there, I saw his long graying hair tangled behind him, with that stupid stone behind his ear. I was dirty and exhausted and my head rang like an empty bottle breaking on rocks. It was too much to take after I'd slept with Terri in my dreams.

And I couldn't help it. I kept seeing the color of his skin. Through my pink-white hands I kept seeing his face, just like the old man's, the same color as the dirt. And I hated him for it, then. I admit it. I hated him for it, then.

You see, for this filth, for this frigid dirty mess, I'd abandoned my wife and my job and my life back at the university. All so I could feel cold and dirty, and sleep with the warmth of a smelly old man.

I kicked Choteau then. Not hard, but harder than I needed to just to wake him. I kicked him in the back, between the shoulder blades, and I told myself it was only to wake him, that's all.

But the old bulldog eyed me and I couldn't lie to myself under that confused gaze. Choteau rolled over, and said, "What's up?"

"Sorry," I mumbled. The old man snorted again, stopped snoring abruptly, and rustled around on the cot. "Let's go," I said. "Let's get out of here. Wherever we are."

The old Indian stirred them, Old Badlands Face from the night before. "Morning, boys," he said brightly. Then he shivered and pulled the gray sheets around him. He sucked in those lips and gummed them some, then yawned and his mouth made a pop as those lips flapped open.

I rubbed my face and shivered, not at the hard cold in the room, but at the thought of sleeping next to that dirty old Indian.

Choteau crawled out of the blankets on the dirt floor, without ever uncovering the old dog. He stopped to tuck the blanket around Protector, then scurried stocking foot over to the wood pile. He grabbed a couple splintered chunks, carried them across the room, and went to work blowing on the ashes in the stove.

"Let's go," I said; I felt a little woozy, like I'd eaten too many cold remedies at once. "We gotta get moving," I said.

Choteau didn't answer. He just fed the splintered wood into the stove as he blew on the coals. One of the chunks of wood said "Pop." on it, but the numbers had been burned off. In moments I heard the crackle of flames beginning to catch.

"Don't you boys want something to eat?" the old Indian said.

I'd had enough of Indian stew the night before. Feeding me dog when I didn't know it. Besides, with the way my head felt, I thought maybe the stew was how they drugged me, because surely somebody had slipped me something.

"Not hungry," I barked, and made my own head ache.

"There's food to eat," the old Indian cackled.

I stood up, waited a moment to keep my balance, then said, "Let's get rolling." I used Choteau's phrase on purpose. Choteau shoved the second piece of wood into the fire, and didn't need to blow anymore. "If you're coming along, better come now," I said.

I reached down to rouse the dog. I felt dizzy and had to lean on the floor and bend my bad knee down to keep my balance. Lights blinked, flashbacks from some drug in my system, I guessed. "You okay?" Choteau said.

I spat out that I was fine. "Let's go."

He tossed a couple more chunks of wood into the stove and then closed the door. Rubbing his hands together, he said, "Whatever you say."

Then he put on his shoes, or I should say he put on my old shoes, and he said to the old Indian, "It'll warm up here in a bit, old man. You stay wrapped up till then."

The shack around me was pandemonium and I just had to get out of there so I could organize myself. I knew it wasn't possible inside that one depraved room. I struggled back to my feet and said, "C'mon, Protector."

Choteau stood up and so did the dog. I already had the car keys in hand. As I unwound the rope door latch, Choteau bent over and hugged the old Indian on the cot. Then he said to Old Badlands Face, "Thank you, Grandfather Ice." All I could think of was how the old guy smelled of smoke and urine, and how this shack was in complete disarray, almost as complete as my soul, and how I had to get away from there to find some usefulness, some orderliness in my mind.

I unwound the rope and pulled open the door and the real cold hit me in the face. The old Indian cackled at the way I staggered. "Walk the good road," he called through his laugh. And then he added, "Little Big Man," to the end.

"C'mon, boy," I said as the dog followed me out to the little Renault. I lifted him in and then got in myself and started the car. In the subzero morning, the little car turned right over. As I sat, letting it warm up, I looked back at the open door to the shack. The cold blew into that little house, and I decided I'd give Choteau until the car was warmed. If he wasn't out here by then, I'd drive away and figure out where I was and then turn myself in. I found myself hoping he wouldn't come, listening for the engine to rest in an easy idle; I was eager to go. I wanted to leave the damn Indians there, with all their problems, and get back to what now seemed comfortable and easy, teaching history to bored college kids.

I put my hand on the shift stick and was about to shove it into first, when I noticed the change. We were sitting outside a one room shack huddled against a broad stretch of Dakota prairie. There wasn't another building in sight. Just snow, drifted in heaps and sharp edged waves wherever there was a roll to the plains. That was it.

But the night before, this had been a little four corners with a housing project around it. There'd been enough here in my headlights for this place to qualify as a town in South Dakota. Now I was looking at a shack and an expanse of prairie.

They moved me, I decided. After I'd passed out, after they'd drugged me, they hauled me off to this shack so I'd never know where I'd been. But why?

Choteau emerged from the shack then. He turned, scuffing the snow out of the entryway, then closed the door behind him and worked at it a moment to be sure it was closed. I lifted my hand from the shifter. It was too late to escape now. I heard the old Indian's laugh again, over the idle of the Renault, through the closed door of the shack, the closed door of the car. And I remembered what he'd called to me. Walk the good road, he'd said, Little Big Man.

But I wasn't Little Big Man. I was an American History prof of French and Irish descent working in southern Missouri, without even a trace of Indian blood in me. I live in the 20th Century. I was not a Lakota from a hundred years ago. I was not Little Big Man.

*   *   *

Choteau pulled open the door and flopped into the car. The bulldog slobbered over his ear, and Choteau laughed as he leaned in to pull the car door shut. The minute it slammed, I put the Renault in gear and we drove off down the frozen lane. Ours were the only tracks in the drifting snow, and in an hour, all our traces would be drifted over, too. But that was all right by me. I just wanted to be gone, out of that mess. Goodbye to the old fart and to Crazy Horse, and all their chums. I was driving Bernard Choteau, escaped murderer, through a bitter cold reality. I was too old to be playing Indian. I wanted to go home.

And most of all, I wanted Terri. The smell and touch of her in my drug-hazed dream seemed more real now than my headache or the bulldog panting in the back seat. Enough was enough.

The only question now was how to get rid of Choteau, safely. It was one thing to go for a spin. But in the last twenty-four hours I'd mugged a cop with him, and then been drugged loony with some dog stew Mickey Finn. I'd had enough, finally. My little midlife career crisis was over. It was time to get back to work. Back to everyday reality.

Not to say all of this clear thinking didn't make my fuzzy head hurt. But suddenly I felt like I was going somewhere. To the closest cop shop, as soon as it was safe. All I needed was a phone and Golman's number in my head. As soon as I could figure out where in hell I was.

"What did you guys slip me?" I said to Choteau's laugh. I looked at his dirty hair and the slouched way he sat, and I wondered then how I ever saw Crazy Horse in him. Crazy

Horse, that great warrior of the past. He was no murdering, dirty convict.

"What?" he said, acting as if he didn't know what I meant.

"What was it?" I said. I didn't need to explain. "Was it in the pipe? Or was it the stew?"

Choteau just shook his head at me, and stopped laughing.

"Oh, it's not funny now, is it?" I said. I trounced on the gas some, and the little car tried to lurch ahead faster, but it was still too cold. The engine raced and we sputtered some oil smoke and jerked for a moment, and then we pushed slowly on. "I'm sure not laughing. You folks knocked me cold, Choteau. And you've been jerking me around for days now. I'm getting tired of it, buddy. Real tired."

"My, my. Aren't we a son of a bitch this morning," he said.

"What kind of shit was that?" I said. "My head is sore."

Choteau was silent for a moment, then he muttered something.

"What'd you say?" I asked.

He looked right at me. "I said I thought you were different."

A day ago I'd have been pleased at that, but not in my new, winter morning clarity. So I ignored it and stuck to my line, "What'd you slip me, Choteau?"

"It's always the same," he said. "Something happens and you can't explain it. But it can't be real to you, can it? Not unless you can explain it. So now, I must have drugged you."

"Don't give me this metaphysical shit, Choteau."

"I ain't giving you nothing. And I didn't 'slip you' anything either. Whatever you remember happening, it happened to you and you were straight as a marine colonel, man. So don't go trying to dump some explanation of yours onto me."

"You expect me to believe that?" I said.

"Just let it be, Professor."

"Who was that old guy?"

Choteau smiled, "Better question, Mr. Professor," he said. "That 'old guy' was John Ice Bissonette. And he's in touch with some big power, Professor." Choteau stopped to whistle at it. "I don't pretend to understand it, I tell you that, man."

"Mumbo jumbo," I muttered.

"Well, you can think what you want," Choteau was grinning wide. "But I didn't slip you any shit. No Grandfather Peyote, man. And no acid or any other shit. The old Ice man there, he don't need any of that, Professor. He's just on to some big shit."

"Listen, Choteau, I'm getting real tired of this." I didn't want to look at him, for some reason. I kept my eyes on the rutted dirt road and drove west. "Last night, you or that old guy Bissonette, or Ice, or whoever, one of you slipped me some kind of hallucinogen. You sent me on some trip. The next thing I know I'm talking to Crazy Horse and all his relatives, buddy, and they're telling me I'm supposed to be Little Big Man. Then I pass out and wake up in bed in some shack in God-only-knows where, South Dakota, I think." I stopped and maneuvered around a frozen clod of dirt in the road. We were getting to somewhere, though; the road was growing better. More gravel, shallower ruts.

"And you, you've been feeding me this line that you're Crazy Horse, born again. Right." I kept on, because I didn't want to hear what he had to say. I'd had enough of his answers. "You think because you've read some history books and you can speak in tongues, and because you can slip me a Mickey in a bowl of dog meat, you think you can use me however you want. Well, I don't buy it. I don't like being used, Choteau, especially when you're just trying to get laid by your old girlfriend. I want out of this, Choteau." I braked and pulled the car to a stop. There was a paved highway running north and south visible out on the horizon. "I'm done with this, Choteau. All I want is you to tell me where you want to be left out." But I was careful not to tell him about Golman, and my own escape hatch.

"You don't have to worry about Mrs. Nordstrom," he said, and sat looking at his feet. "It was a mistake." He was changing the subject, but my curiosity got the best of me.

"What?" I said, trying hard not to fall for this sorry routine.

"When she got wind of how much is following us," he said. "When she realized it was gonna be me and her and half the FBI, she changed her mind about us. Living in Canada and hiding on the Reserve didn't sound too fine to the good doctor's wife. I guess."

"What happened?" I said, thinking of Golman and what he knew.

Choteau looked up and laughed, but it didn't cover anything. A gust of wind rocked the little car. "God damn woman," he said, grinning all the while.

"She went back to being Mrs. Doctor Nordstrom," I said, "didn't she?" He nodded his head and laughed some more, bravely, I suppose.

"Sorry," I said. I was missing Terri, and I knew then that I'd been Terri's own Mary Red Skies these last few days. I'd been screwing up her life, running around the countryside trying to find some version of the truth about myself, or trying to escape it. So it was hard not to feel for old Choteau on his last good run.

"Where you want out?" I said, anyway.

He didn't answer, but I wasn't going to let him get away with it. Sure, I felt sorry for him. But I needed to get home. My own life was a mess, and helping fix his wasn't going to do anything but throw mine away.

201

"You know, Choteau, we've got my brother-in-law. I can call him and we can turn ourselves in to him. Hell take care of both of us." But I still didn't tell him how I could call Golman, how I came to have that number stuck in my head. I did glance in the mirrors though, wondering then whether we were really alone out there. I saw nothing but snow and wind-swept grass, and the hard blue sky.

Choteau just shook his head and chuckled at me. He muttered something about, "He'll take care of you." Still, my suggestion seemed to take both of us off the subject of our hearts. "They won't miss their chance at me," he said. "They've got a score to even up, Professor. There's a couple of dead agents back there on my record, you know. Its Redskins 2, FBI zero. Think they're gonna leave it like that?"

"I may not like him, Choteau. But we can trust him. One thing you can do is trust Mike Golman."

He sat there smiling and shaking his head at me while he gazed out at the snow. "There's a lot you don't see yet, Professor," he whispered, almost as if to himself.

Then he turned and looked right into my eyes. "We didn't drug you, Professor. What you saw is what happened. Think about that for a minute."

"No," I laughed and shook my head back at him.

He kept staring in my eyes. "Think about it, Professor. You didn't smoke any pipes and you didn't eat anything until you were already talking to a roomful of ghosts. Remember?"

He was making my head hurt again.

"No, don't answer that," he said. "You just think about it. And don't get mad at me because you can't figure it out. 'It makes my head hurt,'" he mocked my voice. "Knowing something and being something are different, Professor. When you get done thinking about it, when you're finished with 'research-ing' it, maybe you'll just let it be."

He snorted then. His eyes had turned to a glare and he was angry. "Don't know a gift when you see it," he sneered.

I started to answer, because he was pissing me off. But he held up a hand and shut me up.

"And," he said, "we ain't ready to surrender yet. No sir, Professor, sir," he was still glaring at me. "Not yet."

Out of nowhere, that paring knife showed up in his other hand. Wherever he hid it on his person, he had it easily in hand. "Drive, Professor," he said. There was a cold steadiness in his eyes that was new. "Just keep heading west until we hit the highway. I'll tell you where to go from there." His eyes were too bad to know that his highway was right out there in sight. With his thumb he felt up and down the blade, checking its edge.

But you know, I wasn't afraid of him. I guess maybe I should have been. But that's the funny thing. He'd scared me enough times already, maybe I was getting used to him. But this wasn't really a threat, or at least it didn't seem like one. He just wasn't finished with me yet.

I started the car again, and he said, softly, "Professor, when you get done thinking about last night," and a warm smile crossed his face suddenly, "when you're done being angry and you trust me again, then ask me about last night. Okay?"

He put the knife away. It disappeared as quickly as it came. As I drove down to the pavement, I couldn't help but ponder that weapon and how easily it came into use for him. Everyone claims the charges against him were trumped up. Still, as we drove on in that early winter light, I kept remembering Golman's warnings. I kept seeing that knife. I had my sympathies for him and for his cause yet. But it kept coming back to my mind. All the warnings Golman had given me. It kept coming back. No matter what I felt for him or thought of him, Bernard Choteau had seen more of death than I ever cared to. Violence and cruelty and death were not abstractions for him. This wasn't any history book we were reading from. This was real.

We turned south on the highway. Choteau had hauled us so far out in the middle of nowhere, there weren't even any road markers. Or at least there weren't even any left outside of Old Badlands Face's stove.

"Something else you don't get," he said to me as we drove south and west on the pavement. "We didn't go see Ice for you, Professor. All of that, it wasn't for your sake. You were just lucky to be there. After I finally got in touch with . . . " He paused awkwardly for a moment. "With Mrs. Nordstrom," he said. "After that, I needed to find him."

"So what'd he tell you?" I said, probably more quickly than I should have.

We drove a long way, a mile or two farther, before he said, "When you ask the right questions, Professor, you won't need me to answer."

The land started to change then. The sand, where it was blown clean of snow, turned red, and the gullies grew deeper as the grass ranged thinner. Scrub and sage began to gather in clumps, sticking out of the snowy crust. Before long the little Renault was coasting downhill and limping up against a stiff wind that blew constantly out of the northwest. Choteau just rode along, scruffing the dog's ears, calmly eyeing the landscape as if we were on a Sunday afternoon ride.

"Did you kill those two agents? I said. "I think you owe me a straight answer to that," I added, when he didn't seem to hear me.

"I do, huh?" he said, and was silent again.

204

"Yeah, Choteau, you do. You tell me its Indians 2 and the Bureau zero, and they're gonna even up the score. Peltier is still in jail, and very much alive. So if I count you as one, Choteau, that seems to leave me. Unless you think they'll be satisfied with old Protector here."

"They won't hurt you, Professor," he scoffed at me. Then he paused to reach back and scruff the bulldog's shoulders. "You guys aren't my accomplices. You're my victims."

"So you figure you count for two?" I said. "Aren't we big stuff."

"You know, I lied, Professor. The score ain't two-zip. Its two to one."

"Who?" I said, looking across at him.

I was searching my memory. There were the two Special Agents, Williams and Coler, murdered on that June morning in 1975. They were executed, it seemed, shot at close range in the back of the head.

"Everybody always forgets," Choteau said. His head cocked a bit and he grinned a hard, thin smile. "You remember the feds. You remember how they were shot and where. They made all the headlines. News and trial after trial. But everybody forgets Annie Mae."

"Aquash," I said. "Anna Mae Aquash." He nodded his head. She had been at the Wounded Knee siege, another member of AIM, a Micmac Indian from Nova Scotia.

"It wasn't only about six months after those feds got killed that they killed Annie Mae," he said.

"But there was never anybody charged with that murder," I said, "was there?"

"You know, Professor, she was murdered the same way those agents got killed. A bullet to the back of the head. They tried to cover it up. They said she was drunk and died of exposure, remember? And then they lost her hands, Professor." Choteau held his own out, palms up. "Her hands, Professor.

Cut 'em right off her and lost them. Couldn't identify the body for weeks, you know?

"They screwed the autopsy, too. The fucking BIA doctor said it was exposure killed her. He just didn't notice the little bullet hole in the back of her head. 'A little bullet isn't hard to overlook,' is what he said. Those are his fucking, exact words, man. 'A little bullet.'" Choteau laughed at it and muttered more about, "Lost her hands, man."

"But nobody's ever been even accused of her murder," I said again, as if a little detail like the law made a difference to what Choteau was remembering.

"Like I said, Professor. It's two to one."

We rode for a while then, both of us contemplating the "even score," I suppose. We crossed the Missouri River in silence, and finally I saw a road sign. We were leaving the Crow Creek Reservation, and entering the lower Brule on the other side of the river. Lost in Indian Country, headed for who knows where.

Now there were steep hills all around, topped with flat bluffs. They were red as rust, and where they eroded away, they were whiter than the drifting snow. Slowly the hills and the scrubby bluffs turned to dry plateaus.

"You didn't tell me," I said abruptly out of our silence. "You just changed the subject, Choteau. I still want to know. Who killed those two agents?"

I remembered one of the dry reports I'd read through, one of the dozens of official investigations. The FBI doesn't like having their agents executed. They did a lot of reporting and investigating. They covered everything from wind directions to blood types. But one detail stood out in my mind, one detail in all those thousands of pages. The fingers were cut off one of the agent's hands. Maybe out of some ritual. Maybe because, at the moment of execution, he'd raised his hands to cover his head. but the four fingers of a left hand were cut off at the palm.

"What would you do if I said I did it?" Choteau was still dodging a straight answer.

So I didn't answer him. "You know as well as me, your trial was fixed."

He smiled broadly at that. I saw his flat profile against the red plateaus outside, and he looked like a nickel. And I understood him about as well as I understood that Indian head on the nickel. Who in hell was he, really, behind that Indian face?

"There's still two dead men out there," I said. "And you're doing time for shooting them."

"I was there," he said suddenly. "Two cops got shot. They got dead, so somebody's got to pay. Why not me?" he said. "I been a pretty good martyr for a dozen years."

"You know who did it," I said.

"It was a bad day. There was a lot of shooting." His smile disappeared and he glared at the dash of the Renault. "A lot of people were excited, including them two feds. They came in shooting, you know. That made a few people real angry. There were women and kids and old people around there." His head shook a little, almost imperceptibly. It might have been the bounce in the road, but it wasn't. "Bad day, you know. Bad for everybody, Professor. Better if the sun never came up on that day."

"Who killed them?" I pressed him.

He looked over at me, dead in the eyes, without a grin or a blink, and said, "It was me, Professor."

And I didn't believe him for a minute.

A few miles south of there we cut under the freeway on another dirt road. That led us to a blacktop, patched and pot-holed and lined with skid marks. We were on somebody's fun run to the res', and from the number of burn outs on the asphalt, it looked like maybe it was the whole damn Indian nation.

My head had begun to clear, and it sank into a dull throb that was connected more to my bum knee than to my flashbacks of dog stew and pipe smoke. I'd almost forgotten the Crazy Horse stuff. See, we were getting close to the Rosebud and Pine Ridge, we were heading for the shadows of the Badlands. It was Crazy Horse country, yes, but it was also the country where Leonard Peltier and Dennis Banks had shook up the world, where Bernard Choteau had lived his best days. Where he'd put himself in trouble with the law, and where he discovered who he was. Whoever that might be.

Choteau started to talk then. I think now the memories came at him hard and strong. The shape of the hills and the lay of the road, it brought the past out of him. It had been fifteen years since he'd seen this home ground. I was just lucky enough to be there when he opened up.

"There were good nights, too, Professor," he laughed. "We had some times. You know, there were about two hundred fifty of us that night we pulled into the Knee and took it over. Now, man, that was a party. We were gonna make some noise. We just rolled into that little tourist trap and took over. There was that many of us. Nothing Wilson's goons or the feds or anybody could do about it. They were all over in Pine Ridge town waiting for us, cause they thought that's where we would make our stand. But we surprised them. We just drove right on through Pine Ridge in a caravan, and on to take the Knee. No questions asked, Professor, 'cause they didn't know what to say."

Choteau brightened up the more he spoke, and I guess I did too. Now that my head had cleared enough, I was starting to feel hungry, and I guess that was a good sign. I even took my hand off the wheel long enough to reach around and pat the old bulldog on his flabby chest. It made my knee hurt to turn, but the dog slobbered on my shoulder for a while after that. It was pay enough for me.

*   *   *

"Yeah," Choteau said. "They saw us come rolling by, and we were carrying guns, and boy, did they run."

"That must have been something," I said. "The way you folks held that place and the whole world was watching you. You must have been proud."

"Scared," he chuckled. "That's what I was. Scared and hungry after the first couple days," he said. "We were under siege, you know. And there was plenty of shooting going on. Almost constant. Every night the goons and Feds taking pot-shots at us, and we had to be careful not to waste our ammo. We were always waiting for their big charge, and them feds, they thought we were going to make some kamikaze charge every time we fired a shot. Everybody was on a hair trigger." He paused and then added, "But yeah, we felt pretty good, too. There we were at the Knee and it was like we were setting things right for all the ghosts there, for all them people in that mass grave at the top of the hill."

He was quiet for a moment again. The car sounded loud when he finally spoke, because I could barely make out what he said. "That was when I found out," he said softly.

"Found out what?"

"You know. Who I am," he said, as if I'd missed the obvious connection. "Crazy Horse," he said.

"Oh," he was going to make my head hurt again. "Yeah," I said.

"When I was a kid, after my folks got sent off to Colo-rado, I got sent to the mission boarding school. They had TB, Professor, and the government sent them to a sanatorium down there in Colorado, and they never came back. They both died down there real quick, just a couple months later, I think. I was real little, and even short times seemed like long times to me. But the brothers at the mission told me I was an orphan then, and that was when I started to have these recurring dreams.

"The priest, he just called them nightmares and told me, don't worry, they're not real, you know. But they weren't nightmares, man, because they didn't scare me any. It was the school and my parents disappearing like that," he snapped his fingers, "that was what scared me. It wasn't my dreams. They made me feel good, like I was home or something."

"As I got older, the dreams went away and I forgot about them. They were just bad dreams, that's what the priests all said, and I believed them. The dreams didn't even come back when I was in Korea, man, even in combat. I just forgot about them entirely. Just kid stuff, you know?

"But I know this now. If it hadn't been for Wounded Knee, Professor, I might never have figured them out.

"See, after about the third day, when we were trapped in there, the food started to run out. We figured there were children and some elders with us, so some of us guys went on a fast to preserve the supplies. And to keep ourselves pure for the fight like the old ones used to do. I figured I could go a couple days, and then eat enough to stay well.

"So one night when I wasn't on watch, I was catching some sleep and they came back, man, my old nightmares. More real and vivid than ever. But they didn't scare me, I just couldn't figure them out. A lot of the people there at the Knee, they knew enough to respect dreams. They told me what to do. Go see the Old Man, they said.

"Ice took me off in a corner alone. I told him about how I'd had these dreams as a kid and now they were coming back. 'Tell me the story,' he said. At first I started to tell him about my parents. I could barely remember them, but I talked about their TB and the mission school and all. But he laughed and stopped me. 'No, no. Tell me the real story,' he said and I got it. He meant the dreams, you know?

"So I told him what I dreamed and his eyes got wider and wider the more I explained. See, he was the one who recognized them. He knew right away what they were. I'd been dreaming the visions of Crazy Horse, Professor. Ever since I was a little kid.

"He said to me, 'You have the spirit of Crazy Horse.'

"Now that was something we all talked about there at the Knee, about doing things in the spirit of Crazy Horse, you know, because Crazy Horse was so fearless and sacrificed everything for the people. It was what everybody said at the Knee. So that's how I took it, as a compliment, I guess, when Ice first said that to me. But gradually, I understood the old Iceman. I wasn't living in a way like Crazy Horse. That's not what he meant. What Ice meant to tell me was you ARE Crazy Horse."

"He took me off down into the ditch where Big Foot and his people were massacred, and we sat out there in the February cold and he told me about the four souls."

"Four souls?" I said, because I didn't want to lose him now, not when I was getting close to something big.

"It's what he told me, Professor," Choteau said and then he grinned at me. It was a grin I'd seen before, on that crazy Old Badlands Fart, when he offered me a bowl of dog meat. "See, when you're born, you don't come out of nowhere. Everything comes from another world, a spirit world. That's what we believe, Professor, and it's how the old Iceman explained it to me. Whenever anything is born in this world, whether it's a rock or a crow or a human being, it's born with four other souls, with four parts of itself that are still connected and belong to that spirit world we all came from.

"The first soul is your breath, Professor, your life. It's the part of you that moves. The Niya. And the third soul is the Sicum. That's your power, Professor. Everything has a power

211

that's all its own, that comes from the other world, you know. Some of us have greater powers than others, and some of us have nurtured our powers better than others. When you pray, you are really asking what your power is, and how to use it well.

"The fourth soul, the Nagila, Dr. Gentles, is the little ghost. In everything there is a little part of the holy, you know, the wakan." He held his left hand up between us, pinching his thumb and his index finger together. It was as if he was holding a tiny seed up for me to examine. Then he shook it a little as he spoke, for emphasis. "What is wakan in the whole universe, they say, is in every one of us, in every thing. The Nagila is the little bit of the universe that is in you, but it isn't you."

He nodded his head then at some thought of his own, and let his hand drop to his lap again. "Now comes the crazy part, Professor," he hesitated for a moment, grinned his crazy Old Badlands smile, and then the grin disappeared.

"The second soul is what was important to me. It was what my dreams were all about, you know? The second soul, Professor, is the Nagi. It is the place where everything individual and different lives in you. It's what you mean, nowadays, when you say 'ghost.' A spook, you know. A haunt. But we believe sometimes, when the need is great, you can be born with a Nagi that has lived before. You have the Nagi of Crazy Horse, Ice told me in that old ditch. He talked to me out there until I understood him. My dreams were not my dreams, Professor. And a part of me, one of my four souls, was also the soul of Crazy Horse, the great warrior chief. I had the spirit of Crazy Horse.

"Then Ice told me, at the end, 'We should keep this to ourselves, you know. Don't say anything more about your dreams. This is a great gift, Bernard. It comes because we live in a dangerous time. As we walked back out of the gully toward the store, he stopped and said to me, 'Pray for strength, Bernard. Hard things will be asked of you.'

"I never said anything about it at all. I could hardly understand it myself. I don't know if I do yet. But I don't think the poor old Iceman could keep his big mouth shut. Because by afternoon most of the encampment was talking about me and my vision. Just hearing about my dreams made everybody feel good. It made us strong. It was like a gift when we needed it, you know, over those next couple months during the siege."

"So that's where this Crazy Horse stuff comes from," I said to him. For a moment, I felt like I was on solid ground. I'd figured it out. This whole Crazy Horse line was just the result of some goofy dream analysis by a fruitcake of an old Indian. And it started to explain Choteau and all his delusions away. He wasn't really Crazy Horse, see, he'd been led to believe he was by suggestion. Some nut roll on the Dakota res' had got hold of his common sense, saddled it up and took it for one wild ride.

This new clarity made my headache disappear, and I was most definitely hungry. I felt like I had my hands back on the wheel and I was driving again. I knew where we were going, too. We were headed for the Rosebud Reservation, or maybe for Pine Ridge. We were about to connect up with some of Choteau's old compadres in the revolution. I was going to drop him off with some folk who believed he was Crazy Horse.

Then I could call Golman's number and turn myself in, I could leave them to deal with the FBI while I could get back to Terri and the University, and enjoy my celebrity. I could probably even wheedle a raise and a bunch of release time out of this. I was thinking about myself again. Yeah, I was being a little shit.

But don't give up on me. I still had a lot to learn, and Choteau wasn't done with me yet.

*　　　　　*　　　　　*

213

"See, Professor, you were getting close with that book of yours." Choteau was wiping a hand back and forth on the knee of his trousers. "When you kept asking all them questions about Ghost Dancing and spirits and so on. You were on the right trail then, about those days."

I laughed. "I was, wasn't I? It was about religion and spirits and the past, wasn't it?"

His hand slowed down on his knee, it almost stopped, and he stared blankly out the windshield.

"Is that why you wouldn't talk to me? Is that why everybody shut up when I mentioned your name as the key?"

"I suppose," he said, then stopped moving his hand.

"But I don't understand, Choteau. Why did you and your vision have to stay some kind of secret?"

"Were you gonna believe us if I told you I was Crazy Horse?" He shook his head no. "Man, Professor, we were just gonna come off like a bunch of flakes. You'd a written that book, and you'd be so busy looking down on us and laughing at us, you wouldn't even know you'd a turned us into a cult, a bunch of lunatics. We didn't need any of that, Professor. No sir. We get enough without your help, thank you."

I laughed, but only to cover what I was thinking. I couldn't help it. My head was making sense of it all, and I was already planning that book, and everything it was going to do for me. You know, with a book like that, I might even wind up teaching someplace good. My career was back on track. I was on the rise. Even if I was just driving along somewhere south of the Badlands in old Dakota Territory.

But Bernard Choteau saw right through me. He grinned and talked to the bulldog. "He thinks he's got it all figured out again, Protector," Choteau said. "With everything we've showed him, he's still missing the point, isn't he, old fellow?"

This time, I laughed at him.

"He forgets so easily, Protector. Why, he's even forgotten about his wallet."

"My what?" I said. Then I remembered. Old Badlands Face, or Mr. Ice, or whoever he was back at my psychotic motel. He still had my wallet. We had cash and some plastic, but the rest of it was back there in never-never land. "Shit," I said. I didn't have any ID.

"What's the old guy want with my stuff?" I said.

"Don't worry, Professor, he won't steal anything. Not anything much anyway. He don't need much more than he's got."

I thought it over. I guess there was nothing really to worry about. I had no identification, but it sure seemed to me like the next time we got stopped by the authorities, they weren't going to need it. Next time, they were going to know who we are.

The ghosts of Little Big Man and Crazy Horse, right?

At that moment, the idea struck me as funny.

I was doing my research now, filling in the information gaps, verifying my thesis. I could see the book in my mind, and I decided to use the time I had left with Bernard Choteau who believed he was Crazy Horse, use it to flesh out my ideas. Crazy Horse, see. That was the crux my monograph was searching for all along.

I asked a lot of questions as we drove along; he answered some of them. I began to wish I had a tape recorder along. Finally, I had him talking about Wounded Knee. "Was it the local Indians on the res' who smuggled supplies to you?" I asked. What I really wanted to know was how far into the community this belief in Choteau as Crazy Horse went. Did most of the locals buy it? Or even know about it? Or was it kept a secret? But I didn't think he'd answer those questions directly.

"Wasn't just locals," Choteau said. "We had people from all over in there. By the time we gave up, we had a few hundred more people inside the Knee than when we took it over. We had sixty four tribes represented, man. Supplies got dropped in by airlift a couple times. The Feds had to start patrolling the air space over us with helicopters. It was the big time, Professor"

He stopped and his memory seemed to catch on something, because he sat up straighter and as he spoke he moved his head a lot, shaking it one moment and nodding it the next.

"But at the beginning, you know, it was a little tough, the first week or so. See, we didn't plan to be there more than a day or two. We were going to make our point and split. That was the original idea. We weren't planning any big hold out. But then the Feds and goons surrounded us."

"We almost ran out of food about the third day. Then the arguing started, you know. What should we do? Nobody wanted to give in, so we decided some of us had to sneak out after dark and bring back help. There were a lot of volunteers, but not a lot of good plans. So nobody went anywhere for a while."

Choteau stopped there and rubbed first at his eyes and then his temples. I wondered if it was his poor sight bothering him. But he just creased his brow and let out a long breath, and then went on with it.

"Turns out, we didn't need to sneak out. Soon as it was dark, people started sneaking in to Wounded Knee. Just a few, mostly alone, at first. And at first they didn't bring much with them.

"It was on our sixth night at the Knee. I remember this exactly. I was on watch, carrying an old deer rifle, but it felt like I was toting an old M1 with eight rounds in it, like I carried at Inchon. And I was on my fast, still. My heart was full of what Ice had told me. We were going to do something for the people, and I was going to be part of it. Because I had Crazy Horse's heart in me, and I knew that then.

216

"But it was bitter cold at the Knee that night. It was early march and there was still snow on the ground. When the wind blew, and that was most of the time, it cut right through the wool coat I was wearing. I'd gotten past being hungry, but that cold still hurt, man. I 'spose it was below zero out there.

"The camp was quiet. I could see one dim light on down by the store. I was posted up on the ridge, near the church and the old mass grave where Big Foot's people were dumped. I knew down at that light by the store Buddy Lamont was crouched and trying to stay warm, on watch just like me. Leonard was supposed to relieve me in a couple hours. Leonard Peltier," he looked over at me to see if I was following it all. "It seemed like a long couple of hours then, sitting in the cold. The houses of the town, of Wounded Knee, were all dark just north of me, on the other side of the hill.

"Off to the west and the east, along the highway, I could see the dark cars against the snow. Those were the roadblocks, man. There was one north of the town site, too. I knew that, though I couldn't see it. Just like I knew there were G-men and goons waiting at those cars, and before long there were a good share of South Dakota 'volunteers,' too. Those were the scary folks, you know. The volunteers. They were in it for the fun, I guess? And that's what's scary, man.

"Every now and then, there'd be a little light down at one of those roadblocks. Some Fed lighting a cigarette or some volunteer opening up his pickup door. It would be fast, because we were exchanging fire. Nobody wanted to be caught in some silhouette, and those Feds were freaking at being shot at, man. Shit, it was cold and I felt like I was back in Korea. Except for here it was damn hard to tell who your enemy was. It didn't fall Indian and white, you know. The goons, they were all reservation police. They were Indian, man, even if they were apples.

"So every now and then there would be a little gunplay, just to keep everybody honest, I guess. We wanted them to know we were paying attention, and they wanted us to know the same thing. This was no damn sit in, you know. We weren't screwin' around. And they were armed out on that res'."

He paused there, as if he was remembering something particular from those nights. It gave me time to imagine what it must have been like, shooting to kill in the dark of night, sitting in the cold waiting for them to make a move on you. I realized my life had known nothing like it. There was no joking around here, no saying to somebody, Hey, I'm a nice guy just like you. It didn't matter who you were, or how decent you were. There were just bullets in the anonymous dark. And a lot of emotions I'd yet to experience.

"But like I say," he piped up suddenly, "there were good times out there, too. A lot of good moments, man. That very night, freezing my ass off in the cold, I heard something up to the north and east. There was a thump and somebody cursed. Out in the cold silence, that sound carried, Professor. Somebody dropped something, or somebody fell. But the whole stretch of prairie went on high alert. Man, you could feel it go tense. I was like one gigantic eyeball glaring off in that direction, where the sound came from. And I knew I wasn't the only eye glaring out there. Buddy was listening too, and Leonard and Russell, and so was every goon and Fed out there. Unless, of course, it was the Feds starting to move on us.

"There was still a good blanket of snow out on the prairie grass, so anything moving across it stood out like a clear black shadow on the white. That's when I saw them, like a string of ants hustling across the white sand. They were heading across the rolling hills, must have been half a dozen of them. I kept a bead on the lead runner, but I waited. I couldn't tell from up there on the hilltop just what was going down. Were they more 'skins sneaking in to help us, or was this some goon squad, finally making their move? Man, you had no way to know.

"But I wasn't the only one waiting, either. Out at the Fed's roadblock on the highway east, nobody was firing. Either they knew who was coming at us, or they hadn't seen them yet. But as long as the feds didn't fire, I could figure it was goons coming for us. Still, I wasn't sure. So I held that bead on the leader, and I waited. All I could tell then was those people were carrying a load toward us.

"I'd about decided it was goons and they were trying to set up some kind of operating base or something, closer in to us, you know. I swear I was about to squeeze off a shot at the lead runner in that string when one of them at the rear stumbled again. The bundle he was carrying spilled out on the snow, and that's when the Feds spotted them, I guess. Because the Indians out there scurried around, scooping up what was dropped, until the gunfire started. Then they just ran flat out up the hill. The Feds at the east roadblock started shooting at the smugglers.

"It was obvious then these folks were with us, so I just shifted my aim over to the roadblock. Every time I saw the flash of a gun barrel, I sent a bullet that way. In seconds, gunfire started from down where Buddy was at, and it was more than just Buddy firing, too. Then the goons over at the roadblock to the west jumped in. But I ignored them and just answered the shots coming from the east. We weren't exactly flush with ammunition, but those folks headed toward me needed help. And they were carrying something in. Whatever it was, we needed it, because we needed everything."

Choteau paused to laugh, "The goons and the feds lay pretty low, too, once they were being shot at. They were careful, man. Most of the time, they kept their butts clean and out of range. They were just paranoid, always waiting for our big banzai attack. So the gunplay, it settled down pretty quick. I still don't know if anybody got hurt. Nobody did on our side, not that night. About a month later though, on a night just like that one, it's when Buddy got killed. Took a bullet through the neck." He stopped a moment there, and seemed weak and fat and vulnerable in his quiet. "Some serious shit we were into, man. No freaking peace marches."

Then his head rose a little, and he seemed stronger again. "But that night, nobody got hurt, Professor. And we got our first good supply of food. Those six 'skins were carrying provisions, you know. It was Billy War Eagle who was stumbling around out there. The stupid shit was wearing cowboy boots, man, and he kept slipping on the icy snow. He spilled a whole sack full of canned goods. Soup and vegetables and stuff. That was our first grocery delivery, that night. As they got closer, them skins looked like a whole, damn line of freaking Santa Clauses hauling sacks of goodies, man."

Choteau laughed, shook his head and grinned over at me. "You know who that lead runner was? The guy I had a bead on? Know who that damn kid was?"

He laughed again and didn't wait for me to guess. "It was my kid, Professor man. I didn't even know him then, never seen him, other than old pictures. But he knew me, man." He shook his head no again. "Shit, and I had a bead on him with that deer rifle. If Billy War Eagle hadn't dropped that sack of pork 'n beans, if he'd been smart enough to wear decent shoes, I'd a shot my own damn kid, Professor."

"This is Mary's son?" I said, trying to keep up.

"Yeah," he said, gazing past me now. "Jimmie. Jimmie Nordstrom. He was in school, you know. University of Minnesota, going to college, just like I was supposed to do. When he saw about the siege on the news, he left Minneapolis and headed straight for us. The very first night. Said he knew I was there, you know." Choteau looked down at the floor of the car and said very softly, "That was a time, man."

"Where is he now?" I said.

"He's a lawyer. He went back to school after all the troubles were done with out here; he got back in there and finished, you know. He's a lawyer. Works for some firm in the Cities; you know, Dopie, Grumpie, Sleepie and Bluto, attorneys at law. Some shit like that. Big bucks, fancy cars. The whole deal."

Choteau frowned and shook his head. But then he ran his fingers through his hair, as if he was suddenly aware of how long it was. He was trying to straighten it, I think. But he stopped and laughed at something.

"You know, Professor, when Jimmie showed up that night, he didn't introduce himself as any Nordstrom. No way, Professor. He said to me, 'Mr. Choteau, I'm Jim Red Skies. And that's what he went by then. We called him Red Skies that whole time. So he'll come around, Professor. He may be Mr. Attorney Nordstrom now, but he knows who he is underneath all that shit. He knows who he is."

Right, I thought. He's the son of Crazy Horse. Which made me chuckle. And then Choteau took my laugh the wrong way, and went silent.

We drove down just west of Winner and caught the main highway through the Rosebud. I thought we were finally coming home, but Choteau had me drive straight across the reservation without a stop for gas or food, or even to take a leak. I kept checking the mirror looking for anybody to be following us, but we were alone on the winter highways. If Golman and his chums were out there, they were good at being invisible.

As we passed the road sign on a grassy knoll that told us we were leaving the Rosebud, Choteau asked, "What was that?"

"Bye, bye, Rosebud," I said.

He grunted and nodded.

"Where are we going?" I said, wondering when I'd finally be free of him. "Back to Pine Ridge?" But I was thinking mainly about how he hadn't been able to read that sign.

"Not that far," he gazed out at the snow and grass around us.

It was easy to tell we'd left the reservation, even here in this little square of ground sandwiched between the Rosebud and Pine Ridge. Almost immediately the scarce ranch houses were bigger, sporting new paint and graveled lanes and satellite dishes. They had outbuildings, pole barns and livestock sheds and such. This was hard country to make a living out of; it was dry and windswept and it took a lot of ground just to graze one beef, much less a herd of them. But these were tough people, too. They'd scraped more than a living out of it. Their buildings and fences showed it.

Back on the reservation, it was hard to tell one house from another. They were all government issue. About the only difference between one place and the next was the color of the peeling paint and whether the rusted pickup on blocks in the front yard was a Ford or a Chevy.

"Your eyes are getting worse," I said to him. Protector was snoring in the backseat. My headache was gone, but I was still starved.

"Comes and goes," he said. "Sometimes I can see pretty well."

I nodded yes, but I don't think he really saw it. So I said, "Those sometimes are getting fewer and farther between."

He didn't say anything.

We stopped for gas in Martin and Choteau never got out of the car. I brought back junk food from the station, and he ate a little. Protector and I wolfed down Hostess donuts and Hungry Man jerky. But Choteau seemed worried, distracted.

"This is Martin, right?" he said, when I pulled out of the station drive. I was looking around, but I still didn't see anyone following us. There was nothing around but a lot of pickups and a few big Oldsmobiles. Nothing on our tail.

"Yeah," I said, looking at the big sign over the Martin Body Shop, just around the corner from the big time and temperature sign at the Martin State Bank, as we drove past the Good Food Martin Cafe, with its name painted on both the storefront windows.

"Two miles or so out of town you'll see a dirt lane running to the north. We'll turn there. Okay, Professor man?" He held his head as if he was looking straight down the street. "Anybody following us?" he said.

"I don't think so," I said as I drove out on the highway. I was only partly lying.

I found the turn right about where he said it would be. "Here?" I asked as he turned his head this way and that.

"Are we two miles out?"

"Yeah."

"There's no lane south, is there? It's not a crossroad?"

"Nope."

He nodded his head once. "Yeah, this looks like it," he lied. We rode along another frozen and icy dirt road and every couple miles we'd come to a mailbox. "What's it say?" Choteau would ask. I'd read him the name. We were in Nordic land, because they all went like F. Rasmussen or Per Grunnet or Nils Winther. After each one, he'd say, "Keep going," and we'd drive to the next.

When we came to the place he was using my eyes to find, I knew it right away. "Here it is," I said and turned in the lane.

"What's it say?" Choteau said quickly.

"We're here," I said.

"What'd it say, Professor man?"

"It said, 'R. Red Skies,'"

Choteau nodded his head.

But I pulled the car over beside the lane, set the parking brake and listened to it idle for a moment. I didn't know where Golman's boys were. They could have been anywhere. But I knew they were watching us. And I knew I was about to drag some other people into our little masquerade here. I had to tell Choteau about my visit with Golman the night before. He had to know, so he could decide who was going to be involved. It was time to trust him again, for the sake of the people who lived at the end of this lane.

"Choteau," I said. "I talked to Golman last night."

He didn't budge, he didn't look behind him, or around us, or over at me. He just sat and listened.

"When we stopped for gas, he was hiding there."

"Your wife?" he said.

"I don't know," I lied. "I don't think so."

He didn't say anything, but I don't know if he believed me. I don't know if he cared.

"You got to know this before we drive down there," I said. "He wanted me to stick with you. They want to know who you will lead them to."

He nodded his head, and seemed more alone than ever.

"He gave me a phone number to call," I didn't tell him that it was for my protection. "So we can turn ourselves in," I lied again.

He looked over at me, and put a hand out to touch my shoulder. It was as if he was blind and needed to know I was really there. "When did you see him?"

"Last night."

"Before we turned off?"

I nodded yes and then realized he might not see that. "Yes," I said, and then he broke into a laugh. "What?" I said.

"We're all right," he said, and shook my shoulder.

"Should we still go down there?"

"Well, Professor," he took his hand off my shoulder and then reached back to wipe old Protector's big jowls. He was mopping the slobber off the old dog with his bare hand. "I think we probably lost them last night," he said, and then wiped the dog slobber off on his pants. "And if we didn't," he reached back again then and patted Protector on the head, "then we already led them here. Didn't we?" And he laughed.

But it didn't make me feel comfortable.

Further down the lane we rolled up to a ranch that didn't look Indian at all. It was nestled in a hollow next to a straight row of Osage Orange. There was a new Ford pickup parked in front of a garage that held a station wagon, forest green with the wood on the side. Behind the garage sat a steel cattle barn with a tractor parked near its door. And the house rested sweetly in a yard surrounded by a chain link fence. The house itself looked like it was basically a government issue reservation project, just like its relatives back on the Rosebud. Except this one had a porch built onto the front that wrapped around and became a deck facing south in the windbreak of those Osage trees. A gas grill sat on the deck, with a tiny drift of snow against it. I could see a Christmas tree in the front window, and it came on just as we pulled up.

A collie, and it looked purebred, came darting out from a doghouse next to the porch. Its bark roused old Protector up. The bulldog stared sleepily out the rear window. He woofed once and it fogged the glass.

"Looks like Mr. R. Red Skies is doing all right for himself here." I set the parking brake.

Choteau didn't answer. He was busy straightening the shirt he was wearing of mine and then checking the laces on my old boots. Next came his hair, which he pulled back tight and tied into a ponytail.

That was when the front door of the house opened. Two little heads popped up behind the storm door and one of them wiped the frost off with a sleeve. In a moment, a pretty woman in jeans and an apron appeared and ushered them back in. She was holding a third child, a toddler. She closed the door.

"Are they expecting us?" I asked, because the woman's face sure didn't seem pleased to see us.

I saw Choteau 's hand feel for the door handle and he climbed out of the car. He stood up and looked around him at the snowy hillsides. Then he waved to the house, as if someone was there awaiting our homecoming. The lights on the Christmas tree went out.

"Let's go," he said to me as he flipped the seat up to let Protector climb out. "We're visiting Indian style." By that he meant we were just dropping in, expecting hospitality, of course. He lifted the old dog down and his hand fumbled to find the edge of the door and close it.

I pulled myself out and stretched my bum leg, and said, "Mary's brother?" across the car.

"Cousin," he said, and started around the fence toward the back of the house. The collie followed us around the perimeter of that chain link fence. It growled and barked at us, but Choteau stayed close to the guide of the fence. Protector, just once or twice, let loose with a deep baritone woof, and that'd hush the collie for a moment or two.

As we came around the corner of the chain link and the house, a tall Indian man walked out of the barn and crossed the farmyard to us.

"Bernard?" he said, and a smile filled his face. But at the same time, his eyes kept darting over to examine the car.

"Bobby," Choteau said, and turned toward him at the sound of the voice.

Bobby Red Skies was wearing a felt cowboy hat and a pair of quilt coveralls. As he strode toward us, he adjusted that hat on his head with a hand that wore a beat up, leather work glove. Then his gaze lifted over our heads to check the hillsides all around.

"Pull that car around here behind the garage," he ordered me, as if he knew who I was. Maybe he did.

I followed his orders while he walked over and clapped Choteau on the back. They stood there talking and grinning at one another for a time, standing between the two growling dogs. I left them in a reunion mood. They hadn't moved by the time I had the car parked and came limping back across the clean barnyard toward them, but their mood had changed. And those two little heads were bobbing around behind the storm door at the rear of the house now.

Bobby Red Skies kept checking the lane and the hillsides, and it made me nervous. When I limped back over to them, I noticed his feet. He was wearing an open pair of rubber galoshes. The buckle kind my mother made me wear to kindergarten. The ones I always "forgot" and left at school for weeks at a time. That memory made me crack a grin, but the two men weren't grinning anymore.

"She's gone back to him, you know," he was saying as I came up, and he looked at me like I was intruding.

"It's not what she sounded like in her letter," Choteau said, in a voice that was restrained. "Or on the phone a week ago."

"Well, she don't care for him, I guess," Red Skies said, looking at the frozen ground. "But, hell, he's been good to her and the boy, Bernard. You can't blame her for that."

Choteau introduced me as a way to avoid any response to that. Bobby Red Skies pulled off a work glove and shook my hand. I mentioned what a nice spread they had. Then, looking up the lane again, he said, "Let's get inside. Colder 'n snake's blood out here."

There was an entry room, really a big closet, at the back of the house and Red Skies pulled off his galoshes and coveralls there while we stood and watched. Two cinnamon kids with big dark eyes were waiting just inside. "You know, I don't like this. But I don't have a choice. I don't think you should stay here, Bernard," Bobby set his galoshes down neatly in the corner. "We'll get you some food you can take with

227

you, and I don't know what else you need. Just let us know. But you got to be moving along."

Choteau seemed shocked, maybe even broken at what he heard, but he tried not to let on. My disappointment was hard to hide, though. Here I thought I'd reached the end of the trail.

When Red Skies opened the door to the kitchen, I leaned down to help old Protector up the steps. Bobby Red Skies looked down at the dog. "We don't let . . . " he started to say and then stopped. I guess maybe he was thinking again of hiding us, of keeping us all hidden. The dog included.

"Why not?" Choteau said, standing in the doorway behind Red Skies.

The two kids had backed into the kitchen. They were silent in that way kids have when they sense something serious is happening in the strange world of adults.

"Come in," Red Skies said, ushering us. "I'll explain it, Bernard." Then over his shoulder he said, "Bonnie, get some coffee ready."

We stepped into the warm kitchen and Bobby Red Skies shut the door behind us. He was in Red Wing work boots and jeans now, but he still wore that felt hat.

When I saw how pretty his wife was, I remembered how we must look, Choteau and I. I sported my scrubby growth of beard and I hadn't showered in a couple days. We both probably smelled like a mix of old summer sausage, old bulldog and Old Badlands Face.

But Bonnie Red Skies had long black hair that fell across her shoulders and hid her lovely face, as she held the baby and poured our coffee in brown mugs.

"They been looking for you," Bobby said, maybe too flatly.

"Who has?" Choteau pulled out a kitchen chair and sat at the table. He was hiding his blindness again, but I recognized it now.

"The highway patrol, and then the FBI."

Choteau nodded his head.

"When?" I asked. I leaned up against the doorway to take the weight off my bad leg.

"Yesterday," Red Skies said. "Last evening."

Bonnie Red Skies handed us mugs of coffee then. The two boys moved slowly over to Protector and I smiled at them, so they started to pet the old dog. Their mother tried hard not to frown.

Choteau took a silent sip of coffee, as I asked, "What'd he look like? The FBI?"

He described two men, and just as I knew it would be, Bobby Red Skies described that little military moustache and the marine swagger. It had to be Golman, or someone just like him.

"They may be watching the place right now," Bobby said. "I shouldn't even have you in here, not with these kids around."

The two boys didn't seem to mind though. They had a dog in the house. The older kid, wearing a camouflage G.I. Joe sweatshirt, was hugging Protector. The old bulldog was eating it up, too. He panted and lapped at his chops to keep from slobbering on the waxed linoleum floor. The old boy was on his best behavior.

"Bonnie, help me get some groceries together. We got to get these men back on the road. Those police may be right up the lane. And the feds," he glanced over at me, suspiciously, "they'd just as soon come in shooting. They want his head, man," he nodded in the direction of Choteau, "even if a couple kids might be in the way. That won't slow them down any. Didn't slow 'em any at the Knee or Jumping Bull's, or any-where."

She didn't move for a moment. Then she looked at me with the pretty, dark eyes her children had inherited. "Bobby," she said his name in a scold. "You'll scare the kids. And Bernard and his friend, they're tired." She was hinting around about Indian hospitality, too. "They need to clean up and get rested," she said. "At least."

*　　　　*　　　　*

229

Red Skies took off his Resistol hat and rubbed a hand through his hair. The short hair was pasted against his forehead with sweat, but just as I noticed that he settled his Resistol back down on his head. He was quiet for a long while, thinking. Then the youngest boy lifted old Protector's back foot to look at it, and the arthritis in that dog made him cry out once. Not at the boy, but at the pain and the age and the weariness in him. That one woof set the collie outside barking in answer. Bobby Red Skies raised his head to listen close through those barks. I suppose we all did. Then he stood up and parted the curtains over the kitchen sink. His eyes narrowed as he gazed out against the bright snow.

We were all silent and waiting, until he let the curtain drop. Then Bobby said, with his back to everyone, "I suppose you think I don't want to help these two fellows? You think I wouldn't like to sit around all night and reminisce about the old days with these guys? Tell stories till dawn, and laugh all night? You think I wouldn't like to do that? But, Bonnie, I can't let these two . . . " he looked over at us, trying to decide what word to use next. Then he just changed his tack. "I can't let this fugitive stuff ruin it for us. Not with those feds out there, Bonnie. Not now."

"In the old days," Choteau said very softly, "we didn't just tell stories. We stuck together. We were a tribe, Bobby. Remember the Independent Oglala Nation? Remember, at the Knee . . . "

"Wounded Knee, Wounded Knee," Red Skies said, shaking his head. He turned around and looked at the table, not at Choteau. "That was fifteen years ago, Bernard. It's not like that anymore. You've been locked up too long."

"Okay, Bobby, but in the old days, you . . . "

"Bernard. You're forgetting. In 'the old days' we didn't have enough to eat, but we always found enough to drink. Somehow. In the old days, you wouldn't be here now. You'd have died in your thirties, Bernard, because someone knifed you in a poolroom, or in a prison cell in Minnesota, or because you puked your guts out in some ditch in January and . . . "

He trailed off there, but after a moment Choteau finished it for him. "And froze to death," he said. "Like Lennie."

Bobby Red Skies was quiet a moment. Then he stepped over to the cupboard. "I'm not gonna argue with you, Bernard. But it's not like it used to be out here. We're not a bunch of activists trying to change the world anymore. We're just trying to get somewhere. Trying to take care of our own, you know? The government, they put you and Leonard and Crow Dog in jail, they killed Annie Mae, they got Russell stuck out in California. It's all old news." As he spoke he pulled a jar of peanut butter and a loaf of white bread out of the cupboard. Then came a couple cans of HiC. "But life goes on here, Bernard. In good, old South Dakota."

The baby girl started to sniffle into her mother's shoulder then. It was the hard tone in Red Skies' voice that set her off, and I sensed it wasn't the first time he'd used it in this house. Bobby Red Skies closed his eyes and said, "I've had to swallow a lot to get here, Bernard. You ought to know that."

Then he turned toward his wife, like some trapped animal ready to scrap for his life. "We been working our butts off on this place for five years, Bonnie," he said. The two boys stopped stroking the dog and froze as he spoke. I don't think it was the first time they'd heard this lecture.

"Ever since Nordstrom staked us the money to move off the res', we've given up a lot to be here, Bonnie. These boys are gonna grow up right, and my little girl ain't gonna be some unwed squaw with a baby and a drinking problem at thirteen. You understand? We got out of Pine Ridge. I may have to walk around like some deaf mute in town and be a good Injun' for the wasicu. But, by god," he laid his flat hand on the counter top, and then spoke as if to it, "we got off of Pine Ridge, damn it, and my kids are gonna get a better shake than we got, Bonnie. A damn sight better."

"You're giving up too much, Bobby Red Skies," Choteau said, very softly at first. It was almost as if he was thinking out loud at the start. "You're killing yourself, brother. It's just like it is with Mary. You're giving up too much just to be safe. You're going to kill yourself, just like she has, Bobby." Choteau pushed his chair back with a screech and stood up, hands on the tabletop. "You tell me, Bobby. What's the difference between you and Mary, and what happened to Lennie? What's the difference, really? You're alive, I guess. But beyond that, what the hell's the difference, Bobby?"

"Here's some food," Bobby Red Skies said, in tones that were too even. "I think you'd better be going now."

"Yeah," Choteau said, then he turned quickly and tried to leave with an angry flourish. But as he turned, he tripped over his own chair. It was sitting right in front of him. But his shin got tangled up with it and he lost his footing, and almost in slow motion, reaching out all the way for something he couldn't see, he stumbled over onto the floor.

There was quiet as we all watched Choteau pick himself up. It was clear he didn't want any help. Not from any of us. And even Bonnie Red Skies recognized it. Once he found his footing again, he felt around for the table to steady himself. "You okay?" Bobby said finally and brought the food over in a paper sack.

"I'm fine," Choteau tried to stand at ease. "We better get moving, Professor man." But he didn't seem to know where I was. Then he took a couple steps and reached over to touch the older boy on the head. The two kids still had their arms around the old bulldog.

"You boys like old Protector, huh?" he said, as he scruffed the kid's short hair. "What's your name, son?"

"Leonard," the boy said.

"That's a good name, Leonard. You live up to it, you'll be a big man," Choteau said. "Would you like to keep this old bulldog, and take care of him for us, Leonard?"

"I don't think so, Choteau," Bobby Red Skies said. "Take the dog with you."

Choteau acted as if he hadn't heard Bobby. He kept his hand on the boy's head. "Leonard," he said. "What tribe are you? I'm a Lakota. What tribe are you?"

The boy was silent. He looked across the room at his mother.

"Get out, Choteau," Bobby Red Skies said. "And take your mutt with you." I set my coffee mug down, having only tasted it. Choteau scruffed the older boy's head again. "You're a Lakota, too, Leonard. Just like Red Cloud and Sitting Bull and Black Elk. And Little Big Man." He raised his head, trying to sense where I was, I think.

"And Crazy Horse," Bonnie Red Skies piped in.

Choteau nodded his head yes. "That's right. Crazy Horse, too," he said. Then he patted old Protector on the head. "Let's go, fella," Choteau said.

I stepped over to him so he could follow me out. "Crazy Horse," the littlest boy whispered.

Choteau paused and put a hand on the boy's head. "What's your name, little one?"

"Bernard," he said, in that factual lilt children have.

"You're Lakota, too.," Choteau said, "Bernard."

"And this one," Bonnie Red Skies hugged the toddler she held. "This is Anna. Anna Mae."

Choteau nodded once and picked up the bag of food. "Thanks," he said softly and then followed me out the steps, walking slowly and carefully.

Bobby Red Skies strode out behind us, with old Protector loyally trailing Choteau's every step across the barnyard. The blind and the infirm finding their way.

"Don't tell me where you're going," Red Skies said. "They'll be back asking questions. Sooner than I want to think about. And I'm a lousy liar."

"I noticed," Choteau said with a grin.

The cold snap to the air as we faced it made us hurry to the Renault. As I lifted the dog into the back seat, Red Skies walked around and filled our car up from the ranch's big tank. But the whole time he eyed the horizon on the hills above us.

Choteau settled himself in his seat with the grocery bag between his feet, and he seemed more relaxed now that he was seated and still.

I cranked the car over and put it in gear, but Choteau rolled the window down and called back to Bobby Red Skies. Bobby strolled around behind the car toward Choteau's window, then crossed his arms against the cold. "How's Jimmie?" Choteau yelled, too loudly really. He couldn't seem to judge the distance between himself and Red Skies. "He still in the Cities?"

I watched Bobby's hat nod in the rearview mirror. He didn't come near and bend down to the window, but stood back away from the car. It seemed he didn't want to get too close to us in the open, but maybe it was just the reek of our sweet, lived-in Renault.

"Jim's doing good," he said. "Making good money. He's still not married and settled down, had himself a couple of white girlfriends, but he's doing good."

Choteau nodded. "He ever come back out here? He keep in touch with you? Or with the res'? At all?"

"Never," Red Skies said, shaking his head and looking down for once.

"Well, tell him I asked after him, will ya?" Choteau started to roll the window up. "When you hear from him again," he said. He seemed convinced Jimmie Nordstrom would be back, and soon. Though he didn't tell any of us why.

Bobby Red Skies nodded as he stepped back further from the car. "Let's get outa here," Choteau muttered at me.

So I pulled out with a wave to Bobby Red Skies, but if he saw it he didn't let on. He didn't stand and watch the car drive away either. He was back in the house before we hit the lane in front of his place. The collie barked at us and chased the car all the way around the fence. The dog stood at attention, paws on the chain link, until we rose out of sight. Protector woofed once at him. That was our farewell.

We crested the hill and I turned south again, back for the highway, without asking. I assumed it was on to Pine Ridge now. Someone out there, someone soon, would take Choteau, or Crazy Horse, off my hands. But oddly, I wasn't in a rush anymore. Somehow, I hated to see this all end now. And I surprised myself at that.

Choteau was sullen though. He handed me a piece of plain bread out of the bag and then he fed the dog one. But he was silent. The old bulldog wolfed down a couple more slices, then burped and seemed satisfied to lick his chops. It was pretty simple fare, but I was hungry enough it tasted good. I chewed it slowly, letting it sink in.

Suddenly, Choteau jerked his door open, took that sack and hurled our groceries out like they were some kind of bomb ticking away. Just as quickly he slammed his door shut.

I chewed on the bread in my mouth and thought about how he hadn't eaten anything. For a moment, I yearned for that sweet HiC orange and the jar of peanut butter, long gone out on the snowy plains. It's funny what simple old hunger will do to you. HiC and Skippy, mind you. That's what I was missing.

"Some friends," I said, swallowing that last bite of bread. Choteau stared blindly out ahead of us. "Nothing like old chums you can count on," I said after waiting a while for him to answer.

Choteau cleared his throat, but he didn't speak. The bulldog burped again, then settled down in the backseat with our days old beer cans and Slim Jim wrappers, and his gnawed up highway patrolman's boot. Protector was sleepy, I guess, now that the feeding was over.

*　　　　*　　　　*

Driving down that dirt road out of the rough prairie, I could see our junction to the pavement in the distance. That highway stretched out like a gray ribbon on the horizon. As we pulled up to the blacktop, I steered over to turn right, to the west. "To Pine Ridge?" I said.

Choteau shook his head no.

"Where to?" I said, more than a little surprised. "Back to town?"

He nodded a yes, then said, "And cut south after that, on the highway to Nebraska."

"Where we going?"

He ran both hands back through his long hair, and said nothing.

"You figure they're looking for us to show up at Pine Ridge," I said. My spirits were lifting a little. This adventure wasn't over yet, and I was still in the driver's seat.

It took a long while for him to say, "Probably." But I got the impression he wasn't really thinking about the FBI or the Highway Patrol.

I shoved the car into reverse and wheeled back a little so I could turn east on the highway, and then Choteau started to talk. "There's a memorial ride over at Pine Ridge, Professor. It happens every year; on the anniversary, to remember the massacre. A group of riders take a vow to follow the route Big Foot and his people followed to Wounded Knee, back in 1890. Don't matter what the weather is, man, they ride that trail. It takes about seven days to cover it, Professor. And some of the riders, they fast, and they all pray the whole way. On the anniversary, they end up at the Knee, every year.

"It's not secret or anything like that. But we've always kept it small and quiet. Respectful, honorable. We don't want it to be some tv news special, you know. It's just something we do to pay our respects to the spirits there, and to remember what happened in the old days. We don't want it to become some wasicu Wild West show. You know?"

I shifted the car back into first. "The people you know back on Pine Ridge," I said, "they're on this memorial ride now, aren't they?"

He nodded his head.

"And if we show up there now, every state cop and FBI agent in South Dakota we'll be right behind us. And right behind them will be the media circus," I said. After I paused, I said, "And there might be some violence out of that."

Choteau just stared out the window. And it all made sense at the moment. It didn't occur to me right then that maybe those folks on the memorial ride would want to help Choteau out, that maybe they'd been looking for him to come and waiting impatiently, that maybe the most appropriate memorial of all for old Big Foot would be to help the spirit of Crazy Horse escape. But none of that came to my mind then. And Choteau sure didn't prompt me any.

"So what's in Nebraska?" I said.

"You know, Professor man," Choteau said, shifting around on me again like drifting snow. "Don't be too hard on Bobby. He's a good man, he just let himself get sidetracked. Moved off the res' and left his people; he's just confused. He's trying to be a white man, you know? But he'll come around." He paused, and then added this to his defense of Red Skies, "I'd trust him again." I felt like he was sending some message to me there, but I didn't understand what it was until later.

I turned the car out onto the pavement and drove east toward Martin. "He's still Lakota," Choteau said. "Sort of a reverse apple, you know, Professor. He's white on the outside. But under his skin, man, under that haircut and cowboy hat, he's red yet." Choteau laughed. "And not very deep down, either, man."

"That's why you threw out his food, huh?" I said.

Choteau shook his head and sat a while in silence. When Martin was in sight, he said, "In the old days, Professor, we stuck together." He held up a fist, white knuckled. "Like that," he said.

237

"So what's in Nebraska, Choteau?"

He grinned, opened that hand and rested it on his knee. "Maybe you're ready."

"You know some Indians down there?" I said. We hit the edge of Martin, and turned south at the crossroads.

"Not that," he said. "Were going to Camp Robinson, Professor."

"You mean Fort Robinson," I corrected him. "It's a state park now."

"Camp Robinson," he said again.

I looked over at him and he seemed small and frail then. He seemed lost and isolated, and it seemed everything he counted on out here had changed, or maybe even turned away. He was just a danger to everything he loved, and now he was nearly blind and nearly alone. Except for me. A history professor with an old French car and a new case of the homesick blues.

"You really believe this Crazy Horse stuff, don't you?" I said.

But the only answer I got was when Protector started to snore.

"Terri?" I said when she answered the phone. "It's me."

Choteau was facing me, gazing out the windshield in my direction. I don't know if he saw me, though. I was standing at a drive up pay phone outside the EAT cafe west of Gordon, Nebraska. I should have pulled up and talked while I sat inside the warm car, but I wanted the privacy. Choteau had gone silent on me for the rest of the drive. Ever since I'd asked him that Crazy Horse question. The one he wouldn't answer anymore.

"Are you all right?" Terri said.

At the sound of her voice, I could smell the fragrance of what she wears in her hair. I could see the dark shade of her neck next to that silver-white jewelry. I could feel the smooth soft curve of her hips in my arm.

"Is that you?" she asked when I didn't answer right away.

"I'm fine, Terri," I said. "Except I miss you."

"When are you coming home?" she said. It sounded inside me like some warm, earthy music. I had a home to come to, and it made my heart do the boogie-woogie.

"Soon as I can, Terri," I said. Then I added, "I don't think it will be long."

"Why? Where are you? What's going on?"

"I think we're about at the end of this, Terri. He's taking us to Camp, I mean, Fort Robinson."

I waited then for the idea of that to resonate with her, for it to sink in, the way it had with me. But I forgot. And it took me a while to realize that the whole world wasn't as far into this little time warp as I was.

"Where's that?" Terri said, sounding worried. "Mike left night before last, you know. He left in a hurry."

"I know," I said, and she was quiet, maybe too quiet on the other end. Then, because I had to trust her, I told her. "Terri, I need you to come out here. As soon as you can. To Camp, I mean, its Fort Robinson now. In Nebraska. As soon as you can."

"Nebraska?" she said. "What happened to Canada?"

"Terri, this is probably tapped," I said. "We can't talk forever. I probably said too much already."

"What's going on, Will? What are you talking about?"

"We're coming to the end of this, Terri. Remember when I told you he thinks he's Crazy Horse? Well, Fort Robinson is where Crazy Horse surrendered."

"He's going to turn himself in? Where is it?"

"Terri, listen to me. I don't know what he's planning to do. He's taking us to Camp Robinson. And it's not only where he surrendered, it's also where they killed him, Terri."

"Who?"

"Crazy Horse."

"But what has that got . . . "

"I told you, he thinks he's Crazy Horse, born again, or something."

She didn't say anything for a while, and I guess that goofy idea slowly sunk in. When she did speak, her voice was low and decided. "Will, he's sick. There's something wrong with him, and that's too bad. But he's also dangerous. It sounds like he's suicidal now, or something. And you don't seem to realize that. I want you to get away from him."

"Terri."

"No, you listen. I want you to call Mike. And I want you to get away from him."

"How did you know I have a way to call your brother?" I said.

"You could get hurt, Will."

"How did you know?"

Now her voice just grew sharp and angry. "I didn't, Will. Just get out of there. Please."

I wanted to believe her.

"He says you've been telling them everything."

"Who does?"

"I'll let you figure that out, Terri. I need you out here. I think. And they're probably tracing this call right now, so I've got to go."

"Will, they don't need to trace it. You're telling them where you're headed, for God's sake. This Camp Robington place."

"Robinson," I said. Then I told her I loved her, no matter what happened.

"Will?" she said, then instead of saying she loved me back, she said something better. Words that, right then, had the ring of love and hope resounding in them. "Fort Robinson," she said. "Nebraska." And that's when someone, or something, cut us off.

*　　　　　*　　　　　*

240

"Where to?" I said as we drove into Fort Robinson State Park about nine that night. It was dark, since there was no moon in the clear winter sky, and the park was closed up tight for the winter.

I'd been here before, of course, several times in several different summers of research. I knew my way around and nowhere better than inside the Historical Society Museum. Its library of source materials upstairs was invaluable to research like mine. The research I used to do. Back when I was a professor of time.

But in the dead of winter this place was different. It looked like a small college campus during winter break. There were a few streetlights glowing here and there, for security I suppose. But there was not a footprint anywhere to be seen in the snow that covered every walkway, every lane, every street. It was all blanketed, except where they'd plowed open the main highway, U.S. 20, that cuts across the south edge of the park. The buildings were sealed, the curtains drawn, the porches had drifted with snow and even the street signs were frosted with ice and hard to read.

To the north the black shadows of buttes stretched out around us like a dark crescent under the starry sky. Nestled there under those foothills of the Paha Sapa, Fort Robinson had become quite the tourist complex. The old barracks and officers quarters were vacation lodges now, up for rent from Memorial Day to Labor Day. They lined the dark streets alongside the rows of bare maple trees. Back from the highway were the stables, the rodeo arena, the tennis courts and the covered swimming pool. Tucked over between the elk pasture and the peak of Crow Butte lay the polo field. To the south of the highway, the campgrounds and the now frozen over fishponds hid out behind the baseball diamond. In the center of it all, next to the parade ground, stood the old post headquarters, now the

Fort Robinson Museum, where the doctors of history spent their days and dreamed their dreams about time.

I think that's when it really hit me. There in the snowy shadows of polo fields and tennis courts, my little career with its library carrels and its books and monographs seemed like just one more covered swimming pool on those old, battered grounds. I was just another children's fishpond. Another entertainment, a fancy-assed distraction from what was real and important. I was just another government fed prostitute jerking Bernard Choteau around, using him to get what I needed, and not caring at all about much else.

And what was real and important was sitting right there beside me in that Renault. And it was waiting for me, I hoped, back in Missouri. And it didn't have anything to do with books or carrels or careers.

That may have been the moment I stopped being a doctor of time, you know. I was lost again. Really lost, with no direction home.

All around me, old Fort Robinson had become quite the attraction. In the summer, when I'd been here before, amongst all the fishing and riding and stealing of home plate, there were few signs of the World War II prisoner-of-war camp, of the training facility for the "K9 Corps" where we taught our dogs to be soldiers, of the field where Dull Knife's Cheyenne fought the last battle on their desperate run north from Oklahoma, of the surrender of Crazy Horse's "Sioux." It had all seemed too clean and safe in the summer to be haunted. Though I'd harbored my hopes, back then. But now I saw it again, and even sealed up in the dead of winter, empty and alone, it was just too neat and tidy for any ghosts to wander here.

They had to be driven in from prisons in the East, in little yellow Renaults, I guess.

"Turn here," Choteau said, once we'd driven past the Lodge and the Museum. I knew where he was taking us, of course.

I pulled the car off Highway 20 and hurtled us down a snow covered street beneath signs that pointed to

"Campgrounds" and "Fishing Access." But we weren't going fishing. Camping out was not in our plans.

What was in our plans was still secret from me. Though by this point, I had my fears. And suddenly, the documents and the history were gone. I needed to save Bernard Choteau, and then get back home.

"You know, Choteau," I said, as I let the Renault slide to a stop beneath a tall, stone pyramid. "Crazy Horse did two things here. He didn't just die here. He surrendered, too. Right here, you know."

Choteau didn't even let on I was talking. Just south of the pyramid, two log cabins nestled in the snow. The cabin closest to us had one barred window in its north wall, facing us. "So what are we here for, Chief?" I said. "'Cause if you're here to get yourself killed, I don't want anything to do with it."

He laughed and said, "Do I seem like I want to die, Professor man?" He popped the door open and slipped out of the car, laughing hardily. But not all laughter seems merry.

As I climbed out, stretching my knee again and testing my weight on it, he headed straight for that monument. It was a concrete and stone pyramid, maybe eight feet tall, done in good old 1930 's WPA style. A bronze plaque was mounted on its side. I didn't need to read it to know what it said. I doubt Choteau needed to read it either. But he went over and touched it, as if it was Braille. It said something about near this spot Crazy Horse was killed in 1877.

I reached back and lifted old Protector out of the backseat. I felt the old bulldog shiver as I lifted him out into the cold. Sheltered by this cup of buttes and foothills, the wind did little but swirl here when it managed to get around the Black Hills. It was a lot easier for those northwest blasts to fall down on Rapid City and the Badlands, than it was to cut through these canyons and hollows. But even out of the wind, the hard cold of late December night sat on us. And that old bulldog was growing tired of winter. We may have saved him from a drift, but the living hadn't been easy with us these last few days. His fragile shivering in my arms reminded me of that. There just wasn't much left of this old bulldog. Time had worn him away, like running water on an old rock.

Protector snuggled his big mug into my chest, so I carried him instead of setting him down in the snow. And I reached down to the floor of the car, and got his chewed up boot, too. Then I walked over to Choteau, with his hands still pressed on that bronze plaque.

"The Lakota put this up in the thirties," he said. "Back before the government rebuilt these cabins and made it an historic site. Back when there wasn't anything here but this marker."

A sigh leaked out of me then. I couldn't help it. "Yeah, you know," I said, "you do scare me, Choteau."

"You think I want to die, huh?"

"I told you before, Choteau. I got a brother-in-law who's with the FBI. I can get in touch with him and . . . "

"You don't get it, do you, Professor." He leaned on the stone marker and seemed to speak to it and not to me. "The only way I can surrender to the Feds, man, is in broad daylight and with a crowd watching. And even then, it would be a chance. They don't want me to surrender, man, they want me to resist arrest. They want an excuse to even the score, man. Don't kid yourself, Professor."

"Well," I said, "Golman is my brother-in-law . . . "

"They don't care if this guy is your mother, and it's God damn Mother's Day, Professor," he yelled. Then his voice fell low again, "I'm telling you, it don't matter."

He turned then and walked off to the cabins just south of the markers. I followed him, quietly, hugging the bulldog to me and limping by a series of "historical markers" that explained the layout. But I didn't need any markers. I'd studied them all. I knew them by heart.

Two log cabins sit there, reconstructed by the Nebraska Historical Society. The one to the north is a replica of the guardhouse in 1877. Crazy Horse was lead there one September afternoon, under a guard of soldiers and Indians, with Little Big Man at his side. He struggled in the doorway of that guardhouse and wound up stabbed in the back. Just to the south of there, maybe twenty or thirty feet away, sits the replica of the adjutant's quarters. At about midnight of that day in 1877, Crazy Horse died on the floor of those quarters, refusing at the end to lie in a bed.

So it was with no small measure of relief that I watched Choteau kick in the door of the guardhouse, and disappear inside. In the symmetry I'd set up in my head, it seemed that he was choosing the prison, and not the death of Crazy Horse. But you can read the way he moved that night a half dozen different ways. At least a half dozen.

I left Protector with his trusty boot in Choteau's lap and brought the sleeping bags and blankets from the car. With every squeaking step in the snow, my leg felt stronger and surer, and lifted my spirits. I knew then we could get out of this alive. Maybe even alive and better off.

We shoved the door to the guardhouse closed and curled up on the stone floor inside our bags. This time I held Protector with me, and it seemed the second he was warm, the bulldog dozed straight off. With the boot lying by his head, he snored and drooled on my shoulder.

It felt good to stretch out, and in the cold, even the layers of filth on me were comfortable. Insulation, I guess. But though I kept dozing off, I wasn't really sleepy.

I lay there in the quiet, falling gently asleep and then waking filled with ideas about our situation. And feeling optimistic for the first time in a long, long while. In years, I suppose. Maybe it seemed we'd run out of highways and gas, had come to the end of our road. But I didn't think so.

I have no idea how long I spent like that, but it could have been several hours.

After a while, I started to explain all this to Choteau, to show him the way home, I thought. When I said his name in the dark to rouse him, I found out he was wide awake.

"You know, we could do it in the daylight. And we could make our own crowd, too, Choteau. I've already called Terri, back there in Gordon this evening. I'11 just get a hold of her again, and she'll bring some others."

Choteau rose up on his elbow. Then he laughed out loud at me, that same rich laugh without the old merry in it. "Oh," he said, when he could get a breath, "this gets better and better."

"Surely you know some folks up at Pine Ridge. Folks who weren't on this memorial ride. Right? They'd come down and act as witnesses, and there's Bobby Red Skies and those people up in Dakota. He'd come down, wouldn't he? And bring others?"

Choteau flopped down again on his back, still laughing at me. "Sure. Right," he'd say in bursts. Then laugh some more. He curled the bag up around him against the cold.

"I mean it, Choteau. We could do this." Though I could barely see it in the dark guardhouse, I knew the breath of every word we said was steam in the air. "If we get enough witnesses together and I get Golman out there, we could do it safely."

"Go to sleep, Professor," was all he said. He seemed tired of laughing.

"What about Mary Red Skies?" I said. I was desperate, I guess. I had to reach him. "She would come, if you called? Wouldn't she?"

His laughter stopped and he heaved a weary sigh.

"I bet she'd come, Choteau. If you called her," I said. Then I pushed it too far, I think. "She ought to, Choteau. She's the one got you into this. She's the reason you broke out."

246

There was a sudden moment of deep silence, and even I wouldn't break it. Then the dog snorted in his sleep. Choteau said, evenly, "I'm an adult now, Professor. I'm responsible for what I choose to do. There's nobody else to blame here; nobody but me. Got it?"

So I stopped trying to talk to him. He seemed lost in his own ways, and it was pointless. But that didn't mean I gave up hope. I lay there on the floor, cradling a snoring bulldog, and imagining how it would go tomorrow. I decided I didn't need any of the Red Skies clan; after all, what had they ever been but trouble, anyway? Maybe he was right. You couldn't count on them. But I trusted Terri. She would come. And through her, I trusted Golman too.

"You know, Choteau. I don't believe you," I said and started to crawl out of my bag into the cold. I wrapped the bag around old Protector and tucked him in, while I said, "I'm going to call Terri, and get this set up. Tomorrow evening, Choteau, we'll get us out of this safe. I know we can do it. And I know something else," I stood up and looked down at his back turned to me. "You didn't kill those agents, my friend. You didn't do it, but you know who did."

I didn't let him respond; I just turned and walked out. My knee was sore, but I turned on it and it felt good to put the weight on it. I walked through the ankle deep snow across the old parade ground, headed for the museum, working that stiffness out of my knee with every step. There was a pay phone, on a telephone pole out in front of the museum building. I'd used it several times in the summers before.

Twenty cents got me the operator. I placed the collect call to Terri, and stood listening to the phone ring and planning the way she'd be here to save us in my head. "Drive all night, babe. Come on back to me and save us all," I called out inside my head.

"Doesn't seem to be anyone home, sir," the operator said. "Maybe you could try later."

But I made her let that phone ring five minutes more at least, before I gave up and the operator wore out.

Suddenly I knew I'd just wanted to talk to her, to hear Terri's voice. I wanted to tell her I needed her again. I'd asked her to come before, just that afternoon in Gordon. But at that point, I didn't know why. It was just a need. Now I understood and I wanted to shout it out to her, sing it out to her. Long distance calling: Save us, baby, save us, with your bright green eyes. Be our witness, be our cover, baby, be our salvation.

But she wasn't home. Or she didn't answer.

She was already on the road, on her way here, I told myself. I'd asked her to come and so she was rolling on across those plains. And I worried then about how to reach her, how to find her, how to work this whole surrender deal out.

Walking back across the snowy ground, I saw myself. Dirty, grungy, on the run with some convict, abandoning her during the holidays, and now asking her to drop everything and come rushing halfway across a continent, just because I loved her. Suddenly, I loved her. I cry for help, and expect her to jump to my rescue. But what, really, had I done lately to even hope for that kind of love? I just up and abandon her, drive away to get myself into some loony trouble, and then I decide to say, "I need you, babe."

Would I drive all night across Nebraska in the dead of winter because she called?

"You bet I would," I said out loud to the empty parade ground. But there were no marching bands out there, and part of me wondered. If it was Terri who ran away with some stranger, then called me collect from every small town phone booth on the Great Plains, would I give it all up for her?

By the time I stamped the snow from my feet and stepped back into the guardhouse, I felt lost again. Choteau was still lying on the floor, his back to me. Old Protector lifted his head though, and panted in my direction. If a dog could smile, he was grinning at me with his big ugly mug. Now there

248

was loyalty and love, but I'd done something to deserve it. Hadn't I?

"I'm starved," I said, and Choteau stirred. "We gotta go back to Crawford, get something to eat. Maybe then I'll sleep. But I'm going nuts now, Choteau."

He rubbed the sleep from his eyes, one at a time, with his fingertips. Then Choteau got up, pulled on his shoes and carried loyal Protector to the car.

Thursday, before daylight

A little after midnight we drove into Crawford, a mile or so down the road from the park. Everything there was closed and everyone was sound asleep, except for a roadhouse at the edge of town. The shining beer signs in the windows lured me in, after we'd cruised the U-shaped strip searching for a real restaurant, without any luck. So I pulled up in front of this beer joint without a name. Hank Williams wailed muffled blues at us from some jukebox the minute I killed the engine.

"I'll wait out here," Choteau said.

"Want anything?" I saw visions of beers and burgers dancing with the Hamm's bear to "Your Cheating Heart" inside.

"I'm not hungry," he said. "Dog prob'ly need to pee, though, huh? And he could eat some, I'm sure." He got out holding Protector, and set him gently on the ground. There was a lot of love, and a lot of loss, in the way he cradled that dog.

"How 'bout some beer?" I said, over the top of the car to him. I put all my weight on my bum knee and it felt sore, but sound.

He just shrugged. Like I say, when he acted like that he really scared me. I figured I'd bring out a six pack and a big bag of as many sandwiches as they had. Choteau would eat when he smelled that food. And then maybe he'd be reasonable.

So I strolled in to this old grease and gas to Hamm up. What I'll always regret is I didn't stop to pat old Protector on the head as I strutted past him. The dog was limping around toward the corner of the building, sniffing and searching for

250

just the right spot. But I was too hungry to see, and he'd be waiting in the backseat when I came out. Of course, he would.

I stood at the end of the bar inside while a peach-fuzz kid eyed me. The kid fried up a grill full of burgers for us. Two lonely old men sat sipping draughts at the other end of the bar, beside the big jar of pigs' feet. They eyed me, too. But nobody said a word, and I didn't feel much like offering up small talk. I just looked over the collection of plastic bar lights, the rippling waters and the marching Clydesdales, the Hamm's bear in a Santa suit, and let my mouth water at the greasy smells. The two men looked me over, the scruffy beard and the flannel shirt I'd slept in for days, and shook salt in their beers.

I knew they'd have plenty to say when I left.

I paid the kid when he brought over a six pack and a white bag stuffed full of burgers. Then I pulled out one of the sandwiches and sank happily into my first bite of real food that day. I hung the six pack from my thumb and stuffed the bag under my arm. All so I could keep a hand free to munch that bun full of grease and gristle with mustard and pickle. It tasted like heaven.

"See you, boys," I said as I turned to walk out. "Nice chatting with you."

"Yeah. Right. Uhm," they grunted, and looked startled.

I laughed at them then, and strutted out the door. My mouth was pleasantly full of hamburger.

But I didn't laugh for long.

Outside there was no Choteau and no bulldog to be seen. They'd disappeared somewhere. Instead there were two men in suits and overcoats standing between me and the car. A brown Blazer was parked right up against the Renault, and a

251

third suit and overcoat was leaning in the Blazer's open door, speaking to the CB radio. That one was an overcoat I knew.

"Hey, buddy!" Golman said cheerfully. He hooked the mouthpiece back on the dash and wheeled around straight, out of the Blazer. It was a move he'd made a few times before.

"Where's you partner, buddy?" he said. His white teeth flashed under the little moustache.

I glanced around quickly, not turning my head, just switching my eyes back and forth. I looked plenty suspicious. Wherever Choteau and Protector had gone, they were out of sight.

"Partner?" I said, then swallowed that mouthful of burger hard.

Sirens were crying in the distance, somewhere down Highway 20. The two overcoats took a couple steps toward me, and seemed to go for the pistols tucked under their armpits. All I had stuck under my pit was a bag o' burger meat fresh grilled.

"Hey," Golman said softly and held up a hand. "That won't be necessary, fellas. This is a relative of mine." His little moustache gave me a sweet, toothy smile. "My brother-in-law. Right, buddy?" he began to saunter slowly toward me. His chin was high.

I could see the flashing lights of two highway patrol cars speeding toward us. Red, white and blue flaring like the Aurora Borealis against the December sky.

"Where's Choteau?" Golman said. He came up to me, still smiling sweetly. The two other agents stood right behind him. He whispered under his breath, "Just tell us, chum, I'll take care of the rest." Then he winked at me, with the eye hidden from his compadres.

"Choteau?" I said. "I left him back in Martin. Back in South Dakota."

Behind me, I heard the hinges creak in the cold. Those two lonely drinkers and the peach-fuzz kid pressed out the door of the bar to see what was going on, with all the lights and sirens.

Golman reached out and put his hand on my shoulder. It was a fatherly sort of gesture. "Come on, buddy," he said. "It'll be easier on everybody concerned."

But I couldn't help my reaction. It was pure instinct. I jerked my shoulder back free of his touch, and I glared at him angrily. His mustache curled over his lip then, and his jaw set while Golman sighed out his frustration with me. That's when I first heard this low growl rising out of a ditch clear on the other side of the highway. I looked past Golman over his shoulder, for Protector, and then the growl gathered up into an open mouthed snarl. The three agents ignored it all, concentrating on me, and maybe on those sirens that seemed a constant now behind us. But I was searching for Protector out there somewhere.

He came roaring up out of the ditch then, snarling and frothing, barreling toward Golman with the spirit of some Doberman pup. But he ran like he was locked in slow motion. All his years and that mean arthritis dragged him down, I guess. I watched him as he loped across the pavement, pathetic, nearly dragging his stiff hind legs, all heart and no muscle. Still, with his bared teeth and the hot drool running out of his big mug, and with the snarl roiling up and down in his throat, he was frightening enough. If I'd been Mike Golman just then, I'd be wondering which way to run from a rabid dog.

As soon as Protector reached the pavement, Golman and his two buddies twisted around to see what was causing all that ruckus behind them. For a moment, they forgot about me. And there they were. All three of them, with their backs to me. Three nice little military crew cuts in a row, like little pumpkins on a log. Golman's pumpkin included. All of them, just waiting. But I didn't know what to do about it. I tossed away the burger then, to free my right hand for something.

I think that's when the patrolman driving that lead car saw Protector. That big highway patrol car was bearing down hard on the dog, you see. I wanted to yell out, "No," but the word got stuck in my throat. I guess that cop was a decent guy though, because he started to brake right then and he tried to swerve the car around and miss the old dog. But the big black and white Olds, speeding on those winter Dakota highways, just twisted and went right into a sideways skid. A skid that was headed straight for old, chugging Protector.

I didn't want to watch, but I couldn't look away, somehow. This was a race old Protector was going to lose. That big white and black Olds was screeching right at him, out of control. But the old dog was oblivious to it. The bulldog was pawing on toward Golman, charging to my rescue. Even if he wasn't going to make it, even if he was going to meet the driver's side of a speeding Oldsmobile along the way, he was charging at us with everything he had. That Olds never even gave him pause. It was one of the bravest things I've ever seen, you know. I couldn't turn away.

Golman had a hand raised, and he yelled, "Look out." I'm not sure to who or what. There didn't seem to be anything any of us could do. We were going to watch the old bulldog go rolling under that patrol car. In my mind, I could already see Protector's limp body careening like some piece of meat across the concrete and ice, and it was all out of our hands.

The second patrol car was braking now too, trying to stay out of the way of his skidding partner.

All that dog saw was Mike Golman though. His front paws jerked stiffly in the air, and they bit into the concrete, pulling him as hard as he could at the man who'd just set a threatening hand on my shoulder. It was that little jerk free I made, the hands off shrug I gave to Golman, that's what started this whole deadly race. And Protector meant to save me, if it was the last thing he did.

That's when I noticed Choteau. His head popped up out of the ditch, the same ditch Protector had charged out of seconds before. I don't know if Choteau could see what was happening, but he sensed enough, somehow. Maybe it was the sirens screaming, and the screeching of those hot tires on the cold street, but he understood what was happening. And he knew what to do.

In one smooth leap, Bernard Choteau sprang up out of the ditch. For a while, he seemed the only thing in the whole world that could move quickly. Everything else was nearly in a freeze frame: skidding Olds, chugging dog, pointing cops. But Choteau was moving, floating through the air in a perfect arch. He dove head first and arms out, dove for that old dog.

"That's him," one of the three agents yelled.

The instant they spoke, Choteau landed on the pavement on his curled shoulder, with his arms he wrapped up the bulldog in a hug, and the two of them went into a roll across the highway. The skidding patrol car was spinning around again, until it slid backwards down the pavement. I could see the Nebraska cop inside sitting helplessly out of control, with his hands off the steering wheel.

Golman and his two feds had pistols in their hands then. I never saw them reach or draw. The guns were just there, like absurd fingers pointing at Choteau and Protector, as they rolled across the road. The guns began to fire. I didn't hear them, not that I recall, but I can still see the kick of those pistols jerking in their hands. That "No" was still stuck in my throat.

Choteau and the bulldog rolled just out of the skidding patrol car's path. The rear fender missed them by inches at best, I suppose. Then that Olds slid on about another hundred feet, and came to a rocking halt. The officer inside put his hands back on the wheel, and he sat there with the engine purring and watched the second patrol car behind him slide off the road. That second car slammed down nose first into the same snowy ditch where Choteau and Protector had been hiding. The car's trunk and rear fender sat up in the air, wheels spinning, and its red and blue lights flashed at the sky, reflecting off the snow.

But Choteau and the bulldog just kept on rolling, and those three pistols kept on kicking at them. I heard the gunfire now, but only through a round of loud cheers.

I turned and saw the two drunks and the peach-fuzz kid tumbling over themselves down out of the roadhouse door. They were cheering as they ran. I guess they didn't understand what all the patrol cars and the Feds were about. They'd just seen a man dive in front of a speeding car to save a dog. They had fireworks, crashing cars and a hero besides. They were rooting for Choteau and the mutt.

I don't know what would have happened if they'd run right out into the gunfire. Would those agents have stopped? Or were they so set on killing Bernard Choteau that some innocent bystanders were a sacrifice they'd make? Would they even have paused to think about it?

I shifted the six pack to my free right hand. Gripping the plastic casing hard, I raised those cans, curled back, and heaved all my weight behind them. I swung the six pack around like a club, and smacked those three pumpkin heads as hard as I could. One, two, three bumps they went, with my forearm and then my shoulder following the swing like I was some kind of linebacker. And down they went, all in a row. All three little crewcuts. I watched them fall as I spun around following the swing of my beer can club. The cans had ruptured, and they were spraying beer foam on everything.

I didn't go down right away. I stood there a long moment, saw those three FBI agents lying in the snow and those patrol car lights flashing all around. Somehow, without seeing or hearing them, I knew that Choteau and Protector were rolling on, untouched. I lifted my right arm, and let go of that stringer full of ruptured, foaming cans. It dropped between the legs of one of those agents, and fizzed all over his squirming pants leg. I licked the wet beer off my wrist, and then I finally realized I should run. These feds weren't down for the count. They'd be up and cuffing me away in moments. There was no time to rest on my laurels.

I moved to turn around and run for it, but a pain clapped up through my leg, and then my bum knee folded under me. I don't really remember how I got there. But the next thing I knew, I was lying on the ground, right beside those three Feds. Just another pumpkin in the snow. I smelled those greasy burgers and realized I'd landed on top of the bag and ruptured it open on the snow. One of the agents nearest me was spattered with mustard and pickle relish, the other had half of a bun pasted to his overcoat. The two sirens were whining away and the cheers of the bar gang were still ringing out, but over it all now my knee was screaming in my ears.

I lay there in the trodden snow, my hands wrapped around my knee, trying to hold its screaming down. Through the pain, I watched the two Feds get up, rubbing their crew cuts. Then they ran off somewhere, wearing my buns and relish, and ignored me. Golman had only fallen down on hands and knees. He stood up, dusting snow off his gloved hands. "God damn," he said, shaking his cracked head a little. Then he pulled me up onto my good foot. He mumbled something about, "If it weren't for my sister."

I had to throw an arm around his shoulders to stand. He nearly carried me to the Blazer, but I hopped along with him as best I could.

"Son of a bitch," he said, though he still refused to touch the back of his beer soaked head. "You just don't believe in making life simple," he said. "Do you."

It wasn't a question.

A little ride in the Blazer and I was installed snugly inside an empty yellow-green room down at the Crawford Post Office. I imagine there was a jail in that little town, and I know Golman kept me out of it. But he did leave one patrolmen posted outside the door. Procedure was procedure, and trust was trust. I was under guard, because he was trying to save me from myself. But I was alone for a while. I've no idea how long. The light glowed bright fluorescent inside, and it made a mirror of the window out into the dark. I reached over, saw myself wince at moving the knee, and shut the Venetian blinds. That raised a small cloud of dust. I sat there, watched the particles settle under the white light. I flexed my hand, and felt the

257

cuts my little nightstick work with that six pack had left. My mind seemed numb, though generally I wished my knee was.

Golman came back and brought hamburgers. More burgers. I'm sure they were fried by the same peach-fuzz kid. It was the only food in town at this hour. But I wasn't hungry this time. He had coffee too, in real mugs not styrofoam, bless his soul.

He sat down across a plain wood table from me, unwrapped a burger. Before he ate, or said a word, he reached in his suit coat pocket and pulled out a bottle of ibuprofen. Generic. He spilled some out on the table and took a couple with his coffee. "Good for headaches," he said, grinning.

I scooped up three or four quickly and chewed them up, then chased the bitter taste with black coffee.

"Easy," he said.

What I really needed was a couple stiff shots of something strong. Vodka or Irish whiskey, maybe even straight gin. But I knew there wasn't a chance. Not from Golman, not while we were on duty, you know. I had to be "debriefed" first.

He took a good bite from a hamburger and leaned back in the old, wood office chair. "Listen, don't worry, buddy," he said once he swallowed. While his lips smacked and his tongue cleaned his teeth, he said, "I got your ass covered. You know?" He touched the back of his head. "Even if you did assault a couple of officers. They're good men, buddy. They'll keep their mouths shut, as long as we get Choteau. You know?" A drink of coffee, a couple more smacks. "Connor and Rolston, they won't say anything. Not if they're told not to. But we're gonna need your cooperation now. You gotta play along with this. Okay?"

I drank coffee and looked past him at the line that divided the two-tone wall in half. Pale shit yellow on top, deep shit green underneath. I was sinking in it.

"What about the other one?" I said. "We left that South Dakota cop tied up in his back seat. Remember? Can you fix that too, Golman?" I laughed at him then, and it felt good too. "Do you reach that far, Golman?"

His eyes narrowed at the laughter, then he said, staring right in my retinas, "I can cover your ass, Will. If you let me." He stared at me a moment longer, then he looked up at the ceiling. "You were kidnapped, okay?" he said, while he looked back down at his food and took another bite, avoiding my eyes the whole while. "Nothing to it, buddy. None of this other stuff happened. Not here, not back in South Dakota. But what we need to know is," he swallowed hard and started the smacking and cleaning again, "where was Choteau headed to?"

I laughed. I grinned at Golman. Then I reached into the bag and pulled out a burger. I wasn't really hungry anymore, but it was a nice nonchalant gesture. It kept my cool. "Is he all right?" I asked right back. "Or did you shoot him? Is he dead?" I unwrapped the white paper and saw the greasy burger in the clear, fluorescent light. Hard to believe it had tasted like heaven half an hour before.

"How 'bout you answer my questions first, okay? Then comes your turn. Don't think you can push this connection with my little sister too far. You're a lucky man, chum. I'm your best break in years. Don't blow it." He put his hand on one of his temples and rubbed it. Other than the pills, it was the first concession he'd made to the crack I'd laid on his skull. At least in my presence.

I took a bite of the burger and found out I was hungry. Hungry enough to eat this.

"Where was Choteau headed?" Golman said.

"You know, Mike," I said, "It's not what you think. If you're looking for bombs and conspiracies and so on," I chuckled and rested my elbows on the table. "You're looking wrong. It's a lot simpler than that."

"How so?" he said, obviously letting me talk.

"It's an old lover, Golman," I laughed at him. "His old girlfriend, from high school, if you can believe it. She writes him a letter and calls him up at the joint and says she's leaving her husband. She says she wants him, and so he sneaks out of jail. There's no left wing revolution in the works, Golman. He's not a terrorist. He's just a sucker."

Golman frowned. "You think we don't know about the Red Skies woman and her letter?" he said. "But you're sure that's it? She's not just a cover, or something. She's not a connection?"

I nodded and drank a sip of coffee.

"They had a kid, Mike. She had a little boy, right after they split. Then she married this doctor in North Dakota. Choteau broke out because he loved her, man. You should understand that, Mike. In your situation." I grinned at him.

Golman glanced down and away when I said that. A six pack across the back of the head might not slow him down, but he had some tender spots, I guess. "He was up for parole in six weeks, but she needed him now, I guess. So he blew it, you know. 'Cause he loved her. The sap."

"He wouldn't have got parole," Golman said evenly. It seemed like he was eager to get back to this police work, eager to get away from subjects like love and children.

"It 's almost funny, Mike, if it weren't so sad," I said. "The guys about blind now. He's brokenhearted over this woman. And he's half nuts, Golman. He thinks he's . . . " I dropped it there. It seemed like a sacrilege or something, to tell him about the Crazy Horse stuff. And I don't know, maybe I believed in Choteau again. It's hard to say what's real in the wee hours, in the dark. Maybe I believed him again. I at least had my doubts.

But when I paused, Golman pounced. He sat up straighter in that stiff chair, said, "He thinks he's what?"

"Never mind," I said.

Golman stared up at the crap yellow ceiling and sighed in exasperation.

"There's no big case to crack here, Mike. He's just broken. This woman he loves betrayed him, and everybody he knows on the reservation, all the movement people you're worried about, they're all dead or scattered or locked up or busy. Or they've given up. He's not worth all this trouble, Golman. We should just leave him alone, and let him rest."

Golman leaned forward, "They haven't given up, Will. I know they haven't." His eyebrows arched and he waited for some secrets he couldn't share with me to sink in through my thick skull. Then he picked up his mug and cradled it in both hands like it was the globe. "He thinks he's what?"

"You wouldn't understand."

"Try me."

"Hell, I don't understand it."

"Maybe I will, buddy. We know a lot about these people, you know. I might just understand more than you think."

"I don't think so. Not this time."

"He thinks he's what?" Golman sank back against the seat and threw up an open hand. "What?" he repeated.

"This one is beyond you, Golman. Trust me."

The highway patrolman opened the door just then. "Mike?" he said. These police were all on a first name basis. One for all stuff, you know. And that set me to thinking about what Choteau had said. About how he would never come out of any surrender alive.

Golman got up and strode out. He and the patrolman and at least one other voice talked for a few minutes. I chewed quietly on my burger and tried to listen in, but it was all too muffled. All of it, except when Golman yelled, "What?" not long after he stepped out of the room. Beyond that, all I could sense was a new urgency in their voices. Then I heard him bark out a few orders. I knew that order tone in his voice, even when I didn't know what he said.

He stepped back into the room and closed the door behind him. Leaning on it, he eyed me carefully, thinking something over. He seemed stumped, frustrated. His eyes narrowed a little, and then he said, "Have you talked to Terri?"

"How is she?" I asked him back.

Golman brightened up immediately at that. His white teeth came out, sparkling under the little brown mustache. "She's all right," he said. "Considering what she's been through."

261

I sat back in the plain chair I was in, and tried to adjust my foot so my knee would be comfortable. There was no way for it, though. The pain in my knee helped me to dodge the worry that Golman was shooting my way. I suppose it was why I moved.

"I just talked to her this evening," Golman sauntered over and leaned on his hands on the back of his chair. "She's back in Missouri, a little lonely, but she's getting by."

"When?" I asked, quicker than I should have.

"About seven, eight o'clock."

"You're lying, Golman. I called her about ten and she's gone. She's on her way here."

"Oh she is, is she?" he laughed, walked around the chair and sat down. He looked at the floor for a while, then sat back and picked up the coffee mug. "Need more?" he gestured with his cup. I just shook my head no.

"You must have called the wrong place, Will," he said then. "She's up with my folks, buddy. Up home at the lakes."

He had me squirming, and he knew it. "God damn knee," I muttered as I shifted around the hard chair. But he didn't buy it.

"She still cares about you, brother. I can't figure it out, but she does," he chuckled. I didn't laugh though, so he changed his tack. "This has been hard on her, you know. You put her in a tough spot, chum. Between me and the Bureau, and you and your Indian pals. That's not real fair of you."

I nodded my head. I wanted to say something about how it wasn't entirely my fault, that she was all for it at the start, but that would have sounded stupid.

"Hey, brother-in-law, listen up. Please," he said, and looked dead serious again. "She called me. Got it. She's the reason we know you're out here, near the park."

I couldn't look at him. Suddenly I was identifying with Choteau, the broken Choteau in my mind. The betrayed one.

"She told us about the Red Skies woman, buddy. She tipped us off to that and to where you two were in South Dakota. We've been following you, thanks to Terri, since Tuesday. Since you left Tecumseh, Kansas."

262

I felt weak then, like I was going to crack up or something, but I tried to hide it. It was fear, I guess, but it was more than just that. It was as low as I'd ever felt, lower than hospitals and wakes and funerals. Lower than ever. And Golman knew it, too. Because he kept on pushing.

"We lost you, too. You disappeared somewhere in South Dakota on Wednesday night. Couldn't find you anywhere. But then Terri called us again, buddy. She told us you were headed for Fort Robinson State Park. And so," he grinned and raised his hands. "Here we are."

"It was you guys, wasn't it. You got to Mary Red Skies, didn't you," I said, but I wasn't asking any questions. The little bit of anger rising in me felt good. It was better than sinking into the dark.

"We sent some people to find her, yeah," Golman sipped from his coffee. "Seemed like she was just a doctor's wife on a little spree. She went home, soon as we talked with her. As soon as we explained what she was getting into. She claimed she had nothing to do with Bernard Choteau. Not in twenty-five years, anyway."

"You bastards," I said. They had turned her over. They had talked their sense to her, and she'd turned him in. And if they could do it to Mary Red Skies, then they could turn Terri over too. After all, I'd left her there in Golman's hands, with nothing but the night news and her brother to trust. He could turn her over.

"He killed two agents, buddy. You know we don't forget that," Golman said in that flat voice again. There were depths to that even voice I'd never heard before. "Now he wants to be a home wrecker, too."

"That's rich, Golman. That's really rich. Take out your own problems on him." I laughed in his face, and he steeled himself enough at my bitter laugh that I knew he hated it, and he hated me. I was real close to burning my bridges here, but at the moment it seemed worth the warmth of the fire. It might make me feel stronger. "How is Jacki, anyway? Did you talk to her at Christmas, Mike?" Just using her first name was enough to set us off.

"Help us bring him in, buddy," Golman said, "and I'll get you home to Terri before you can say 'There's no place like home,' man. Maybe before you lose her." Then he said my name. Not "buddy" or "chum," but my name. "Will," he said. It made him sound genuine. Almost.

I thought about the offer, and then it dawned on me what it all meant. What the hot conversation in the hallway was all about.

"He got away," I smirked at him. "Didn't he?"

Golman's eyes glanced away from me.

I started to laugh, and though it made my knee speak in obscene tongues, I tilted back in my chair.

"Let's see now," I chuckled. "You had a couple of patrol cars full of state cops. And there was three of you Bureau boys. There's probably more, besides, right?"

Golman nodded. "Crawford's got a cop. There's a couple Park Service patrolmen down from the Black Hills. Two more plain clothes men with the Bureau. And we've got two more S.A.'s on a plane coming from Denver."

"From Denver," I chuckled. "And probably some local volunteers."

"I tried to avoid that," Golman said. "But. You know. BIA police from up at Pine Ridge, and some locals, too. Yeah." I noticed the way he saw the white volunteers as "locals," the Indian police as different, almost outsiders.

"All them folks," I shook my head slowly. "Trained and motivated," I said.

"The two agents coming from Denver," Golman nodded. "They were friends of Jack Coler."

"All of those folks," I let my chair flop back to the table. "And you can't even find a blind Indian toting an arthritic old dog around in the snow."

"Funny," he said, but he didn't laugh.

I did.

After listening a while, he said, "Where's he at, chum?"

"How am I supposed to know?"

"You can guess," Golman said.

He was right. Maybe the last time I saw Choteau and Protector they were rolling across Highway 20, but I knew where they were. Maybe not now, not right at the moment. It would take him a while. But I knew where I'd find Choteau, eventually. He was headed back to "Camp Robinson," to that guardhouse out there, because he believed he was Crazy Horse. He'd get himself back to that site, one way or another.

"You saw him last?" I tried to lie my way out of it. "You know better than me."

Golman rubbed at his temple again. He glanced at his wristwatch.

"You know, were going to find him," he said to the table. Then he looked me in the eyes. "Terri tipped us off, remember? You're out at Fort Robinson Park, we know that. It's a big park, a lot of buildings. But well go through them all. One at a time. So we'll find him.

"The thing is, buddy, somebody might get hurt in the process. Understand? A cop. Maybe another agent, again. That's not gonna help your friend out any. Not to mention," he paused and thought a moment about the right way to phrase this. He was choosing his words carefully now, I could tell. "Who knows? Wrong agent gets to Choteau first, and the Indian puts up a fight. I don't know. Choteau could be the one who gets hurt, maybe."

"Is this some kind of threat, Golman?" I jumped on him, because he was so cautious.

"I'm only setting out the possibilities, Will. That's why I'm asking. If you can lead us to him, and we make a clean arrest. Everybody wins. Right? Choteau keeps his scalp," he grinned and cocked his head a bit. "You come off as cooperating with us. We get our job done safely." Then he stopped, and his best sparkle came out under the little, trimmed mustache. "You get your ass back to Terri and we all do a little Christmas. There's some presents waiting for you under the tree, chum. And my sister's still waiting too." He chuckled once. "Though I can't figure out why."

Maybe it was late. Maybe I was tired. But he started to make sense. Not with his Christmas present line, but with all his other plans. It was what I wanted, after all. A safe way to surrender. It was the point of my last call to Terri, wasn't it? No matter what she might have done with that information.

"Not tonight," I said.

He spun his chair around and sat down straddling it. I could see victory in his eyes. I'd just admitted I could take him to Choteau. Agent Golman was making progress.

"What's up?" he said. He leaned down on his crossed arms on the back of the chair.

"We've got to wait for Terri to get here. Then I'll take you to him. I don't know where he is right now, Golman. But I know where he'll be."

"Where?" he said softly.

I shook my head and picked up my coffee cup. "No," I said and then drained the lukewarm coffee out of the mug. "I'm not saying anymore until Terri gets here. It's the only way I'll trust you."

He stared at the tabletop for a moment. "She's not coming, bud. Understand that, will ya'? She's with my folks. I made sure she got up there, Will, where she's safe."

"When she gets here, I'll . . . "

"It doesn't work that way. She's not going to be here."

266

"Well, screw it then," I said and thumped the empty mug down. I was just angry then, at being alone, at being caught, at Terri.

We both sat there, divided, waiting for something to change. After a few moments, he said, very quietly, "We'll find him, you know, sooner or later."

I got his point, the one about how it might not be the best for Choteau to go that way. Or for me.

"He won't surrender to you in the dark," I said. "He doesn't trust you. And I don't either."

"I don't trust us, chum," he said. "There's too many old wounds on a case like this."

"So I'll take you to him tomorrow. Tomorrow afternoon. Let me get some of his friends here, some people to witness it." I paused there. I almost said we would wait for Terri. But I didn't want to hear him deny it anymore. "Let me make some phone calls."

"You know, I'm gonna be honest with you," Golman said. "I don't think I can hold it off 'til then. There's too many of us, and too many emotions here. I can't guarantee something won't happen before tomorrow afternoon. How long do you think I can hold these local volunteers off?"

"Or those Denver agents?" I was tired.

"They'll follow their orders," he said curtly, and then relented. "But they'll be watching for Choteau to give them a chance."

Still, I could see his point, and I thought he was being straight with me. As straight as he could. He wanted a clean arrest without any trouble.

"How about we split the difference, chum?" Golman said. "We wait until morning. I think I can hold it all off 'til it's daylight. But then you take us to him, right?"

"And the witnesses?"

267

"I'll give you access to a phone. If you can get a couple people here by morning, okay by us," he said. "But, only a couple. We don't want this turning into another Wounded Knee scene, okay? Nobody from Pine Ridge is in on this. Is that a deal?"

"Except the goons," I said.

I'm not sure, but I think I agreed to Golman's terms because Choteau himself seemed to want it that way. Nobody wanted the Pine Ridge Lakota involved.

"There aren't any 'goons' anymore. We straightened out that problem years ago," Golman said.

"No," I laughed at him. "You just call them local volunteers now."

"It's the way we got to do it," Golman said, then he stood up straight. "Is it a deal?" he said.

"Let me think about it," I said to his back as he stepped out the door, because he didn't really need an answer.

I sat there alone in that yellow room trying to decide whether I could trust Mike Golman or not, and the only thing I could remember was an old argument we had. It was the biggest argument I ever had with Terri. That's all I could think about. With everything else going up in smoke around me, all I could remember was what Golman did that night.

The funny thing is, I can't remember now what we argued about. I remember the weather. It was one of those cold, weary evenings late in winter. The snow outside had melted all afternoon in warm, spring sun. But once that sun set, the snow froze hard again. It was crusted on top with a layer of ice, brittle and shiny under the streetlights.

And I remember what we were eating. I made fettuccini with red sauce filled with clams and garlic. I baked bread sticks and then dipped them in garlic butter. We were drinking a bottle of some Chianti.

But I can't remember what it was we were talking about on the night Terri and I had our biggest fight. I guess that's because it didn't really matter.

She stood up and set her fork on the table. I had my mouth full of bread. She walked away from the table then, and said, "You don't mean that. It's just an act."

I remember she was right. Whatever it was we were fighting about, I was acting like a professor. I was out to make some sort of logical kill as I dissected what she said. She was talking about her thoughts and feelings, and I was listening for the logic in her choice of terms. It was the old seminar table instinct, and I'd always done well with it in the past. It earned me my "A"s in school, and my tenure too, I suppose.

"Don't use that tone of voice with me," she said.

"What tone?"

"That one right there," she said. "We just disagree on this. Okay? But don't talk to me like I'm wrong, or foolish, or something. Like I don't know how to think. We just disagree."

"What do you mean 'tone of voice'?" I said, though I knew perfectly well what she meant.

"I don't know," Terri walked away across the room toward the front door. Then she turned, swept her coat off the hall tree. "And don't think you can tell me what to think," she said.

"Why does this have to be a fight?" I said. "I'm just trying to make my point that . . . "

That's when she hurled her key ring. She could have been throwing them at me. But they missed me by a yard or more, and went jingling off across the floor, tinkling like little bells. She didn't want to hit me. If she'd wanted to hit me with those keys, I was close enough I'd have gotten them full in the face.

"You made your point, buster," she said.

Then with a dancelike step that seemed strangely graceful, she twirled and was gone out the door. She didn't slam it, but it closed behind her, solidly.

Buster, I thought. That one name in all the world that can never be said with true affection. Buster. Like an exclamation point.

I strode back over to the table where all that nearly untouched food sat growing cold. "Why does this have to be a fight?" I said. Then, like an idiot, I slammed my fist onto the table top.

The pain shot through me immediately, telling me how stupid I was. But I wasn't done. The ache of my hand seemed like one last indignity, then. I picked up her plate and hurled it at the front door.

Of course, for once in my life I made a perfect throw. The dinner plate flew across the room, spraying clam sauce and fettuccini over the furniture and the carpet. The plate rode right up into the antique, cut glass window in the arched door, then sailed straight through it with a crash. There was a thump, and it cracked the window pane in the storm door, and then fell to the doorstep.

All of this in a second. But a long enough second for remorse to hit me.

"Shit," I said. I wasn't ready to laugh at myself yet. I was still too busy being an ass.

I walked slowly over, opened the door and picked up the dirty plate, broken cleanly in two. A long crack split the glass in the storm door into three big pieces, still sitting precariously in place. The glass was wobbling in the frame still, wanting to fall. I opened the storm door carefully. Shards of antique glass tinkled out of the doorway onto the brick door stoop.

Outside on the stoop, I sat down holding the broken plate in my hands. Terri was nowhere in sight. But her footprints in the hard crusted snow trailed across the yard and down the street.

She is a tiny woman, you know. All of maybe 95 lbs, after a full meal. And there was a layer of ice on that snow I could have walked carefully across and not broken once. But sitting there, I saw her footprints hard and clear, punched through that ice in a trail all the way to sidewalk.

I sat there for about fifteen or twenty minutes, trying to figure out what this argument was really all about.

It wasn't my "tone of voice." That was too easy. And obviously, Terri knew how to tell me where to go when I let my academic jets kick in. She'd done it before. And it didn't lead to flying plates and broken windows.

I sat on our stoop, feeling cold, wondering through all this without finding any answers. I loved her. She meant more to me than blue skies or mountain air. But if I was hurting her this much, if what we had was this awry, then why should we stay together? Unless there was a need, or a fear, holding us that I didn't see.

I decided that night I would find Terri, hand her back her keys, and then leave her alone. Leave her for long enough to let both of us know what was right. Together, or apart.

But a creak of tires on the hard snow startled me out of those thoughts. Headlights swept over me, blinded me for a second. When they were switched out, I could see it was a jeep Cherokee. The door swung open at the same instant I connected and knew who it was.

"Sort of cold for playing porch potato, pal," Golman said.

I rubbed my eyes, from the headlights I swear, and set the pieces of plate on the stoop. "Golman," I said.

"Aren't you freezing?" Golman said.

"What are you doing here?" I said.

"Well, buddy. I was in the neighborhood. Thought I'd drop by." He let the door of the Cherokee slam shut and walked over through the yard toward me. I just sat. Golman was being close mouthed about his secret work for the Agency, again. I guess when you work for the FBI you get used to people wondering why you're around. But he loved it. He loved sidestepping questions, letting you wonder what big case was going down across the street. He loved feeling he knew more than you did.

"What are you doing sitting on the step, buddy?" He wore prescription aviator shades, along with cowboy boots and a suit, under a leather overcoat. The crusted snow clicked and cracked as he strode across it toward me.

But he had a hard time keeping his balance, since those boots were made for negotiating with a horse, not for negotiating with ice crusted on top of wet snow. And it's real tough trying to do the old macho stride while you're skating toward a slide on your behind.

"Oh," he said as he got close, "Domestic bliss, eh, pal?" He stood towering over me and eyed the broken windows on the two doors. Then he dusted off the stoop with a boot, and sat down next to me. He arranged the leather coat carefully so he wasn't sitting on it. "You two having problems?"

"You ought to know. You're the expert." It was a cheap shot, but I was not in the mood for his advice. Or his condolences.

"What? Did she kick you out, pal, and toss dinner at you, too?" Golman laughed, ignoring my crack about his marriage to Jacki.

"Actually, I made dinner. And I threw the plate."

He laughed again, adjusted his glasses, and said, "Figures."

"I'm freezing," I stood up. Sitting on my doorstoop in the snow sparring with "Special Agent Golman" about my marriage didn't sound attractive. I opened the storm door carefully, trying not to shake the broken panes loose. "Come on in, Golman," I said.

"Where's my sister?" Golman said inside, as he eyed the damage in the living room: the broken glass, the spattered sauce and noodles. He stuck his hands in his pants pockets so that leather overcoat bunched back behind him in a way that looked casual and contrived all at once. He'd been watching those Clint Eastwood movies again. He spun around slowly as he walked in, giving the place his investigator's eye. He laughed. "Whoa! Can't get no deferments from this war. Eh, pal?"

"Cheap shot, Golman. Too bad it doesn't bother me." It was the oldest game we played. Golman, the Viet Nam vet, versus Mr. Student Deferment with a lucky lottery number.

"Some things you can't avoid, pal."

"Like your Jacki?" I said.

"Where's Terri?" he said. But he meant it as a genuine concern.

"I don't know, Golman. We argued and she walked out, about half an hour ago."

"Damn," Golman said. Suddenly I liked him. He hadn't asked what the fight was about.

"I think I know where she might be, though," I said. "Is it important? Do you need to see her?" I walked across the living room and picked up Terri's keys from the carpet.

"Go get her, pal," Golman said. He tossed me the keys to his Jeep. I think he winked at me behind the shades. "Don't let it rest. Go straighten it out."

He meant it, too. And not just because Terri was his sister. It was the voice of a guy who'd messed up too many of his own chances to "go straighten it out." But he didn't wish his own screw ups on anyone else, not even me.

"Right," I said.

He nodded his head in a parental way, and that almost stopped me. "Get goin'," he said.

My guess was right. I drove the Cherokee down to Louie's Java Shop, a couple blocks away. Terri was sitting by herself at a table, both hands holding a cup of hot cocoa. She watched me come in. Patsy Cline sang from the juke box speakers across the room.

I intended to hand her those keys and tell her we needed a vacation from one another. I would move out at the start of the week and we could give it all a month or two. Then we'd see what happened.

But as I walked over, her hair was a wonderful mess of curls, and she wore some tiny silver earrings I'd given her. Her face was dark and rosy from the walk in the cold. And her eyes were just a little red. Somehow, I didn't set the keys on the table and make my little speech. Instead, I strolled over and stood there, looking stupid.

She let me stand there like an idiot for a long minute or so, then she cracked a smile.

"Cup of coffee, sailor?" she said.

"Only if you need a ride."

She laughed, and her laugh seemed like the trickle of spring melt. "Home?" she said.

"Anywhere you want to go, babe."

"Well, I am on foot."

When she saw the Cherokee outside, with its government plates and its suburban wood on the side, she said, "Mike?"

I nodded.

"He's here?"

"Yup. "

"Oh great," she rolled her eyes. "What timing, big brother Mike."

"You're telling me," I said as we walked outside and climbed in the jeep. "I was sitting on the stoop in the broken glass when he pulled in the drive."

"Glass?" she said, her eyebrows lifting. God, she was pretty then as she laughed at me.

"You'll see," I said.

But she didn't. By the time we walked in, just moments later, the glass was gone. Golman had swept it up, cut a chunk of cardboard for the door and duct taped it in where the window arch had been. He'd even duct taped the pane in the storm door.

When we strolled in, he was on his knees in his suit pants, wiping clam sauce off the carpet. His tie was off. The sleeves of his white shirt were rolled up. But he still wore the shoulder holster, and his gun, of course. He was still with the Bureau, you know.

"Well," he said from the floor, "it didn't take you two lovebirds long to make up."

He seemed genuinely happy there, looking like a scrub maid. I guess any couple staying together was a hope for him. And salvation for some abstract ideal he held to about marriage and family.

"Thanks, Golman," I said. I offered him a beer then, and I thought how he almost seemed like a brother, except for the gun.

Later that night, as we got ready for bed, I told Terri, "I was going to offer to move out, so we could decide what we need to do. That's what I was thinking about. But I just couldn't quite say it when I saw you at Louie's."

Still I knew these arguments, these things we say to one another when we fight, they don't go away. There's no evaporation. No disappearance. Once they're said, they ride our words out into reality. They're solid as marble columns. They taste of salt and they smell of smoke. They're part of creation.

They get forgiven, maybe. But forgotten, no. They don't disappear.

"I was going to leave you the keys, Terri, and go."

"I know," she said. "I could see that the moment you walked in. But the main thing is," she said, "you didn't."

Her eyes were green as a shamrock.

Sitting there looking at the shit yellow walls and that plain fluorescent light, I could remember all of that, the food and the words and the way Golman walked. But I still couldn't remember what the argument was about, what had started it all. My knee ached and my head ached and the table in that office was bare of everything but our coffee cups and the wrappers. I was too tired to be sick, and I wondered where Choteau and Protector were. Then Golman came back and helped me up on my feet. "You need some rest," he said.

He hauled me off to a room in the Cowpoke Motel, a couple miles back to the east toward Chadron. I think it must have become FBI headquarters. There were only five rooms there, but they were all lit up. There was a Nebraska HiPo parked in front next to some Chrysler sedan with federal government tags. He parked the Blazer next to it and he put me in a room alone with a phone. I knew they were listening, though.

275

If it wasn't tapped, then I could see a row of them with their ears up against the thin walls. But I'd grant him this, Golman left me alone to make those calls.

I sat for a while trying to think who I could try. I didn't know anyone nearby. But a call to information got me the number of a Dr. Nordstrom, M.D., in Grand Forks. What the hell, it was a start, I thought.

The good Doc himself answered, sounding gruff and angry. He's probably not a half-bad guy, just got himself into a half bad marriage. Still, it was past 2 a.m., and doctors should be used to these late night calls, even in a time of office visits and fully staffed emergency wards. "Could I speak to Mary?" I said.

"Who is this? Who's calling?"

"You don't know me, Doctor Nordstrom, but I really need to talk to your wife." I stopped, thinking over how to phrase it. "I'm a friend of Bernard Choteau's," I said, finally. What else could I do?

There was a loaded silence on the other end.

"Who are you?" he said, and he sounded both hurt and compassionate then.

"Listen, Doctor, just tell her this. Tell her that Choteau is in trouble and she should come to Crawford, Nebraska, to the state park near there, as soon as possible. By morning, if she can. This is critical, sir. By morning, if she can."

"You know, friend, it's after two o'clock."

"Just wake her, and tell her that. It's all I can say. Unless you let me talk to her myself."

There was another long pause. Very softly he said, "Leave her alone." Then he hung up.

I am still amazed that he listened to me even that long.

I woke Bobby Red Skies next. The drowsiness disappeared from his voice the moment I said my name.

276

"You're the guy was here s'afternoon," he said, "with Bernard."

I told him where we were, carefully leaving out any mention of the guardhouse. "He's going to surrender to the FBI in the morning," I said. "We need as many people as you can gather at Camp Robinson, by daybreak."

"Daybreak! That's only four-five hours from now," he said.

"We need witnesses, Bobby. I don't want it to be just me and Choteau alone with the FBI and a bunch of goons."

"Right," he said quickly. Then he added, "Damn it." I heard him turn away from the phone and say, "Nothing. Its okay."

"Bobby," I said. "Do you know anybody from the old days? Anybody you can call over on the reservations . . . ?"

"Most folks from the Knee are on this ride, now, you know?"

"To Wounded Knee, I know. Choteau told me about it. He said he didn't want to mess with it. But I think that's our chance, Bobby. You got to get a group of folks together . . . "

"Be tough to find them." Then Bobby Red Skies laughed, not at us, but with one of those bitter Indian laughs I was beginning to understand. "You think Indians will qualify as witnesses?" he said.

"It's our best chance, Bobby. Find those people from the reservation and . . . "

That's where the line went dead. I set the phone on the cradle and tried to figure it out. Was it the feds listening in, and cutting us off before we got it all set up? Or was it that Bobby Red Skies had hung up?

After that I was stumped. But I called home again and listened to my phone ring and ring and ring. I thought about trying Terri's folks, but I told myself it was too late. I didn't want to wake them. When it came down to it, I really didn't want to know. With what I was headed into at daylight, I needed to keep my illusions alive. I didn't need to know I'd been left alone. Not now.

*

    I stretched out on the double bed in my room at the Cowpoke Motel. I wanted a shower, but I didn't have the will anymore to get up. Yet I couldn't sleep either. I guess I'd driven myself beyond all that. The whole week began to catch up with me then, the constant driving, the living in these same dirty clothes, the struggling to stay warm against the bitter cold of the winter prairies, the broken diet of Slim Jims and cheap beer and coffee, and the almost nothing to eat in the last twenty-four hours. I'd not been in the best of shape when we'd driven off on this adventure, and now I think I'd reached some sort of physical limit. My will was gone.

    I lay there on the too soft bed staring at the cracked ceiling. There was just one lamp in the motel room, by the bed. It had an old bulb in it that would make a loud snap now and again, and then change its intensity. I could see the patterns of its filament on the ceiling. So I found myself awake, lying there waiting for the next crackle from that bulb, watching for the shade of that yellow-white light to change and create a new pattern on the walls.

    The ceiling was coated with an old plaster, and as I lay there I began to imagine it was a map. The cracks were highways, and the rough, stucco edges were white mountains changing colors in the varying light of day. I followed the roads around with my eyes, trying to see where they would lead, but they always, eventually, disappeared off the map into the shadows of the walls that held them up. Then snap would go the bulb, and I was off on another highway, wandering around until I reached the end of the map again. I think, finally, that wore me out. I closed my eyes and I may have dozed off.

It was his burp that startled me. I never heard him come in. Just this loud belch, and then I could smell it: old stew cooked to a mush and tobacco wet from spit. Old Badlands' belch. Before I even opened my eyes, his hoarse cackle broke out and followed the gas. I looked over and he was lying right next to me in the bed. "Hoka hey, Little Big Man," he said, looking into my eyes from inches away. I could smell the rot in his toothless gums as his hello blew into my face.

I sat up in the bed, or maybe I jumped up. I don't know. I was barely awake. "What are you doing here?" I said. But he only laughed in response.

He was stretched out on the mattress, wearing some dirty old jeans and a flannel cowboy shirt that hadn't seen a laundromat since it got sewn together in Indonesia. His gray white hair, yellowing from dirt, was spread out on the bed behind him. But then, I didn't have much to brag about. I wasn't much cleaner than he was.

"How did you get in here?" I looked around the room in the dim light and saw nothing but shadows. We were alone. "Did anybody see you?"

That brought another round of laughter out of him. Then his tongue poked out of that caved in mouth and mopped around his wrinkled lips.

I lowered my voice, and said, "Have you seen Choteau?" I found I couldn't help but stare at the thin walls of the motel room. "Is he all right?"

He shut off the laugh at that, just grinned and slowly sat up beside me in the bed. "Did he send you here?" I said, as the old man curled up his legs and sat beside me like some Chinese monk. I was ready to whisper to him the deal I'd made with Golman, to see what he thought.

But Old Badlands just held up a hand to silence me, chuckled twice at something, and then reached inside his shirt. He pulled out a pipe in two long pieces and casually fit it together. I remembered the one lesson I'd learned from them before: stop asking questions of these people and just listen. That way, you learn what they want you to know. It's the only way. So I shut up.

The light bulb clicked then and the room went to a dim orange that trembled a little. There was a flash from Old Badland's lighter and he puffed on the pipe. "Good evening, Grandfather Bissonette," I said, feeling a lot more clever about all this.

He held the pipe out to me, smiling. "All my relatives," he said, but in Lakota.

I smoked, and it tasted of plain, straight tobacco. But there was something relaxing about it. I seemed to move into step with time as it carried me along. I gazed down at the sheets on the bed and they seemed as gray with filth as the sheets on that bed in the old man's shack.

"Bissonette," I said to him. "does that mean Little Buffalo, Grandfather?"

He laughed again, and we passed the pipe back and forth a while. When I stopped wondering entirely what he was there for, Old Badlands Face seemed to sense it, because he got up and went over into a corner of the room. He left me holding the pipe.

The old man bent down into the shadows in the corner, and as he reached around for something, a long, plump fart leaked out of him. It made a low rumble for a while and then ended with a happy squeak. That made him shake with laughter and lose the strength he needed to pick up whatever it was he had there. I laughed with him, and in a moment I could smell him all over the room.

"Grandfather smells like a big buffalo," I said.

He turned around then and he was holding my mask. Against his chest, hugging it to him, he held up the bear mask that hangs above our mantel back in Missouri.

"How did you?" I started to say; and then remembered that my questions wouldn't get me anywhere.

Old Badlands Face struggled around to where he held that big mask cradled in one arm, and he tucked his other hand behind it, to where he could control it. I know that piece was heavy, because I'd hung it on the wall myself. It weighed an easy twenty pounds. Old Badlands may have been a tough old coot, but it was taking something out of him to hold that mask

281

still and in place. Enough so that he broke wind again. This time, he smelled like the dusty insides of an old corn bin.

I took a deep draught on the pipe, trying to cover up that old man's raunchy stink. The harsh tobacco, though I coughed it through my nose, helped.

"See this, little white man," the old guy said, and as he spoke, the light bulb popped and the room switched to bright chrome yellow, like it was show time suddenly.

He opened up the bear's head, but there wasn't a raven inside. Not like there was inside the mask I had at home. Inside this bear I saw a painted likeness of Bernard Choteau's face. He was young and scowling out at me, his gray hair was darker than it is now, and I knew it was the face of Choteau back at Wounded Knee, or back in North Dakota planning on his love and his law school. But while I sat and watched, the old man worked the mask and Choteau's eyes angled down and narrowed. His scowl cracked and turned up into a sneer. It was a face hardened by years on the run and a decade of incarceration. It became the painted face of a man who could murder my brother-in-law's friends. A man who was angry and proud enough to commit murder, if it was needed.

But Old Badlands wouldn't leave me there. He laughed, and I heard Choteau's voice loud right beside me. "You can call me Crazy," he said, "for short." It was so clear, I turned my head expecting to see him there, in the room with me. This was going to be rich. I was hiding out with Choteau and his relatives in the room where the FBI put me up. I laughed and forgot that murderous sneer on the mask of his face.

But Choteau wasn't there. I was alone with the old man. His cackle brought me back to the mask, and the scowl inside the bear was someone else's now. It was Crazy Horse. I knew who the face was because the cheeks were painted with a white streak of lightning, though it was really the same painted likeness of Bernard Choteau. It had become Crazy Horse now, with his proud chin in the air, Crazy Horse the victor of the Little Big Horn, the conqueror of Yellow Hair, the scourge of Custer. Old Badlands worked the mask's mouth and I saw it click open and shut, as if the dead man was talking. But no words came out. He was silent.

"This is his surrender," Old Badlands laughed. Click, click went the teeth on the mask. The proud chin was up still, but the hollow clacking of those teeth broke it in two, rattling like some rusted tambourine, laughing at all that courage and pride.

The light bulb made a pop and we were plunged into a soft brown light, darker than anything we'd seen before in the room. The old man started to hum, and the clacking of Crazy Horse's teeth stopped. He was humming some tune I'd heard before, but I couldn't make it out. Then the big mask made a heavy wooden crack, and the eyes of that painted face snapped shut. Though the red and black mouth of it didn't really change, it still seemed to relax. Old Badlands hummed along with his sad tune.

For a while, I forgot Old Badlands was there. I just sat and heard his voice and gazed at that face inside the bear. I found out if I concentrated, I could make it into any face I wanted, with just a little imagination. I could see whoever I wanted on the blank slate of that mask. I think, after a while I saw Mary Red Skies there, as she was when Choteau fell in love with her, and I could see her too as I saw her in that photo he carried, with her hair curled up and their son in his little bow tie. I saw Terri then, because I wanted to see her. It was what I wanted most. I guess I forced it. Because at first I saw the face of her anger, the way she glared as she hurled her keys at me and stomped out the door into that frozen, crusted snow. I struggled and fought with that, but I turned it into another face, eventually. It became Terri on the night she bit my shoulder in the hot August dark, on the night I came home late and she made love to me on the hardwood floor. I held that face as long as I could, until Old Badlands broke my concentration. He stopped singing to lift a leg and then he blew another loud, tweeting fart.

Quick as I could, I took up the pipe and pulled another long draught. Anything to cover the corn bin smell of his bowels. I sucked as much in as my lungs could hold and blew it through my nose. It made me cough again, and my eyes watered, but it was still better than the alternative.

When I wiped my eyes clear, the mask was back to the plain, painted face it was when it started. Just a glaring, human face with a sharp nose and angry eyes, all painted red and white and black. It was no one, not Terri, not Choteau, not Crazy Horse, not anyone. Just a blank face. Human.

I shook my head to clear it, and I held my brow for a moment. "You put something in the pipe, didn't you, old man?" I said.

Old Badlands just laughed, then he sucked in a big breath, enjoying the smell of his own gas.

"You slipped me something again," I said. I laughed at myself. "Son of a bitch," I said.

Then the old man shook his head at me. I noticed he was trembling now, trying to hold up the big Kwakiutl mask. "Put it down," I said. "Show's over."

Old Badlands snorted once, but he leaned back down and set the mask in the corner. This time he must have been clean. He didn't lose any gas in that effort.

"Feeling better?" I said, and I laughed at him. My own head was starting to clear, even if the air wasn't. I shook it again, blinked my eyes a couple times.

The old man hobbled over toward me. His step was shaky, and he seemed tired now. I felt sorry for him. I'd discovered his little trick, even if I couldn't tell yet why he was doping me. The light bulb, without a sound, suddenly switched to a bright white, and the pattern of the filaments shook stiffly, almost trembled on the ceiling.

Old Badlands worked his way around slowly toward that lamp. His head hung down, and his face wrinkled in like a sinkhole, and he seemed about to cry.

"Why did you try to drug me again?" I said. Then I remembered what I'd learned about questions and this old coot, and I gave up asking him anything.

He stepped feebly around by the light. Then he looked up at me from under that wrinkled brow, and the laughter seemed gone out of him, as gone as the gas in his bowels. "Little Big Man," he said.

"I'm not Little Big Man," I told him. "My name is William Gentles."

"Little Big Man," he reached over and put his hand right on the hot white bulb. "How can you tell the dancer from the mask?" he said.

"What?" I mumbled, but he broke that bulb with his bare hand then. It snapped like a cracker, and I heard the electricity pop. I reached out and tried to stop him, but the bright flash blinded me for a moment.

"Mr. Bissonette?" I said. There was a hot spot in my eyes, turning green and yellow and bright blue. I couldn't see for moments. I flailed an arm out, trying to find the old man. "Are you all right, Mr. Bissonette?" I said. "Grandfather?" But I couldn't find him.

Gradually my eyes cleared, and I got up and limped over to the bathroom. I switched the fluorescent on there, and its plain, white light cast out the door and half lit the bedroom. The old man was gone.

I limped all around, and hopped when the pain was too much, but he wasn't there, and the doors and windows were locked. Over in the corner, where he'd set the big Kwakiutl mask down, there was nothing but an old tin trashcan. It was gray and round and rusted, and it looked nothing like a mask.

I flopped down on the bed because my bad knee was torturing me. It couldn't stand even that gentle use. So I gave up looking for what had slipped away into the night. There was nothing left of the old man but his sacred pipe. I still held it in the crook of my arm and the stench of his rotten gas.

"Little Big Man," I said, carefully imitating his words. I spoke to the dark room, hoping he'd hear me. "Little Big Man, my ass."

*

daybreak

Golman woke me with a prod to the shoulder. The room was dark. A crack of light cut like a razor out of the bathroom. I heard the shower running. "It's almost light, buddy," he said. "Let's get cleaned up."

He strolled over and sat at the bureau near the phone, and waited. "I got the shower all steamy and flowing for ya', chum," he said.

I sat up in bed and immediately my knee reminded me that it wouldn't move without yelling. I rubbed my face, and just felt hung over. "What time is it?" I growled, squinting at the sharp bathroom light. My head ached. Then I remembered the pipe. But it wasn't in my arm, so I reached down and felt around in the sheets for it. It was gone.

I leaned over then and looked up inside that funky lamp. The old, weak bulb was there, unbroken, whole.

"Get in the shower," Golman brushed his mustache with a finger. He sniffed the stale air in the room. "You stink like a bum. A bum with the shits. You feeling okay?"

"You didn't take anything from me, did you, Golman? There wasn't anything on the bed here? Was there?"

"Like what?" he said, waiting coyly to hear more.

"Never mind," I said. "It's nothing." I was still glancing around, looking for it, as I hopped to the john.

Clean clothes were waiting for me when I crawled out of the bathroom. But my conscience wasn't quite ready to wear them. I put on my old blue jeans and flannel shirt while Golman griped about spoiling the "new car scent" in the Blazer. He had donuts and coffee, too, and those I took to without any

286

prompting. I may have been a betrayer, but I was a Judas who needed his caffeine.

"We know where he is," Golman said, while I slurped down the coffee. It was still black outside the windows of the room.

"He started a fire to stay warm in one of the old restored cabins out there. One of our volunteers spotted the smoke," he said. He didn't have to say I told you so. But to be honest, he was letting my conscience off the hook.

"So why do you need me?" I said. I was hoping maybe this bitter cup would pass me by, but I knew better. Now that they'd found him, it was even more important I get out there to stop the bloodshed. At least I hadn't turned him in, I told myself. I think it is my old academic training that helps me rationalize so well.

"We're out watching the place," he said. "But it seems like I promised you the chance to get him out, last night. So we're waiting." He grinned at me, "And it'll help you a lot to be the one who turns him over to us," he said, "brother-in-law."

"He's in the old guardhouse, isn't he?"

Golman nodded. He stood up. "My men will follow orders," he said. "They're not supposed to even show themselves until we get there. But if Choteau tries something, or . . . "

"Or if some of your volunteers decide to help out."

What he really meant was there would be no waiting for my witnesses. It left me uneasy, to be facing them alone in the middle of Nowhere, Nebraska, but Golman was right. Waiting would only be pushing our luck.

"Let's go," I said.

He picked up an aluminum cane and tossed it at me. "You might need this," he said. It had a big rubber tip on the end and it was all shining and silver. Agent Golman had been busy through the night, but I have to say this was damn thoughtful of him.

I stood and used it to walk a few steps. He was right. It not only helped, I needed it. "Don't I get to lean on you anymore, Golman," I said.

"Don't push your luck, chum," he grinned. With one hand he rubbed the back of his head. Then he turned toward the door and the grin disappeared. "This is serious shit, Will," he said. "Be careful."

Golman closed the door to my room in the Cowpoke Motel, and then he stepped up next to me. It wasn't hard. I was about two steps ahead of him, trying to get a feel for the cane in the ice and gravel of the parking lot. "Helps, huh?" he said.

I nodded, and set the red rubber tip firm in the gravel and ice. He watched me limp a moment. Then he said, "What was it you were looking for in there?"

"Where?"

"In the bed. Just now, when I woke you."

"It was nothing," I said. "I was dreaming about something. That's all." I was talking to myself as much as to him. There was no sign anywhere that there had ever been a pipe.

Golman nodded his head, and he seemed to believe me. He opened the door to the rider's side of the Blazer, and he waited there for me.

"You know, Will," he said, "there's one thing you and Choteau still got us on. After I talked to you in that gas station, right after that, we lost you. You two just disappeared, pal." He laughed, shook his head, and paused then to think about something. "We didn't catch up with you until you called Sis, buddy. That's when Terri told us you were heading for this park out here." He laughed again.

I stopped, but I didn't look up at him. I kept my head down, and I set the cane's tip in the gravel.

"Where did you guys disappear to?" he said. "That was really something. We had you, buddy, and then poof, you're gone. Where'd you guys go to?"

I thought a minute about who I was giving away, because I knew he was trying to pry information out of me. It seemed hopeless for a moment, though. As hopeless as trying

288

to find that vanished pipe. So I told him. "Medicine Wheel?" I said.

"Where?"

"At Medicine Wheel."

"Never heard of it. Is that a town, or what?"

"It's what the sign said, Golman. Medicine Wheel."

"Was somebody there?"

I started working toward the car again, one step and then set the cane, and then another step. "I don't know," I said.

"What was this place?"

"I don't know," I said again, and he got the point. I wasn't telling him anymore. But it didn't matter. I didn't know as I limped across the dark parking lot that no one would ever find Medicine Wheel, South Dakota. Never again. Not with any amount of searching. But I didn't know that then, so I just shut up.

We rode in the Blazer as dawn broke behind us across the rough foothills and buttes. The bare face of Crow Butte glowed pink and bronze above the black pines on its collar. About half a mile from the Fort, the Highway Patrol waved us through a road block. Four Nebraska Patrol cars cut off all but a channel down the middle of U.S. 20.

Golman slowed and drove us straight through the block, nodding to the phalanx of patrolmen. A camera went off when I looked out the car window. The flash blinded me, but not before I realized the press was here. I saw the camera trucks from at least one Rapid City tv station.

"Every road in here is sealed," Golman gave a cop at the roadblock one of his casual, two fingered salutes.

"You promised," I said. "How are my witnesses supposed to get in here? How are they supposed to get past these blockades?"

"You give me the names of anybody you think is coming. I'll radio it back and they'll get through. I'll do it right now,

Will. Who's coming to visit, pal?" He reached down and plucked the mouthpiece from its hook. He seemed a little too eager.

I thought a moment about who I could name, and whether I should. But I didn't see any other way. Besides, anyone I could name was not going to be news to them. "Bobby Red Skies," I said. "And anybody he brings with him."

"We won't let anybody we know from Pine Ridge in. Anybody with a record, or, well, you know. This is not gonna be any new Wounded Knee, pal. No way."

"So what am I supposed to . . . "

"Red Skies is okay. I'm just telling you, anybody who comes with him will have to be checked."

"Right," I said, because I had no choice anyway.

"Who else?" Golman said. We drove slowly down within sight of the campus now.

"Mary Nordstrom and anybody with her. Or anybody using her name, too, I guess."

Golman was grinning again, driving along without looking at me. "That's it?" he said. He didn't have to say a word about my few and not so choice friends. He called in those names and left the orders, and made no comment about my lame chances of drawing a crowd.

"And Terri, " I said.

Golman sighed and shook his head at me like I was some sort of stubborn child. He hung the mouthpiece back on its rest. Then he pulled the Blazer over into a gravel lot behind the post playhouse. Parked in neat rows around us were at least fifteen or twenty vehicles: State patrol cars, jeeps, a few sedans with federal plates, and more than a few "deputized" volunteers sporting South Dakota tags. These were the retired goons, the old reservation cops from the days at the Knee, I guessed.

"Where's the National Guard?" I said.

"You'll see Terri," Golman set the parking brake with a jerk, "when we get you the hell out of this mess and back to Missouri. That's when you'll see her again, because that's where she is. If you focus on that and think real hard, buddy, maybe you'll understand it. Maybe."

290

*   *   *

A row of six white cabins lies across the old parade ground from the guardhouse and the adjutant's office. Golman and I came at them from the east. The snow was trampled and hard from footsteps. As we approached, I saw the "cavalry" and realized what Choteau was up against.

About twenty or twenty-five men in a motley of different uniforms and hunting gear were huddled in and around those six cabins. Of the twenty-five or so, there were six Indians by my count. It stung me to see them. Because it was the oldest of our many tricks, you know, the old divide and conquer. It made me feel angry, and I wondered how it must make Choteau feel to see something like that. Choteau and all the generations of warriors behind him. But I had to ignore that anger. The day was not ours. There was no time now to be angry.

The back doors to all six cabins were open and every window held at least one marksman. Every one of them was waiting, and not patiently. All this to arrest one blind man and his old dog. The overkill made me laugh out loud, and Golman hushed me quickly.

"You think he doesn't know you're here?" I said.

"No," he said curtly, under his breath.

"He may be blind, Golman," I said, "but Choteau's not stupid."

"I never said he was, Will." Golman was a few steps ahead of me. Then he turned and asked me, "So how do you want to do this?" I got the feeling he was just looking for a graceful way to tell me what he wanted me to do. It was orders time, but at least he was trying to let me have a say in it all.

"You don't want him hurt, do you?" I said, because I wasn't sure suddenly.

"No. I don't. I don't like him. And whatever he gets, he deserves. But I'm in charge, so I want this one by the book.

291

Which means Choteau gets out of here safe and sound. Then he can spend the rest of his damn life rotting in jail, as far as I'm concerned." He jerked his head at the small army of feds and cops and volunteers behind him, hunkered down and waiting in that row of cabins. "I don't think I speak for everybody here, though."

"This is an execution."

"No," he said. "Not if we do it right. And that means you and I both stay close to him. Skin close."

"How do you think we should do this?" I asked, because I didn't know what else to do. Golman had been here before, he'd been in situations like this since before he was twenty. What did I know about arrests, or battles?

"You and I should both go out there. Then I'll wait outside, right by the door, or close in, anyway. Then you go inside, Will," he stopped there, took a breath. He winced at the growing brightness of the snow, and suddenly he looked as hard and old as the crow's feet wrinkled around his eyes. "You bring Choteau out, Will. Then we'll cuff him, and I'll stay right in front of him and you stay behind. We'll just sandwich him between us, and we stick close until we get him all the way back here to the Blazer. Then we're out of here before anybody has any trouble."

I shook my head no. The wind swirled cold out across the parade ground and I saw it knock the smoke down in Choteau's stack. "He won't go along with that."

"Then how?"

"I'll go in there alone. Once I'm there, so he knows what's happening, I'll wave to you and then you can drive the Blazer around close. Right out on the parade ground. Then you get out and come up to the door. Then we'll do like you figured."

Golman nodded his head.

"But one thing, Mike. You can't have any guns on you. When you walk up to that door, you're not armed and you're in your shirtsleeves," I was pointing my finger at him now, giving him orders. "Your hands are in the air, so Choteau can see that you're clean."

292

Shaking his head no, Golman said, "I got to come in armed, Will."

"It won't work that way," my tone had switched to something close to desperate then. "Choteau won't come out that door, not if you've got a gun on him."

"But tell me this, Will, what keeps you and your Indian pal from pulling a gun on me?" Golman said coldly. "What keeps him from kidnapping me, Will?"

"My word," I said, quickly. Perhaps too quickly.

Golman looked up at the tops of the tall trees that circled the parade ground for a moment, and then his eyes fell from that clear blue sky and they stared directly into mine, and he held them fixed there for a long while. I just stared back at him, and never blinked. Finally, he nodded, once.

"And I want you to clear everybody out of here," I waved my cane at the row of cabins. "Everybody you can't control."

"I can't do that, Will."

"Are you telling me, Mike, that you can't control these people of yours, and you can't get rid of them?"

He shook his head no. "I'm telling you that I can't," he paused and corrected himself. "I won't let this become another Wounded Knee."

"Which one do you mean?" I said.

"Very funny," he said. "But you know exactly what I'm talking about. This is not turning into some grandstand for you and your AIM chums. That's why these men are here. To make sure of that."

"It's no good, Golman. It's not safe. It's not even close. Why should I have anything to do with . . . "

"Because you're smart, Will, and you've looked at your options," he pointed an angry finger back at me. "You and I can go over there and walk your friend out safely. Or you can go back to the roadblock and wait while these guys bring him out." He waved that accusing finger around at the "cavalry" waiting to move in. "One way or another, the guy who killed Jack Coler is coming out of there."

"You told me we could . . . " I said.

"Listen, Will, it's for your sake and my sister's sake, I'm putting my ass on the line out there. As long as Choteau behaves himself, we got no problem, buddy. You just make sure he understands that." He stopped and squinted at the cabin across the grounds. "It's the way it's gonna be," he said.

I nodded my head. I'd just become one of the boys, another member of the "cavalry." I was just taking my orders.

"When you're ready, Will, you wave that cane and I'll drive the truck around just like you figured."

"I don't like this," I said. But it sounded lame even to me.

"Well, there's a lot of things here I don't like," he gazed down at the snow at his feet now, his eyes relaxed again and he seemed resigned suddenly. "But it's the way things are."

"Just give us some time, would you?" I pleaded and hobbled past him on the cane. "At least give us that, Golman. Don't rush it. And if anybody shows up . . . "

He nodded, "If they come, and they're clean, they'll get through," he nodded a curt yes to me. "But just to watch," he said.

"Let's get this over with," I tried to stride angrily away, but a step or two away from him, I stumbled and then got my footing again. I walked on, more slowly, more carefully, using my cane.

Just above the bluffs, the sun shone down clear and rose hued now, and I cast a long gray shadow out across the smooth snow. It wasn't an easy walk. The rubber tip of my cane poked through the crust on the snow and sunk six inches or so every time I put my weight on it. But my feet, about half the time, stayed on top of the snow. I waddled along, breaking through here and there, limping like some hobbled old man. Other shadows on the whitened ground spoke to me, then. The echoes of what happened here in 1877 sounded all around me. This neat and tidy campus of a state park suddenly came alive with ghosts. I heard Black Shawl, Crazy Horse's wife, weeping softly in the wind. She was dying of TB. And I heard He Dog whisper at us, from over near the adjutant's office. "Look out. Watch your step," he said. "You are going into a dangerous place." Then he repeated it all again, over and over softly, blending with the sound of Black Shawl's weeping.

The wind whispered across the snow then, and blew some tiny flakes up like dry dust where my footprints had broken through the hard crust. I stepped and heard the creaking under my feet as that gust of wind sighed away into the hills.

Red Cloud was there too, with a group of Indians, all silent. He nodded to me, and seemed concerned, but satisfied. "Look out," He Dog whispered. And American Horse was there then, standing between me and the adjutant's cabin. And his men were all around him, wrapped against the cold in the plain army blankets they'd gotten when they surrendered. He smiled sadly at me. "Watch your step," came He Dog's whisper. And the crust of snow groaned under my weight.

"Choteau," I called out over the weeping and whispering ghosts all around me. But nothing came from the guardhouse, nothing but a trail of smoke out the fireplace. "Choteau, it's me," I yelled again louder. "I'm coming in." My voice echoed against the buttes and merged with the whispers of He Dog and the low weeping of Black Shawl. I wondered then if this is what Choteau heard all the time, these voices from another time whirling around him in a funnel. This is the way Bernard Choteau lived, I thought. In two times at once.

But at the sound of my voice, I heard the row of soldiers behind me cock their guns, and rise to their places in the windows across the field. I heard them collectively hold their breath, and for a moment the wind seemed to stop.

Somewhere up in the bluffs above us all, to the north, Touch-the-Clouds rode up. All seven foot of him, at the crest of the foothills. "I've come to watch," he said, almost dwarfing the horse under him. "I was not here to help, the last time," he said, as he gazed down at us.

"Choteau," I yelled. I was just a step or two from the door to the guardhouse. "I'm coming in," I said loud enough for all to hear. "It's just me. It's just Will Gentles."

I limped up to the door and pushed it open with my free hand. It swung in easily. "Watch your step," He Dog whispered in my ear. "You are going into a dangerous place," he said.

I stepped in the door and closed it behind me. The whispering and weeping and watching all stopped the moment the door closed. Time folded around me like an envelope. I turned around, and found Crazy Horse waiting inside.

He sat there on the other end of the one room, in the shadows. A deep red blanket was wrapped around him, taken from the cot inside the cell. The stove in the middle of the room glowed warm. I was nearly blinded, though, coming from that morning sun on snowfield glare into this dusky, shaded cage.

"Watch your step," he said, as I limped forward. I almost tripped over a body I hadn't seen on the floor.

"What the hell?" I said, and scuffled around it in the dark. But then I recognized him. I bent down, put my hands on the cold body, and then my damn knee buckled under me with the pain. So I fell over onto my knees on the plank floor beside Protector. Slowly I picked myself up.

"What happened to him?" I said. "When did this . . . "

"When they shot at me last night," Choteau laughed once bitterly. "The old fella took it in the chest. The bullets aimed for me. You know, Professor, I guess I named him right after all."

I stroked the old bulldog's broad head. Protector was cold as the floorboards.

"You've got to watch yourself when you give someone a name, Doc," Choteau said. "It may become the truth."

As I stroked the dog along his shoulders, my hand brushed against the slash on his neck. I began to see the dark bullet holes in Protector's ribs, as my eyes adjusted. And I understood, slowly, what must have happened. Choteau had cut the old dog's throat, to free it from a slow, cold death.

For a while I didn't speak, I just let my hand rest on the dog's quiet ribs. Choteau filled the empty air with words. "Funny, you know, but the old boy seemed to understand. We gave him an extra day or two when we pulled him out of the snowstorm, Will. A couple more days of jerky and beer to enjoy, and a nice ride in the country." Choteau nodded his head.

Then he said, "How many are there?" though his tone didn't change.

"Fifteen. Maybe twenty," I lied. I wanted it to look safe to him out there, but I wasn't sure how. I wanted him to believe in this surrender. It seemed like the only way.

He kicked back his head and laughed loudly at that. Then he said, "They must be scared."

"I am, too, Choteau," I said.

He nodded, but it didn't slow his laughter any. As my eyes adjusted to the shadowy room, I saw him more clearly too. He wore his hair loose and draped over his bare shoulders. He was bareback, except for the red blanket. On his cheek he had painted that bolt of lightning, and his chest was speckled with the painted hailstones in his vision. I knew without being able to see it that he wore that little brown stone behind his ear. If I didn't recognize all those markings from all my old research, if I hadn't ridden with him for this last week and come to see him as some sort of Crazy Horse, the way he saw himself, if I was just some cop bursting in the door, he'd have been frightening. He would have been some painted savage psycho. I'd have shot him dead, out of fear. Fear of that crazy face paint I couldn't understand.

But I did know him, and all of the lightning and hail had come to seem right to me. It seemed appropriate now, even familiar. It was as if I expected to see him there in all his ritual glory. I wanted it that way.

But what was under the paint? How little I really knew of what was there, when I thought about it. I stared at his bare shoulder, its dark ochre shade, like wet, clayey soil. And under it coursed blood that was richer and older than mine on this ground. But it was all foreign and odd and, though I believed we were the same deep down, I'd been taught that, I wasn't sure of it then. Not at that moment. I wasn't sure of anything then, except that he and I were different. And I didn't have even a wisp of a notion about what made him work. Did he have any notion of me? He seemed to understand me like my heart was made of clear glass. But did he really?

Still we were about to walk out onto a flat stretch of ground in front of twenty-some waiting guns and a hundred-some years of ghosts, together. And when I got down to the bottom of it, to the end of the wells of truth, the only thing I understood less than Choteau was myself.

So, just like I always did, when times got tough and the emotions grew raw and scary, I fell back on my book learning, on the safety zone of my education. "You know the one thing I always loved about Crazy Horse," I said. I must have sounded mad to him, talking like that with him dressed as the old chief. But he never let on to any of it. "Out of the whole of his life, it's the one thing that always stuck in my mind about him. You know, when he surrendered to Clark, just a couple miles north of here, the white men were expecting his war bonnet. He was supposed to hand over his war bonnet, you know," I chuckled, and then felt dumb for chuckling. I felt like I was telling Crazy Horse what he already knew. And maybe I was.

"But he just wore that one hawk's feather, from his vision, you know?" I pointed to where it should hang in his hair then. "So he shook hands with Lt. Clark and said, 'I want this peace to last forever.' Then He Dog rode up and handed over his own war bonnet." I paused, and the room seemed very quiet. "I love that," I said to fill up the silence. "He had to borrow a headdress to surrender."

"And four months later," Choteau said, "he was dead."

He reached down and felt around on the floor for something. He didn't even try to look. I wondered then how he'd found his way back here, because his sight seemed entirely gone. Whatever he was searching for on the floor, he didn't find it and just stopped.

So I told him about the surrender plans, because I needed to, but also because it changed the subject. He nodded his head at the set up, but he seemed not to care. At least until I mentioned the witnesses and the roadblock.

"Who did you call?" he wanted to know. He seemed lonely asking that.

"Bobby," I said. "But I don't know whether he'll come. And, well, it depends on who he brings." Choteau lowered his head. He ran a hand through his hair, and then pulled the blanket up over his shoulder tighter. "They won't let anybody who was at Wounded Knee through the roadblock. The Feds are afraid this might become another embarrassment. That's the reason for the small army out there."

He sat up straight again and held a fist in the air in front of him. "We had 'em once, Professor," his knuckles were white as he shook that fist. "When we were together," he held the fist up before him, and looked for all the world like an old warrior. "But see what's happened to me and old Bobby, man," he spoke to his fist, and he let it loosen with each word until it was open. "We just never could stick together, man. Oh, every now and then we'd get wise and we'd all pull at once and, shit, we'd make some noise, one for all. But then, right away, it'd be back to the old one on one game." The hand dropped, and after a moment, he said, "And I'm the worst of the bunch, Professor. I let everybody down."

"I talked to Dr. Nordstrom, too," I said.

His head jerked up at that.

"I left a message for her with him," I said. "Will she get it?"

"I don't know," he said, and he seemed so frail he might tremble.

"Choteau?" I asked him. "She was the reason you broke out, I know. But I'm still not sure why."

His shoulders hunched and he had nothing of Indian chiefs or Crazy Horse or even AIM in him. The warrior of moments ago was gone. He was just a hard timer on the run, cornered and desperate.

"She called and told you she was leaving him, but why not wait? You were up for parole right?"

"They'd never give it to me," he said. "They'll never let me out, Professor. Not until they're all dead and I'm long forgotten."

He was talking about those agents at the Bureau who knew Coler and Williams. They'd all have to die of old age before he ever saw the Black Hills, or Fort Totten, or anything he'd call home, again.

"You've never spent fifteen years in jail, Professor," he said. Even his shoulders seemed sunken. Then, so softly I could barely hear him, he said, "I just wanted to **see** her again."

The way he said that word, I suddenly understood some small part of him. At least I think I did. For a moment, his ochre skin and his ancient blood seemed clearer, and not so opaque. He was going blind, so he meant that word literally. He wanted just once more, just once in a long lifetime of being a martyr for a cause behind the bars of one federal prison or another, just once more he wanted to look at her. I suppose only he could have known how quickly the darkness was closing in, how little time he had left. He sat there now, hunched over, remarkable for what he could accomplish, but blinder than any of us ever realized.

"Who else?" he said, rising from that crouch.

"No one," I lied. Or maybe it wasn't a lie. It seemed pointless now to mention Terri, because Golman was right. I'd screwed it all up with her. She was back in Missouri, she was with her parents, she was safe at home. I was alone on this one.

"Choteau?" I said. He seemed lost in himself then, and I didn't think he heard me. "I saw the old man last night. I think."

He turned his head sideways, and he looked over at me. "And?" he said.

I believed at that moment he could see me.

"Last night, at this motel where they kept me locked up. He showed up after everybody was asleep. I think he did anyway." I stopped there, trying to remember it all clearly, thinking about that missing pipe again. "There wasn't any trace of him this morning, though. I looked around and there was nothing. Nothing at all."

Choteau nodded his head, his smile faded away. But he didn't speak.

"So maybe it was just a dream, you know. But I could've sworn he was there in the room, Choteau." Then I shook my head, "I was probably just dreaming it."

"Probably," he said, but a little smile crept back to his lips.

I laughed. "Right," I said. "I see what you mean," and that made him laugh too and nod his head yes.

"So tell me, Professor," he pulled the blanket up around him and covered that bare shoulder from the cold. It was a good sign, I thought. If he wanted to stay warm, then maybe he wanted to surrender, too. Maybe he didn't want to die. "What did Grandfather Ice have to say?" He didn't add "in your dream" to that.

"Not much." I limped over to the hot stove and held my free hand out toward it. "Mostly he had things to show me."

"Like what?"

So I told him about the mask, and Choteau nodded his head with recognition. "The one in your house," he grinned at remembering it. I told him the way it kept changing, the way it was his face and it was Crazy Horse's face, and I even told him about Mary Red Skies. But when it came time to mention Terri, I left her out. I didn't want to remember it, and I was afraid that, in describing her, I might understand something in that dream I didn't want to face. Not now, not with all those hungry cops and loaded guns outside. Not when she wasn't going to show up.

So I switched the subject, and told Choteau about the disappearing pipe and the broken bulb that wasn't broken, and then about the way the old man smelled and how he farted at every turn.

"Some things never change," Choteau chuckled. "Some smells never grow old, they just grow riper. Even in your dreams."

"What do you suppose that all means, Choteau?" I said, in the end.

He shrugged. "It could mean a lot of things," he grinned. "But there is one thing that it means, Professor. It means that you're not angry at Grandfather Ice anymore. And that means maybe you'll trust in him. Someday."

"He asked me a question, before he was gone," I said. I could hear the old man's cackle again. "How can you tell the dancer from the mask?" I repeated his words.

Choteau nodded his head at that.

"What does that mean?" I said.

"It means, Professor, you are finally asking the right questions." He laughed, and seemed proud of me. His head was still nodding at what I'd said. "This is a good dream, Professor Gentles. It will take you a lifetime to understand it. But now, we should give you a name from it."

"In the dream," I said, "the old man, he kept calling me Little Big Man."

Choteau smiled broadly at that. He looked in my direction, though I don't think he saw me. At least not clearly. He put his palms on his knees and leaned up. "Well, Little Big Man," he snorted, "it looks like it's you and me, then."

I limped back over to the doorway and said, "It doesn't feel right, Choteau. I still feel like Will Gentles."

"Let's get this over with," he said, as if he wasn't changing the subject at all. As if what happened next might change my mind. "Call this brother-in-law of yours in."

"We can trust Golman," I told myself as well as him. I opened the door and waved the cane outside. I heard the ghosts out there whispering and weeping again, but I shoved the door closed and said. "Golman doesn't like you, but he wants you alive."

*   *   *

302

In a matter of moments we heard the Blazer pulling down the lane and then jumping the curb. It was so fast, it surprised even me. Golman must have been waiting out there, with the engine idling. The Blazer pulled up out in front of our little log guardhouse.

"Let's get rolling," Choteau said again, smiling a little. He stood up.

"Wait," I said, with my nose out the cracked door. "I want to be sure Golman's alone. And everything's the way we planned it."

"I thought you trusted him," Choteau chuckled at me and took a few steps toward me, and the doorway.

I didn't answer, because Golman stepped out of the truck then. He raised his arms in the air and walked around the fender. Everything looked right. The Blazer was empty. Golman was without his jacket. The shoulder holster in the pit of his white shirt was empty. His pockets were turned out. From his belt the handcuffs dangled. He stopped about twenty feet from the door.

After a moment, Golman said, "I'm freezing my ass off out here, folks. Let's go."

"Let's go," Choteau repeated.

He walked up to the door and, taking it from me, opened it wide. I think he needed all the light he could to see, but he never let on for a moment. "Wait," I said. I bent over and scooped up some dust from the doorstep with my free hand, and then I took it and rubbed it in his hair. I tossed the rest of it over him like some kind of incense. "Remember your dream," I said. "Now you're safe from your enemies. Right?"

He just stepped past me and out onto the snow. He never let on that he knew what I was talking about. But he did. I know he did. Then I saw the shock in Golman's eyes. He was seeing the war paint and the bare shoulder and the draped red blanket for the first time. He was seeing Crazy Horse, only to him this Indian just looked like some psychopath. And Golman was scared. And it was the only time I've ever seen him that way.

But if Golman was scared, how did this look to the twenty some men out there waiting for a shot at Bernard Choteau, the old cop-killer himself? How did it look to them?

I hobbled out the door behind Choteau, staying close to him, and I carefully scanned the grounds all around us. He Dog was there, somewhere, because he whispered to us again. "I warned you," he said. Red Cloud and his men were huddled just over to my right, and they seemed to rise up and stand taller, wanting to see what would happen. "I warned you something like this would happen," He Dog whispered. American Horse and his followers stepped back, they wanted to be clear of the growing trouble. The morning sun was glaring right in our faces now. I scanned the row of cabins where the feds and their volunteers were waiting. But they were all just gray silhouettes against that sun breaking off the snow behind them. They weren't real, but all these spirits were. Up in the bluffs near Crow Butte, with the sun at his back, Touch the Clouds heaved a sigh and turned his horse away. He rode back to the north, off into the hills, never looking behind him. He hadn't seen it before; he couldn't stand to watch it now.

"I warned you," He Dog whispered. I looked around, but I couldn't see him anywhere. I just understood it was his voice. "You are not even with friends," he said. "Except for me," he whispered.

Choteau stopped about four steps out of the guardhouse. He turned his head, his chin was high and proud, and he seemed to survey the world around him. I doubt if he saw anything. It was all part of the act. But maybe, when I think of it now, maybe he was seeing that field of ghosts.

With his head high, Choteau began to sing then. At first it was just soft and it sounded like a moan. But before long it rose up out of his chest and became a chant, a full-blown musical prayer, sung from deep in his chest.

Golman's arms dropped a little and his eyes squinted. The paint and the blanket had scared him, but this song stuff, I could tell it was making his insides squirm. He was not worrying about the cold anymore. He had some deep craziness on his hands.

But this Indian blues Choteau was chanting out to the hills, to the ghosts, to the retreating shape of old Touch-the-Clouds, to the spirit of Protector, to us all, I recognized it. I think all of us did, in some way. We'd all heard it before, in our hearts. But I'd heard it just recently. And not in my head.

It was the same song Choteau sang our first night on the road. The one he'd told me I'd understand soon enough, way back in Hounddog, Kansas. And it was the same tune I heard Old Badlands humming last night, in my dreams.

It was his death song.

"Let's move it now," Golman said, but his voice cracked. The marine in him made him walk toward us to cover his fear. But this singing stuff had just plain rattled his soul, I think. As he came near, he lowered his arms and took the cuffs from his belt. "The sooner we get him in that truck and out of here, the better off we'll all be," he hissed at me.

Just then a station wagon, forest green with brown wood panels on its side, came ripping down Highway 20 from the east. It slid to a stop up on the highway at the far end of the parade ground. He Dog fell silent. Red Cloud and American Horse and the others all turned and looked toward it.

"Let's get these cuffs on, Choteau," Golman said. "Hold out your hands."

Choteau's chant softened to a moan again, but he ignored Golman's orders. The Indian already seemed part of another time.

The door to the station wagon swung open. Choteau didn't move. He was looking straight at Golman. He chanted low, almost under his breath, but I could still hear it. Bobby Red Skies stood up out of the station wagon, and slammed the door shut behind him. He stood there, in a sheepskin coat and bareheaded. The rest of the car was empty.

Golman put a hand on Choteau's elbow. "C'mon, pal. Don't make trouble," he said.

"Don't touch me," Choteau spoke suddenly, and pulled his arm loose. "I am Crazy Horse."

305

"Bernard," Bobby Red Skies yelled through his cupped hands. "It's me. Bobby."

Choteau's chin rose again and he turned toward Red Skies. But I've never been more sure that he was blind.

"C'mon, hands out here, buddy," Golman said, but his voice wavered. "Let's go."

"Be careful, Bernard. There's pigs and goons all over hell," Bobby yelled. It must have sounded like some old, rebel yell from back at Wounded Knee to Choteau, because it sure did to me. It lifted my heart.

At the same moment, Golman took hold of Choteau's wrist. But with a great, defiant roar, that would be his last, Choteau twisted away from him. Then, from under the blanket somewhere, that little paring knife flashed in the bright sun. Choteau slashed it once through the air at Golman's side. Mike slipped, and fell backwards onto the snow, as he moved to dodge the blade.

I remember yelling, "No." I remember I grabbed hold of the arm that held the knife and jerked it behind his back. We struggled for a moment or two and then we both fell onto the ground. He had years on me, but Choteau was still stronger than I was. I was tangled up in my cane, and in his arms. I pulled both his arms behind his back, but I couldn't hold onto him. He kept slipping loose. I just pulled harder, and he kept struggling loose. Then he groaned and I felt the warm blood on my chest and stomach.

I didn't know right away whose blood it was. It was just red all over my hands, quicker than I thought possible. It scared me enough I let out a heavy groan too.

I turned over and rolled away from him in the red snow. And that was what did it for him. You see, I cleared the way then. I rolled free and left him like a red target in the snow. And the instant he was clear of Golman and me, though he lay on the ground bleeding and helpless, the guns started.

It was all one heavy blow, really, the way it came. They all were ready, all poised. They seemed to fire at once, though I know it must have been a ragged unison at best. Still, it seemed to fall on him in one blow.

Choteau's body recoiled at the strike. He slid a few inches in the snow. His body was freckled black, and then red, all at once, and then it was still. It didn't seem possible that he could be dead so quickly, but he was. He was gone.

And with him went all the ghosts. Red Cloud, and Black Shawl, and He Dog. All of them gone. Crazy Horse is dead. The parade ground was empty.

It was just the remains of Bernard Choteau, a full blood Lakota and an inmate who'd escaped, lying dead in the snow, now. And there was nothing left to do about it. Nothing left to change, nothing to escape. Nothing.

In the moments after that the world changed its shape. I was surrounded by cops. I shook myself and found I was holding that bloody knife in my hand. There was a deep slash at the base of my thumb, and it was bleeding in streams, but other than that I was untouched. I got up and pushed past Golman and his, "You okay?" The cops let me walk over to the body, they just parted out of some silent respect that reached even them for a moment or two. I walked, without the cane, limping, but I didn't feel that knee. Not at all.

Bobby Red Skies was standing near the body, gazing at Choteau 's bare shoulder. Except it was torn now and oozing blood. Bobby was too stunned to speak.

"We're not done yet," I said to him. Bobby looked blankly at me. I slipped the knife in my belt and I bent down to the body.

"I'm sorry, man," Red Skies muttered, to who I'll never know.

"Let's do it up right, Chief," I said and I picked Choteau up. I think of it now, and I know my knee must have been screaming in pain at me. But didn't feel it. Not then.

A couple of patrolmen started for me, yelling stuff about not messing with the evidence. But Golman and Bobby held them back. "Leave him alone," Red Skies said. I suppose

I looked crazed myself, covered with blood and snow and mud, stumbling and limping under the body's weight.

I carried him over to the adjutant's quarters, to that other cabin where Crazy Horse had died in 1877. He was already gone, but we needed to finish it right. Golman and Red Skies followed me.

With one kick of my bum leg I knocked the door open and carried him in. There was a cot inside, but I laid him on the floor beside it. I put him there where he had died before, right on the floor, right where Crazy Horse had refused to die in the white man's bed.

In his back he had two deep wounds from my knife. How in that flash of struggle I managed to stab him twice in the back I'll never know. But I did. Like two old thrusts of a bayonet. Like William Gentles of old. Like Little Big Man holding his arms.

I stretched him out there and covered him with a blanket, and closed his blank, open eyes.

Suddenly it was just me and a bunch of cops and a dead man. It was just now. My leg was back to its old shape, and I lay down on the floor next to him, because I couldn't stand up any longer. All the past had disappeared. There was only now, echoing through the years. All those ghosts were gone, as if they'd never been there, never even existed. And it struck me then: there was one spirit who never showed, the one ghost I've never seen. Because maybe, like they tell me, he lives under my skin.

Little Big Man.

My life has seemed pale since that moment. When you lose someone, even someone you don't understand, even such a stranger as Bernard Choteau was, it leaves a gap. And there are some gaps which never close.

After a while Golman helped me up. He shoved the cane back in my hand. "C'mon, pal," he said. "Buck up now."

He slipped the knife out of my belt too, I suppose to prevent trouble. But it was evidence, too. Important evidence. You see, it was my knife that stabbed Choteau and saved an agent's life. I wasn't thinking about that little detail, but he was. It was my back door out of this deal.

After the coroner came and declared Choteau dead, they hauled me and the remains back to Chadron in an ambulance. Golman followed in the Blazer, and Bobby Red Skies in his station wagon. But I refused to ride with them. I'd come this far with Choteau, or with Crazy Horse, take your pick. It was time for me to finish the trip. Full circle, from one hospital escape to one hospital morgue.

The medics in the ambulance bandaged my hand up while we waited for the coroner. On the ride to Chadron they wrapped my knee. "Better get it looked at," they said, "if you want to walk without that cane again." They left Choteau alone. There was nothing they could do for him.

One of the cops came to me then, while we sat waiting there. "What's this?" he said. He held up that patrolman's boot. Old Protector's favorite chew toy.

"I don't know," I said.

"Hey, there's a dog in here," I heard someone yell. "He killed a damn dog in here."

Out at the road block, along with all the cops and the press, a group of half a dozen Indian men stood beside an old Ford pickup. Bobby waved to them as we drove past. They were all long haired, and I realized they were the men who didn't get through, the men with Wounded Knee in their past. They watched the ambulance roll by and they seemed to understand what it meant, with no lights and no siren and no rush. Because they didn't follow us. I watched them out the back window of the ambulance turned hearse, as they all climbed, somehow into the cab of that one pickup, and drove away to the north.

*   *   *

I waited with Choteau's body at the hospital, too. The morgue was just an over-air conditioned room in the basement. I sat inside there on a folding chair beside the gurney where he lay. When it got too cold for me, I took the chair and sat outside the door until I warmed up. Then it was back to his side again.

Golman and Bobby Red Skies tried to talk me out of it. "This is getting ridiculous," Golman said. But like the doctors and the officials at the Chadron hospital, he saw my eyes. They left me alone, because they didn't want a scene. They watched my every move, but they let me stay. And I suppose Golman saved my behind again. I'm sure he was behind their tolerance. "The family will be here soon," Red Skies told them, so I stayed by Choteau's side. "For the time being," was ringing in all their ears.

A string of federal cops came and asked me questions. The second one took my fingerprints. They seemed mostly interested in that knife: where it came from, how it had disappeared, how long it had been hidden, and especially how it had appeared again, out on the old parade grounds at the state park. They liked my story about how the knife had spent the night in a toilet tank in a Kansas motel. But mostly they wanted to know about that moment it came flashing out of Crazy Horse's blanket, slashing at Special Agent Michael Golman, and slicing my hand. I may have saved that agent's life, several of them said. I think they'd been well prepped by my clever brother-in-law.

But whatever they said and did around me, I stayed there at the morgue, like I was on guard duty, mainly because I didn't know what else to do. I suppose I was in shock, now that I think back on those hours. I know I felt emotionally numb. The day passed.

*   *   *

About three or four that afternoon, the "family" showed. The other people Bobby Red Skies called. Though I'd never seen them before, not in the flesh anyway, I knew them immediately. And they knew me.

Close to thirty years had passed on them since that picture was taken, the one Choteau carried with him so far and so long. The photo that disappeared somewhere along our way to that old parade ground and his end.

Bobby and an aid who was wearing whites showed the two of them off the elevator at the end of the hall. He indicated the door, and then gladly left them to me, and the cop watching me. The boy was in his mid-thirties now, just a few years younger than me. His haircut was worth more than all the clothes I had on, and he wore a dark suit with a camel overcoat and a gray scarf. In my old jeans and flannel, even with my bright blue eyes, I looked more Indian than he did at the moment.

She was in her early sixties, I suppose, but still beautiful. Her long hair was dark and shot with a frost of gray. It may have been a hair dresser's work, in fact it probably was, but however it got there, it looked right on her. Her deep eyes drew you to them, and had just the hint of the high plains in them. They were made up, but the make up had run off.

"Mrs. Nordstrom," I said.

She looked at me with those brown, youthful eyes and corrected me. "Mary," she said. Cousin Bobby stood by silently. He looked relieved to be passing them off to me.

"And you must be Jimmie," I said and he shook my hand. I think he'd rather I'd called him James, or Mr. Nordstrom.

As I took them inside the air-conditioned room, leaving Bobby and my friendly cop outside the door, I tried to hate her. After all, she'd been the fulcrum, when you got right down to it. She had pried all this destruction loose. Now she strode in here, in some fur fringed coat and an appropriate black dress,

311

with her big eyes all red and her mascara rinsed off. But what had she really done for Bernard Choteau, beyond breaking his heart? Like I say, I tried hard at hating her for it all.

I led them over to the gurney and, with no little animosity, I lifted the sheet from his face. She caught her breath and her hands rose to cover her mouth. Then with her right hand, she gently reached down and stroked his cheek, where the streak of lightning still flashed. She seemed to cradle Choteau's head then in her hand, and the tears welled up in her eyes.

It was a real gesture, that last touch. And it brought me around, out of my anesthesia. Whatever hurt and harm they had done to one another, however long the chain of mistakes they had made, I realized then it had never been deliberate. It had always been desperate. And I quit trying to hate her for it.

But the boy surprised me. You see, she seemed, considering the situation, composed and strong. But the boy came apart. This big time lawyer from the Twin Cities in his fancy suit of courtroom clothes, he buried his face in both hands and he wept. It was silent, but only because he struggled to hold the rock of his weeping in.

Suddenly my anger flared up and I felt something from this death, for the first time. It rose up out of my shock and cracked my numbness. "You know, none of us are at fault here," I said. I think I believed it too, at that moment. I know I said it as much for her as for myself.

"You know why he's dead here?" I said. "It's not anything of ours." Jimmie's head lifted from his hands and he looked at me, and there was something hungry or fearful in his eyes. But it didn't stop me. Not for a moment.

"It's what happened out there at Oglala thirteen years ago," I said. "It's those two dead agents out there. They had to even the score. Choteau said it himself. They wanted him dead, and now that's what they got. But us? All of us? We were just trying to save him."

Jimmie Nordstrom slouched down into his hands again, but she seemed to stand at attention and gaze quietly at his remains there.

312

"And you know?" I went on. "He told me he did it; he told me he murdered those two agents out there at Oglala. He said he was guilty. He said he killed them. But I don't believe it, not for a moment. They killed him for it; that's why he died. But he didn't do it. I know he didn't do it."

She turned and walked away from the gurney, wrapping that fur coat around her tightly, and not just at the cold. She stared at the bare white wall of the morgue, seemed emotionless, with her back to me. He wiped his eyes and his cheeks with his fingers. I'll always remember that. I know little Jimmie had a silk hanky on him somewhere, but he forgot it. He just wiped his face with his bare fingers.

"He died for nothing," I said. "Because he didn't do it."

"I think you've said enough," Jimmie Nordstrom straightened up and sniffed and put his professional face back on. "We can take it from here. I believe."

That was when a new silence fell over us, and not one that seemed fair. It was a blaming quiet, it separated us into camps. I stood there, angry still, and I looked at the boy, at Choteau's son, and over at her back.

And suddenly, my duties were over. I was done with it, and not the way I wanted to be done with it, either. But there was nothing more I could do. Everything would be taken care of, now, and without me. It was all over and done.

"Right," I said in a whisper. I didn't look at Choteau anymore. I let the sheet cover his face and I limped slowly and deliberately out of the room.

When I opened the door I heard her say, "Thank you." Other than her own name, they were the only words I ever heard her speak. But I didn't look back, and the door closed behind me on the cold air of the morgue.

The early dusk of winter had fallen outside, and I didn't know what to do, or where to go. Golman was waiting in the lobby and he seemed to brighten up when he saw me. I suppose it was relief.

Quickly he took me out a side door to the Blazer and said, as he helped me in, "Don't worry, brother, you're all taken care of." Then he walked around the truck and got in behind the wheel. "You know, you maybe saved my life out there. I won't forget that."

"Let's not exaggerate, Golman."

"Who's exaggerating?" he laughed.

Then the press found us. Ten or twelve of them came bursting around the corner of the hospital at a full run. Video cameras and microphones and popping flashes, all on the gallop.

"Let's get out of here," Golman started the Blazer and we screeched past them. But not before someone got the photo of me that made the front page of most papers, next to little headlines that all read like "Hostage Prof Saved in Gun Battle." I was on my way to celebrity status, if I wanted it.

But at that moment I just wanted to be alone. "Can you take me to my car?" I said.

Golman looked at me and didn't answer immediately.

"I just need to get away for a couple hours, just need to think about it all," I said. "I don't need those reporters just yet."

"We can keep you away from them, chum. No problem."

"But I need to get away from you guys, too," I said.

Golman nodded his head with some understanding. I realized then he might be my lone ticket back to Terri. But for the time being, I mostly needed to be alone.

"We'll need a formal statement from you sometime. But I can write that up for you," he said, pausing. Then he seemed to like the idea. "Why don't you disappear for 24 hours or so? Yeah."

The little Renault, speckled with salt and mud, was still parked near that tavern on the outskirts of Crawford. On the rear fender I saw the chips and dents of that buckshot blast back in Kansas, back when Choteau and I were "foraging" our way north to the promised land, back when Mary Red Skies didn't seem so much like Mrs. Nordstrom. Back when I thought I knew where we were heading. Golman helped me over to the little car; he leaned in and laid my cane over on the rider's seat, on what I'd come to think of as Crazy Horse's place in the last week. He took a scrap of paper from that same notebook in his coat and scribbled a number on it again. He tore it out and shoved it, along with a fifty dollar bill, in the pocket of my flannel. "Get lost at some hotel out here somewhere tonight," he said. "Call that number tomorrow, and we'll find you. Okay?"

I nodded and slammed the car door shut. The Le Car turned right over in the cold, though the idle sounded like a tractor. Golman rapped on the window and I rolled it down.

"Don't worry about a thing, brother-in-law," Golman said. "I got your ass all covered." Then he winked at me.

I drove north on a cold, icy blacktop out of Crawford. It cut through foothills and scrub, and then out onto snow covered prairies. Another pair of headlights followed me at a distance, but I barely noticed. I was driving the only paved road for forty miles in every direction, so being followed didn't seem unusual.

But the old Le Car was not really eating up the highway. Out there, in the shadow of the Black Hills, the prairie rolls in heavy waves. At first I thought the car was just cold. But even after an hour of driving, it lost power climbing hills, and it began to knock if I didn't let up on the gas. We were not breaking any land speed records out there.

After a while I began to notice those headlights behind me. They seemed to stay about the same distance away. Either

315

that vehicle had some knocking problems just like this old Renault, or it was hanging back and pacing me. Golman had hooked a tail on me.

About the time I saw my tenth billboard for the Reptile Gardens and the Wall Drug, I decided to lose my FBI accompaniment. Since that was next to impossible to do on an isolated road like this, I headed into Rapid City.

In a way, this chase was what I needed. It was fun playing hide and seek with the fed-mobile on my tail. It was a fine distraction. On most of my two and a half hour creep from Nebraska to Rapid City, I concentrated on my tail. I barely thought about Bernard Choteau or Crazy Horse or the parade grounds at old Fort Robinson. About the bloody body or the knife in my hands. About the doctor's wife and Choteau's kid lawyer and their too little, too late grief. About Terri. I just drove. I sputtered up hills and rolled down them, and I watched those headlights in my mirror. They would disappear behind me into a hollow, flash against the clear black sky and then crest a hill after me. Closing in, fading back, watching. But always back there.

I didn't really know or care where I was headed. I was only looking for more traffic, for some busy city street, where I could lose him. Once he got too close and I caught a glimpse of the car. I saw enough to know it was a fairly new sedan, not a truck or a patrol car. That's all I could tell, in the dark.

I stopped for gas at the edge of Rapid City, and I watched the cars roll past me on the divided four lane. Then I drove through the hills east of town, in new housing subdivisions filled with cul-de-sacs and dead ends, and I even tooled around in the empty, unplowed parking lot of a race track. It wasn't long before every car behind me seemed to be a fairly new sedan. After about an hour of driving the outskirts, I turned west and rode down through the heart of town. Abut twenty years ago a great flood had rolled down out of the Black hills and cut away a wide swipe of the old town along Rapid Creek. It was urban renewal, Paha Sapa style. So now I drove along a pretty parkway of young trees and landscaped banks that the old flood had left open. There were late model sedans all around, but none of them seemed to be following me. All they cared was that I stayed out of their way. I'd lost my tail, I was sure.

I saw a sign and headed west on the Interstate. After a week of back roads and side trips, this big broad runway of a road seemed a luxury. The Renault was still stuttering every time it had to pull up a hill. But at least the inclines were smoother and gentler on I90. Freeways, you know, with their sweet illusion of escape, are great therapy. I didn't want to feel. I just drove. And it worked.

Outside of Sturgis, though, my headlights caught the brown sign for Bear Butte State Park. Of course, I thought. Where else but Bear Butte? The oldest, holiest site on the plains. Old Noahves. That sacred place where the Crow and the Blackfeet and the Cheyenne and the Arapahoe and all the Lakotas, where they all had reached for and maybe touched something divine. The place where Sweet Medicine brought the law and the four sacred Arrows down, where the White Buffalo Woman who brought the sacred pipe had disappeared. The Bear Butte. Where else could I be headed but there? It was just too neat and tidy and appropriate to just drive by now, and besides, I think something was drawing me there.

I turned off at the Sturgis exit and wandered through town, heading north gradually with the dark lines of the Black Hills at my back. It was right along there, on the north edge of Sturgis, I noticed I'd picked up my late model sedan again. I had my tail back.

But if the feds wanted to visit Bear Butte with me, it was okay by me. Maybe they'd learn something there, I thought. But deeper down I knew that was why I was headed to the Mountain, that ancient holy place. Maybe I'd learn something, too. Something more.

I wheeled through a scattering of trees and down to a parking lot by a darkened Visitor's Center. The FBI sedan's headlights pulled in across the lot behind me and stopped. I opened the door and stood up, leaning on the car. The mountain rose up like a black shadow behind me, like a big brother protecting me. It felt like a bodyguard, and I felt strong.

The sedan snapped into reverse, wheeled around and then with a jump, drove away. I laughed at his tail lights. I'd led him down a dead end and caught him. But while I laughed, I also noticed the sedan was a rental car with South Dakota plates, and there was only the driver inside. Would the feds be renting cars from Avis? Wouldn't they have their own local fleet? And I wondered whether the FBI would send a loner out to tail me. And if he wasn't alone, then where was the other agent?

A gust of wind out of the west slapped me in the face, and forced me to turn around. It may have been the mountain calling me to attention. Its big black shadow towered in front of me. I took my cane and hobbled across the snowy lot toward it. I stepped over the curb and gazed up at the dark face of the mountain.

A gully filled with brush huddled around the base of it. The scrub and snow there lay between me and the sides of the Butte. A trail led through the brush and disappeared into the hollow. I assume it led to a trail up the mountainside. But there was no way my bad knee would let me get any closer. I'd come to another end of the road. Still, the mountain stood there in front of me dressed in the snow and the cold and the night and asked me, "So?"

I was afraid suddenly. I'm not sure of what, but I began to tremble in the cold wind, and I kept seeing Choteau's body sliding in the pink snow. I kept hearing him say, "Do not touch me. I am Crazy Horse." But there was none of it I could understand.

So I asked the mountain. "Why?" I said to it, but I didn't dare to speak out loud. I whispered that word, inside my head.

That's right. Little old me, Mr. Twentieth Century Man, an usher boy at the Church of Reason, the tenured Professor of

Time. I was reduced to standing there sheepishly talking to a mountain. "Why?" I said. And it didn't answer.

I felt like it was what I should do, what Old Badlands Face and Crazy Horse and Choteau and the whole load of them, what they wanted from me. What they would have done. With all my dreaming and driving and then my vigil with the body, it all seemed to lead right then, to the foot of Bear Butte, and to me asking a mountainside what I should do next.

And for all that, I got nothing.

The mountain just sat there like a lifeless slab of rock and ice, wearing away in the wind and the rain. It didn't say anything.

And then I felt stupid. I remembered how pale I was, and how dark they all were, Choteau and Old Badlands and all of them. They were all different than me. I was done. I had tried. But I couldn't play Indian. I was just a damn history teacher who'd read too many books and started talking to the hills. I was trying to turn myself into some kind of Indian Quixote, but it wouldn't work. Because after it was all over, in the end, at the bottom of this snowy hill, I was white.

I limped back to the car and crawled in the tiny back seat. I was cold and lonely and this Thursday that started with hopes of surrender and homecoming had become the longest day of my life.

The sleeping bags were still lying back on the floor of the guardhouse at Fort Robinson. I curled up tight into a ball, trying to absorb the warmth left in the car, and I listened to the wind sweep around the mountain.

The Lakota have a myth, and I remembered it then, curled up at the foot of their holy mountain. They believe that at the beginning of time a buffalo stood up way off in the west to hold the waters of destruction back. Every year that old buffalo loses one hair, and every age he loses one leg. When all of his fur and all four legs are gone, the waters will rush in and it will be the end of our time.

I fell asleep that night in the cold back seat of the Le Car, and dreamt of a buffalo, crippled, dying, trying in the end to stand on its one, last leg.

*

now and then

I tried to go back to teaching after all of this. My big adventure was over, and there were a couple weeks of Christmas break left to rest and recuperate. Ahead of me, I had a schedule I once would have enjoyed: two sections of the second half of American History and a course on the history of the Mississippi and the West. The Department even went easy on me as far as committee duties, considering the "stress" I'd been through. And noticing my new celebrity, too, which they hoped to benefit from as well.

I started out all three of my spring courses with Wounded Knee. Maybe this would help me bring my anger and confusion to some point. At least, that's what I hoped. I could use my experience to teach with real passion. And it worked, too, for the first day or so.

You see, on the opening day of classes I didn't bring in course outlines or rattle on about papers and tests and textbooks. None of that. Instead, I drew a vivid mental picture for my students, so vivid it startled them. I showed them Chief Big Foot and the remainders of his band trapped and trying to surrender on a bitter cold day, on December 29, 1890. They were herded down into what is really little more than a ditch, though they were knee deep in the high plains snow. Then the Seventh Cavalry gathered around that gully, the same Seventh Cavalry who'd taken it full on the chin at the Little Big Horn fourteen years before, at what we had named Custer's Last Stand. With that battle in their memories, the Seventh Cavalry fired into the ditch at Wounded Knee, and killed Big Foot and over 300 of his people. The Lakota died, bleeding on the ground, and I made my students see the pink streaks in the snow and the black of the powder burns at close range. "Twenty-five sol-

320

diers from the Seventh died that day, in their own cross fire," I told them. And in each class, without really planning it this way, I ended my lecture standing in the middle of the room, my arms waving in the air, telling them how twenty Congressional Medals of Honor were awarded to the soldiers of the Seventh Cav. Twenty brave, gold medals for a massacre, and only a mass grave for the "Sioux." Then I marched dramatically out of the auditorium and left those classes wondering whether it was all right for them to go.

That was how I survived the first day. All three classes were the same. It went downhill from there.

You see, as we worked on into the semester I realized I was supposed to lay it out for them in order. It was my job to make it all clear to them, to talk about the causes and the results, so they could understand. I should have asked the cogent questions about Progress and Manifest Destiny, and lectured like I once did about the fatal, inevitable clash of cultures. Because, after all, I was the Professor of Time. It was my job.

And I tried. I really and truly did. I had all the notes I'd used in the past, and I had done it all before. More times than I dare to admit to myself, even now. But it seemed every time I began to lecture, every time I tried to make all those neat, ironic connections, I got lost. I'd find myself halfway through the class period discussing the idea of the perpetual now, or that maybe time wasn't a straight line the way we've always seen it, how it might fold back on itself. That it might move in a circle, or maybe a spiral at best, and how could we know really about anything like a cause. Didn't history repeat itself? Didn't I repeat it over and over, each semester?

I found out later, from an old student who'd become a friend, that I terrified those poor classes. They tell me I glared at them with such fervor, as I rambled on and on, my eyes burning, nearly frothing at the mouth in a fit, my students were afraid to come to class, and more afraid of what I might do if they dared to cut.

After about four weeks of that, the University gave me a medical leave. I didn't object.

Bernard Choteau's not really named Choteau, you know. There's no Mary Red Skies, either. And I'm not Will Gentles, though I told you that already at the start. You realize I've changed all the names here. There are people still in prison over this whole deal and some people who might go to prison if I used their real names. So nobody who's anybody here is real. As far as you're concerned, I made this all up. It didn't even happen.

But while you think about that, I want to remind you of something an old man said once. It was a deal just about like this one. He said, "Whether it happened exactly like this or not, I don't know." I suspect he stopped right there to chuckle at the people listening. "But if you think about it long enough," he said, "you can see it's true."

It was old Badlands Face, the Grandfather of Gas, who said that.

Amen, I say. Amen, Grandfather.

A rapping came at the window. I sat up with a jump and saw someone in a suit and overcoat standing outside the Renault. It must have been after midnight, in the early hours of Friday morning, because the winds at Bear Butte had blown all the warmth out of the car. I was freezing, and I might have frozen to death I suppose, if I hadn't been roused.

I shivered and looked out the back window. The rented sedan was parked across the visitors lot from me, its headlights still on. The rap came on the window again. The suit of the FBI agent was waiting for me out in the cold night. A stranger's voice, but one I'd heard before, said my name. My full name. He even attached the "Dr." in front of it that I never used.

I lumbered out of the car, fighting my stiffness from the cold.

"You okay?" the suit said.

I didn't answer; I just wrangled my way out of the tiny backseat, feeling as arthritic as poor old Protector, rest his soul. When I stood straight and turned around, I saw him.

"Are you sure you're all right?" Jimmie Nordstrom said. "You looked like you'd passed out or," he took off his camel overcoat, "or something in there."

"You," I said, glancing over at the rented sedan.

He wrapped the overcoat around me.

"You've been following me," I said. "From Nebraska."

He nodded his head. "I've been driving around all night."

"It was you."

"I've been trying to decide whether to talk to you or not." Jimmie looked away from me and at the side of Bear Butte. I believe he knew what he was looking at.

"About what?"

"About my father," he said.

I didn't speak and he stared at the mountain. We both understood he meant Choteau.

"You said, you know, back at the hospital. You said he died for nothing."

"Well," I muttered, "I was still pretty upset about. . . "

Jimmie Nordstrom held up a hand to silence me. "No. You were right," he said. "My father didn't kill those FBI agents back at Oglala. He wasn't guilty."

"But he knew who did kill them," I pulled his overcoat around me.

He nodded his head and then he looked at me and said, "But he didn't die for nothing, Professor. He had his reasons. And I just wanted you to know that."

"He died to protect the one who did it. Didn't he."

Jimmie Nordstrom nodded his head, but his eyelids shielded his eyes.

"You were just a kid, weren't you," I said.

"Barely twenty one," he hung his head a little.

"Just a kid," I said. "And it was a rough situation."

Suddenly he spoke in one burst. "There were guns going off all over, you know. And everybody forgets there were children and old people at the house. Later on Little Joe Killsright got shot dead in the gunfire. Everybody forgets that." The lawyer's head and shoulders began to bob and he scuffed his feet around in the snow as he spoke. Suddenly he looked like a naive teenager dressed up in a four thousand dollar suit. "I was so pissed off, man, I just couldn't believe it. Here they come rolling in with the guns blazing. We were just camped down by the stream. No big deal. And then . . . "

He stopped there and he looked right at the mountain. His eyes narrowed, as if he was staring into a hard glare. "We went over to the car there in the hollow, you know. All of its tires were flat, shot out in the fight before that. There were six of us. Me and Leonard and my father." The other names he conspicuously left out. It was the two men serving time for the murders, the two men convicted of it, and himself. The others carefully never got mentioned. "The one agent was passed out, and he was lying in the back seat of the car. The other guy, he was bleeding from the shoulder and the fingers on one of his hands were broken. He couldn't even hold a pistol up anymore, you know. But he could sure talk yet. Calling us all fucking redskins and yelling that he would get us all. If any one of us fuckers got out of there alive, he was going to make sure we died in prison, Professor, that's what he said. Because we killed his buddy, see. That other agent wasn't even dead yet, but we were gonna pay.

"Then he said, 'Just like them redskins up on the hill.' I remember my father looked at Leonard, and you could see they were both thinking about Grandpa and Grandma Jumping Bull, 'cause they lived up on the plateau above us. My father says to Leonard, 'I'll go check.' So he hands me his rifle, and he set off at a run up the side of the hill. He wasn't even there, Professor." Jimmie snorted a laugh out. "He wasn't even there when somebody said, 'What are we going to do with these two?' It was Leonard who said they'd never let us get out of there alive. Not after this. Then that agent laughed, you know? I remember what he said. 'When you fuckheads are all dead and gone,' he goes and starts laughing at us, 'I'll be down here teepee creeping, man. Dicking with your sisters.' That's when I said, 'It's a good day to die, brother,' and I put my father's rifle right up to his head. He was nuts, you know, 'cause he laughed right up to the end, Professor. That fed just lost his shit. The poor fucker."

Jimmie was still gazing at the mountain in the dark. He never once during that whole time even glanced away from it.

"So Leonard said no, and my father wasn't even there. I hauled the other one out of the car and finished him off too. Right on the ground beside his friend. Just like that. And Leonard kept saying no. It isn't right. And my father, it was all over and done with by the time he got back. He wasn't even there.

"But they got me out of there. Nobody ever knew I was even in South Dakota, you know. I went back to school, back to Minneapolis. And nobody ever said a word about it. Through all those trials, you know. And all those years Leonard has spent in jail. And all his appeals, Professor. My name never came up once. Not once. And my father, he never even tried to get an appeal. He turned them down, Professor. My father just . . . "

He trailed off there and nobody needed to say anymore. What he'd said echoed around in my mind, making a lot of connections.

"Does your mother know?" I said, piecing it all together.

He shook his head no, but he said, "She's maybe heard rumors, you know. She doesn't believe them, though."

I nodded to him. After a long while, I lied to Jimmie Nordstrom. "Your father didn't die for nothing," I said, though I didn't believe that. It felt wrong to be telling lies there at the foot of that mountain, too.

"Well," he said. "I guess I just thought you should know that." He took a couple steps back away from me, as if we'd drawn too close. The barriers, whatever they were made of, went back up. "I should get back. There's a lot of arrangements to make." He started to walk away. "Keep the jacket, man. You need it," he said.

"Jimmie," I said, and he stopped. But he didn't turn around. "He asked after you, you know." I told him then about the way Choteau had asked Bobby Red Skies about him. About the way Choteau reacted to the news, to the story of his lawyer son. "What he said to me that night, Jimmie, is that you would come around. He believed that. Right up to the end."

Jimmie Nordstrom nodded his head once. I suppose it meant thanks, and goodbye, and some other things besides. But who knows what it really meant. He walked over to his rented car, in his suit and his tie, and he drove away.

When the University gave me my leave, I decided there was only one thing I could do to get straight again. But it could be I was wrong. Maybe there are other ways to heal. But this is what I decided. I sat down and tried to write it all down. At first, for the first three months or so, I just sat at the desk with paper loaded in the typewriter and drank enough coffee everyday to make myself jittery. But then, slowly, I started to put some words on the page. Maybe just a sentence or two, in a day, but gradually it all went down.

I figured when I started writing this it was the only way I could understand what has happened to me. To write it all down. Now, here I am, hammering away at the old keyboard, and with almost the whole story down on paper, and I'm not so sure of that anymore.

The mask sits in the corner by the desk now, near where I write this. It's a beautiful thing, a comfort to me, with its deep black eyes and the red streaks along the bear's nose, and along the raven's beak inside. I've taken it down off the wall. When the words on the page have me stumped, and I don't know what to say anymore, it gives me something to do, I guess. I play with the mask. I pick it up and use the strings in the back to open the bear's mouth and look at the raven hidden inside. I can open the raven's beak too, and see that glaring human face within. But I have to do that by prying at the beak from the outside. I haven't learned yet the trick that Choteau knew that first night, how to open it from inside, the way the old Kwakiutl shamans did when they danced. That part of the great mask is still a mystery to me.

The old Le Car sputtered like it was running out of gas, we jerked and thumped for half a mile, and then all the dummy lights came on at once. It was done for. I'm afraid my little run with Crazy Horse had worn it out. There was not much left of it when we started out, and we'd pushed it now to the end. The old Renault died right there on top of the hill and I let it coast off the pavement into the ditch filled with drifted snow.

I climbed out and pulled out my cane, then I slapped the car on the hood to say farewell. I had no complaints. It had brought me all this way, and now it left me at the top of the hill. All that remained was a long walk down into the valley, to the gully at the bottom. I pulled Jimmie Nordstrom's overcoat around me tighter and started limping down into Wounded Knee.

Pale yellow sunlight glowed just off to the east. The broad rolling hills of the reservation were still baby blue, covered with snow in the moonless night. A stiff wind blew across the highway, and I hobbled against it at the edge of the pavement.

Just moments ago my headlights had flashed across the Pine Ridge Agency's big road marker for Crazy Horse. Eight or ten feet of sign planted in concrete, it bore his whole life story on its two sides. It also bore the graffiti of a lot of local anger. I'd stopped there in the past, in the summers of my grants and my old research, and I'd read it all, including the defacers' comments and changes. I even made notes about it back then. But what I remembered now was the end of it. Out here somewhere, the sign claimed, the parents of Crazy Horse had taken his remains. They'd hauled Crazy Horse's body away on a travois and disappeared with it into these prairies and badlands. Several people claimed to have seen them with that travois. But in every story, they were headed in a different direction, it seemed. In the end, no one knows where they went with him. Crazy Horse's body just disappeared somewhere into these deep, rolling hills.

That road sign is the closest we'll ever come to a grave for him, the Strange Man of the Oglala.

Though it seemed right, my headlights flashing across the marker as I drove past it on that night after Choteau died, it wasn't where I was headed. It wasn't my destination.

After Jimmie Nordstrom left me at the foot of Bear Butte, the old history professor in me reared his head. I thought he was long dead, but then I remembered what day it was. Friday, December 29, 1989. Almost a century too late. And that told me where I had to go next.

So I found myself limping down along the pavement with yellow dawn breaking over the valley. The only sounds were the squeaking of the snow and the slow pant of my breathing. It was ninety-nine years ago, in that gully down below me, cowering among the bare trees, that the slaughter occurred. The mass grave lay near the church, on top of the hill across this valley.

There weren't any cars out on the road, and the few houses were dark and clustered on the other side of the hill, beyond the church. So I was alone. There was just me and the ghosts of ninety-nine years ago, and of Bernard Choteau. He seemed to still be with me, because I could hear his voice and his laugh yet, I could still remember his snore, and the way we smelled of cheap beer, and old bulldog and Slim Jims. I remembered his laugh when he told me we were "foraging." Maybe here, at Wounded Knee, he'd tell me why he died.

The slow, limping walk in the cold helped, too. It gave me time to think. The sky above the valley had turned a pale green, just before the sun cracked the horizon. Everything but the old wind was still, frozen hard and solid. And I tried to give it all some sense.

Maybe it was the years in prison, I thought. That occurred to me first. Choteau knew the parole would never come; with those agents dead and the Bureau always ready to find someone to testify against him, the judges would never set him free. He would die in one prison or another, in some jail house infirmary, forgotten and alone. And the days between now and that death stretched out like some useless desert road, heading nowhere.

And it was even worse for him than it was for Leonard. At least Peltier could fight the flaws in his case, he could write newsletters and paint pictures and work with the moviemakers who wanted to tell his story, and he could hope one day to get out. But Bernard Choteau's only way out was exactly what kept him in. Because if the truth set him free, it also risked his only son. When they could prove Choteau didn't do it, they'd have to be steps and steps and steps closer to knowing who did. And they'd be looking to make it even again. Maybe it seemed to Choteau there was no way for him to be innocent, and for Jimmie to be safe. They were opposite sides of the coin, and only one of them could be up at a time.

So the days in jail stretched out forever ahead of him.

And then there was Mary Red Skies. Once before when he was just a kid he'd lost her. Then late in his life, in the darkness of that prison cell, it must have seemed he had a chance to be with her again. Maybe they could be together, even for just a little while, and he could at least remember his old, his spoiled dreams. And so he risked everything. He even risked his son's future when you think about it. Everything, just to come to her, to be with her. He had used me to find his way to her.

I could hear my heart beating in my ears then. It was louder than the squeaking of the dry snow. I was only halfway down the long hill, and the gravel and ice along the side of the

329

highway seemed loose and treacherous, and the metal cane was so cold it seemed futile. The long, faint shadows I cast on the pavement were gray and broken. The dark gully of Wounded Knee seemed farther away than it did at the top of the hill, and the whole reservation around me was desolate. Winter had drained out the life.

He must have known, I kept saying to myself. All along our free ride toward Mary Red Skies, he must have known they would kill him for it. For taking his freedom back, for trying to live on his own again, for daring to hope. Given the chance, the FBI would even up the score. He knew that. He told me so himself, over and over. And in the end, he was right.

Mike Golman and his clever pals got to her first. They found Mary Red Skies before Choteau did. And one last time, she left him alone. Whatever he had inside him, however strong and determined he was, however committed or crazed he might seem, that must have broken him finally. To lose her again like that, it must have made the idea of a prison cell seem smaller and darker, and time seem longer than ever before. It took the hope out of time. Maybe it made death seem like an answer.

The sun broke clean over the snowfields then, a huge, bare, white ball, and the clear sky above Pine Ridge turned quickly to bright orange. I squinted at the sun's glare on the snow. And suddenly Choteau didn't seem so clear and simple as all of that. It was all too easy, and he was a lot harder than that.

Because I remembered the way he'd hidden his blindness, and I remembered the way he got around on his own and refused to be helped, even going as far as offering to drive. I remembered how blind he was at the end, in that dark cabin guardhouse. Maybe it terrified him, to sit in a cell everyday and see the walls of his vision close in and lock him inside his own head. It must have been like the cell doors closing, maybe it was even like death itself.

So it wasn't just her, and it wasn't just the kid. It was too easy and too logical to just blame them. The Red Skies clan. That was too easy. There was his eyesight. And there was the movement, too. There was AIM, and "the Knee." What about them? He was dedicated to that cause, and his glory days were right here at what he called "the Knee." But why did he refuse the help he could have found among his old compatriots from here? Why did he run to Camp Robinson, and not to here? To Wounded Knee? It didn't make any kind of sense, and I was as lost as ever.

I came to a snow covered dirt lane that cut off from the highway. The church steeple was high on the knoll above me to the north. The church itself, along with the mass grave, had disappeared behind the hilltop. The gully beside the pavement was the gully where they'd died, almost a hundred years ago. I stuck the cane into the drifted snow and slowly, stepping against the pain in my knee, I worked my way toward the bare trees beside the gulch. Just past their shadows, I could see the burned out remains of the museum and store over among those trees. They were still standing there, rusted steel poles and the old, broken bricks of a chimney. That was all. I looked around for something, for an answer, I guess, but it wasn't there in the rust and the brick. Those cheap ruins stood for nothing, not in the shadow of all that had happened here. Those remains were no kind of symbol, though I wanted them to be. I tried to make an answer out of them. They meant nothing.

Bernard Choteau was a symbol, though. And he knew he was, too. Along with Crow Dog and Peltier and a handful of others, he'd become some kind of guiding light, he was the jailed up inspiration of Indian Liberation. He knew that, and he didn't take that role lightly, either. It was the role he had to play, for his people. For their cause.

So maybe he was thinking about what he looked like at the end, maybe that was going through his mind during those hours. Here he was, on the run with nowhere to go, really. Especially after she left him alone again. There was nowhere to run. He would certainly be caught. Sooner or later, it would happen. And then it would all come out their way. Bernard Choteau had broken out of jail to see a woman, skipped out just months before he was up for parole. He couldn't wait, because she'd run away from her respected doctor husband. And then she'd given him the cold shoulder anyway, gone running back to her safe life. But he was out of control, he was crazed, just a criminal on the loose. He was no martyr; he was a dangerous, irrational savage like we'd always known he was. No matter that they all knew the parole wouldn't come. No matter that it wasn't just a woman, it was love. No matter that there was an only son involved. No matter, that's the way it would come across. That's the picture they would paint. A crazy Indian, out of control.

But he knew he could do it differently. He could become an escaped Indian leader, a dedicated activist from the old days, killed by the police at the very place where Crazy Horse was murdered. And that would be a different picture, a picture that might linger in the memory, might inspire some young leader, might urge some old freedom fighter on the res' to rise again. This was a different way to die, proud and undefeated. A warrior's death. One last good run. In the spirit of Crazy Horse.

The snow was dry and powdery where I limped through it, and the sun was breaking full above the hills now. Working my way through the drifts, I understood this different way to see him. Maybe Choteau had given himself this choice. He could become a blind, forgotten prisoner in a federal prison, or he could become a tragic martyr bursting into our conscience, into his people's memory. He could be part of this people's history, or he could be just another forgotten, besotted fool. Another white man's Ind'in. He may have given himself that kind of choice.

As I set the tip of my cane down carelessly into the snow, it slipped on something. It skirted out loose, wagging in the air. I lost my footing and nearly fell down in the snow. My good foot went sliding out from under me and I had to land on that injured leg to stay standing. I pulled myself up, and laughed at my clumsiness. For a moment I could see my laughter in the cold, dark air. But then the sharp ache in that bum knee stopped it. It was sharp enough it made my eyes tear. I rested both hands on the cane and took my weight off that weak leg. I stood like that, like some out of place flamingo, until the pain died down.

And the slow way the pain faded away made me angry, angry at myself, and angry at him. I mean, what the hell kind of choice is that to give yourself? Did he really work himself up until he thought he was more important dead than alive? Did he really think his death, if done right, meant more than his life? It was one way I could explain him, to explain it all away. And that made me angry.

I poked around in the blanket of snow with the cane looking for what had almost made me fall. It was cold enough that the snow scattered like dry particles of sand, none of it sticking to the rubber tip of the cane. Underneath the snow cover, all kinds of gravel and trash were hiding away. But nothing there was big enough to trip me up like that. Nothing.

And I still couldn't figure why he'd done it all alone. Why not find help on the Rosebud or Pine Ridge among the hundreds of traditionals there? Even if he had to die, in his own eyes, why go down to so lonely a death?

That's when the tip of my cane thumped against something. I dusted the snow off carefully, with the cane, like I was working some archeological dig. It was a bottle, round and slick and buried in the smooth snow. You see, I'd stepped on it with my good leg, and it had nearly sent me sprawling in the snow. It had jerked my knee around and twisted it again.

I turned the bottle over gently, so the torn label was up, until I could see what it was: Thunderbird, an empty bottle of Thunderbird. Thunderbird wine. That was all.

I suppose he was thinking of them again. Maybe he didn't want anyone hurt but himself, and a few cheap white lives. He didn't want any other skins dying in this last, heroic gesture of his. And the last thing he expected out of some white man like me was that I'd go risking my neck to stop him.

Or maybe it was just that he was embarrassed. After all, he'd thrown his life away and trashed his reputation among his people, wasted all the expectations built up for him, and all for a woman who just left him again. Left him cold. There was no way he could know about Golman and his tricks. Not all of it anyway. And I suppose it didn't matter to him anyway. Maybe it was just Choteau's stupid, bruised pride that made him want to die alone, and never face those people on the reservations. Even if they chuckled at him, shook their heads, and understood.

I reached down, though it made my knee ache, and I picked up that bottle of old Thunderbird. I hefted it once in my hand. It was my bandaged hand, but the pain felt good and solid there. It felt good to move the wound inside the bandage, to grasp the bottle. Then I coiled back with it. I threw that old Thunderbird off the road and down into the gully where they all died. Then I waited for the chime or at least the thud of it breaking, but it never came. It must have slid softly down in the snow. It rested somewhere now on the old bloody ground.

The remains of the museum were in front of me, just a few twisted and charred steel beams, and a fireplace. Everywhere I stepped, I seemed to be walking on broken glass. Beer bottles, whiskey bottles, wine bottles. It was a glass floor under the snow at the new Wounded Knee. I listened a moment and heard no ghosts. Not even the wind so I could imagine them. Ninety-nine years had passed, and now one more was dead, and I heard nothing. Nothing but the crunch of broken glass under my feet.

Then a rustle came from the gulch, and it startled me. For a moment I was afraid I might get my melodramatic wish. The ghost of Choteau or Crazy Horse would come walking up out of the hollow to explain it all to me. I was still for a moment, until I saw a skunk skitter out of the trash in the ditch, near where I'd tossed the empty Thunderbird, and disappear into a culvert under the highway.

But there it was, you know, the strangest motive of all. Right there in the way I'd let a skunk startle me. Bernard Choteau believed he was Crazy Horse. Choteau had arranged it all, and included me, Will Gentles, gave me a starring role as his own Little Big Man. He walked into my house, took over my life, and then did everything he could to reenact the death of Crazy Horse. And I didn't know what to make of that. Was it all some sort of strange play acting? If it was an act, believe me, Choteau was convincing.

Still, there isn't any doubt. Bernard Choteau died because he was Crazy Horse, or because he believed he was Crazy Horse. He died to fulfill his Crazy Horse dream.

Standing there amidst all that broken glass, from all those broken bottles, I remembered what Choteau had said about Lennie Red Skies. Lennie died because he forgot he was an Indian. He knew he wasn't white, Choteau told me somewhere along the way, but Lennie forgot the Lakota side. He forgot who he was.

It seemed to me, right then, that Choteau was exactly Lennie's opposite. Bernard Choteau couldn't forget he was an Indian. And it had killed him. If he hadn't been this visionary, if he'd just been some broken hearted Korean war vet with eye problems and not some missionary soul from the past, he'd be alive right now. Hell, he'd be taken care of.

But he wasn't. He had dreamed the dream of Crazy Horse, and he was Lakota, and so he was dead.

And now Wounded Knee stretched out around me there and it had become a dump. The ground was littered with garbage buried in the snow. This is what ninety-nine years had wrought. Another death and a lot of garbage. And it made me angry, and it made me tired.

It was light enough now that my shadow was long and blue and smooth on the snow. I looked at it and I saw the cane there, and I saw the way I was bent down to use it. But that shadow was soft and fuzzy. It could have been anyone. Any old man bent there in the snow, but not me. It could have been anyone but me.

Choteau had used me. That fact came roaring up out of my guts like a startled bear. I trusted him, and I risked my home and my living and my life for him. And for all that, he just used me to commit some sort of suicide.

I remembered his death song, then, that chant he sang at the very end as we left the guardhouse. He was ready to die then. But there in the dump that Wounded Knee had become, I remembered the other time I heard him chant that song. Way back, days before, when he switched our plates in Kansas, on our first night out there, he'd sung that song. At the very start of all this. And it had sunk into me, because I'd heard it in my dream.

I asked him what it was, and I remembered what he said then. "You'll know," he said. "You'll know all too soon."

Because he knew where we were headed that night, from the start of it. Right from the very beginning we were headed for that guardhouse at old Fort Robinson. We were on our way to fulfill his dreams.

I was so angry at him then, at the way he'd used me, and at the way I'd fallen for it, a sucker for his Indian act and my bleeding heart sympathies, I was so angry, I began to kick at the trash around me. Who did he think he was? Who was he to use me to stage his own death? To put my life in danger so he could take his own? Just who the hell did he think he was? I swung my cane around and shot beer cans and bottles from under the snow into the air. I was even kicking at the crap with my bum leg.

That's when I finally did slip and fall, and landed flat on my back. I heard the crunching and snapping of the glass under me. I think it was that big heavy coat of Jimmie Nordstrom's with all that sleek camel hair and silk lining that shielded me, because I wasn't cut. I landed hard on that bed of old blood and broken glass, but I wasn't cut. I wasn't even touched. But I did wind up on my back looking at my bandaged hand in front of my face. And I started to laugh.

I heard the skunk out by the road skittering in the snow again, and I laughed. I laughed at myself, and at the frightened skunk, and at the whole damn, pitiful Red Skies clan, and at Bernard Choteau. But I didn't laugh at Crazy Horse.

Because, stretched out in the snow and the trash there, I realized this was all so much foolishness. The whole blasted deal. There I was lying on the ground stamping my feet like an angry child, because I didn't understand. Because it wasn't fair. But I never would understand. In some strange way Bernard Choteau was Crazy Horse, and in some stranger way--only because it seemed like common sense--he was only Bernard

Choteau. But I would never know why he died. I could stamp my feet in the snow and glass until Wounded Knee became the bottom of the ocean, and I'd never know. I knew it wasn't fair, that it was tragic; I knew he was partly at fault, and I knew he was a victim, too. A victim of his love for Mary Red Skies, and of the reservations, and history, and the color of his skin, and of me, and of himself. I knew all of that. But none of it told me why he was dead. That I never would understand.

No more than I would ever really understand the beautiful story his people told. The story they believed, about two hunters out for deer in the long ago times, before the world was upside down. Gazing way off in the far distance, the two hunters saw a beautiful woman with a bundle walking toward them. As she came near, they saw how lovely she was. Her buckskins were white as the eagle's head, and her long smooth hair was black as the eagle's eye. She walked toward them with that kind of grace and litheness that made them both watch her, made their eyes linger on her steps. one hunter was filled with desire and said, "I want her." But the other one said, "No, brother, you mustn't. She is sacred; she is wakan. Can't you tell?"

The woman came near and stopped, setting her bundle down on the ground. Then she waved to the hunter who was hungry for her, and he hurried over to her. While the other hunter watched, the man reached out to touch her and a cloud descended over them.

When it parted there was nothing left of the bold one but a stack of bones lying in the dust. The woman said, "Do not fear." But the hunter who was left trembled. "I have something for you," the beautiful woman said, picking up her bundle.

She was the woman who gave the Lakota the sacred pipe and all the rituals of their religion, and the way to live in the world. This was what she carried in the bundle, and she gave it to the hunter who was left, and to all the people through him.

Then she walked a short distance away, and she lay down, rolled over and became a buffalo as white as the puffy clouds in a blue summer sky. She rose up from her wallow and galloped away, disappearing over the distant hills.

The White Buffalo Woman gave him great gifts: the pipe, and the law, and a way to live in the world. But she didn't give him back his friend.

When I grew tired of looking at those blank pages in the typewriter, I took a trip that summer. I went looking for Old Badlands Face. I drove around in the middle of South Dakota in circles, and never found a trace. I spent a week at the Lower Brule and the Crow Creek reservations, asking questions and describing the old man to anyone who'd listen. They smiled a lot and suggested some names, now and then. But I never found him or even any sign of his Inipi Motel, or of Medicine Wheel, or anything.

After two weeks I drove home discouraged. I was convinced that if I found Old Badlands, he could explain at least some of what has happened. But from all that driving and searching, I learned only one thing. And that was about myself.

I had come to believe, most of the time, that Bernard Choteau was Crazy Horse. Though I couldn't explain how.

The nights out here seem especially dark, darker than they ever seemed in the city, or even at Fort Robinson. On this old dead tobacco farm, it sometimes seems very lonely.

Sometimes, on those nights, I remember that moment when Choteau said, "Turn here," and we headed off to the west to Fort Robinson by way of the Rosebud, toward that morning when we killed him, maybe killed him again. I'm drawn back to that moment, during my nights here, when I'm alone, that moment when I turned the corner and got lost in that mysterious Medicine Wheel. That was the moment, you know, when I

338

took a left turn out of time and wound up someplace where the past and the present crisscrossed enough to create a wave or a wrinkle where everything from every time seemed entirely possible. And there was nowhere to run. I went that night to a place I'll never find again, because it's gone like the petals on last summer's asters. Gone.

Choteau took me there, and he took me there on the darkest night of his life. I realize now that rutted dark drive rode across his loneliness, because he was learning that those things you love are always meant sometime, eventually, to leave you. And when they're gone, and when you're left, you have the past, and it's all you have for a future. All you have, in fact. And the nights out there then, out here now, are very dark. They're black.

But, even on old, dead tobacco farms, even when you're alone at night because you've hurt all the people you loved and betrayed everything you value, even when you know in the end you'll be alone, and probably it will be because you deserve to be alone. Even in those dead, dark nights, there are stars in the sky.

They're faint, and they flicker. They're anything but constant. Sometimes when you need them most, they're gone entirely. Clouded over and obscure. But now and then, there are stars.

Remember this.

You haven't earned them. They're a gift.

"Are you all right?" she said.

I was still lying on my back surrounded by broken bottles, laughing at Choteau and me and at Wounded Knee. Laughing at the circles that Time had spun me in. I suppose to anyone walking up, I looked like I was drunk, or mad, or both.

But the sound of her voice stopped me.

"Terri?" I said.

Maybe I'd died and gone to some place where forgiveness doesn't need to be deserved. If I heard Crazy Horse speak next, I'd know for sure. I was dead and in paradise.

She said my name, but it sounded like a question.

I flopped over awkwardly, like some decked fish. I propped myself up on one elbow, dodging the broken glass with my hands.

"Is that you?" I said lamely.

She was standing there in the snow, wrapped up tight in the white parka I'd given her for Christmas years back. Her face stuck out of the hood, along with pretty shocks of her black curly hair. She was rosy pink. She looked cold. "Are you okay?" she said. She looked beautiful.

I laughed, realizing how I must have looked, wallowing around in the snow laughing out loud. So I used the cane and climbed up to my knees, then my feet. I still wasn't entirely sure I hadn't crossed over some line into la-la-land. Was it really her, or was I hallucinating? It had been a hell of a week. At that point, I was more surprised at reality than at hallucination.

I dusted the snow and garbage off the front of Jimmie Nordstrom's coat, remembering how I hadn't shaved in a week, wondering how I smelled after rolling around in the frozen trash and vomit. "Yeah. Yeah," I said, "I'm fine."

We stood there and looked at one another beside the gully at Wounded Knee. I hadn't seen her in an age of time, an age that had rattled me to my core, obviously. But we didn't seem to have anything to say to one another. There was this awful awkward silence, and I felt like I had to break it before it began to speak on its own, before it began to tell us how different and lost from one another we were.

"How did you find me?" I said.

She nodded at something in my direction, and said, "Mike told me."

My eyes, instinctively, switched to scanning the hillsides above us nervously. "Where is he?" I muttered.

"No," she said, "he's not here. It's the cane. It's got a transmitter in it. He was worried about you. They've been keeping track of you since he let you go."

I lifted the aluminum cane and looked at it. It seemed so obvious now. I seemed so stupid.

"He wasn't sure what you might you do," she said, "after . . . "

I grabbed the cane by the rubber tip on its end and hurled it off into that bleak gully. Let 'em track that, I said to myself. Then I tried awkwardly to stay standing, fighting to keep my balance on my good leg after that big, dramatic javelin toss.

"He was just worried about you," she said. We were still standing twenty or thirty yards apart in the snow and the trash.

"So Golman called you and flew you out here. So he could take care of his witness. Gotta be sure they keep me quiet about what happened."

She lowered her head. But I wasn't done.

"Well, its not gonna happen that way. I saw that mass of cops murder Choteau, and I'm gonna tell the world about this, because the blood is on my hands too." I held up my bandaged mitt. "Golman and his chums are not slipping by that easily. Not this time."

"You asked me to come," she said. She lifted her head. "Mike didn't have anything to do with it."

"Right," I stuck my hands in the pockets of the overcoat and tried to look calm and in control of myself. It didn't work. Not when I wobbled on my good leg. "I asked you to come out here, and instead you ran home to your folks, and then you told Golman and his Bureau buddies where we were. Just like you tipped them off to Mary Red Skies and where we were headed. Don't act innocent now. Maybe you did it because you thought it was right, it was good for me, but Golman told me the whole damn story, Terri."

She stood there quiet a moment, letting what I said sink in. Letting my attitude sink in. "Mike told you what?" she whispered, eventually.

"You turned us in and ran for home. And now Choteau is dead." Blaming her was a lie, but I spit it out angrily anyway.

341

"Mike told you that?" her voice was rising. "That son of a bitch," she said and walked around once in circle. She scuffed the snow around with her feet and thought a moment. Then she stopped, looked up at me again, and said, "And you son of a bitch. You believed him."

She gazed at me a while, as if she was trying to understand me. She looked rosy and cold there. "It's so stupid," she shook her head at me. "You know they were listening on the phones. And the Red Skies woman, you think she was some big secret? You think they didn't know all about her?" Terri stopped there, too angry to speak for a moment. "You believed Mike because you wanted to believe him, Will. You wanted me to turn you in, you bastard."

She looked down into the gully and spoke, without looking at me. "You called and said you needed me, and then you believe my son of a bitch brother." Her mouth set closed then, hard and final.

"Terri," I said, but nothing followed her name.

"No, you listen for a change, buster," she said. She shook her head so the white hood of the parka came down, and her dark hair bounced loose. "You run off with some convict and with some dusty old set of ideals of yours, and you leave me all alone. And I was all for it. You drive around the countryside, making yourself a joke on the evening news, and making my life a mess. And I'm still right behind you. Then you call me up out of Nowheresville, South Dakota, and say, 'Terri, come here, I need you.' And what do I do?

"I drop everything and come driving out here to find you rolling around like a bum in a ditch. And you," she paused there to collect herself. She swallowed, but she wasn't going to let herself cry. "And you believe my brother when he lies to you. You trust the god damn FBI, and not me. This is what I get for . . . "

She stopped then, and didn't finish that sentence. She left it at that, I guess for fear of what might get said.

I just stood there with my weight on my one good leg, in my borrowed overcoat with my hands stuffed in the pockets, wobbling in the wind. Suddenly it felt mighty cold out at Wounded Knee.

After a while, Terri said, "I'm freezing my ass off out here." Then she walked toward me through the glass and snow. "Let's go," she said. She didn't say where.

In the southwest, high on plateaus above the desert, the Hopi carve masks for when their gods dance. And they raise their children there to believe in the kachinas who come down dancing from the mountains. It is kept a great secret from the children who the dancers really are. As the kachinas enter the kiva, the children always know they are seeing spirits from on high. There is no trickery here, there is only truth. The magic happens.

But one day you grow old enough that a turning point has come, though you don't even know it. Your parents place you in the kiva waiting for the gods to come and, for the first time in your life, you see the kachinas enter carrying their masks. Suddenly, with no warning at all, there are no gods. There is only old Uncle Davey the car mechanic, toting around a big bulky mask. Only your neighbor Johnny Begay who sleeps too much on Saturdays and yells at the little kids, and only that old shepherd from way out on Black Mesa who comes to town once a month or so for mail and supplies, and maybe a drink or two. Their big bellies hang out over the ka-china costumes they wear. And that's all you have, and there aren't spirits or dancing gods anymore, nothing from on high. The magic is gone.

And it seems cruel to you at first. You want to scream, but instead you just weep to yourself for a while. You keep the confusion inside. You feel like everything worthwhile has been stripped away.

But then Uncle Davey and the others put on their masks, and they tell you to be ready. Because the children are

343

coming in now. You mustn't let on. And as the kachinas dance, the old ones gather around you and you begin to see. There is a deeper magic in the world, something beyond the tricks. You're old enough now to know this. Though it takes you a while, and it isn't as easy as it was before.

You see, it's easier to turn a mask than an uncle into one of the gods. Easier, but not better.

I'm holding that old mask in my hands right now, as I sit here at the desk. I can touch the smooth wood, carved and sanded down by hand. I can run my fingers around the oval of the bear's black eyes, and smell the mustiness of its old age. I turn the thing over, and I can see the two other faces hidden inside: the raven, the man.

Way back at the start of all this, on those few nights before Christmas, Choteau told me there was a fourth face behind this mask. I didn't understand him then. There are only three, I said. Human, raven, bear. And he laughed at me.

But it was the dancer that he meant, of course. The first face. The one who wears them all. At least I think that's what he meant. But I didn't know that then.

I set the mask down a moment ago. It's on the floor now, and the bear is grinning up at me. The raven hides inside, I know. And past that, there is a man. But the bear is grinning at me because, like a Hopi child, I see. There is a magic deeper than just learning to pull the strings. It's a transformation, after all. The bear becomes the bird, you see, just the way the dancer becomes the bear. It's not the mask that matters. It's what happens to the dancer.

Once I was a Professor of Time. But Bernard Choteau changed all that.

I called it reincarnation the first time he told me, in that snowstorm in a car in Nebraska, and I laughed at it. But I'm different now. I know it isn't easy to tell the mask from the

344

dancer. And the part of me that needs to know the difference, I'm learning to ignore.

Bernard Choteau taught me that.

I live now in the country. I took the little money I had from my retirement fund at the University, when I resigned, and used it to buy this old decrepit tobacco farm. It's just sixty acres, worn out with abuse and over use. It needs some restoration. Come spring, I'm going to turn it into a truck farm, raise vegetables and sell them at the farmer's markets in town. And I decided I'm going to keep a little garden of endangered plants, too. It seems the least I can do.

Every now and then, when I'm in town, I run into one or another of my old friends from the U. They always look sad and ask me how I'm doing. I think some of them assume I'm doing research out here, still looking for the answers to all the questions I raised in that old monograph of mine. I suppose I seem eccentric to them. But you know, they're still looking for the effect to every cause and, if you want to know the truth, it's me who feels sorry for them. They have so much to think about.

As for me, I worry about my knee. The cane is permanent now and they tell me it is the start of arthritis. That could make my gardening tough some day, so I might have to find a new way. But when that time comes, I'll face it. Who knows, maybe I'll go back to teaching. Maybe I'll know enough then to try it.

The most amazing thing of all is this: Terri is still with me. She's put up with all the changes I've made, and she seems to like it here in the country. She says she enjoys using the sun for a clock and the snow for a calendar, and I guess I do too. But her hair has the first signs of gray in it. I wonder sometimes if I deserve her, with what I am.

Sometimes she says she likes me better now.

Sometimes she's just quiet.

345

       *   *   *

In her car as we drove away from Wounded Knee, Terri switched the radio to a weepy country station, and we listened in silence to one sad, broken song after another, separated only by bad market reports. In the back seat she had a Christmas present for me, though I don't think it was what Golman had been planning. It was a bottle of Rhine wine with a bow around its neck, the same brand I bought way back on the night we met. It sat in the back seat now, like some sort of bad joke, and neither of us mentioned it. But she knew that I saw it, and that I knew what it was.

That night in a motel in Rapid City, after I'd collapsed in exhaustion on the bed, she made love to me. It was like in the old days, when I'd come back from one of my research trips. It was filled with that physical hunger that comes from absence and distance. Like she does sometimes, Terri began to laugh. She was on top of me and we were going hard, and her dark hair had fallen all around her white, freckled skin, and she was laughing. At the peak of it, I swear, I heard her, or I heard someone inside a crazy laugh, say, "Hoka Hey, Little Big Man."

Probably I imagined that. After all, I was exhausted.

In the morning we were silent again. We didn't really begin to talk much until we got home.

Golman showed up out here at the farm one evening. It was about a month after we'd moved in, and he stopped by with a bottle of wine for our housewarming, and to say good-bye, I guess. He was in jeans and a wool shirt, and he looked about as casual as I've ever seen him look. But his haircut was too neat, and the jeans were too new. It looked like a costume.

346

"It's got possibilities, Will," he said, as he strolled around our big, empty front room with its bare wood floors. "You could do a lot worse," he said, nodding his head.

"Thanks," I said, mainly wanting him gone.

"Where's little Sis?"

"You're lucky she's not here," I set his gift on the floor by the door.

He looked a little startled that I was going to be abrupt about it all. He grinned, and said, "Well, I knew she was mad, but I figured it would blow over, you know, with time. It's been months."

"It hasn't been long enough," I said.

"Oh, come on, buddy, it was just . . . " he said.

"You lied to us, Mike," I walked away from him and stared out the window at his Jeep in the lane back by the barn. "The biggest mistake I ever made was trusting you. I was down about as low as I've ever been, you know, and I leaned on you then."

"Leaned on me, shit, pal, you saved my life."

I tried to hold my voice in check, but it began to shake as I spoke. "You told me she turned us in, Mike. You fucking lied to me. And I trusted you. I believed you. And you just about tore us apart." I limped over and picked up his bottle off the floor where I'd left it. "You wanted Choteau so bad, you were willing to throw me and Terri away to get to him. We didn't matter. Your own sister's marriage didn't matter. Nothing did. All that mattered was Choteau, and some kind of cheap revenge for the Bureau."

"That's not true, Will, you know that's not true."

I walked over to him and handed him back the bottle. I noticed then it had a little pearl ribbon tied carefully in a bow around its neck. "You better go, Mike."

He brushed his trimmed mustache with his thumb a couple times. Then his eyes darkened as he looked at the bottle in his hand. "Oh hell, that's bullshit, buddy. I wasn't risking you two. Shit, not even for a minute. She still loved you, even if you are half nuts. And the proof is right here, pal." He waved

347

the bottle around at the farmhouse. "You two are still together, happier than ever. Aren't you?"

"Terri'll be back any minute," I said. "You better go."

I walked back and opened the door for him. It was fall already out there, the leaves were drifting down out of the old maples in our yard. As he strutted past me, I couldn't stop myself, because I still found what he did hard to believe. And because I knew that blaming him was a lie, and a lie that wouldn't help anything anyway. "Why'd you do it, Golman?" I said as he stepped outside.

He looked back, as if he couldn't believe I'd even asked. "It was the law, Will," he said. "I swore I'd uphold it, you know. It was my duty."

I wanted to laugh at him, but I knew he wouldn't understand, and I knew my laugh would hurt him more than I had it in me to hurt him then. So I just shook my head.

Golman turned around out in the yard. He stopped and set the bottle on the step and left it there. Then he looked up, as if he'd forgotten something. "How's the book going, buddy?"

It wasn't the old argument between us. He'd helped me with my research before, and he knew I was struggling now to write this all down. I think a part of him figured a book would get me out of the country and back to teaching and being fruitful again, at least in his eyes. He was trying to help out, I think, in his way. He was being the good marine.

"Not so well," I said. But then I added, "I've got a lot of new information, though. A lot."

He nodded his head.

"You know, Will, we never found him," he said. He was looking down at the gray and brown leaves. I was looking at him, at the way his hair stayed in place when his head was down. "His body just disappeared, Will. We can't even find a record of who came to pick it up."

He was right though. Bernard Choteau's body had disappeared. A hearse came to pick up the remains in Chadron and it drove off to the north. And that's all anyone knows. The hearse headed north and never returned. Some people say the Lakota at Pine Ridge took him, and on the reservation they

348

know where he lies. There's others who say the FBI managed to have the evidence disappear. If that isn't true, I know it is true the boys from the Bureau didn't search very hard for his remains. If the feds didn't snatch Choteau, they're sure pleased the body's gone.

It could be Mary Red Skies is behind the disappearance, though. A part of me thinks that she may know where he lies. She may finally have brought him home, you know. It's what I'd like to think.

But the main thing is, just like Crazy Horse, he's disappeared into those prairies again. Where he's gone, no one knows. Or no one's saying.

Maybe someday he'll be back. For one more run.

I didn't say anything more to Golman, though he stood there looking at the dead grass. He waited a minute for me to respond, and then it slowly grew clear that I had nothing more to say. Golman shrugged and looked confused. "I thought you'd want to put that in your book," he said. He nodded his head yes, and after a moment he walked away. As he got in the Blazer he raised an arm and waved to me in the doorway. I almost shut the door without waving back, but at the last moment, as the blazer backed down our lane, I raised an arm and waved to him. I don't know if he saw it, or if he saw me pick up the bottle on the steps and bring it in the house.

That's the last time I saw Mike Golman. Not long after that he got promoted and he moved to D.C. Later that year, not even a month after he was gone, Jacki filed for their divorce.

I noticed an article in the St. Louis paper yesterday morning about a big fishing rights disagreement somewhere up in northern Wisconsin. The case has to do with an old treaty, and with the Indians up there, and with the tourist trade that wants to limit where and how they can fish the lakes they used to own.

Probably I would have found that article anyway, because I sort of keep tabs on these treaty wars now. I have a special interest in them, since my ride with Crazy Horse. But there was something else in that article that caught my eye. There was a name that jumped out at me, and made me clip those columns out of the paper and keep them. I keep them here in my top desk drawer.

I guess one of the lawyers at the hearing refused to answer to his legal name, and that upset the judge. He's been threatening this hotshot of a lawyer with contempt of court. Get the name changed legally, son, or shut up. That's what the judge says. But this young Indian lawyer still won't answer to any name but the one he claims is his real name. He just sits there and ignores the judge, unless he hears what he calls his true name.

He wants to be called Red Skies, the paper said.

From the looks of it, this kid seems like a born troublemaker, the genuine item. In the blood, I'd say. And I don't think we've heard the last of him.

To leave Wounded Knee, I had to lean on Terri. Wearing Jimmie Nordstrom's coat, I put my arm around the shoulders of her white parka, and she helped me limp without my cane back out to the highway. It wasn't easy, because almost the whole way the ground was littered with broken glass and old beer cans under the snow, and because Terri is not very big. Once we nearly fell, and that made us laugh. But it only lasted a moment. Then it was back to the angry silence between us.

After we'd limped along a few yards on the pavement, she decided it was too slow. She ran up the road toward her car to drive it down closer to me. I stood teetering, my weight on my good leg, and the wind tried to knock me down.

Alone, I watched her jog up the highway, and realized it was pity that was hauling me out of there. This was not a fresh start for us. It was more likely a limping, pitiful end. Because it was what I had earned for myself. See, she wasn't taking me home. She just had no way to leave me there.

It was just as she reached the car that I heard the first drum beat. I guess the wind carried it over the hill, because I looked up out of the valley and saw nothing. Terri heard it too. She stopped by the car and looked back at me. Maybe she thought I'd fallen or something. The frown on her face said, What was that? But she didn't speak.

Then the first riders pranced over the knoll beside the church, and the lone drumbeats came regularly to us. With them came the sound of three or four voices, chanting high and soft on the wind, sounding almost oriental.

I turned to watch, and for a moment forgot my little worries and the way I'd wronged her.

Slowly the procession appeared over the top of the knoll and began to collect there. Many were on horses, some were on foot leading a mount, and in the center of the random line walked four or five old men wrapped in blankets against the cold. It was one or another of those old men who sang the chants, and kept it going, as the song passed around among them and their steps seemed in rhythm to it. Somewhere, someone beat on one lone drum. I knew what it was they were gathering around. It was the mass grave from the old massacre. This was the Big Foot memorial ride that Bobby and Choteau had talked about. These were the women and men who'd spent a week in prayer and fasting. Now they came like dancers to the end of their road, the end of their ghost trail, on the ninety-ninth anniversary of the Massacre at Wounded Knee.

As they glided and stepped over the top of that hill, I tried to count them, but then I gave up. There must have been a hundred-and-fifty or two hundred of them. They filled the top of that knoll. As they gathered, the chant drifted around among them and their hunched shoulders followed, swaying with the drum beat.

Some of those faces on the hill I recognized from the day before. Some of them had been at that road block down in

Nebraska. Some of them I'd seen out the rear window of that ambulance made hearse.

I couldn't help but think, at first, what might have happened. If Choteau had tried to reach them, if Bobby had been able to get them through, if Golman had found a way to let them in, if we could have gathered these two hundred at Fort Robinson, then Crazy Horse would be alive right now. It would all be different now. Bernard Choteau could have been saved. And I felt my anger rise again at what should have been.

One of the old men in the center raised a staff then, and the chanting stopped. The old man began to speak, but not in English. He made an offering of tobacco. The staff he held was lined with feathers, and each one was a gift from one of the riders. It represented the vow someone had made to ride in the memorial and to follow the good red road of the Lakota way for a year. This is what I learned later, when I came back looking for Old Badlands Face in the summer. But that morning, I sensed as much as I listened to the old man on the hill speak in Lakota.

I think Terri sensed it too. Because she came up behind me then, and put her arms around me. She hugged against my dirtied, borrowed overcoat, partly to feel my warmth in the cold.

But we stood there on the side of the pavement and listened to the ceremony. It was all in Lakota, so we couldn't understand a word. But we did understand it wasn't just to remember, it was to wipe the tears away. To somehow close the circle of time, and learn how to go on. And the riders knew we were there, too. They never acknowledged us, but they knew we were part of the circle.

We didn't leave until the riders, even in their weariness, came lightly down from the knoll and danced into the gully, and made another tobacco offering there. In the ditch where the old ones had died in that long ago time.

Then Terri helped me limp back to her car. Along the way she grinned at me, and then she pinched my ass.

*   *   *

They spoke in Lakota that morning, and now they speak every night in my dreams, praying for every dancer in every mask. It is not the mask that matters, they always say. Run your fingers over the grain in the wood, smell the mustiness of its old age. Touch the smooth shells that make its crazy eyes. Metakuye oyasin, they say. We are all related. But it's not the mask that matters.

When it is all related.

It's what happens to the dancer. On his last good run.

ALSO BY SANDRO DARIOSTO

BURTON THE RED
An omnibus edition

forthcoming from *per sempre Anita Edizione*

BURTON WITH THE THOUSAND

IN THE NORTH

BEYOND ASPROMONTE

HANDS OF THE BIRD AND OTHER STORIES

THE WISDOM RUN

www.ingramcontent.com/pod-product-compliance
Lightning Source LLC
Chambersburg PA
CBHW070800180626
46818CB00001B/41